Francine Pascal's

HORROR IN LONDON COLLECTION

including
LOVE AND DEATH IN LONDON
A DATE WITH A WEREWOLF
BEWARE THE WOLFMAN

BANTAM BOOKS
TORONTO · NEW YORK · LONDON · SYDNEY · AUCKLAND

SWEET VALLEY HIGH
HORROR IN LONDON COLLECTION
A BANTAM BOOK : 0 553 81283 1

Individual titles originally published in U.S.A. by Bantam Books
First published in Great Britain as individual titles in 1994
Collection first published in Great Britain

PRINTING HISTORY
Bantam Collection published 1999

1 3 5 7 9 10 8 6 4 2

Copyright © 1999 by Francine Pascal

including
LOVE AND DEATH IN LONDON
First published in Great Britain, 1994
Copyright © 1994 by Francine Pascal

A DATE WITH A WEREWOLF
First published in Great Britain, 1994
Copyright © 1994 by Francine Pascal

BEWARE THE WOLFMAN
First published in Great Britain, 1994
Copyright © 1994 by Francine Pascal

Conceived by Francine Pascal

Produced by Daniel Weiss Associates, Inc,
33 West 17th Street, New York, NY 10011

Bantam Books are published by Transworld Publishers Ltd,
61–63 Uxbridge Road, Ealing, London W5 5SA,
a division of The Random House Group Ltd,
in Australia by Random House Australia (Pty) Ltd,
20 Alfred Street, Milsons Point, Sydney, NSW 2061, Australia,
in New Zealand by Random House New Zealand Ltd,
18 Poland Road, Glenfield, Auckland 10, New Zealand
and in South Africa by Random House (Pty) Ltd,
Endulini, 5a Jubilee Road, Parktown 2193, South Africa.

Made and printed in Great Britain by
Cox & Wyman Ltd, Reading, Berkshire.

LOVE AND
DEATH IN LONDON

Written by
Kate William

Created by
FRANCINE PASCAL

BANTAM BOOKS
NEW YORK · TORONTO · LONDON · SYDNEY · AUCKLAND

To Mia Pascal Johansson

Chapter 1

"Look, Liz!" sixteen-year-old Jessica Wakefield cried with excitement. "I see England!"

Leaning across her twin sister, Elizabeth peered out the airplane window. Sure enough, the sparkling Atlantic Ocean had given way to a patchwork quilt of lush green farmland sprinkled with little villages. "England," Elizabeth breathed, clasping her hands together. "I can't believe we're really here!"

"We're not actually on the *ground* yet." Jessica bounced impatiently. "I feel as if I've spent my whole life on this plane. If I don't get off soon, I'll scream!"

Elizabeth was just as restless as her sister. It had been a long two days of traveling: they'd left Sweet Valley, California, on Saturday morning and switched planes in New York Saturday night. With the time change, the overnight flight to London was putting them into Heathrow Airport after lunch on Sunday.

"Just think," said Elizabeth. "Tomorrow we start our internships at the *London Journal*! It's going to be such a thrill to meet Mr. Reeves, to actually *work* with him."

Stars sparkled in Elizabeth's blue-green eyes. Jessica's eyes, meanwhile, crinkled up in a big yawn. *Elizabeth gets fired up about the strangest things*, Jessica thought. "Henry Reeves just looks like any old gray-haired geezer to me," she remarked carelessly.

Elizabeth looked shocked by Jessica's lack of awe and respect for the *Journal*'s venerable editor-in-chief. "He's a *legend*, and the *London Journal* is the classiest, most intellectual newspaper in the world. This is an incredible honor. We're going to learn so much from him!"

"Well, I for one refuse to learn *too* much," Jessica declared. "It's summer vacation, after all— my brain cells need a rest."

"It won't be like school; it'll be fun," Elizabeth promised. "Remember what a blast we had interning for the *Sweet Valley News*? And that was just our local paper, ten minutes from home. This time we're going to be in London, *England*!"

Elizabeth sank back in her seat. The month-long internship aside, excitement enough for a would-be writer, a trip to England was a dream come true. "Think of all the wonderful poets and playwrights and novelists who were from England." Elizabeth listed the names rapturously.

2

"Wordsworth and Shelley and Keats. Charles Dickens and Jane Austen, Virginia Woolf, and the Brontë sisters. And Shakespeare!"

Jessica clapped her hands over her ears. "Don't even *speak* those names," she begged. "It makes me feel as if I'm back in Mr. Collins' English class. Remember, we're on *vacation*, Liz. V-A-C-A-T-I-O-N." She spelled out the word to give it a better chance of penetrating her sister's bookwormish brain. "Try not to be such a nerd, for once!"

Not surprisingly, the twins had very different reasons for looking forward to their stay in London. Although identical in appearance, with the same sun-kissed blond hair, turquoise eyes, and slim, athletic figures, their interests tended to propel them in opposite directions. Elizabeth made schoolwork a priority and spent hours every day writing for the Sweet Valley High newspaper, *The Oracle*, or in her journal. Jessica, on the other hand, inclined toward nonacademic activities like cheerleading, shopping, boy-watching, and sunbathing—she could only do homework if the stereo was blasting one of her favorite CDs, and if she took a break every five or ten minutes to yak on the phone with one of her friends. Elizabeth was a fixture of the Sweet Valley High party scene, but she also enjoyed spending quiet time with her best friend Enid Rollins, or Todd Wilkins, the boy she'd been dating steadily for as long as anyone could remember. Jessica had had a few steady boyfriends herself, but all in all preferred the life of a swinging single—why tie yourself down to just one boy when the world was filled with so many cute ones?

"Our old boss from the *Sweet Valley News* was great to help us line up these internships, but let's get our agenda straight, OK?" said Jessica. "*I* plan to shop on Sloane Street, and hit the London music scene, and hobnob with royalty. *That's* what travel abroad is all about, if you ask me, not visiting musty old museums and making pathetic pilgrimages to the birthplaces of boring old authors who died *centuries* ago."

Elizabeth laughed. "Lucky for us, a city like London has something for everyone."

"It sure does. Remember the movie we watched at Lila's the other night?"

Elizabeth rolled her eyes. "How could I forget? *An American Werewolf in London*—nice choice for a friendly bon voyage party!"

Jessica laughed. "That girl has quite a sense of humor," she agreed. Lila had thrown a huge bash for the twins at her family's mansion, Fowler Crest, inviting everyone who was anyone at Sweet Valley High. A lot of people had worn costumes—the British royal family put in an appearance, as well as Sherlock Holmes and Watson, James Bond, and even Jack the Ripper. Lila had rented the horror movie *An American Werewolf in London*, and they'd all screamed themselves silly.

"Two teenaged American guys go to England on a backpacking trip and are attacked on the deserted moors by a werewolf." Jessica hugged herself, enjoying a pleasant shiver. "One of them's ripped to shreds right then and there, but the other guy, David, lives and turns into a werewolf himself during the next full moon."

Elizabeth wrinkled her nose distastefully. "Really, Jess, do you have to remind me of all the gory details?"

"Yes, I do," said Jessica with a mischievous smile. "Because David ends up in *London* and goes on a total rampage, killing like half a dozen people before the entire London police force finally corners him in a dead-end alley and shoots him with a silver bullet. *Pow!*"

Elizabeth jumped. "Stop! You're scaring me all over again. Once was enough—I'd rather not even *think* about that movie."

"I liked it," Jessica declared with bloodthirsty relish. "Maybe there'll be a nice, ghoulish *murder* while we're working for the *London Journal*, something gruesome and creepy!"

Elizabeth shook her head. "Don't get your grisly hopes up," she advised. "It was just a movie, thank goodness!"

Just then, the head flight attendant's voice came over the intercom. "Please fasten your seat belts and bring your chairs to an upright position," she requested in a crisp British accent. "We've begun our descent into Heathrow and will be landing shortly."

Elizabeth and Jessica exchanged excited smiles. "Look out, London," announced Jessica. "Here we come!"

•   •   •

"I love this, I absolutely love this," Elizabeth said twenty minutes later as they scurried through the bustling airport. Having passed through customs, they were headed for the baggage claim area. "Listen to that." Elizabeth stopped in her tracks and Jessica followed suit, cocking her ear. "English accents," Elizabeth explained when Jessica looked at her blankly. "Aren't they the coolest?"

"The coolest *and* the sexiest," Jessica agreed. "I just can't wait to meet some of these adorable English boys!"

Thirty seconds later, it was Jessica's turn to slam on the brakes. "Liz! Is that who I think it is?"

She pointed to a tall, elegantly dressed young man with a thatch of unruly chestnut hair, ruddy cheeks, and a wide grin. "I don't know. Who *do* you think it is?" replied Elizabeth.

"A prince," Jessica gushed. "Or the cousin of a prince, or at least the *friend* of a prince . . ."

Grabbing her sister's arm, Elizabeth dragged her forward. "Not every good-looking rich guy in England will turn out to be a member of the royal family, you know."

"No, but some of them are bound to." Jessica's gaze was already roving in search of more potential celebrities. "They're out there somewhere! Isn't it just great to be in a country where there are kings and queens and *aristocrats*?"

They reached the baggage carousel to find a mob of travelers waiting for luggage to begin appearing. Wandering over to a row of newspaper

6

vending machines, Jessica and Elizabeth halted in front of the first one. "Speaking of the royal family," Elizabeth said, "take a look at those headlines!"

Every newspaper on display, including the *London Journal*, trumpeted the same startling news. "'Princess Eliana Missing,'" Jessica read out loud. "Wow, that's terrible!"

"Here." Elizabeth fumbled in her pocket for some change. "Let's buy a paper." She started to stick a quarter in the slot, then caught herself with a laugh. "I almost forgot—we need to trade in our American money for British currency! Be right back."

While Elizabeth dashed off to the currency exchange, Jessica bent over to look at the grainy black-and-white picture accompanying the *Journal's* story about the missing princess. An unsmiling, fair-haired girl stared out at Jessica from the front page. "Missing," Jessica breathed. "I wonder where she is? Did she run away? Was she kidnapped?"

Elizabeth had returned with a handful of pound notes and coins. "We'll find out," she said, inserting a coin and removing a copy of the *Journal*.

Their heads close together, the twins read eagerly about the disappearance of the British queen's youngest daughter. "She looks spoiled and bored," Elizabeth commented, examining the photo.

"According to this, she's 'a darling of the British press and public,'" Jessica quoted. "And did you know she's sixteen, exactly our age?"

"They don't have any clues to her whereabouts—there's been no ransom note, nothing." Elizabeth shivered. "Pretty scary, huh?"

Behind them, they heard a beeping sound. The luggage from their flight began to roll onto the conveyor belt. Tucking the newspaper under her arm, Jessica hurried over just in time to snatch her suitcase as it rumbled by.

When Elizabeth's appeared a moment later, they were ready to head outside and hail a cab. "Look at the big, black taxis!" Jessica squealed. "Aren't they wild?"

They joined the queue waiting for a cab and soon were being helped into one of the spacious, lumbering Austins by a burly driver. "Americans, I see," he grunted cheerfully through his thick black beard. He tossed Elizabeth's bag into the trunk as if it weighed no more than a feather. "Is this your first visit to London?"

Elizabeth and Jessica nodded. Shutting them into the backseat, the driver returned to the wheel and revved the engine. "I suppose you've heard about the missing princess," he remarked as they merged with the traffic heading for the city. "Biggest story in years."

Jessica gasped suddenly, clutching Elizabeth's arm. "Stop!" she shrieked at the cabbie. "You're driving on the wrong side of the road!"

To her surprise, a bearlike chuckle rumbled from his chest. "We drive on the left side in England," he informed her, "and that's the *right* side, in our view."

Jessica collapsed weakly against the seat. "I'll

never get used to it," she told her sister.

"Me, neither," Elizabeth admitted. "I keep thinking we're going to have a head-on collision!"

A short, swift ride took them from the outskirts of London into the heart of the city. Jessica and Elizabeth looked from one side of the taxi to the other, devouring the exciting new sights and sounds. "Look, it's the Parliament buildings and Big Ben!" Elizabeth pointed to the famous clock.

"You said Winchester Street, didn't you, miss?" the cabdriver called back.

"That's right." Elizabeth glanced again at the brochure from HIS, Housing for International Students, the room-and-board youth hostel where they'd live during their internships. "One thousand and twenty Winchester Street."

"A safe enough neighborhood," the cabbie said approvingly. "But mind you don't wander around the city overmuch by yourselves. It's easy for strangers to lose their way, and scenic as it is, London can be a dangerous place." He made a worried tsking sound. "I fear the worst for the young princess, I'll tell you that."

Elizabeth clasped her hands together tightly, sobered by the cabbie's warning. Jessica tossed her hair, unconcerned. "We'll be fine," she said carelessly. "It's not like we've never been away from home before."

The taxi began winding its way through a spiderweb of tree-lined residential streets. "Nevertheless," the cabbie insisted, "you don't want to learn your lessons the hard way. Don't forget to look both ways before crossing the street—the traffic comes from the right, not the left the way you're used to. I've seen more than one of my American passengers leave the taxi and nearly lose their lives with their first step in London."

With those ominous if well-intended words, the driver coasted to a stop in front of an unadorned yet elegant brick Georgian house. "Here you are," he announced.

As she paid the cabdriver, Elizabeth realized her heart was pounding with nervous anticipation. Jessica gave her sister's hand a quick squeeze and then flung open the door of the taxi, not waiting for the driver to assist her.

She stepped onto the curb with Elizabeth close at her heels. Staring eagerly ahead at the group of young people gathered on the front steps of HIS, Jessica didn't notice the hunchbacked old bag lady hobbling along the sidewalk toward her until they were face-to-face. The woman was dressed in grimy rags, and her wildly tangled gray hair looked as if it might provide a home for bats. Jessica yelped in surprise.

"Beware the full moon," the old woman hissed, her wart-covered nose just inches from Jessica's. "Beware the full moon."

The bag lady hobbled on without a backward glance. Jessica shook her head, laughing at herself for being so startled, but Elizabeth couldn't quite muster a smile. As she watched the old crone disappear around the corner, an unaccountable shiver chased up her spine.

Chapter 2

"Are you coming, Liz?" Jessica asked.

Elizabeth took a deep breath, shaking off the creepy sensation. Bending, she picked up the suitcase the cabbie had deposited on the curb.

A dozen boys and girls were hanging out in front of the youth hostel, chatting and laughing. Some were speaking English, but Elizabeth also heard French and German—even what she thought might be Russian.

"This is so cool!" Jessica whispered in Elizabeth's ear. "Kind of like an international version of Sweet Valley High. Check out that gorgeous guy on the left—he's *got* to be Italian!"

As the twins approached, the other teenagers stopped talking and looked at them curiously. "Hi," said Jessica.

They were greeted by smiles and a chorus of hellos in various languages.

11

An auburn-haired girl with a splash of freckles across her upturned nose hopped to her feet and stepped up to the twins. "You must be the Americans," she guessed, her emerald-green eyes twinkling with friendliness. Grabbing Jessica's suitcase with one hand, she opened the front door with the other. "You're just in time for tea," she announced, striding across the foyer to the staircase. "I promise we won't bore you with tales of the missing princess. Stash your stuff in your room and then come on!"

There didn't seem to be anything to do but to chase after the red-haired girl. "I'm Elizabeth Wakefield and this is my sister, Jessica," Elizabeth said.

"Of course you are. Oh, I'm sorry!" The girl burst out laughing, her eyes crinkling. "Emily Cartwright. Nice to meet you."

"Your accent," said Jessica. "It's not English, it's . . ."

"Australian. I'm from Sydney. Lovely town, if I may say so myself." They paused on the second-floor landing to catch their breath. "I'm taking you all the way up to three," Emily said. "That's where the girls are—the boys are on two. Mrs. Bates is putting you in with Lina and Portia. It's a big airy room—you'll like it fine."

"What brings you to London?" Elizabeth asked Emily as they continued up the stairs.

"An internship at the BBC—the British Broadcasting Company," Emily replied. "I'd like to go into television production."

Trooping down the blue-carpeted third-floor hallway, Emily stopped at the last door on the left, nudging it open with her foot.

Jessica and Elizabeth peeked inside eagerly. The room had two sets of bunk beds, one made up with sheets and blankets and the other bare with the linens folded and stacked on top. There were two dressers, and one corner of the room had been turned into a conversation nook with easy chairs, a coffee table, and a reading lamp. A door stood open, revealing a walk-in closet already half full of clothes, shoes, and other feminine odds and ends. White lace curtains fluttered at the open windows, and the scent of a delicate floral perfume filled the air.

"Top or bottom bunk?" Elizabeth asked, dropping her suitcase on the floor with a thump.

"Top," said Jessica.

Emily made herself comfortable in one of the easy chairs. "Pretty room, isn't it?" she chattered. "I've got both good and bad news about your roommates, however. The good news is Lina Smith— she's a real sweetie pie. The bad news is Portia Albert. *She's* a royal pain in the you-know-what."

Jessica and Elizabeth laughed.

"Lina's from a poor family in Liverpool," Emily went on, without pausing for breath. "She's working for the summer at a homeless shelter and soup kitchen. They only pay her pennies and she doesn't get much help from home, so I really don't know how she manages. You'll like her," Emily promised. "She comes across as a bit quiet and shy, but she's got a bold streak."

13

"What about Portia?" prompted Jessica.

Emily rolled her eyes. "*Portia* is the daughter of Sir Montford Albert. Have you heard of him?"

"Have we *heard* of him?" Elizabeth squealed. "He's the most famous Shakespearean actor in the *world*!"

"So, you can imagine how stuck-up Portia is," said Emily. "She came to London from Edinburgh, where her dad runs a theater company, to be an actress herself. I've never met a snobbier, ruder, more self-absorbed girl in my life."

"Then you've never met Lila Fowler," Jessica kidded, referring to her best friend and chief rival at Sweet Valley High.

"Is she really that bad?" wondered Elizabeth as she unzipped her suitcase and started placing her clothes in the bottom dresser drawers.

"Ask anyone in the dorm." Slinging one slender leg over the arm of the chair, Emily swung her foot idly. "Nobody can stand her. She thinks she's the bee's knees because she landed a part in a new play opening later this week in the West End—thanks to Sir Montford's influence, I don't doubt."

"So, what's it like living here?" asked Jessica. Her unpacking technique differed somewhat from Elizabeth's; she simply held her suitcase upside down and shook its contents unceremoniously on the bed. "How's the food? Are there a lot of rules?"

"The food is plain but there's plenty of it. A big English breakfast at eight, tea from four in the afternoon till six, and a light supper later. You're on your own for lunch. As for *rules* . . . Didn't I mention Mrs. Bates, the housemother, is the epitome of ironclad propriety? If you want to stay on her good side—not that she has one, mind you—you'd better plan to follow HIS rules to the *letter*."

As she and Elizabeth exchanged a glance, Jessica smiled slyly. *Follow the rules, eh? Talk about an invitation to do just the opposite!*

"No boys on the third floor," Emily elaborated, "and the girls aren't to linger on the second-floor landing *or* to set foot—not a single toe!—into the second-floor hallway. Then there's the *curfew*."

Jessica wrinkled her nose. "Curfew?"

"Curfew," Emily repeated. "Eleven o'clock, and Mrs. Bates locks and bolts the front door promptly. If you're not inside, you'll spend the night on the street."

"I can't believe we have a curfew," Jessica complained to Elizabeth. "We might as well still be at home!"

"That's the whole point," Elizabeth reminded her. "Why do you think Mom and Dad *picked* this place for us?"

"You'll meet Mrs. Bates at tea, and I'm sure she'll go over everything." Emily cocked her head to one side. "You're the first Americans this summer—I wonder how she'll treat you? It's highly possible you won't be up to snuff in her book. She fawns over Portia because she's got 'bloodlines,' but she's a bit chilly to the rest of us." Emily laughed heartily. "Especially me, being from Australia. 'Why, my dear, do you *know* who your ancestors are? The whole *country* was settled by *convicts*!'"

15

Emily's laughter was contagious, and Elizabeth and Jessica joined in. "She sounds like a real ogre," Elizabeth commented, hanging two cotton dresses in the closet. "I'm almost afraid to go down to tea!"

"She takes good care of us, in her own way," Emily assured her. "And you *mustn't* skip tea—it's the perfect time to meet the rest of the gang, and it's a grand bunch." Checking her watch, she hopped to her feet. "In fact, tea is served in five minutes. Let's go down to the dining room, shall we?"

Sticking their empty suitcases under the bottom bunk, the twins sped off in Emily's energetic wake. "Now that you know about a few of the girls, I'll tell you about some of the boys. David Bartholomew is from Liverpool, like Lina. His mum's a charwoman and his father is on the dole—disability, I think. He's attending the London University summer session on a scholarship, studying literature. Quite the serious, bookish young man—a very nice fellow."

They reached the second-floor landing, and Elizabeth fought off the urge to dash into the hallway in violation of Mrs. Bates's stern rules. "Gabriello Moretti's at the university, too, taking a summer course in music," Emily continued. "Classical, but he also plays rock. He's Italian and gorgeous, an absolute work of art." She winked playfully. "Michelangelo's David springs to mind."

Jessica's eyes sparkled with interest. "Sounds like the boy of my dreams."

"Sorry." Emily patted Jessica's arm. "He already found a girlfriend—Sophie from the summer session—it took him about five minutes. But *Rene* . . . I don't think *he's* attached."

"Rene?" said Jessica.

"From France. He's interning at the embassy." Emily sighed dreamily. "He's handsome and charming and, well, *French*, if you know what I mean."

Rene from France . . . At the sound of the name, Elizabeth's heart skipped a beat. Apparently, Jessica had the same thought. "Rene," Jessica whispered in Elizabeth's ear as they reached the bottom of the staircase. "Do you think it could be . . . ?"

Elizabeth put a hand to her face. It grew hot as she felt herself transported back to the spring break she and Jessica had spent as exchange students in southern France. They'd stayed in Cannes at the home of Madame Avery Glize and her son, Rene, while Rene's sister, Fernie, visited the Wakefields in Sweet Valley.

At first, the twins found Rene unfriendly to the point of rudeness. It turned out that he resented Americans because his American father had divorced his mother and, after remarrying and starting a new family in the States, he'd wanted nothing to do with the family he'd left behind. Elizabeth had finally managed to break through Rene's defenses, however. *I'll never forget what a hero he was*, Elizabeth thought, pressing the palm of her hand to her pink cheek. *That day he overcame his fear of water to save Jessica's life after the sailing accident. And then we kissed. . . .*

She'd returned to Sweet Valley before anything

17

had a chance to develop with Rene, and that was just as well, as she had a boyfriend at home. But Elizabeth had always wondered. *What if . . . ?*

"It can't be him," she whispered back. "There must be a million Renes in France."

But as they walked into the oak-paneled dining room a moment later, there he was, standing by the bay window with a steaming cup of tea in his hand. His dark eyes moved to Jessica and Elizabeth as they entered and instantly lit up with pleased recognition. Putting his cup down, he crossed the room with long, quick strides. "Elizabeth and Jessica Wakefield!"

"Rene, fancy meeting you here!" Jessica cried.

As Emily watched in astonishment, Rene took both Jessica's hands in his and kissed her with enthusiasm twice, first on the left cheek and then on the right. "What a wonderful surprise," he exclaimed, turning to Elizabeth.

Releasing Jessica's hands, he seized Elizabeth's, squeezing them warmly. "Elizabeth, you haven't changed a bit," Rene murmured as he bent to kiss her. Did she imagine it, or did his lips seem to linger on her cheek? "Except, *si c'est possible*, you've grown even more beautiful."

Rene's dark eyes smiled down at her, and Elizabeth blushed. *Si c'est possible*, you're *even taller and more handsome*, she could have responded. "This is such an incredible coincidence," she gasped instead.

"We have to sit and talk," he declared. Taking

Elizabeth's arm, Rene led the three girls to a table by the window. As he dashed off to pour tea and fill plates with sandwiches and cookies, Emily leaned forward to whisper to the twins.

"I can't believe you already know the cutest boy in the dorm!"

Jessica lifted her hands and smiled smugly. "What can we say?"

Rene returned with the tea. As he handed Elizabeth her cup, his fingers brushed lightly against hers, making her skin tingle. "I know you've probably just arrived, but before Emily whirls you away to meet everybody else, you must tell me how you've been and what brings you to London," he said. "It's been too long since we corresponded."

"Jessica and I have summer internships at the *London Journal*," Elizabeth told him.

"Ah. You still want to be a writer."

Elizabeth smiled. "And you?"

"My interests have been changing and evolving lately," Rene replied. "You see, I've reconciled with my father."

Elizabeth touched his arm, her eyes glowing. "I'm so glad to hear that!"

"Fernie and I visited him and his second family in Massachusetts, and recently he invited me along on a business trip to Japan," said Rene, choosing a small egg-salad sandwich. "All this travel has given me the idea that I might like to study international relations when I go to university next year."

"Emily says you have an internship at the

19

French embassy," said Elizabeth. "Are you enjoying it?"

"Immensely," Rene told her. "But it's very busy. Almost every night, I have to attend a reception or function of some sort."

"We never see him," Emily confirmed as she reached for the pitcher and sloshed some milk into her tea.

"But now that *you're* here . . ." Rene smiled at Jessica and then turned his gaze on Elizabeth, staring deep into her eyes. "I'll just have to make some free time."

Elizabeth felt Jessica kick Emily under the table and blushed furiously. She had a boyfriend at home—she was in love with Todd Wilkins, and always would be. But she couldn't deny it; the sparks were still there between her and Rene Glize.

She'd arrived in London just that afternoon, and it looked as if the first adventure of the summer was starting already!

"I am *so* tired, I think I could sleep for a *year*," Jessica moaned as she and Elizabeth walked slowly up the stairs to the third floor.

"Your internal clock is all mixed up—jet lag," Elizabeth said, yawning widely.

After supper, the sisters had hung out for an hour in the library gabbing with some of their new housemates. There were two people they still had yet to meet, however: Lina and Portia. According to Emily, Portia usually missed tea and dinner because of play rehearsals. As for Lina, the twins had only gotten a glimpse of her, when she ducked late into tea, grabbed a scone, and hurried off again.

They found the door to their room ajar. As they entered, Lina Smith turned toward them, in the act of slipping her arms out of a worn gray wool cardigan.

"Why, hullo!" she said in a cheery Liverpudlian accent reminiscent of the Beatles. "You must be Jessica and Elizabeth. I hope I didn't seem overly rude at tea, not stopping by to introduce myself properly, but it was my night to captain the soup kitchen supper crew and I had to dash right back out."

Lina was a slender girl of medium height with cropped brown hair and big blue eyes sparkling intelligently behind wire-rimmed glasses. Elizabeth liked her immediately. "It's nice to meet you," Elizabeth said. "The soup kitchen must be hard work."

Lina flopped down into one of the easy chairs and kicked off her loafers. "It's exhausting, but also rewarding. I don't know what could be more satisfying than providing needy people with a square meal and a clean, safe bed." She heaved a sigh. "Unless, of course, we found a way to eliminate homelessness altogether."

"It's a problem in the U.S., too," said Elizabeth, hunting in her drawer for a nightgown.

"Well, what is *your* government doing about it?" Lina sat forward, her elbows on her knees and her eyes flashing. "Do you think the American political system is better constituted to cure social ills than the British system? Because I think we English tend to . . ."

As she and Lina talked politics, Elizabeth could see Jessica fighting to suppress a yawn—and losing the battle. It didn't take Jessica long to categorize people, and Elizabeth could tell her sister had already decided she had nothing in common with unglamorous Lina in her plain navy-blue dress and gray knee socks; spunky, flashy Emily the undisputed gossip queen of HIS was more Jessica's style. *Although with a bit of a fashion make-over, Lina would be very pretty,* Elizabeth found herself musing. *She reminds me of someone . . . but who?*

At that moment, the door to the bedroom was flung wide open from the other side. As it banged against the wall, Lina shot an ironic glance at Jessica and Elizabeth. "Here comes her royal highness," she whispered.

A tall, curvy girl with a cascade of wavy raven-black hair took one step into the room and then paused dramatically, surveying the scene through lowered lashes. Disdainful gray eyes raked Jessica and Elizabeth up and down. "Twins. How quaint," the girl drawled, as if to herself.

She breezed across the room without another glance at the girls. "Portia, this is Elizabeth and Jessica Wakefield, our new roommates from California," said Lina.

"Hmm," Portia murmured, stripping off her unstructured raw silk jacket and flinging it into the closet. "Delighted, I'm sure."

22

She sounded anything but. Elizabeth looked at Lina. Lina shrugged as if to say, *Your move, if you really want to make one.*

"We hear you're an actress," Elizabeth ventured, addressing Portia's back. "Emily says you have a role in a new play."

Flouncing from the closet to her dressing table, Portia sat down in front of the mirror, her back still pointedly turned to Elizabeth, Jessica, and Lina. "Hmm, yes."

Elizabeth made another attempt. "Actually, my sister's very interested in theater, aren't you, Jess? She's a member of the drama club at school. And I just love reading plays in English class, especially Shakespeare," Elizabeth rambled on.

Slowly, Portia pivoted in her chair and fixed Elizabeth with a withering look. "We *must* continue this fascinating chat sometime," she said in the haughtiest British accent Elizabeth had ever heard. "A cultural discussion with Americans, whose idea of theater is the thirty-minute situation comedy, promises to be immensely . . . *refreshing.*"

With that, Portia faced the mirror again and began removing her makeup. After brushing her hair for thirty strokes, she undressed and slipped into an elegant, lace-trimmed satin nightgown. "I do hope you're ready for lights-out," she announced, her hand hovering over the light switch.

Quickly, Jessica, Elizabeth, and Lina scrambled into their sleep attire. Lina and Jessica hopped into the top bunks and grinned across at each other, smothering giggles.

Elizabeth watched, fascinated, as Portia pulled back her covers, climbed into bed, donned eyeshades and earplugs, and then lay gracefully back on her pillow. *Emily wasn't exaggerating,* she marveled silently. *Portia's everything she promised, and more!*

For fifteen minutes, the room had been dead quiet. *They're all asleep,* Elizabeth thought, rolling over in her bed to face the window.

The waxing moon shone brightly, bathing Elizabeth's face in eerie light. The night breeze, as soft as a sigh, lifted the curtains gently and then let them drop again. Elizabeth was bone tired, but she couldn't sleep. Her head whirled with thoughts of home and her parents and Todd . . . and Rene and what the next day would bring.

"Jessica?" Elizabeth whispered after a moment, hoping her twin was still awake.

"Hmm?" Jessica mumbled sleepily from the top bunk.

"What do you think that old woman on the sidewalk meant when she said 'Beware the full moon'?"

The bunk creaked as Jessica rolled over. "She meant beware of werewolves, of course. Remember the line from *An American Werewolf in London*? The villagers tried to warn the Americans about werewolves, but they didn't listen. And look what happened to them!"

Jessica's tone was lighthearted and teasing, but Elizabeth felt spooked. "You don't *believe* in werewolves, do you?" she asked, pulling her covers up to her chin and eyeing the moon with apprehension.

A muffled snort floated down from the top bunk. "*I* don't," Jessica said, "but obviously that nutty lady did!" She howled softly, and they both broke up laughing.

Chapter 3

Monday morning dawned wet and cool and foggy. "Pretty different from summer in Sweet Valley," Jessica said to Elizabeth as they dug into their hearty breakfast of eggs, sausage, and baked tomatoes. "Does it rain here all the time, you guys?"

"Pretty often," Lina acknowledged, digging into a bowl of muesli. "I can't imagine living someplace where it's always warm and sunny. No wonder you two are so bronzed."

Jessica felt a momentary pang, thinking about how she would while away the first day of summer vacation if she were back in Sweet Valley. *I'd sleep until noon and then head to the beach with Lila and Amy, where we'd spend hours just lounging on the white sand, reading fashion magazines and scoping guys.* "By the end of this internship, I'll have lost my tan completely and be pale as a ghost," Jessica predicted mournfully.

"A month in London is worth it, though, don't you think?" said Emily.

"Yes, we'll try to make it up to you," promised Lina.

Jessica's expression brightened. "Maybe I'll cultivate the pale, aristocratic look of a British royal," she mused. Imitating the newspaper photo of the missing princess, she pursed her lips in a sulky, blue-blooded pout.

Lina smiled. "That's it exactly."

After finishing breakfast, the four girls bused their dishes and headed into the front hall, where they converged with David and Gabriello. Only Portia still lingered in bed, having grumbled about how much noise the twins and Lina made getting ready for work earlier.

"I'm off to the BBC," Emily declared, sauntering out to the sidewalk. "Have fun at the *Journal*, Liz and Jess. Can't wait to hear all about it!"

Elizabeth and Jessica waved after Emily, then turned to bid good-bye to Lina; the soup kitchen was in the opposite direction. "See you tonight!" Lina called back to them.

David and Gabriello shouldered backpacks weighted down with books; Gabriello also carried a violin case. "We're walking to the corner to catch the bus to the university," said Gabriello, shaking back his shaggy black hair. "How about you?"

"We take the tube," Elizabeth told him. "Have a good day, guys."

"The tube—that's such a funny name," Jessica chattered as she and Elizabeth walked toward the street and prepared to cross. "Why don't they just call it a subway? I mean, isn't it the same thing?"

Looking over her shoulder, Jessica tossed one last wave to Gabriello and David and then stepped off the curb. A piercing horn sounded and Elizabeth grabbed Jessica's arm, yanking her back onto the sidewalk with a warning cry. "Jessica, watch out!"

A blood-red double-decker bus roared past them, right over the spot where Jessica had been standing only an instant before. Jessica gasped. "You looked the wrong way, just like the cabdriver said you would!" Elizabeth exclaimed, giving her sister's arm a shake. "You'd better be more careful. Do you want to get *killed* on your first day in London?"

Jessica took a deep breath, trying to slow her racing heartbeat. Shaken by this close call, she looked both ways with exaggerated care. "How come it's always me who makes all the dumb mistakes?" she muttered as she and Elizabeth scurried across the street and continued on their way to the *Journal*.

"This part of the city is very ancient and historical," Elizabeth told Jessica as they walked from the tube station to the offices of the *London Journal*. "It was laid out in the seventeenth century by the famous architect Sir Christopher Wren, after a big fire burned most of London down to the ground. The streets are like spokes in a wheel, all radiating outward from St. Paul's Cathedral."

They stopped in front of a tall building with the newspaper's name blazoned over the door. "This is it." Elizabeth patted the shoulder bag, which held a notebook and her new miniature tape recorder. "Ready to report some news, Jess?"

They pushed through the revolving door to find the newspaper office in chaos. Past the reception desk, the twins could see *Journal* staffers running to and fro like hamsters in a cage. "We're looking for the editor-in-chief, Henry Reeves," Elizabeth told the receptionist. "He's expecting us. We're—"

The receptionist waved them in without bothering to take their names. "Go ahead. If you can find him, more power to you."

"I wonder what's going on?" Jessica whispered as they made their way through a sea of desks. Telephones were ringing everywhere, and the hum of voices and clattering computer keyboards was deafening.

"A big story must be breaking," Elizabeth surmised, her heart leaping with excitement. "Let's find out!"

"Excuse me." Elizabeth waved to catch the attention of a young woman sprinting by. "We're looking for—"

The woman didn't even break stride to glance at the twins. "Excuse me, sir," Elizabeth tried again, this time reaching out to touch an older man's sleeve. "Can you tell me where—"

The man brushed past her. "Ask the receptionist."

Jessica had a different tactic. Planting herself squarely in front of the next person to approach, she put her hands on her hips and demanded loudly, "What's all the fuss about?"

The middle-aged woman, her gray hair flying in every direction, stopped just long enough to say, "You mean you haven't heard? It appears that Cameron Neville, a prominent London doctor, was murdered last night. His body was discovered only *minutes* ago!"

Clutching an armful of manila folders, the woman bustled off. Jessica and Elizabeth gaped at each other. "A *murder*," Jessica squeaked.

"Looks like your wish is coming true," said Elizabeth, referring to her sister's flip remark on the plane.

"Maybe Henry Reeves will put us on the story!" Jessica said hopefully.

Elizabeth couldn't deny that this prospect was very appealing. *We'd work with Scotland Yard to solve the case,* she fantasized. *Our story would be on the front page and we'd have our very own by-lines: 'Reported exclusively for the* Journal *by Elizabeth and Jessica Wakefield'!*

"Henry Reeves can't put us on *any* story if we don't find him and introduce ourselves, though," she pointed out.

"Which may never happen, as everybody in this crazy office is ignoring us." Jessica craned her neck. "I'm going to the ladies' room and reapply some lipstick—be right back."

As Jessica disappeared in the direction of the rest rooms, Elizabeth continued the search for Henry Reeves. "He'd have a private office, of course," she murmured to herself, walking down one of the short hallways that sprouted out from the central office space. She peeked into a couple of empty conference rooms. "Maybe around this corner . . ."

Around the bend, the hallway ended in a large, open work area. Here, away from the frantic activity of the main office, a boy sat alone at a desk, writing in a notebook. "Excuse me," Elizabeth began, her voice sounding loud in the silence.

The boy jumped, startled. Slamming his notebook shut, he looked up at Elizabeth. Their eyes locked.

His were a clear, alpine-lake blue. His skin was fair and his hair, a long lock of which fell over his forehead, was almost black. He reminded Elizabeth of pictures she'd seen of the Romantic poet Lord Byron, and she caught her breath.

"I—I'm sorry if I startled you, but I was wondering whether you could tell me—"

Before she could finish her question, the boy sprang to his feet, still staring at her, his face pale and frightened as if he'd seen a ghost. Elizabeth would have repeated her apology, but she didn't get a chance. "I must . . . take care of something," the boy muttered vaguely. Then he bolted past her and disappeared.

Still puzzling over the strange encounter, Elizabeth retraced her steps. She bumped into her sister halfway. "I found Henry Reeves," Jessica declared triumphantly. "Come on!"

Together, they hurried to the editor-in-chief's

office. The door was wide open, and Henry Reeves was inside, talking to two of his reporters.

Elizabeth recognized him immediately from the photograph in a recent magazine article about the world's most influential newspaper publishers and editors. Under the stewardship of Henry Reeves, the *London Journal* had won a slew of journalistic honors and consolidated its position as the most widely read paper in England.

The three men continued their discussion, in argumentative tones, as Jessica and Elizabeth approached. Elizabeth cleared her throat. "Excuse me," she said hesitantly. "Mr. Reeves?"

The tall, silver-haired editor-in-chief turned toward her impatiently. "What do you want?" he snapped.

Elizabeth blinked. "Uh, I'm Elizabeth Wakefield and this is my sister, Jessica," she stuttered, shifting her feet. When Mr. Reeves stared at her without comprehension, she added, "We're the new summer interns from Sweet Valley High. We—we *were* supposed to start today, weren't we?"

"Yes, of course, today's fine. Just stay out of the way," Mr. Reeves said briskly. "Get over to Frank in society—the desk by the east window—tell him he can do whatever he wants with you."

With a distracted, shooing gesture, Mr. Reeves hustled Jessica and Elizabeth out of his office and slammed the door. The twins gaped at each other. "He acted like he'd never even heard our names before!" Jessica said, her eyes flashing indignantly. "What a jerk!"

Elizabeth's shoulders slumped with disappointment. So much for her dreams of working with Scotland Yard and being personally mentored by Henry Reeves, the perfect English gentleman-editor. "He's not what I expected," she conceded glumly. "I thought he'd have special assignments for us—I thought he'd take us under his wing."

"Instead, he's shoving us aside like unwanted furniture. This internship is really getting off to a great start," Jessica complained as they trooped back across the office. "I can't believe we flew all the way across the ocean to be assigned to the *social* page! Society," she muttered disdainfully as they stepped up to a cubicle with a nameplate reading: TONY FRANK, SOCIETY EDITOR. "What's that, tea parties?"

A sandy-haired man in a wrinkled blue Oxford shirt glanced up at the twins. His mouth twisted in a sardonic smile. "They're not just *any* tea parties, mind you, but the tea parties of the very rich and well-bred," he said dryly. "The *aristocracy*." He drew the word out, giving it a nasal, hoity-toity inflection. Elizabeth and Jessica giggled. "By the way, I don't think I've had the pleasure."

"Oh!" Elizabeth laughed. "We're Elizabeth and Jessica Wakefield, new interns from—"

Tony Frank held up a hand. "Let me guess." He grinned. "Sunny California."

"Bingo," said Jessica.

"So, how can I help you?" he asked, sitting on the edge of his desk.

"Mr. Reeves sent us over," Elizabeth explained.

"He didn't seem to remember that we were coming. He said to tell you you could do whatever you wanted with us."

"Ah." Tony Frank tapped a pencil on the desk. "And writing for the society column isn't exactly what you had in mind."

"Not really," Jessica confessed.

"Well, I don't like it any better than you do." Tony Frank's eyes glittered with sudden fire. "What I wouldn't give to get my hands on a story like the Dr. Neville murder. . . ." He refocused on the twins, a thoughtful smile on his lips. "Tell you what. Since Reeves doesn't seem to care what you do, let's see if we can't drum up something a little more interesting than tea parties."

Once again, Jessica and Elizabeth plunged into the whirl of the *Journal*. Following Tony, they made their way to a cubicle on the opposite side of the office. A big white storyboard was labeled: CRIME.

"Crime—now, *that's* more like it!" Jessica whispered to Elizabeth.

A beautiful tawny-haired woman in a forest-green silk dress was furiously typing on a computer. She glanced at the trio over the rims of her glasses. "Not now, Frank," she said, still typing.

"I'm not here to pester you for a date," Tony assured her, winking at Jessica and Elizabeth. "Orders from Henry. We have a couple of fresh new interns—twins, you see, a package deal—and he says we're to flip for them."

"We're working on the biggest murder in *years*, Frank, not to mention the missing princess," the woman reminded him crisply. "I don't have time to be a Girl Guides leader. They're all yours."

"Fair is fair," said Tony, taking a coin from his pocket. "Heads or tails?"

With an exasperated sigh, the woman pushed her glasses up on her nose. "Heads."

Tony flipped the coin, then showed her the results, a broad smile on his face. "What luck—heads it is! Elizabeth and Jessica Wakefield, meet your new boss, our distinguished crime editor, Lucy Friday."

Lucy narrowed her hazel eyes at Tony. *If looks could kill!* Elizabeth thought. Tony just grinned, his eyes fixed on Lucy's. Their staring contest lasted for a long, supercharged minute. Then, with another conspiratorial wink at the twins, Tony stuck his hands in his trouser pockets and sauntered off, whistling.

Surreptitiously, Jessica pinched Elizabeth's arm. The sisters were ecstatic. "We're going to cover the murder story with Lucy!" Jessica mouthed.

Lucy, meanwhile, was drumming her fingers on the desk. "I don't need a couple of interns tripping me up today," she grumbled. "You'll probably do fine on your own if the story's nothing too big. . . ."

She contemplated the storyboard, with its long list of crimes to be reported. Then she tore off a scrap of paper and scribbled rapidly. "Here," she said, handing the paper to Elizabeth along with two press cards she'd removed from her top desk drawer. "You'll cover Bumpo's beat. He's a Scotland Yard detective, and this morning he's looking into the case of Lady Wimpole's missing Yorkie. This is the address. Report back to me." With that, she turned back to her computer and resumed typing, apparently forgetting instantly that the twins even existed.

Press cards in hand, Jessica and Elizabeth headed out to the street. "A Scotland Yard detective!" Jessica gushed. "What's a Yorkie, anyway? A type of gemstone? A car?"

"A little yappie dog," her sister informed her flatly. "Our first crime story for the illustrious, high-toned *London Journal* is going to be about a lost *dog*!"

Jessica felt deflated, but only for a moment. "Let's make it fast, then," she recommended. "After Lady Wimpole's, we have to get to Essex Street."

"What's on Essex Street?" asked Elizabeth.

Jessica grinned triumphantly. "The scene of the crime—the big murder everybody's talking about. I saw the address written in Lois Lane's datebook."

Elizabeth grinned. "Very clever, little sister. Very clever!"

A maid in a crisp black uniform with a white apron and cap admitted them into Lady Wimpole's fashionable Knightsbridge townhouse. Stepping into the front parlor, Elizabeth and Jessica found the plump society matron seated on an overstuffed couch with a red-faced police detective, looking at photographs in a leather-bound album.

"And here's poor Poo-Poo on his third birthday," Lady Wimpole told the detective. Sniffling loudly, she dabbed her eyes with a lace-edged handkerchief. "We gave him the *loveliest* party. All the other doggies in the neighborhood were invited, and they brought the most generous, thoughtful gifts." She flipped to another page in the album. "And here is Poo-Poo at the seashore last holiday. Isn't he just darling in his little sunsuit?"

"Um, yes, yes, quite," Sergeant Bumpo mumbled, sliding a finger into his shirt collar as if it were choking him.

When Jessica and Elizabeth proffered their *Journal* press cards, Lady Wimpole beckoned them forward eagerly. "Oh, *do* write a thorough report, girls," she begged, "and see to it that it's featured prominently. Tell the editor I *insist*. We simply must find Poo-Poo—we *must!*"

Jessica put a hand to her mouth to smother a laugh. "Of course, of course. Ahem," Sergeant Bumpo spluttered. Patting his pockets for a minute or two, he finally located a small, dog-eared notebook and pencil. "Perhaps you could provide some details, Lady Wimpole," he requested, his expression remaining utterly serious. "When did your pet disappear and what were the circumstances?"

Their own pencils poised, Jessica and Elizabeth also waited politely for Lady Wimpole's response.

"It was last evening, at sunset," Lady Wimpole began, stifling a sob. "After supper, Grimsby, our butler, put Poo-Poo out as usual. But the careless man, not to notice that there was a hole in the garden fence!" Lady Wimpole's distress made her breathless; she gasped like a fish out of water.

"When Grimsby went to let Poo-Poo back in a quarter of an hour later, he was nowhere to be seen. Grimsby and Olivia the maid and Lord Wimpole traipsed up and down the street for *hours* calling Poo-Poo's name, but to no avail. I'm deathly afraid . . ." Lady Wimpole sank back against the sofa cushions, half fainting. "I'm *deathly* afraid it's the work of *dognappers*," she concluded in a weak but emphatic whisper.

"I see, I see." Sergeant Bumpo furrowed his brow and made a note of this theory. "Um, yes, hmm."

Jessica shot a mischievous glance at Elizabeth and then turned to the detective. "Dognappers," she mused, adopting a serious and professional air. "Has Cruella DeVille been rounded up for questioning, Sergeant?"

"DeVille, eh?" Elizabeth struggled not to laugh as Sergeant Bumpo put pencil to paper. "How did you spell that first name?"

As Jessica spelled the name of the villainess from *One Hundred and One Dalmations* for Sergeant Bumpo, Elizabeth turned away, trying to hide her laughter by pretending to be overcome by a fit of coughing.

"I think we have all the information we need for our story," Jessica declared, rising to her feet. "But do call us at the newspaper, Sergeant Bumpo, if you get any leads on the case."

"Oh, just one more thing," Lady Wimpole cried. Removing a photo from the album, she presented it to Elizabeth. "A picture of Poo-Poo to accompany your story." Her tiny eyes brimmed with tears. "And please mention that there will be a *sizable* reward to anyone who returns our darling to us."

Elizabeth pocketed the photograph. "We'll do that," she promised.

They left Sergeant Bumpo still in Lady Wimpole's clutches, squinting in a befuddled fashion at yet another doggie photo album. The maid showed them to the door. Safely outside on the sidewalk, Jessica and Elizabeth exploded with pent-up laughter.

"Oh, poor Lady Wimpole," Elizabeth gasped. "And poor Poo-Poo!"

"Dognapped—what a dire fate." Jessica clutched her sides. "Do you think Sergeant Bumpo will ever escape from that stuffy parlor?"

"At some point, Lady Wimpole has to let him go if she wants him to find her dog." Elizabeth wiped her eyes, hiccuping. "Fat chance of *that*, though. He couldn't find the notebook in his own pocket!"

"Obviously Scotland Yard gives him all the stupidest, most trivial cases. He couldn't be trusted to solve a *real* crime."

"Lucy probably thought she was keeping us out of trouble, assigning us to his beat," Elizabeth agreed.

"Lucky we know how to find action on our own!" Jessica pulled a London city map from her shoulder bag and quickly determined the quickest route to Essex Street. "There's the bus we want to take," she said, pointing to the corner. "Let's go!"

They got off at a bus stop half a block from the Essex Street address of the deceased Dr. Neville. Approaching the elegant Victorian-era townhouse, they saw signs of frantic activity in the otherwise quiet residential area. Sober-faced police officers bustled in and out of the building, which was cordoned off by bright yellow police tape; a stern-looking London bobby stood watchful guard at the wrought-iron gate.

Jessica and Elizabeth paused in the shadow of one of the spreading oaks that lined the street. "I don't know, Jess," Elizabeth said doubtfully. "How can we sneak past an entire *army* of police officers? I'm sure they won't want us snooping around!"

Jessica folded her arms across her chest and considered the situation. "We might as well try the oldest trick in the book," she said. "We've got nothing to lose if it doesn't work, right?"

Tiptoeing to the next tree, Jessica stooped and picked up a good-sized stone. Winding up like a major-league ball player, she pitched it as far as she could.

It hit the sidewalk twenty yards to the other side of Dr. Neville's gate. The bobby on guard heard the clatter; stepping onto the sidewalk to see what had caused the noise, he turned his back momentarily. Quick as a wink, the twins dashed from behind the tree and slipped through the open gate.

It was a short, tense sprint across the front

lawn. Diving into the cover of a rhododendron bush, Elizabeth and Jessica crouched close to the house, catching their breath and listening for sounds of pursuit. There were none.

"We made it!" Jessica whispered.

"Yeah, but now what?" Elizabeth wondered. "How do we get inside from here?"

"Maybe we don't need to go all the way inside," said Jessica. "I hear voices. There's a picture window above—let's just peek in."

Cautiously, the twins got to their feet again. The rhododendron continued to shield them, and they found that, when standing, their chins were just level with the windowsill and they could see inside. What they saw . . . and heard, however, almost made them wish they couldn't.

Elizabeth pressed a hand to her mouth, a tidal wave of nausea crashing over her. Then her journalistic instincts took over and, pulling her minicorder from her bag, she began describing what she saw.

The body of a man in dark flannel trousers and a camel's hair cardigan lay facedown in the middle of the parlor floor; underneath him, the pale carpet was soaked with blood.

"It's him," Jessica gasped excitedly. "It's the dead man!"

Lucy Friday stood close to the corpse, looking down at it and reciting something into a hand-held tape recorder similar to Elizabeth's. A flashbulb popped as a police photographer snapped shots of the body from various angles.

"Who do you suppose *they* are?" Elizabeth whispered to Jessica. There were two other people in the room, both well-dressed, middle-aged men. "They don't look like police."

"Private detectives? Friends of the doctor? The guy on the left looks pretty upset." Raising her camera, Jessica took a quick picture of the scene through the glass. "What's that thing he's holding?"

The man was staring down in disbelief at something flat and silver lying in the palm of his hand. "A cigarette case, maybe," Elizabeth guessed.

The side window was open a crack, and at that moment Lucy Friday's clear, dispassionate voice drifted out to them. The sight of the body was horrible enough, but her words were even more disturbing—they chilled Jessica and Elizabeth to the very bone. "The victim's throat has been ripped open," Lucy recorded, "as if by a wild beast. . . ."

Chapter 4

Five minutes later, Elizabeth and Jessica were riding a red double-decker bus back toward the *Journal.* Elizabeth sat with her shoulders hunched, still tense with dread; Jessica slumped, drained as if she'd just run a marathon.

"I think we got more than we bargained for when we set out looking for an exciting story," Jessica whispered.

Elizabeth nodded, shivering. Jessica's words on the airplane and Lucy Friday's observation over the body echoed through her brain. *I wouldn't mind a nice, ghoulish London murder. . . . The victim's throat has been ripped out, as if by a wild beast. . . .*

The twins relaxed somewhat as the bus carried them farther and farther from the scene of the crime. Still, when their stop approached and they stood to walk to the front of the bus, Elizabeth realized her knees were still shaking.

It was a sunny day, and the busy city seemed vibrantly alive—a stark contrast, Elizabeth couldn't help thinking, to the lifeless corpse in the dim parlor. As she jumped onto the sidewalk, she took a deep breath of fresh air, willing herself to feel a renewed sense of courage. *You're supposed to be a crime reporter,* she reminded herself, *cool and collected like Lucy Friday.*

"That was totally gruesome," Jessica said with relish as they trotted up the stairs to the *London Journal's* revolving doors. Having put a safe distance between herself and the dead body, Jessica had brightened up considerably. "Too bad Lucy would probably fire us if she found out we snuck over to Dr. Neville's." She patted her shoulder bag with the camera inside. "It would be so cool to write this up as our first article for the *Journal*—we have pictures and everything!"

Elizabeth didn't even like to think about that roll of film. "Just don't let anything slip to Lucy," she advised. "We were at Lady Wimpole's this whole time, OK?"

"Gotcha," said Jessica.

When they reported to Lucy's desk a few minutes later, they found the crime editor taking off her jacket and hanging it on the back of her chair. *She just got back from Dr. Neville's herself,* Elizabeth speculated, shooting a glance at Jessica.

"We got the story from Lady Wimpole," Jessica said. "What would you like us to do now?"

"Lady Wimpole?" Dropping a stack of folders and her datebook on the desk, Lucy blinked distractedly at Jessica. "Oh, right—the dog. Well, let's see. Why doesn't one of you write a blurb for this evening's 'Crime Reporter' column?"

"I'll do that," Elizabeth volunteered.

"Here's yesterday's paper. 'Crime Reporter' is at the back of the second section—take a look at how we present the short pieces," Lucy recommended. "As for you, Jessica . . ." She checked the storyboard once more. Quite a few items had been checked off as reporters divvied up the prospects and headed out to research their stories. Lucy's lips twitched, as if she were trying not to smile. "How about another Bumpo case? He's scheduled to look into a problem at Pembroke Green this afternoon—a theft of some sort. Get a write-up to me by four and we can squeeze that in tonight's 'Crime Reporter,' too."

Jessica rolled her eyes. "Not Bumpo again!" she groaned to Elizabeth as soon as they were out of earshot.

"Would you rather write up the Poo-Poo Report?" Elizabeth asked.

The two giggled. "I guess not." Jessica grinned. "If the rest of the Sweet Valley High newspaper staff could see you now!"

Tucked away in the remote corner of the office where Tony Frank had located a vacant desk for her, Elizabeth typed a few more words. She had nearly finished the Poo-Poo story, but it had taken much longer than it should have. She just couldn't concentrate. The report was fairly straightforward, but her thoughts kept drifting . . . back to Essex Street and the horrible fate of the unfortunate Dr. Neville.

Rewinding her mini-corder, Elizabeth played back the last part of the tape. As she listened to her own frightened whisper, a chill raced up her spine, making her teeth chatter. *The poor man's throat was ripped out,* Elizabeth thought, hugging herself to stop from shaking. Along with distress and revulsion, she couldn't help feeling curiosity, too. Who would commit such a vile crime, and why? What kind of person had Dr. Neville been; did he have enemies? Who were the two men standing over the body with Lucy?

Elizabeth hit the off button on the mini-corder just as someone spoke behind her. "Excuse me," a voice said timidly.

Elizabeth jumped, her heart leaping into her throat. Swiveling, she found herself face-to-face with the handsome, dark-haired boy she'd seen earlier that day, the one who'd run away when she tried to talk to him.

The boy tossed hair back from his forehead and gave her a rueful smile. "I came to apologize for being impolite this morning—and, look, now I've practically scared you to death," he said in a lilting, adorable English accent. "You'll have to forgive me twice over now. This morning, I was just so absorbed in my writing that you took me by surprise." His smile deepened, making his eyes crinkle at the corners. "I felt guilty, you see. Caught in the act." Leaning closer, he confided, "I was writing poems instead of working on my newspaper story."

Elizabeth couldn't tell him why she'd been so jumpy, so instead she stood up and extended a hand. "I'm Elizabeth Wakefield," she told him. "My twin sister, Jessica, and I are summer interns, from the States."

"Luke Shepherd." He gave her hand a light squeeze. "It's a pleasure to meet you."

"And to meet you." For some reason, Elizabeth felt herself blushing; maybe it was Luke's touch, or the shyly admiring look in his intensely blue eyes. She dropped her gaze. "Well . . ."

"I say, Elizabeth." Luke glanced at his watch. "Would you let me take you out to tea, to make up for my rudeness? I know a place just a few blocks away where the sandwiches are as thick as your arm and the Devonshire cream is the sweetest you'll find anywhere in London."

Elizabeth glanced down at her not-quite-finished report. Bending, she quickly keyed in a concluding sentence and then pressed the print command. "Let me just turn this in to my boss," she told Luke after the printer had spit it out. "If she gives me permission to leave early, I'd love to have tea with you."

"Pembroke Green," Jessica murmured to herself. The Pembroke family's stately residence, situated on one of the most fashionable squares in town, was encircled by lush gardens. "I see where it gets its name."

49

A minute after she rang the bell, the door was opened by a uniformed maid who might have been the twin of Lady Wimpole's. Jessica exhibited her press card. "I'm here to ask Lady Pembroke a few questions about the theft," she said in her most serious and self-important manner.

The maid led her to the rear of the house. Green filtered sunlight poured into the large, airy drawing room from an attached solarium filled with potted plants.

Sergeant Bumpo was standing awkwardly at attention in front of a regally seated Lady Pembroke. The thin, jewelry-bedecked woman, who was coiffed and manicured within an inch of her life, didn't bother rising when Jessica entered the room. "It's about time," Lady Pembroke said somewhat peevishly. "I certainly hope my story will be included in the P.M. edition. People should be *warned* what can happen when they check their furs at Brown's!"

What is she talking about? Jessica wondered. "I need you to start at the beginning," she requested, perching gingerly on the edge of a brocade-upholstered wing chair, even though Lady Pembroke hadn't invited her to sit down. Taking out her notebook, she tried her best to look professional. "What was stolen, and where did the theft occur?"

Lady Pembroke heaved an impatient sigh. "I was just telling the Sergeant, but I *suppose* I can go over it again. I was having tea at Brown's Hotel yesterday afternoon, and I made the mistake of checking my new mink."

Jessica bit her tongue to keep from saying, *You were wearing a* mink *in the* summer?

"Imagine my dismay when I claimed it," Lady Pembroke continued, "and wound up with a wretched chinchilla instead!"

"Wretched chinchilla," Jessica repeated, dutifully making a note.

"There it is, over there." Lady Pembroke waved a languid hand across the room at something brown and furry lying on the piano bench.

"Ah ha," grunted Sergeant Bumpo. Eager to examine the evidence, he hurried over to the piano, catching a toe under the edge of the Oriental rug as he went, nearly falling flat on his face.

Jessica swallowed a giggle. "Did you point out the mistake right away, or didn't you notice until you got home?" she asked.

Lady Pembroke arched an overplucked eyebrow. "Of course I realized *instantly* that I'd been given the wrong fur. But the scatterbrained coatcheck girl insisted that I'd checked the chinchilla. I demanded that the maître d' intercede and he searched high and low, but my mink had vanished. The dismal, stupid girl had sent it home with someone else!"

"How upsetting that must have been for you," Jessica murmured. *Especially as you probably have a whole closetful of minks upstairs!*

"Oh, it was." Lady Pembroke sighed. "It was."

At that moment, a movement in the hallway caught Jessica's attention. She turned her head just as a remarkably handsome young man in formal

51

English riding gear passed by the entrance to the drawing room. *Wow!* Straining to get a better look at him, Jessica nearly fell off her chair. *Yoo-hoo, over here!*

To her profound disappointment, the debonair young man didn't enter the sitting room, but rather turned on his boot heel to exchange a few words with another man who'd just entered behind him. The second man was quite a bit older, but there was a distinct family resemblance. *Father and son,* Jessica guessed. *Lord Pembroke, a.k.a. Mr. Wretched Chinchilla, and Lord Pembroke Junior.* Then something about the older man triggered Jessica's memory. *It's the man with the cigarette case!* she realized with a jolt of excited recognition. *The one who was standing over Dr. Neville's body!*

The two men moved out of sight, and Jessica did her best to refocus on Lady Pembroke and Sergeant Bumpo. Wrinkling his nose distastefully, the detective held the chinchilla at arm's length as if it were still alive and might bite him.

Jessica sneezed to disguise the laughter bubbling up in her throat. "Achew!"

"Bless you," Bumpo said solemnly. Then he turned to Lady Pembroke, clicking his heels together. "I'll need to confiscate this."

"By all means, take it—take it out of my sight."

"Is there anything else you think I should know?" Jessica asked Lady Pembroke, looking for a way to prolong the interview so she might get another glimpse of the handsome horseman.

"That's all, I believe," Lady Pembroke replied.

"Well, let's just go over this one last time," Jessica suggested. "I want to be sure the story is accurate in every detail."

With painstaking slowness, Jessica read back her notes to Lady Pembroke, keeping one eye on the hallway. Sergeant Bumpo, meanwhile, continued to prowl around the drawing room, occasionally colliding with something; a Ming vase came perilously near to sliding off a shelf and a fragile lamp teetered precariously.

Finally, there was nothing left for Jessica to do but tuck her notebook back in her shoulder bag. "Thanks for your cooperation," she said to Lady Pembroke. "I hope you get your mink back."

"Never fear," proclaimed Sergeant Bumpo.

"Well . . . so long." Jessica stood up just as the young man she'd spotted earlier strode into the room. Having showered and shaved, he now wore the clothes of an English gentleman, ascot and all. *He can't be real,* Jessica thought. *I must have wandered onto a movie set!*

The young man directed an amused glance at Sergeant Bumpo and then fixed a pair of dazzling midnight-blue eyes on Jessica. The frank admiration she saw there made her heart somersault.

"Exercising your power over the minions again, eh, Mother?" the young man teased. He continued to gaze at Jessica, his chiseled, aristocratic lips curling in a smile. "I'm Lady Pembroke's son, little Lord Pembroke. But you can call me Robert. And I can call you . . . ?"

Anytime! Jessica thought. "Jessica Wakefield,"

she said breathlessly. "From the *London Journal*."

"The *Journal*—yes, of course." Still smiling, Robert gave her a quick, practiced look up and down. "A bit young to be a reporter, aren't you? And if I'm not mistaken, your accent is distinctly American."

Jessica conceded the American part but hedged about her age in case Robert, who appeared to be about twenty, might lose interest if he knew she was only sixteen. "I'm a summer intern from the States. This is my first day on the job."

"And what an exciting day it's been, eh?" he kidded. "Somebody made off with Mother's mink. What's the world coming to?"

"Oh, Robert," Lady Pembroke said with mock exasperation. "Must you be flip about absolutely everything?"

"I'm not flip, I'm deadly serious," he swore. "So serious that I intend to do some of my own investigating. Have you gotten all the pertinent details, Miss Wakefield?"

When Jessica nodded, Robert took her left hand and hooked it through his arm. "Then how about tea at Brown's?" he suggested in the brash, confident manner of someone used to having his every wish gratified. He winked rakishly at Lady Pembroke. "There's no substitute for a visit to the scene of the crime, wouldn't you say, Mother?"

Luke opened the door to the pub. "The Slaughtered Lamb's not fancy, but the grub's first-rate," he promised.

54

Before stepping into the dark, wood-smoky interior, Elizabeth glanced up at the old wooden sign. It depicted a wolf standing over the body of a dead lamb, blood dripping from his fangs. "What a creepy name, though," she said. "And it was the name of the pub in this really scary movie I just saw, *An American Werewolf in London*. Did you ever see it?"

Luke's lips curved in a smile. "I did, as a matter of fact. Several times. But this is a different kind of pub, on my honor. Warm and cozy. You'll like it."

As they slid into a booth near the stone fireplace, Elizabeth smiled at Luke. "You're right, it is different. I like it already."

"It's the real thing. Not many pubs like this left in the city nowadays." He smiled wryly. "They've all given way to American fast-food restaurants."

Elizabeth laughed. "Don't blame me! I'm American, but I'd rather eat someplace like this anyday."

They ordered sandwiches, scones, and a pot of tea, and then a shy silence descended over them. "So . . ." Luke looked down at his hands, folded on top of the table, and then up at Elizabeth. "You and your sister are from California, ay? Just here for the summer?"

"Sweet Valley, California," said Elizabeth. "On the coast, north of L.A."

"Sweet Valley." A smile touched Luke's lips. "Sounds like heaven."

"It's beautiful," Elizabeth had to admit. "But we couldn't wait to come to London. This is such an exciting city, and there's so much *history*."

"Where are you staying?"

"HIS—Housing for International Students. It's like a dorm, with kids from all over the world."

The waitress placed a pot of steaming tea, cream and sugar, and two mugs on the table. "What do you think of the *Journal* so far?" asked Luke, pouring Elizabeth a mug of tea.

Tipping her head to one side, Elizabeth decided to be honest. Her instincts told her she could count on Luke's sympathy. "I was a little disappointed—no, a *lot* disappointed!—that Mr. Reeves basically forgot we were coming. But I know he's really busy, and it will probably work out fine. He turned us over to Tony Frank, who turned us over to Lucy Friday, who turned us over to Sergeant Bumpo of Scotland Yard."

"Scotland Yard—that sounds promising."

Elizabeth grinned. "Yeah. We reported on an investigation into a big disappearance."

"The princess?" guessed Luke.

"No, Poo-Poo the Yorkshire Terrier." Elizabeth related the episode at Lady Wimpole's, taking pleasure in Luke's hearty laughter. "Yes, you could say we're on the fast track. But what about you? What's your position at the *Journal*?"

A platter of sandwiches and scones was deposited on the table. After offering them to Elizabeth, Luke selected a fat, buttery scone, fresh from the oven. "I'm fairly new at the paper myself," he said, splitting the scone and spreading it with thick Devonshire cream. "I write for the arts and literature section, film and book reviews mostly. I'm hoping I'll have time to keep up with it when I start at the university in the fall—the cash would come in handy."

"And you write poems, too," said Elizabeth, topping her own scone with a dollop of strawberry jam.

"Yes. Just for myself, of course. As I said, that's what I was doing when you came upon me this morning. Sometimes the inspiration just strikes . . . there's nothing I can do but give in to it." His face reddened. "It probably sounds silly to you."

"Oh, not at all." Elizabeth reached out impulsively to touch his hand, her eyes shining. "I understand perfectly. I have a notebook, too, where I keep my journal, and I wouldn't go anywhere without it. I love poetry—it's my favorite thing."

Their eyes locked and a warm current of sympathy coursed between them, binding them close. "Thanks for not making fun of me," Luke said softly.

"I wouldn't, ever," Elizabeth replied.

Another spell of silence followed, but this time it was comfortable. Though she still didn't know much about him, Luke had ceased to be a stranger to Elizabeth, and she could tell he felt the same way about her.

Finishing her first scone, Elizabeth reached for another. "Did you move to London when you got the job at the *Journal*, or does your family live here?" she asked.

"My family . . ." Luke toyed with his teaspoon.

"My father is my only family. My father, and Mrs. Weldon, our housekeeper. We live in a house on the outskirts of town. A nice enough old house—I was born there, and so was my dad—but in desperate need of a new coat of paint, I'm sorry to say. My mother . . ." Luke's eyes dropped and Elizabeth saw his jaw clench. "My mother died of pneumonia when I was a boy."

"I'm sorry," Elizabeth whispered. "Oh, that must have been so hard."

When Luke looked up at Elizabeth, his eyes were damp with unshed tears. "I was very close to her—she was my whole world."

He pulled his wallet from his trouser pocket and removed a faded, creased photograph. Wordlessly, he handed the picture to Elizabeth. The lovely young woman looked very much like Luke. She had the same sweep of raven hair, the same spectacular blue eyes, the same shy, warm smile. "She's beautiful," said Elizabeth.

"She was even more beautiful on the inside," said Luke. "She was smart and kind. She was a writer, too—in fact, she staffed for the *London Journal* for a time. Working there . . ." Luke's voice cracked with emotion. "I feel painfully close to her."

Sympathetic tears sparkled in Elizabeth's eyes. "I can imagine." She shifted the subject somewhat, hoping to cheer Luke up. "How about your father—is he also a writer?"

Instantly, the sorrow on Luke's face gave way to a look of disdain. "My father doesn't have an ounce of creativity in his bones. He runs a shabby little corner drugstore—he's a pharmacist."

Luke's sudden hostility took Elizabeth by surprise. "Well . . ." she murmured awkwardly.

Luke studied her face. "I know what you're thinking. Such a tragedy *could* have brought my father and me closer together. Maybe if he'd shown some emotion when she died . . . but he didn't even seem to feel it. And when she fell sick, he should have known." Luke's hand tightened around the mug of tea, his knuckles whitening. "Of all people, as a druggist, he should have known how serious it was, how quickly pneumonia can take a turn for the worse and be fatal."

Luke shook his head. "I guess there are times when, even after all these years, I still can't believe she's gone. Forgive me for getting so emotional. And for talking so much about myself! I hope I haven't scared you off." His manner brightened; he smiled. "Because I want to learn about *you*, Elizabeth, and about life in the United States. Do you have any other brothers or sisters? What is your school like? Do you belong to clubs and play sports?"

Luke listened with an animated expression as Elizabeth told stories about her family and Sweet Valley. He prompted her with questions, as if hungry for conversation. *He's lonely*, Elizabeth sensed. *He must not have many people to talk to—he's eager for us to be friends.*

That was fine with her. She was incredibly glad she'd bumped into Luke on her first day working at the *Journal*. He'd struck a chord deep inside her. She felt tremendous compassion—and attraction—for this solitary, motherless poet.

"Another cup of tea, Jessica?"

Jessica nodded. "That would be lovely."

Robert lifted his chin and a waiter came running to ascertain his wishes. Within moments, their delicate china cups were refilled with hot tea and their plates with a fresh assortment of exquisite little cakes and tiny sandwiches.

This is the life, Jessica thought, gazing at her companion with something like awe. *Robert Pembroke, you are the man of my dreams!*

It was almost too good to be true. Here she was, sipping fragrant tea at the poshest hotel in London with the suave and handsome Lord Robert Pembroke, whom she'd met only an hour before. And *everyone* seemed to recognize him. It was such a thrill, being the object of admiring, envious glances—Jessica felt like a movie star.

Robert resumed the story he'd been telling, with a smitten Jessica hanging on his every word. "It really wasn't so bad, getting kicked out of Eaton," he drawled. "My parents just packed me off to auntie's for the summer. They thought perhaps my cousin would be a good influence on me. My cousin . . . Prince Malcolm," he added casually.

Jessica's jaw dropped. "*The* Prince Malcolm?"

"None other," said Robert.

"So, 'auntie' is . . ."

"The queen," he confirmed.

Jessica's already high opinion of Robert

Pembroke now soared up into the stratosphere. "You're *related* to the royal family?" she squeaked. "They're your *cousins?*"

"Well, it's a rather distant connection," he admitted. "Third cousins, once removed—something like that. But we've always been quite close."

Jessica tried to keep a grip on what was left of her composure; it was hard not to come across as a total starstruck idiot. "Umm," she murmured encouragingly, hoping to hear juicy details about his royal relations—maybe even get the inside scoop on the disappearance of Princess Eliana.

"But what about *you*, Jessica?" Robert leaned forward, his foot brushing hers under the table. "How do you come to be working for my father's newspaper?"

"Your father's newspaper?" Jessica echoed, worrying that she was starting to sound like a parrot.

"My humble clan owns the *London Journal*, didn't you know that?" Robert grinned wickedly. "Why do you suppose you got exclusive rights to Mummy's tragic tale?"

Jessica laughed. "It was the first story I've investigated on my very own. It could be my big breakthrough, the stepping-stone to my own byline."

Robert patted the pockets of his jacket. "Now, where are my cigarettes? Just as well I haven't got them—I really should kick the habit. So, you want to be a journalist, Jessica."

"Not really," she admitted. "My sister does— I'm mostly along for the ride."

"And how's the . . . ride . . . so far?"

Jessica dimpled flirtatiously. "We only arrived yesterday, but already I have a feeling it's going to be the ride of my life."

"We'll make sure of it," Robert declared. "You know, my father takes quite an active interest in the paper, and he's always hoped I'd follow his example, take over the reins someday. Can't say I've lived up to his expectations . . . although I did stop in last week to hobnob a bit with ol' Henry. He seemed to be frantically worried about the *London Daily Post* stealing away our readers. Not bloody likely if you ask me. But now . . ." The look Robert gave her made Jessica's heart melt like butter. "It appears that I'll have to find more excuses to drop by the office. In the meantime . . ." Reaching across the table, he touched her hand. "Are you free tomorrow evening? May I show you around my city?"

Jessica forced herself to take a sip of tea before replying. She didn't want to come across as too eager, to reveal that she was totally infatuated. Rich, handsome, elegant, sophisticated Lord Robert Pembroke had taken her out to tea, and she'd obviously passed muster because now he was asking her for a *real* date!

"I'd love that," she said casually, thinking meanwhile, *If Lila and Amy could see me now!*

Chapter 5

Elizabeth was sitting with her legs hooked over the arm of an easy chair, her eyes half closed and a dreamy smile on her lips, when Jessica burst into their room at HIS just before dinnertime.

"You won't believe what happened to me this afternoon." Tossing her shoulder bag onto the bed, Jessica flung herself into the other chair. "You won't *believe* who I've fallen madly in love with!"

Elizabeth opened her eyes and fixed her sister with a mischievous smile. "Sergeant Bumpo?"

"Actually, that imbecile played cupid, in a manner of speaking. If Lucy hadn't assigned us to his beat, I wouldn't have gone to Pembroke Green on a story. And if I hadn't gone to Pembroke Green, I wouldn't have met Lord Pembroke Junior, and if I hadn't met Lord Pembroke Junior, he couldn't have taken me out to tea at Brown's Hotel!"

"Lord Pembroke Junior took you out to tea at

Brown's Hotel?" repeated Elizabeth. "Who's he? Where's that?"

"Liz, you wouldn't believe their house, and it's just their *London* residence—they have a castle in the country. A castle, a real live castle! And not only *that*." Jessica paused dramatically. "They're related to the *queen*. The queen! Robert practically grew up in Buckingham Palace, playing cricket and polo and what have you with Prince Malcolm."

"Wow," Elizabeth said politely.

"I'll never be able to date a Sweet Valley High boy again," Jessica concluded with a rapturous sigh. "Now that I know what it's like to go out with a *nobleman*."

Elizabeth smiled. "I had a feeling it wouldn't take you long to elbow your way into the royal family."

"I didn't elbow my way anywhere," Jessica insisted righteously. "Can I help it if Robert Pembroke took one look at me and fell head over heels for my sexy American style?"

Her sister laughed. "I guess not."

"So what about you?" Jessica kicked off her shoes and tucked her legs up on the chair. "How did you spend *your* afternoon?"

Elizabeth glanced out the window, the dreamy look returning to her eyes. "I went out to tea with a guy from work," she replied. "Luke Shepherd. He writes for the arts and literature section—I'll introduce you to him tomorrow."

"I don't suppose *he's* related to royalty," said Jessica with a superior sniff.

Elizabeth shook her head. "No, but he's very

nice. And smart and sensitive. . . . We had the most interesting talk! It was as if we'd known each other for years instead of hours." Her cheeks warmed, remembering the intimacy of their booth at the Slaughtered Lamb. "After tea, he took me for a walking tour of literary London. It was wonderful, like stepping back in time." Her eyes sparkled with animation. "We saw places that Dickens and Trollope and Thackeray wrote about, and where E. M. Forster and Virginia Woolf and the rest of the Bloomsbury group lived, and where Henry James went for tea and an afternoon stroll. Luke's read more books than anyone I've ever met, including Mr. Collins. He's so different from . . ."

The sentence trailed off, unfinished. Elizabeth's blush deepened. *What am I doing, comparing Todd to Luke?* she wondered with a pang of guilt.

Elizabeth knew she should be pining for her boyfriend, but it was useless to pretend that Luke Shepherd hadn't made a striking impression on her. She shrugged, trying to sound more casual. "There's just . . . something about him."

"Yeah, something incredibly *boring*," Jessica remarked, yawning. "A walking tour of literary London—blech. You have a warped idea of fun, Liz."

"To each her own, I guess."

"You'd better believe it. Lord Pembroke's taking me out tomorrow night and, I can tell you, *we* won't be *walking* anywhere. It's going to be limousines all the way!"

"Well, la di da. Excuse *me*, Lady Robert Pembroke *Junior*."

"Lady Pembroke—I like the sound of *that*. Am I glad I didn't decide to settle for one of these run-of-the-mill HIS boys."

Luke's pale, romantic face faded from Elizabeth's mind, and the bronzed, chiseled features of Rene Glize took its place. "I almost forgot about Rene," she mused out loud. "We never really got to explore our feelings for each other in France."

"Well, if you want my opinion," said Jessica, "this Luke guy sounds like a dud. Rene, on the other hand, is a total— Hey, what's that on your bed?"

Elizabeth hadn't noticed it before, but now she saw that someone had placed a red rose on her pillow. Padding over, she picked up the rose and the folded note that lay beneath it. "It's from Rene," she told Jessica.

"Read it, read it!" Jessica clamored.

"'*Chere* Elizabeth, I'll be at an embassy function all evening, but didn't want to waste a minute making a date with you. Would you have dinner with me tomorrow night? I know a wonderful little French café. . . . I hope you are free tomorrow, as it's my only night off all week and I want to spend it with you. Please leave me a note. Love, Rene.'"

"Ooh la la," Jessica teased, pursing her lips and blowing a noisy kiss. "Sounds like Rene's ready to explore *his* feelings."

Elizabeth blushed more furiously than ever. "I'm sure we both want the same thing—to be very good friends. Unlike *some* people, I didn't come to London looking for romance."

66

Jessica shook her head. "Still . . . two new suitors in twenty-four hours, Liz?" she teased. "I'd say that's moving pretty fast for somebody who's not looking for romance. Poor, poor Todd!"

I didn't come to London to look for romance, Elizabeth repeated to herself as she scribbled a note to Rene, accepting his invitation to dinner the following night. An image flickered through her mind—a boy's lake-blue eyes, milky skin, and sweep of dark hair. . . .

Quickly, Elizabeth banished the picture of Luke Shepherd, summoning up instead Todd's warm smile and coffee-brown eyes. "Are you ready?" Jessica asked impatiently.

Folding the note, Elizabeth followed her sister out of the bedroom. As they walked downstairs, she glanced at her watch. "Dinner doesn't start for five minutes," she said. "Let's run out and buy the evening edition of the *Journal.*"

"I can't wait to see my story about Lady Pembroke's mink. If it's not on the front page, I'm quitting," Jessica joked.

"You know what *will* be on the front page—Dr. Neville's murder," Elizabeth reminded her.

"I almost forgot about that. This was such a long day. It feels like years since we looked in the window and saw . . . *him.*"

Elizabeth shivered. *I'll never forget,* she thought. *The body, the blood* . . .

"C'mon." Jessica pushed open the door to the street. "Or we'll be the last ones into dinner and we'll get stuck sitting with Portia."

They jogged to the nearest newsstand, three blocks away near the tube entrance. Fishing in her purse for change, Elizabeth paid the vendor while Jessica picked up a copy of the *Journal*.

Side by side, they peered eagerly at the headlines. "Where's the murder story?" Jessica asked.

Elizabeth's eyes ran up and down the front page. "I don't see it," she said, surprised. "Maybe it's on the second page."

Jessica snatched the paper from her. "Let's find our stories first. Lucy said 'Crime Reporter' is at the back of the second section."

Sure enough, half of the second-to-last page of the local news section was devoted to the London 'Crime Reporter,' edited by Lucy Friday. "Look!" Jessica squealed, delighted. "There's my piece, 'The Fur Flies at Brown's.' Doesn't it look great?"

"Great title." Elizabeth found her own piece sandwiched between write-ups about a downtown traffic accident and a foiled bank robbery. "No picture of Poo-Poo—Lady Wimpole will be disappointed!"

"Liz, look." Jessica pointed to a box set next to the 'Crime Reporter' column. "The Dr. Neville murder story!"

It took only a moment to skim the article, which wasn't much longer than the 'Crime Reporter' blurbs. "What's a big story like this doing buried back here?" wondered Jessica.

A puzzled frown creased Elizabeth's forehead. "It's not a big story anymore. Listen to this: 'Prominent physician Cameron Neville was killed in his home late Sunday night. He was pronounced dead on the scene by London Police Department emergency medics. Memorial services will be held . . . ' Et cetera."

"They left out all the gory details!" Jessica cried.

"You can't even tell from this that he was *murdered* as opposed to being killed accidentally," Elizabeth agreed.

"People don't get their throats ripped out by accident," Jessica declared. "It's not like falling down the stairs or something. I don't get it. After all the fuss everyone was making, why would Lucy play down the story like this?"

Elizabeth chewed her lip. "She wouldn't. This can't be the article she was working on all day. It simply can't be."

Thoughtfully, she turned back to the front page. "Maybe that's why Dr. Neville got shoved to the back of the paper," Jessica speculated. "The missing princess is still hogging all the headlines." She indicated the biggest one. "'Princess Eliana Kidnapped?' Wow, that's terrible! Did they get a ransom note? Who did it?"

Elizabeth ran her eye down the column of print. "According to this, there hasn't actually been a ransom note. They don't have *evidence* that she was kidnapped—it's just a theory."

"So, that huge headline's just to catch people's eyes and sell more papers."

"I guess so. I didn't think the *Journal* stooped to sensationalism—I thought it was intellectual and objective."

Jessica shrugged. "It's a big story—you can't blame them for playing it for everything it's worth."

"Then why wouldn't they do the same with Dr. Neville's murder?" Elizabeth countered. "What could be more sensational than that?"

"Good point."

For a minute, the sisters stood reading the paper in silence. Accompanying the story about Princess Eliana was an interview with Andrew Thatcher, the London chief of police. Suddenly, Elizabeth's eyes widened in startled recognition. "This man!" she gasped, pointing to the photograph of the police chief. "Jessica, wasn't he . . . ?"

Jessica studied the picture and then nodded excitedly. "The other man we saw through the window at Dr. Neville's!"

Elizabeth blinked at her sister. "The *other* man?"

"Didn't I tell you?" Jessica slapped the palm of her hand to her forehead. "I can't believe I forgot—I guess I was so wrapped up in Robert that I—Lord Pembroke!" she explained disjointedly. "Or rather, Lord Pembroke *Senior*. Robert's father. I caught a glimpse of him at Pembroke Green and I'm ninety-nine percent positive he was one of the two men standing over the body, the one holding the cigarette case."

"And the London chief of police was the other," Elizabeth mused. "Lord Pembroke Senior . . . hmm. Do you suppose he was a friend of Dr. Neville, or a patient? Or could he have been there just by coincidence?"

"I have no idea," said Jessica. "I didn't think to ask Robert about it."

"It's better that you didn't, since we weren't supposed to be spying through that window in the first place. Officially, we don't know anything."

"Unofficially, we don't know anything, either," Jessica pointed out. "Lord Pembroke Senior and Police Chief Thatcher were at Dr. Neville's, but so what?"

"It may mean something," Elizabeth insisted. "It *has* to mean something. If the chief of police himself went to investigate Dr. Neville's death, then it must be a high-profile crime, so why wasn't it given bigger press?"

"Something's fishy," Jessica concluded.

"Something's *very* fishy," Elizabeth agreed.

"Well, take your pick," Jessica whispered in Elizabeth's ear as they stood in the entrance to the HIS dining room five minutes later. "There are two free seats at that table . . . and a few more over there."

Elizabeth stifled a giggle as she surveyed their choices. Lina, Emily, David, and Gabriello sat at a table for six near the big bay window, while a solitary Portia occupied a small table in the corner, the book in her free hand held to eye level as if to block out any offensive view of her dormmates.

The twins made a beeline for the group by the window. "Hi, everybody!" Jessica said brightly, slipping into an empty chair.

She tossed the folded newspaper onto the

71

table, front page up. Lina jumped.

"Not more missing princess headlines," Emily groaned, seizing the paper and throwing it under the table. "Does anyone mind if we *don't* spend the entire meal discussing who might have kidnapped her?"

"Fine with me," said Gabriello, tearing off a hunk of fresh-baked bread and then passing the loaf to Elizabeth.

"And me," murmured Lina.

"Tell us about your first day at the *Journal*," invited Emily as the kitchen staff began distributing plates piled high with pot roast, peas, and potatoes. "Did you get a good assignment or is it going to be deadly dull?"

Elizabeth shot a glance at Jessica, knowing her sister had the same thought. *Deadly yes, but not dull!*

"We're covering the beat of a Scotland Yard detective who couldn't solve a crime if it happened right under his nose," Jessica told Emily and the others. "Sergeant Bumpo."

David chuckled. "Is that really his name?"

Jessica nodded. "And it suits him perfectly. He's like a bull in a china shop—he crashed into just about every breakable thing in the drawing room at Pembroke Green. Which reminds me!" she exclaimed, turning to Emily with sparkling eyes. "Guess who's taking me out on the town tomorrow night?"

Emily laughed. "Don't tell me you've already met Prince Charming!"

"*Lord* Charming, actually," said Jessica, dimpling. "Robert, the only son of Lord and Lady Pembroke of Pembroke Green and Pembroke Manor."

"The Pembrokes own half of England, and the *London Journal* to boot!" Emily cried.

Elizabeth's eyebrows arched in surprise. "They own the *Journal*?"

Jessica nodded. "Isn't it exciting, Em?"

"You're the luckiest girl in the world," her friend declared. "Now if some of your luck would only rub off on me . . . !"

As Emily begged Jessica for a blow-by-blow account of tea with Robert Pembroke, Elizabeth smiled at Lina. "How was *your* day?"

Lina pushed a strand of hair back from her forehead and smiled back wearily. "Long. Tiring. But we fed forty people, found an apartment for a family of five, and helped a dozen or so fill out job applications. Sometimes I see the faintest glimmer of light at the end of the tunnel."

"You know, Lina, I . . . um, I think what you're doing is very admirable," a male voice ventured hesitantly.

Elizabeth and Lina both turned to look at the speaker. David ducked his head, hiding his eyes behind a shock of hair. "I know what it's like to go without, that's all," he continued, speaking down to his plate. "You're good to help them who are hard up."

Now it was Lina's turn to drop her gaze and blush. "It's nothing," she mumbled.

It was the first time Elizabeth had heard quiet

73

David Bartholomew utter two sentences in a row, and she waited with interest, hoping he'd pursue the conversation. Instead, he retreated back into his shell. Lina, too, fell silent, eating methodically with her eyes downcast. *Either she hasn't noticed that David has a huge crush on her,* Elizabeth mused, *or she doesn't want to notice.*

Jessica had finished reenacting every look and word that had passed between her and Robert Pembroke, and now she heaved a grumpy sigh. "This curfew is really going to cramp my style," she complained. "How am I going to tell Robert that Mrs. Bates will have my hide if I'm not back by eleven?"

"It's a total drag," agreed Gabriello. "A friend of mine from the music department at the university plays bass for a rock band, Lunar Landscape. They're booked at Mondo tonight and I'd love to go hear them, but the show doesn't even *start* until eleven."

"Mondo," Jessica raved. "Robert says that's the hippest club in London right now!"

"Robert's right," confirmed Gabriello. "So, what do you say we all sneak out after curfew and go dancing?"

Elizabeth could tell he was just kidding, but to her surprise Lina, of all people, took the suggestion at face value. "Let's do it! I haven't been to Mondo in the longest—" She checked herself. "I mean, I'd really like to hear some live music."

"I'm up for it," David announced boldly.

Emily and Jessica didn't need their arms

twisted. "Rules are made to be broken, that's my motto," Jessica declared. "How 'bout you, Liz?"

Elizabeth was gazing thoughtfully at Lina, curious about Lina's sudden, unexpected animation and about what she'd started to say: "I haven't been to Mondo in the longest *time*." *An odd remark for a poor working-class girl from Liverpool!* "Hmm? Yeah, sure," Elizabeth told Jessica. "Count me in."

"This is going to be so much fun!" Emily exclaimed. Then her face fell. "There's only one problem."

"Mrs. Bates?" Jessica guessed.

"I'm confident that between the six of us we can come up with a scheme to fool her. No, I was thinking about . . . *her*." Emily nodded toward the corner table.

They all turned to gaze at Portia. If she was aware of their scrutiny, she didn't show it. Daintily licking the tip of one red-nailed finger, Portia turned a page in her novel and once again raised it high.

"She'll snitch on us," Emily predicted gloomily. "She'll get us evicted from HIS."

"It's true we can't sneak out without her knowing," said Elizabeth. "So we need to get her on our side. Why not ask her to come along?"

Emily wrinkled her nose in distaste. "Hmph."

"It may be our best shot," Lina agreed reluctantly.

"*I'm* not asking her," Jessica told Elizabeth. "But if you want to set yourself up to get shot down, go ahead."

Elizabeth rose to her feet and strode purposefully toward Portia's table. *We're going to be roommates all month,* she reasoned. *It would be nice to be friends, too. Maybe I just didn't try hard enough last night.*

"Portia, hi," Elizabeth said.

One long beat passed, and then Portia lowered her book to nose level. The gray eyes that met Elizabeth's were expressionless. Without speaking, Portia arched her eyebrows inquiringly.

"Um, the rest of us were just— We were talking about— There's a great band playing tonight at Mondo," Elizabeth stuttered. "A friend of Gabriello's plays bass and we thought— It'll be after curfew but maybe we can sneak— Would you like to come along?" she finished in an incoherent rush.

Portia let a few more seconds tick by, seeming to enjoy watching Elizabeth squirm. "You all have a good time," she drawled, mimicking an American accent. "I personally prefer not to rub shoulders with the hoi polloi. But don't worry, I won't tattle to Mrs. Bates." In an unmistakable sign of dismissal, her eyes dropped from Elizabeth's face back to the pages of her book. "*That's* beneath me, too."

"Well, fine," Elizabeth muttered.

Whirling, she marched off, fuming silently. *See if I ever try talking to you again, Portia Albert! Who do you think you are?*

Chapter 6

At quarter past eleven that night, Jessica, Elizabeth, Emily, and Lina tiptoed down the dark staircase. David and Gabriello were waiting for them in the shadows on the second-floor landing. "So, who's going to lift Mrs. Bates's key?" whispered Gabriello.

"I am," Lina whispered back.

"How?" asked David.

"Watch this," said Lina.

With Lina leading, the six crept down to the foyer. As the others huddled in the dark dining room, Lina knocked loudly on Mrs. Bates's door across the hall. "Who is it?" Mrs. Bates called out suspiciously.

"Mrs. Bates, it's me, Lina. I have a terrible headache and I know I won't be able to sleep a wink if I don't get rid of it."

Jessica and Elizabeth peered out from the dining room, watching breathlessly. When Mrs. Bates yanked her door open, light spilled suddenly into the hallway. The twins jumped back, clutching each other and trying desperately not to giggle.

"Do you have any aspirin, Mrs. Bates?" Lina asked in a mouselike and apologetic manner.

Mrs. Bates pulled the belt of her bathrobe more snugly around her plump middle. "Come in, dear, come in," she invited impatiently. "Now, you wouldn't have a headache in the first place if you didn't squander your time tending to those ungrateful, good-for-nothing . . ."

Her voice trailed off as she shuffled across the floor, Lina trotting after her. A minute later, Lina reappeared. With her right hand, she waved an aspirin bottle at Mrs. Bates; her left arm was bent, her fist held behind her back. "Good night, Mrs. Bates. Thanks again—you're very kind."

Lina backed out of Mrs. Bates's room. The instant the door clicked shut, the others exploded out of their hiding place. "While Mrs. B. fetched the aspirin, I switched my room key for the front door key she keeps on a hook by the door." Lina displayed the purloined key triumphantly. "I'll switch them back in the morning when I return the pills. Now let's get out of here before the old hen pops out and catches us standing here!"

The well-oiled front door swung open soundlessly and the six teenagers flew out to the sidewalk. "We're free," Jessica sang.

"Which way to Mondo?" asked Elizabeth.

Gabriello pointed west. "It's walking distance,

but I say we head to the corner and hail a cab. Let's do this in style!"

They squeezed into the first taxi that came along. Elizabeth gazed out at the bright city lights blazing by, a rapt expression on her face. *We're going to dance until dawn, and Mrs. Bates will be none the wiser,* she thought, feeling daring and sophisticated. *Wait till I tell Todd and Enid about this!*

In a few minutes, the cabbie pulled up in front of a renovated warehouse marked by a neon globe proclaiming: MONDO. Elizabeth, Jessica, and the others piled out onto the sidewalk and joined the queue waiting to be admitted to the club.

Elizabeth eyed the stylish young people, suddenly feeling provincial in her plain, short knit dress. "It looks like a pretty hip crowd."

"It's *the* place in London if you want to see and be seen," Emily promised. "The people watching will be fantastic, I guarantee!"

"But we're here for the music," Gabriello reminded her as they received the nod from the bouncer and squeezed through the door.

"Speak for yourself," Emily teased, winking at Jessica.

The dark, smoky club was packed with bodies and pulsing with music. Strobe lights flashed, illuminating funky outfits, wild hairstyles, animated faces. "The dance floor is that way," Gabriello shouted, gesturing. "That's Basil's band playing right now. Let's head over!"

They pushed through the crowd, Jessica pausing occasionally to elbow Emily or Elizabeth in the ribs. "Look at that dress!" Jessica gaped at a girl in a leopard-print mini with holes cut down the front to her belly button. "Even Lila wouldn't show that much skin."

"How 'bout that one?" Emily pointed to a dress of black velvet and chiffon that looked to Elizabeth as if someone had gone at it with a pair of scissors.

"Ohmigod." Looking the other way, Jessica yanked on Emily's arm. "Em, isn't that . . . ?"

Emily clapped a hand to her mouth. "Lady Anne Binghamton. Her photo is *always* in the tabloids. She used to date Prince Malcolm!"

"Actually, she dated Malcolm's younger brother, Douglas," Lina corrected.

Emily snapped her fingers. "Right."

"There sure are some great-looking guys here," Jessica observed happily. "None as handsome as Robert Pembroke, of course, but still. Check *him* out."

Following Jessica's gaze, Emily gasped again. "I know that face," she declared. "It's . . . it's . . ." Elizabeth could see her mentally thumbing through the last issue of her favorite British celebrity magazine. "It's Percy Camden, the prime minister's son!"

"No." Once more, Lina shook her head. "I'm pretty sure that's Harry, the prime minister's *nephew*."

Emily raised her eyebrows. "Why, Lina, I had no idea you were on a first-name basis with the young London jet set!" she teased.

Lina smiled sheepishly. "What can I say, Em? Your bad habits are rubbing off—I've taken to fishing your tabloid newspapers out of the trash and reading them myself."

Within moments, Jessica and Emily were approached by two passably cute boys. As they melted into the hot whirl of bodies on the dance floor, Gabriello spotted his girlfriend, Sophie, and followed.

That left Elizabeth, Lina, and David. *Two's company, three's a crowd*, Elizabeth thought as she caught David gazing hopefully at Lina.

"Go on, you guys—take a spin," Elizabeth suggested with an encouraging smile. "I think I'll buy a soda."

"No," Lina said quickly, "you two should dance. I'm happy just listening to the music."

"So am I," David announced, clearly determined to stay by Lina's side. "I like this band. They remind me a little of a group from Liverpool. Monkeyshines—heard of 'em?"

"Um, no, I don't think so," said Lina.

"Where do you go to hear music in Liverpool?" David asked her.

Lina shifted her feet, looking poised for flight. "I don't think we're from the same part of town. We probably hang out at different pubs."

"Liverpool's not that big a city," David persisted amiably. "Try me."

"You wouldn't— Hi, Em! Hi, Jess!" Lina greeted the two returning girls with distinct relief. "Having fun?"

"Are we ever," declared Emily, lifting her auburn hair off her neck and fanning herself with one hand. "The music's outrageous. You've got to dance, all of you."

"Isn't Gabriello's friend Basil cute, Liz?" Jessica asked. "I can't wait till the band takes a break so I can meet him."

"Good luck tearing Gabriello away from Sophie long enough to get an introduction!" joked Emily. Then her gaze shifted from Gabriello and Sophie to another glamorous couple on the dance floor. "Ohmigod, look! It's Princess Gloria!" she squealed, pointing. "I was dancing right near her and I didn't even realize it!"

Jessica, Elizabeth, and David turned to gape. The beautiful young woman in high heels and a short, black sequined dress wore her fair hair piled loosely on top of her head; jewels glittered at her ears, throat, and wrists. "Wow," Jessica breathed.

"She's twenty-one—the queen's older daughter," said Emily. "There are pictures of her in magazines all the time—I can't believe I'm seeing her in person!"

It was pretty exciting, Elizabeth had to admit. Living in southern California, she and Jessica were used to spotting celebrities, but there was something special about royalty—unquestionably, Princess Gloria was more intriguing than any Hollywood movie star.

"What do you natives think about the royal family?" Elizabeth asked David and Lina. "Lina, had you ever— Are you all right?"

Lina's face was ghostly pale; she looked as if all the blood had been suddenly drained from her body. Elizabeth put a hand on her friend's arm and repeated the question. "Lina, are you OK?"

"No." Lina shook her head. "I don't feel well—I don't feel well at all. I'd better go home. Now!"

Abruptly, Lina spun on her heel and darted toward the exit. "I'll go with her," Elizabeth offered. "It's late. Maybe we should all go."

"But I'm not ready to leave yet!" Jessica wailed. "We just got here—I want to dance. I want to meet the guys in the band!"

"Tell you what—we'll leave the front-door key under the flowerpot," Elizabeth proposed. "Just don't stay out *too* late. We managed to sneak out undetected, but Mrs. Bates gets up at the crack of dawn. You wouldn't want her to catch you sneaking back *in*!"

Elizabeth caught up to Lina on the sidewalk just outside Mondo. "Lina, wait!"

A chill fog had crept into the city while they were inside; Lina's woolly cardigan was buttoned up to her neck. Elizabeth was relieved to see some color in her cheeks, however. "You look better," she said.

Lina nodded. "I *feel* better. For a minute in there, I thought I was going to faint. I guess I just needed some fresh air."

"You should probably go straight to bed." Fumbling in her pocketbook, Elizabeth was only able to come up with some small change. "Shoot. I don't have enough money for a cab."

Lina pulled the empty pockets of her cardigan inside out. "Me, either. But it's probably just a fifteen-minute walk back to HIS. The exercise will do me good."

They headed east into the fog. Two blocks from Mondo, they turned right onto Spencer Street. "This is a nice residential neighborhood," said Lina. "And it should connect straight through to Winchester."

The fog, curling thickly around trees and houses, dimmed the yellow globes of the street lamps. Cold, white fingers of mist brushed the girls' faces and sprinkled their hair with dew; they walked quickly and close together.

"I'm sorry to tear you away from all the fun," Lina apologized. "You're very sweet to look after me."

"It works out just fine," Elizabeth assured her. "This way, I'll be well rested for another day at the *Journal*." Her lips curved in a smile. "Anyhow, I'm sure there'll be other midnight escapades!"

"It's a fun bunch at HIS, isn't it?" Lina agreed.

"I like everyone a lot." Elizabeth thought of Portia Albert. "Well, *almost* everyone." She glanced at Lina out of the corner of her eye. "David is really nice, isn't he? The two of you must have a lot to talk about, being from the same hometown and all. And he's awfully cute."

A telltale blush stained Lina's fair cheeks. "Umm," she murmured. "He *is* that."

"You know, I think he likes you," Elizabeth ventured.

Lina hunched her slender shoulders, tucking her chin into the neck of her sweater. "He's a pleasant fellow. So sweet and serious . . . so different from other boys I've known. But I'm *not* looking for a boyfriend this summer," she added emphatically.

Something about Lina's tone discouraged further discussion. *What* are *you looking for?* Elizabeth wondered, deciding that underneath her plain surface, Lina Smith was really a very complicated girl.

They crossed a couple of side streets and then the road ended in a T. "Spencer dead-ends here," Lina observed. "We can go left or right but not straight."

Elizabeth peered through the fog at the cross streets. "Rochester. Does that ring a bell?"

"'Fraid not." Lina bit her lip. "But I think HIS is over . . . there." She waved a hand vaguely. "I say we turn left."

Elizabeth glanced back over her shoulder. The mist had closed in behind them, obliterating the path they'd just taken. The swirling white made her dizzy and disoriented. *We're lost—lost in the English fog,* Elizabeth thought, her heart contracting. *Just like the boys in the werewolf movie . . .* "Left is fine with me. I've lost all sense of direction, anyway."

They proceeded on, their steps tentative. The dense blanket of fog muffled all sound; the street was eerily silent, and the girls fell silent, too.

Suddenly, the night was shattered by a high-pitched shriek. Elizabeth's heart leapt into her throat; with a cry of fear, she grabbed Lina's arm.

A black cat sprang out of the mist, darting across the sidewalk in front of them. The two girls collapsed against each other, laughing with relief. "A cat. It was just a cat," Lina gasped.

Elizabeth took a deep breath to slow the pounding of her heart. "Look at us, scared to death by a little fog."

"It's too silly. C'mon." Lina hooked her arm through Elizabeth's. "Let's step lively, or we'll never get home!"

They lengthened their strides and Lina began whistling softly. Elizabeth knew her companion was still just as edgy as she was, though; the muscles in Lina's arm were tense, and her eyes darted continually from side to side.

And then Lina stopped dead in her tracks and screamed—a scream of pure terror that raked Elizabeth's nerves with teeth of ice. "Look," Lina choked, pointing with a trembling finger.

Something lay on the edge of the sidewalk—a tiny, crumpled, furry body. "It's a dog," Elizabeth whispered. "A dead dog." Then she saw the distinctive jeweled collar . . . and something else that made her blood run cold.

"Poo-Poo," she murmered. It was Lady Wimpole's missing Yorkshire terrier . . . dead, with his throat ripped out.

Elizabeth closed her eyes, swallowing hard.

Lina was crying softly. "Poor little thing. That horrible gash—it almost looks as if he were attacked by a wild animal. But how could that happen here in London?"

Elizabeth shuddered. *Attacked by a wild animal* . . .

Just then, a beam of light shone down on the body of the hapless dog. Glancing up fearfully, Elizabeth saw the moon glinting through a ragged break in the clouds. It was pale yellow . . . and nearly full.

Suddenly, the old bag lady's words of warning echoed in her head. *Beware the full moon.* . . .

"So, then what did you do?" asked Jessica in a horrified whisper.

After much tossing and turning, Lina had finally fallen asleep, but Elizabeth continued to lie awake, restless and troubled by the light of the moon coming through her window . . . and by the thought of Poo-Poo's dreadful end.

She was thankful when Jessica tiptoed in and sat on the edge of her bunk to tell her about all the boys she'd danced with at Mondo. It was a relief to tell someone about Poo-Poo.

"I had my camera and mini-corder in my bag," Elizabeth whispered back, "so I did what Lucy did at Dr. Neville's—I took some pictures and recorded a description. Meanwhile, Lina ran to the nearest telephone booth—thank goodness they're painted red, or she never would have found one in the fog!"

"What did the police say?"

"They weren't terribly interested. They took the

address from Lina and said they'd send an animal-control car over in the morning to pick up the body and take it to Lady Wimpole's." Elizabeth shivered. "They didn't seem to understand that he hadn't just been hit by a car, that . . . something else . . . had happened to him."

"Poor Poo-Poo. Poor Lady Wimpole!"

"She's going to be heartbroken." Elizabeth's throat tightened with tears. "It was horrible, Jess," she whispered.

"I'm telling you, Liz, it's werewolf season," Jessica said lightly. "Just like in the movie we watched at Lila's. Looks like Poo-Poo tried to make friends with the wrong kind of dog!"

Elizabeth tried to laugh, but it came out sounding more like a sob.

Jessica squeezed her sister's arm. "Don't take it so hard," she advised gently. "It's too bad about Poo-Poo, but there's nothing anyone can do for him now."

Elizabeth nodded without speaking.

Rising, Jessica slipped off her dress and pulled on an oversized sleep T-shirt. The bunk squeaked as she clambered on top. Almost instantly, Elizabeth heard a muffled snore from above.

As Jessica said, there's no point fretting, Elizabeth told herself. *No one can help Poo-Poo now. Just go to sleep. Stop worrying . . .*

But she couldn't stop worrying; she couldn't stop puzzling over the mysteries that suddenly seemed to haunt her. Dr. Neville's murder and its downplayed coverage in the *Journal*, and now Poo-Poo . . .

One thing was for certain, Elizabeth thought. Movies were one thing, and real life was another. Jessica wouldn't have laughed if she'd been there in the fog on Spencer Street, if she'd seen the dog's twisted, mutilated corpse with her own eyes. Who—or what—had done that to him?

Chapter 7

"I suppose we can't sneak out every night," Gabriello murmured to Jessica as they stood in the HIS foyer after breakfast on Tuesday, "because I'm going to fall asleep in class. But it really was a blast."

Jessica nodded, rubbing her eyes. "I'd better get an easy assignment at the *Journal* today— something that doesn't involve much walking or talking." She yawned widely. "Maybe a story about the important health benefits of taking an afternoon nap!" The yawn was contagious; Elizabeth, Emily, Lina, and David all followed suit.

As the six shuffled with heavy footsteps to the front door, they were overtaken by Rene, looking crisp and elegant in a double-breasted, navy-blue summer suit. Stopping by Elizabeth's side, he put a hand on her arm. "I'm late already, or I'd offer to escort you to work," he said, his eyes bright. "My only consolation is our dinner date this evening—I look forward so much to finally having a chance to talk with you."

Elizabeth gave him a sleepy smile. "Me, too, Rene."

He waved to the others. "Have a great day, everyone!"

As Rene strode off briskly, Emily put her hands on her hips and shook her head. "Astonishing, simply astonishing," she declared. "Lord Robert Pembroke, Rene Glize . . . you Wakefields have managed to snag all the gorgeous guys already. American girls have all the luck!"

"I wonder what Lucy will give us today?" Jessica said to Elizabeth as they waved to Tony Frank on their way to the crime editor's desk.

"I want to tell her about Poo-Poo," said Elizabeth. "Maybe she'll let us do a follow-up with Lady Wimpole."

When they didn't find Lucy at her desk, the twins wandered back toward Tony's cubicle. As they passed a glass-windowed conference room, Jessica halted, gripping her sister's arm. "There she is, with Reeves."

As if someone had yanked it shut in a hurry, the curtain over the conference-room window wasn't closed all the way. An inch or two of window remained uncovered—just enough for Jessica and Elizabeth to peek through.

"This is some heavy-duty meeting," Elizabeth whispered. "Lucy looks really mad!"

92

They couldn't hear what Lucy was saying, but her gestures and expression spoke volumes. Tossing her hair, she stalked up and down, her eyes flashing angrily. Words spilled from her lips in a furious torrent.

Strangely enough, in the face of this display, Henry Reeves appeared calm and undisturbed. Hands folded, he sat at the conference table quietly watching Lucy pace.

"How can he be so mellow when she's so upset?" Jessica wondered.

"Maybe that's *why* she's so upset," Elizabeth guessed. "Whatever it is she's saying, he's not listening."

Lucy raised her voice, her words reaching the twins through the conference room's thick, nearly soundproof window. "I quit!" Lucy shouted, flinging her arms into the air.

Jessica and Elizabeth glanced at each other, shocked. Reeves didn't so much as blink an eye. Nor did he try to prevent Lucy from storming from the room—his lips remained pressed together in a stern, thin line.

The conference room door banged open and Lucy burst out, her hazel eyes shooting sparks. The twins flattened themselves against the wall, hoping it wasn't too obvious that they'd been spying. It didn't matter; Lucy didn't see them. With the momentum of a freight train, she careened off down the hallway, her tawny hair bouncing and her high heels clattering.

Jessica and Elizabeth hurried after her, not wanting to miss any of the action. As Lucy swept past Tony's cubicle, he called after her. "Friday, what's wrong?"

"I'm quitting, Frank," she shot back, not slowing her pace. "And don't try to talk me out of it!"

Leaping to his feet, Tony joined Jessica and Elizabeth in chasing Lucy back to her desk. Without a moment's hesitation, Lucy began sweeping her personal belongings into a roomy, battered leather attaché.

"Now, Friday, take a deep breath," Tony urged in a soothing tone. He placed a hand on her arm. "Let's talk this through. What set you off this time?"

Lucy shook off his hand impatiently. Yanking the top drawer right out of her desk, she upended it into the attaché. "You know darned well what set me off, Frank. One of the most shocking and mysterious murders in years, and Reeves hides the story at the back of the paper!"

"It was a big news day, what with the princess still missing," Tony reasoned. "Perhaps Reeves thought the murder story didn't rate—"

"And he didn't just edit my piece—he didn't just trim it," Lucy interrupted, pausing in her cleanup to slam a fist on the desk. "He butchered it! He left out all the pertinent details such as—"

Tony cleared his throat loudly, shooting a pointed glance at the twins, and Lucy caught herself. *Such as Dr. Neville's gruesomely ravaged throat,* Elizabeth thought, gulping.

"He made it sound as if Neville could have died of natural causes. It's a cover-up, plain and simple, and I've had enough. I won't work for a dishonest newspaper."

"Now, Friday." Tony lifted a hand to gently push back a strand of Lucy's tousled hair. "Let's not be so hot and hasty. You've worked hard to build a career—don't throw it away on a whim. Reeves revised your story, granted, but that doesn't necessarily indicate—"

"Don't defend him, Frank," Lucy warned. "You know as well as I do that Reeves is in a sweat about the competition from the *Post*. This isn't the first time he's . . ."

Jessica and Elizabeth strained to hear what came next, but Lucy had lowered her voice. She and Tony moved off slightly, continuing their conversation out of earshot.

"A cover-up at the *London Journal!*" Jessica whispered excitedly.

"And Henry Reeves himself is behind it!" Elizabeth whispered back.

"So, while Liz is writing up the dead dog story, what should *I* do?" Jessica asked Tony.

Lucy had exited the office like a tornado, leaving a ransacked desk and a trail of whispers in her wake. A mere twenty-four hours after first arriving at the *London Journal*, the twins were under Tony Frank's wing once more.

"Well, let's see. I may have an upper-crust tea party for you," he kidded.

"I know I was kind of scornful about writing for the society page yesterday," Jessica said contritely, hitching herself up on the edge of Tony's desk. "But as it turns out, I think I'll be very well-suited to it. You see, I now have an *in* with the aristocracy. I'm *dating* the younger Lord Robert Pembroke."

Tony looked suitably impressed. "That was fast. Swept him off his feet, eh?"

"He's putty in my hands."

Tony dropped into his desk chair. "Putty, eh? Somehow, I never thought of young Pembroke as being made of a soft, malleable substance," he reflected. "I would have said he was more the unpredictable volcanic type."

"Really?" Jessica said with interest. "Do you know him?"

"He's the *Journal* owner's only son and heir-apparent, that's all," Tony said carelessly. "Though he doesn't toe the line as much as Lord P. Senior would like."

"How do you mean?"

"He's sowed some wild oats and rumor has it old Bob worries that he won't ever settle down to being a proper lord of the manor and newspaper owner. I say give the boy a chance—blood will tell."

Wild oats . . . blood will tell. Jessica was more intrigued by Lord Pembroke Junior than ever. She felt a pleasant shiver of anticipation. *And I'm having dinner with him tonight!*

"Don't get me wrong—I've always liked the chap." Tony winked at Jessica. "And I'd say he's shaping up already, casting his eye on one of my star interns. Speaking of which, before I send you off on assignment, let's just check Lucy's desk in case she left anything behind for you."

Lucy's desk was a mess of scrap paper: half-written stories and notes relating to matters she'd deemed unimportant. "But she took her file on the Dr. Neville murder," Tony murmured to himself. "Hmm . . ."

Next to the telephone was a small notepad. As Tony read the top sheet, his lips twitched with amusement. "Lucy didn't forget you, see? 'Liz and Jessica, Scotland Yard, shoplifting chauffeur case.' Here's the address. You're all set."

"Oh, no," groaned Jessica. "Don't tell me."

"I'm afraid so." Tony's grin widened. "It's a Sergeant Bumpo case!"

"Thank you for talking to me, Lady Wimpole," said Elizabeth. "I know how hard this must be for you."

Replacing the phone, Elizabeth resumed typing, her brow furrowed. "The Wimpole family does not know who might have had a motive to harm them or their pet," she murmured as her fingers flew over the keyboard. "Nor has it been determined whether the terrier ran away or was abducted. His body was found more than three miles from Knightsbridge on Spencer Street. . . ."

Just typing the words "Spencer Street" gave Elizabeth goose bumps. She could almost feel the clammy fog closing around her; she could almost hear Lina's bloodcurdling scream. . . .

A hand touched Elizabeth's shoulder, and she

nearly jumped out of her skin. "Oh, Luke, it's you!" she squeaked.

"I did it again," he said ruefully. "I'm always scaring you!"

"I was already scared," Elizabeth confessed, "just reliving last night."

Quickly, she told him about sneaking out after curfew, and walking home from Mondo in the fog with Lina. "I recognized the little dog right away, from the photos Lady Wimpole showed us. And he wore a little leather collar with gemstones. . . ." Elizabeth crossed her arms, hugging herself. "His throat was torn open, just like—" She stopped herself, remembering that Luke didn't know the true details of Dr. Neville's death. "It was awful."

Luke narrowed his eyes. "What do you mean, his throat was torn open? You mean, with a knife?"

"No, it wasn't a clean cut. The wound was . . ." She shuddered. "Jagged."

"Jagged, as if perhaps . . ." A worried frown creased Luke's forehead; his eyes clouded.

"Luke, what is it?" Elizabeth asked. "What are you thinking?"

Luke blinked. "Nothing," he said, though he still appeared troubled. "Nothing."

An instant later, his expression cleared and he smiled. "Tell you what. Finish typing your story and then ask Tony if he'll give you the afternoon off. I'll take you sight-seeing."

Fortunately, Tony was amenable to the idea. "Get to know the city," he urged Elizabeth. "It will help make you a better reporter."

98

Luke and Elizabeth grabbed their sweaters and headed for the door. "Now, forget about last night," Luke ordered Elizabeth. "London is a warm and delightful city by daylight, I promise!"

Warm and delightful . . . I don't know about that, Elizabeth thought as she and Luke wandered through the vast, shadowy, echoing spaces of Westminster Abbey.

The abbey was certainly awe-inspiringly beautiful, and rich with history. "I can't believe how many famous people are buried in here!" Elizabeth whispered to Luke as they paused to read the memorial stones in the poets' corner. "Kings and queens, writers and statesmen . . . I've never seen anything like it."

"Think of all the ceremonies that have taken place here over the centuries," he murmured back. "Royal weddings, and christenings, and funeral processions. The stained-glass windows, the vaulting arches, the very stones under our feet have silently witnessed it all for hundreds and hundreds of years."

Despite her fuzzy cardigan sweater, Elizabeth felt chilled to the bones. "I'm ready for some sunshine," she told Luke. "What's the next stop on our tour?"

"The Tower of London," Luke answered, taking her arm. "I'll tell you about it on the way over."

The day was warm and clear, so they walked to the tower, pausing on a bridge spanning the Thames River to savor the view from a distance.

"Kings and queens, starting with William the Conqueror in the eleventh century, used the tower buildings as a prison," Luke explained. "Mary, Queen of Scots, was beheaded there in 1587 for conspiring to seize the English throne from the rightful queen, your namesake, Elizabeth I."

Arriving at the tower, they purchased tickets and joined a guided tour. "I'm sure the tour guide will tell the story of the little princes," Luke said to Elizabeth in a low voice as they crossed a stone courtyard. Huge black ravens perched on a wall, cawing mournfully. "It's featured in Shakespeare's historical play about Richard the Third. Do you know it?"

Elizabeth shook her head. "Who were the little princes?"

"The sons of Richard's older brother, King Edward the Fourth. The tragedy unfolded during the Wars of the Roses, in the fifteenth century. Upon Edward's death, Richard seized power, declaring himself the young princes' protector." Luke laughed mirthlessly. "Some protector. He had the little boys imprisoned here . . . and then he ordered them murdered."

Elizabeth gasped. "How horrible!"

"Or so the story goes," Luke concluded in a lighter tone. "Some modern-day historians claim that Richard wasn't quite as villainous as Shakespeare made him out. They never did find the bodies of the little boys. . . ."

As they entered a dimly lit passageway, Elizabeth glanced fearfully over her shoulder. Shadows danced on the dank stone walls; she could almost imagine they were the ghosts of the murdered princes. "What a gruesome place," she said, shuddering. "It must have been so awful to be imprisoned here, knowing you might moulder and die in one of these dark cells, never again seeing the light of day."

"Or perhaps you'd see the light of day one last time, as they led you in chains to that courtyard where the ravens were—in order to behead you."

"I can't imagine living in such a brutal time," Elizabeth reflected.

"It's fascinating, though, isn't it?" said Luke. "Throughout history, the things people have done to their own flesh and blood out of greed, ambition, jealousy, fear."

"Fascinating," Elizabeth agreed, "but also frightening!"

After admiring the crown jewels, housed in the tower for safekeeping, Elizabeth and Luke hurried back outside. "There's one more place I'd like to show you," said Luke.

Elizabeth laughed. "As long as it doesn't have any graves or dungeons. I've had my share of old bones for the day, thank you very much!"

Luke grinned. "No old bones, I promise. It's history, in a way, but just for fun."

A few minutes later, they stood on the sidewalk in front of the wax museum. As Luke paid for two tickets, Elizabeth smiled. "You tricked me," she teased. "There are bound to be lots of murderous scenes depicted in here."

101

"But they're just wax dummies. It's not real blood!"

The wax museum proved highly entertaining. Elizabeth was captivated by the wax models of British royalty, from the unfortunate wives of Henry VIII to the present-day queen and her family. "The costumes are wonderful," she exclaimed, curtsying to the wax queen. "That's just the sort of funny little hat she always wears!"

"They make new models of the royal family's younger members every year or so," Luke told her, "and I believe the family donates the clothes so the dioramas will be authentic."

Elizabeth gazed thoughtfully at the model of Princess Eliana, the queen's youngest daughter, who was still missing. "I wonder where she is?" she mused.

They moved on, past famous characters from fiction, film, and folklore, as well as history. As they moved back in time, the path grew dimmer; flickering candles replaced the electric lighting, creating an aura of mystery and suspense. Elizabeth's scalp prickled. *What will be around the next bend in the hall?* she wondered.

When she saw the next exhibit, she clutched Luke's arm. "A werewolf!" she cried.

The figures of the diorama illustrated the stages of the werewolf's terrifying transformation, from ordinary man to a hairy, crouching, red-eyed creature with blood dripping from its fangs. *It's so lifelike,* Elizabeth thought. *It looks like it might spring right out at us.*

She buried her face against Luke's woolly sweater. "Let's get out of here," she whispered.

"In a minute," Luke murmured, wrapping a strong arm around her shoulders. "It's just wax, remember, Liz? Look up. It won't hurt you."

Reluctantly, Elizabeth turned back to the exhibit, but she remained pressed close to Luke's side. "The werewolf is one of the most fascinating creatures in all folklore," said Luke. "The superstition dates back to medieval times. The transformation from man to wolf is performed at will in some cases; in others, it's involuntary, triggered by passion or the phases of the moon. The full moon, of course, is when the werewolf comes into possession of his greatest powers—his greatest strength and ferocity. It's when he kills."

Elizabeth clenched her teeth to keep them from chattering. "You know an awful lot about this." She forced a nervous laugh. "I guess you've seen more than one werewolf movie!"

"It's an interest of mine," Luke admitted. "I picked it up from my mother—she was intrigued by the legends. She collected books and artifacts relating to the subject." Luke pulled a wolf-fang keychain from his pocket and held it up for Elizabeth to see. "This belonged to her. Do you think it's a strange hobby, Elizabeth?"

She shrugged. "I . . . I guess not."

"I'd understand if you thought it odd," he assured her. "I'm sure *your* mother doesn't believe in werewolves! But I've never been able to forget something my mother once said to me. She believed that to acknowledge the reality of the were-wolf is merely to acknowledge our own dual nature. Mankind is composed of both heaven and hell; we are bad as well as good. We *all* have an animal side, Elizabeth."

Elizabeth nodded, her eyes on Luke's face. He continued talking softly. "Like vampires, werewolves are immortal and indestructible. They often pass their curse on to their unfortunate victims, who become un-dead."

"Isn't there any way to stop them?" wondered Elizabeth.

"The curse can only be lifted if the werewolf's bloodline is severed—if the werewolf himself is destroyed, by fire or by a weapon made of pure silver, such as a silver bullet."

Luke spoke matter-of-factly, as if there were no doubt in his mind that werewolves were real. Elizabeth knew she should be skeptical—she remembered scoffing at Jessica. *An American Werewolf in London* was only a movie. . . . But after an afternoon spent immersed in the shadowy side of England's past, she didn't *feel* skeptical. She was entranced by Luke's words; they entered her mind in a strange way, taking root. *History is full of murderous monsters, human and nonhuman,* she thought, still staring, mesmerized, at the figure of the werewolf. *Who am I to say werewolves don't exist?*

Chapter 8

When Elizabeth and Luke emerged from the wax
museum, the sun had dropped behind the buildings, sinking the city streets in shadow. A cool,
slightly damp breeze fingered Elizabeth's hair. *It's
going to be another foggy night,* she guessed. *A
good night to get home early . . . and stay home!*

"Is it really that late?" Luke asked as the bells
of a nearby church chimed the hour. "We didn't
have any tea—you must be ravenous."

"I wouldn't mind a bite to eat," Elizabeth admitted.

"Then do me the honor of dining with me,"
Luke said gallantly. "There's a wonderful old pub a
few streets from here—a bit fancier than the
Slaughtered Lamb. They have a fireplace big
enough to roast an ox—it'll warm you up in no
time."

The invitation was enough to make Elizabeth

feel warm inside. The wax museum had given her the creeps, but she couldn't deny she'd enjoyed an excuse to be close to Luke. She was happy to extend their excursion for an hour or two longer. "Sounds divine," she said with a smile. "But what about your father? Isn't he expecting you for dinner?"

Luke shook his head. "I tend to come and go as I please. He won't wait for me—we rarely have a meal together."

Tactfully, Elizabeth let the subject drop. Luke's tone verged on gruff; it didn't encourage further inquiry. *Poor guy*, she thought, her heart swelling with pity. *To be motherless, and for all purposes fatherless, too!*

The Gloucester Arms was bustling and bright. Within minutes, Luke and Elizabeth were tucked away at a cozy corner table, big plates of hearty stew and crusty homemade bread in front of them. Slipping out of her cardigan, Elizabeth dug into her food, suddenly starving.

"I feel like I haven't eaten in days," she said, tearing off another piece of the warm bread. "I guess all the excitement at the *Journal* is giving me an appetite."

"You mean Lady Wimpole's dog?"

Elizabeth gazed somberly at Luke. He looked back with clear, honest eyes. *I might as well tell him*, she decided. *Maybe he can help me make sense of it all*. "The dog is only part of it. You heard that Lucy Friday quit, didn't you?"

"Sure. Everyone at work was talking about it. She had a falling-out with old man Reeves."

"That's an understatement." Elizabeth leaned forward, lowering her voice. "Lucy accused Reeves of covering up the murder of Dr. Neville. He suppressed her story of what really happened—that's why she quit."

Luke's eyes widened. "What really happened? You mean, they know more than they printed?"

Elizabeth nodded. "*Lots* more. And Jessica and I know it, too, because we were there . . . at Dr. Neville's house. We looked in the window and saw . . . and saw . . ." Suddenly, the memory seemed too terrible. She couldn't go on.

"What?" Luke prompted gently. "What did you see?"

"Doctor Neville lying on the floor, dead. Lucy was there, and two men—Lord Robert Pembroke Senior, who owns the *Journal*, and Andrew Thatcher, the chief of the London police."

Firelight flickered on Luke's face; Elizabeth saw his jaw tighten. "What else? How did Neville die?"

"There was blood everywhere." Elizabeth pressed her hands to her eyes as if she could wipe out the vision. "The body was facedown, but Lucy must have seen . . . the other side. She said into her tape recorder that—that the doctor looked as if he'd been attacked by a wild animal."

"Meaning . . . ?"

"His throat was torn out," Elizabeth whispered. "Just like Poo-Poo's."

The color drained from Luke's face. "I didn't want to believe it," he said, his voice hoarse. "I didn't say anything when you told me about the dog, but this—this confirms my worst fears."

"Your fears about what?" asked Elizabeth, her heart thumping wildly.

"The deaths—Dr. Neville's and the little Yorkie's. I think they're connected somehow." Luke's eyes were wide and frightened. "And it sounds like the work of a . . ."

Elizabeth braced herself for his next words. A draft of clammy air brushed her bare arms; her whole body trembled.

" . . . a werewolf!"

"It can't be," Elizabeth breathed.

"Have you seen wolves at the zoo being fed? Have you seen them tear into the meat with their fangs? The wounds you've described weren't made by any ordinary weapon. And a dog will bark at a werewolf. Poo-Poo may have . . . antagonized . . ."

Elizabeth pictured the encounter and shivered again. The theory was incredibly farfetched, but Luke managed to be very convincing. "So, why the cover-up?" She pushed back her plate, her appetite gone. "Do you think Lord Pembroke knows something about it?"

"Pembroke." Luke spat out the name, startling Elizabeth with his vehemence. "He was viewing the the body—he must know something," he declared. "And he owns the *Journal*. It's common knowledge that he has immense influence over Reeves and editorial decisions. The chief of police was there, too, you say? Yes." Luke nodded, his expression grim. "Pembroke's involved, I'm sure of it. For some reason, he's making both Reeves and the police department cover up the murder of Dr. Neville!"

"I keep thinking I must be dreaming," Jessica said to Emily on Tuesday evening. Taking one of her sister's silk blouses from the closet, she held it up to herself in front of the mirror. "I mean, I never have a problem meeting guys, and I've dated some rich ones. But let's face it, nobody in California has a *title*. There aren't any lords and ladies in Sweet Valley!"

"In Sydney, either," said Emily. "Robert sounds like he stepped straight out of a fairy tale. What a story to tell your friends back home!"

"They'll die," Jessica predicted with satisfaction. "They'll just die."

She faced Emily, displaying the blouse. Emily wrinkled her freckled nose thoughtfully, then shook her head. "It's pretty, but a bit too . . . *red*."

"Too flashy, huh?" Jessica ruffled through the closet some more. "You're right. Robert's used to dating very high-class girls. I don't want to look like a cocktail waitress. Nothing too bare, nothing too bright. . . . How 'bout this?"

She held out Elizabeth's navy and white sailor dress for Emily's inspection. Once more, Emily shook her head. "Too schoolgirlish."

"Right again," Jessica agreed. "He probably thinks I'm at least eighteen, and I don't want to disillusion him!"

"Too bad Portia's such a nasty piece of work," Emily commented. "She has the most stunning wardrobe."

Jessica turned to Portia's side of the closet and sighed. "What I wouldn't give to borrow this," she said, fingering an elegant silk chemise. "With that raw silk jacket of hers over it . . ."

"And her *accessories*. Scarves, belts, shoes, hair thingimabobs—every inch of her is always perfect, from her fingernail polish to her panty hose."

Rifling in the back of the closet, Jessica came across a hanging garment bag. She unzipped it, gasping with surprised pleasure. "Now, how about this!" She showed Emily the emerald-green taffeta party dress. "It's too dressy for a dinner date, but Robert's bound to invite me to a more formal event one of these days—a function at Buckingham Palace, maybe! I'll just have to butter Portia up. I don't care what a witch she is—I have to borrow this dress."

Emily studied the dress with interest. "That can't be Portia's, though. Look how short it is in the waist—it wouldn't even fit you, and Portia's inches taller yet."

"Well, it's not mine and it's not Liz's," said Jessica. "So it must be . . ."

Emily's eyebrows shot up. Jessica's mouth dropped open. "Lina's?" said Emily, puzzled. "But where would she get the money for a dress like that?"

"Maybe someone donated it to the homeless shelter," Jessica guessed, stroking the lush fabric of the dress.

"Or maybe she . . ." Emily bit her lip, not finishing the sentence.

She didn't need to. *Maybe she stole it,* Jessica thought. *Oh, the poor, poor deprived thing, to do something so desperate!*

Just then there was a sharp rap on the door. "Put the dress away, quick!" Emily hissed. "It's Mrs. Bates—we don't want to get Lina in trouble!"

Jessica shoved the dress back in the garment bag and slammed the closet door, then threw herself into the easy chair opposite Emily's. "Come in!" she called.

Mrs. Bates stepped into the room, her expression disapproving, as usual.

"What ho, Mrs. Bates!" Emily caroled with irreverent cheeriness.

Jessica stifled a giggle. Mrs. Bates pursed her lips. "I heard that you have a *date* this evening, Jessica." She made "date" sound like a dirty word. "I hope you and your young man will not forget that we have a *curfew* here at Housing for International Students."

"Thanks for the reminder," Jessica said with a falsely sweet smile. "I'll be sure to tell my young man . . . Lord Robert Pembroke."

"*The* Lord Robert Pembroke?" Mrs. Bates croaked.

"None other," Jessica drawled. "Robert *Junior*, of course—Lord P. Senior would be much too old for me. Why, he's probably as old as you!"

The insult slipped right by Mrs. Bates, who appeared to be experiencing heart palpitations. She patted her ample bosom, and then raised her pince-nez to her nose to peer at Jessica with new interest. "Why, my dear, a date with Lord Pembroke!" Mrs. Bates fluttered over to Jessica and gave her arm a motherly pat. "How splendid—how *delightful*. Well, under *these* circumstances, of course, an exception *could* be made . . . if you should be the teensy, weensiest bit late . . . I'll wait up for you, just in case. The door won't be locked against you, not while you're accompanied by Lord Robert Pembroke. . . ."

Still babbling like a brook, Mrs. Bates scurried out. The moment the door shut behind her, Jessica and Emily burst out laughing. "What a sly way to exploit the old biddy's weakness for the upper class!" Emily exclaimed. "You've got her eating out of the palm of your hand. Congratulations."

Jessica grinned. "Just chalk up another victory for the Americans!"

"Thank you for a wonderful day, Elizabeth."

Luke had ridden back with her on the tube and now they stood on the sidewalk in front of HIS. Dusk had fallen. The leafy branches of a tree blocked the light of a nearby street lamp, making it difficult for Elizabeth to read Luke's expression.

He was very close; she could feel the warmth from his body. Elizabeth's heart skipped a beat. The day's startling revelations had flung them into an unexpected intimacy; she knew she would never forget his face in the firelight at the Gloucester Arms, or the feel of his arm warm and strong around her at the wax museum.

I want him to kiss me, Elizabeth realized suddenly, glad that the shadows hid her blush. "Thanks for going out of your way to bring me home," she said. "I'll see you at work tomorrow."

"Good night." Bending his head, Luke grazed her cheek with his lips. An electric current shot through Elizabeth, warming her entire body. Then he turned and disappeared into the night mist. Elizabeth watched him go, one hand held to her burning cheek. Though the kiss had been as light and soft as the brush of a butterfly's wing, perfectly chaste and proper, it held the unmistakable promise of a real kiss in the not-too-distant future. . . .

Her head spinning, from the kiss and from all the events of the day, Elizabeth walked slowly up the path to the dorm. The front door of HIS was open, and a tall figure stood there, as if waiting for her. Elizabeth focused on the boy, and then clapped a hand to her mouth, horrified at her thoughtlessness.

"Oh, Rene!" she gasped, her face turning as red as a London phone booth. "I completely forgot about our plans. I'm so sorry! But we were sight-seeing, and I lost track of time, and . . ."

She smiled apologetically, but Rene's expression remained stiff and cool. *Did he see Luke kiss me?* she wondered, wishing she could think of a way to diffuse the awkwardness of the moment. "I'm sorry," she repeated. "Let's make a rain date. How 'bout tomorrow night?"

"I'm busy," Rene said curtly. "This was my only free evening all week."

"Oh." Elizabeth bit her lip. "Well . . ."

"I have some paperwork to do," Rene muttered. "See you around, Elizabeth."

Turning on his heel, he stalked off. With a sigh, Elizabeth trudged up the rest of the steps and into the foyer of HIS. *I guess I really let him down,* she thought with regret. *Or maybe I just hurt his pride,* she mused, heading down the hall toward the library, where she intended to curl up with a book. *Either way, he overreacted. It was a simple mistake, and it's not like he's my boyfriend. He doesn't have any claim on me.*

There was an alcove outside the library containing a chair, a small table, and a telephone. As Elizabeth approached, she heard a girl speaking. "No, Daddy, I haven't landed a part yet, but I'm going to keep on trying. . . ."

It was Portia. Elizabeth resisted the temptation to slow down as she passed by, not wanting Portia to suspect her of eavesdropping. But the fragment of conversation was tantalizing. *What about her role in* A Common Man? Elizabeth wondered. Portia had to be lying to somebody: either to her father, or to everybody in the dorm. Which was it, and why?

Elizabeth's brain was too tired to grapple with another mystery. She didn't have the mental energy to think about Portia, or about Rene, for that matter.

In the library, she crossed to a wall lined with old books and ran her eye along the titles. She chose a slim, leather-bound volume—*The Strange Case of Dr. Jekyll and Mr. Hyde* by Robert Louis

Stevenson—and then settled into an overstuffed chair by one of the tall, brocade-curtained windows. Opening the book, she skimmed a line or two but soon her gaze strayed to the reflections in the window and her thoughts turned back to the chilling mysteries of London, past and present . . . to werewolves . . . and to Luke.

"I think that was the most elegant meal I've ever eaten," Jessica confessed as Robert Pembroke helped her into the backseat of a long black limousine.

"This is my favorite restaurant in London," said Robert. Climbing in next to Jessica, he grinned up at the chauffeur. "Clifford can tell you, we stop off here at least once a week."

"We certainly do, sir," Clifford confirmed solemnly before closing the door and walking around to the driver's seat.

Jessica leaned back against the butter-soft leather upholstery. *Imagine having your very own family chauffeur to drive you around to a different fancy restaurant whenever you wanted. Every night would be like prom night,* she thought. *I think I could get used to it!*

"Where to now, sir?" Clifford inquired politely.

"Hmm . . . let's see." Robert pondered the options, tapping his jaw with his forefinger. "Fashion is so ephemeral—last week's hip spot will be dead as a doornail this week. You'll have to be my lucky charm, Jessica. I say we try Club U.S.A. on Thames Street."

When the limousine rolled to a stop in front of

Club U.S.A., Robert and Jessica waited for Clifford to walk around and open the door. Stepping out onto the sidewalk under bright neon lights, Jessica felt like a movie star arriving at a Hollywood premiere. Dozens of people clustered around the entrance, waiting to be admitted to the club. When the bouncer spotted Lord Pembroke, he waved them right in. "It pays to be a Pembroke," Robert whispered jokingly in Jessica's ear. "Stick with me, kid, and we'll go places."

Stick with you . . . don't worry, I'm planning to! Jessica thought.

The packed club's clientele was, if anything, even more glamorous than at Mondo the previous night. Immediately, Jessica spotted Princess Gloria, this time wearing a peacock-blue strapless dress. "I saw her at Mondo last night," Jessica told Robert, trying to sound casual. "But she was with a different guy."

"She's a bit fickle, cousin Gloria," Robert agreed. "She's dated every fellow in the U.K. with a drop of noble blood in his veins—this is the second time she's toyed with poor Burton."

Jessica's eyes darted around the room, dazzled by the designer-original dresses, the jewels, the general air of sophistication and gentility. Suddenly, it seemed completely improbable that Lord Robert Pembroke would want to date someone like her—an uncouth, untitled American nobody.

Maybe he's already dated every girl in the U.K. with a drop of noble blood, Jessica speculated. *Maybe he's just toying with me, just for tonight.*

116

But as Robert whisked her onto the dance floor, his muscular arms wrapped tightly around her waist, Jessica decided she didn't care. One magical night with Lord Robert Pembroke would be enough to last her for the rest of her life.

"When the song is over, I'll introduce you to Lady Amanda and Lord Charles Darlington." Twirling her, Robert nodded toward a group of people chatting and laughing nearby. "They're the two redheads, brother and sister, and jolly good company. And I bet you'd adore Lady Catherine Rangeley and her current flame, Neddy. He's a duke, you know."

Jessica burst out laughing and Robert's lips twisted in a wry smile. "You think it's silly and pretentious, don't you, this antiquated social system of ours?"

"Oh, no," Jessica assured him. "I was just imagining how it would translate back home at Sweet Valley High, if all my friends from school had titles. Lord Winston Egbert! And Lady Maria and Lady Amy, and of course *Lila* would insist on being queen." She dimpled mischievously. "I could be the Countess of Calico Drive."

"You'd make a splendid countess," Robert declared, dipping her backward, tango style. "But you're probably better off the way you are. I actually envy you equality-minded, unstuffy Americans."

Jessica raised her eyebrows. "You can't tell me you don't like being a lord!"

"It has its advantages, of course, and I shamelessly make the most of them," he conceded with a rakish smile. "There *are* times, though, when the expectations are downright inconvenient and inhibiting. Take school, for example. I was packed off to Eaton as a boy, like my father and every male Pembroke before me, even though anyone could have predicted that I was primed for rebellion. It was an utter disaster. I was expelled from a grand total of six of the finest schools in England before I ended up in one that wasn't full of overbred, conformist, gutless ninnies."

Jessica laughed. "You would like Sweet Valley High, then. There are a few ninnies, but lots of other types of people, too."

Robert grinned. "I could have been a California surfer instead of an English lord. What a concept!"

"So, what exactly does an English lord *do?*" asked Jessica as they stepped apart to dance to a fast tune.

"Now, that's a good question, and you'd get a different answer from my father. *He* feels that each successive Lord Pembroke should live exactly like the one before him. Manage the estate and the family business interests in the most conservative manner possible, marry the richest and most boring girl you can find, and in general keep up the good old Pembroke name."

Jessica recalled her conversation with Tony at the *Journal*. "But you have different ideas."

Robert smiled. "A few."

The tempo of the music slowed, and Robert drew Jessica close once more. She looked up into his cool, sexy gray-blue eyes, her lashes fluttering and her heart giving a telltale thump. *I'm falling in love,* she thought blissfully.

"Tomorrow night . . . are you free?" Robert asked.

Jessica nodded.

"Good. And how about this weekend? I'll be at Pembroke Manor, my family's country seat. It's an easy train ride from London—would you like to join us? Bring your twin sister, and her beau if she has one."

A weekend at Pembroke Manor! Jessica nearly swooned. "I'd love to."

"Grand." Robert gave her a little squeeze. "There's nothing like a canter around the estate on a breezy summer afternoon." His eyes twinkled. "And I know my mother would be delighted to renew her acquaintance with you. Sergeant Bumpo actually managed to recover her mink!"

A weekend at Pembroke Manor . . . As she slow-danced with Robert, Jessica's eyes grew misty with visions of herself riding around the English countryside with Robert. He would want to show her every inch of Pembroke land . . . because someday it would be her home, too. *I'd give up Sweet Valley in a minute. Lady Jessica Pembroke,* she thought with a rapturous sigh. *No doubt about it, it's my destiny!*

Chapter 9

"Elizabeth, there you are."

Elizabeth looked up from *Dr. Jekyll and Mr. Hyde* to see Mrs. Bates beckoning to her from the door to the library. "You have a call on the hall telephone. Long distance from America."

Mom and Dad! Elizabeth thought. Tossing the book aside, she sprinted to the phone where she'd seen Portia talking earlier. "Hello?"

"Liz, it's Todd."

"Todd!" Elizabeth nearly dropped the receiver. "Todd," she repeated. "It's you!"

Todd's laugh crackled warmly over the line. "It's me, all right. How are you? How's London? How's the internship?"

"Oh, it's all wonderful. I was going to write you a letter tonight. . . . I can't believe you called! It's so expensive to call overseas—your parents will kill you when they find out."

"I told them how much I missed you, and they said it was OK," Todd assured her. "As long as I keep it under five minutes."

Elizabeth laughed. "In that case, I'll talk fast." Quickly, she told Todd about HIS, and about Lucy Friday, Tony Frank, Sergeant Bumpo, Henry Reeves, and the mysterious murder of Dr. Neville. "We haven't had a dull moment so far," she concluded. "Guess where Jessica is right now? On a date with someone named *Lord* Robert Pembroke."

"Better her than you," he joked.

"Yeah," said Elizabeth, remembering supper at the Gloucester Arms with Luke and her broken date with Rene.

"Well, I should go." Todd's voice was husky with emotion. "I just had to hear your voice. I miss you so much, Liz."

"I miss you, too," she said, suddenly feeling a rush of love and homesickness. "I hate being so far away from you."

"Don't forget about me, OK?"

"Never," Elizabeth promised. "Bye, Todd."

"Bye, Liz. I love you."

"I love you, too."

Hanging up the phone, she rose and slowly padded down the hall toward the staircase. She'd told Todd just about everything that had happened to her since she'd arrived in London except for the episodes involving Rene and Luke. *I just kind of . . . left them out. Is that as bad as lying?* she wondered.

Mixed feelings battled inside her. *Of course*

*Todd wants me to have fun while I'm in London—
he wants me to make new friends, and some of
them are bound to be boys. There's nothing wrong
with that.* Even so, Elizabeth knew Todd wouldn't
be happy to learn she was going out on dates. And
maybe after tonight it wouldn't be hard to stay on a
platonic level with Rene, but what about Luke?

Reaching the end of the third-floor hallway,
Elizabeth pushed open her bedroom door. For an
instant, she found herself wishing desperately that
she was home in her own room in Sweet Valley.
She wanted to be alone with her thoughts, but
there was Portia, sitting at her dressing table in a
lavender silk robe with her hair in a turban, removing her eye makeup with a cotton ball.

Without greeting her roommate, Elizabeth
flung herself onto her bunk. Portia had made it
abundantly clear that she couldn't be bothered
with even the most fundamental civilities—there
was no point trying to chat with her.

Curling up on her side, Elizabeth hugged her
pillow. *Oh, Todd,* she thought, wishing he were
there to put his arms around her . . . and obliterate
the memory of Luke Shepherd's lips brushing her
cheek. . . .

She heaved a deep, heartfelt sigh. Portia
glanced up from the mirror. "Is anything the matter?" she inquired.

Elizabeth sat up on the bed. *Is she actually
deigning to speak to me?* she wondered, surprised.
She didn't know quite how to respond—she wasn't
about to expose her innermost feelings to someone

as cold and unsympathetic as Portia Albert. "No, nothing's the matter," Elizabeth said. "I guess I'm just a little homesick."

Portia twisted in her chair to look at Elizabeth. "You *are* an awfully long way from California."

"I'm used to talking over my day with my parents, getting their feedback. It's strange not being able to do that. I feel kind of . . . adrift."

Elizabeth hadn't intended to confide in Portia; the words just spilled out. She waited for Portia to make a disparaging remark. Instead, Portia tipped her head to one side, her gray eyes thoughtful. "You have that kind of relationship with your parents? You share things? They take an interest?"

"Sure." Idly, Elizabeth reached for a pair of wire-rimmed eyeglasses that someone, Lina she assumed, had left on the night table. She lifted them to her eyes. To her surprise, they didn't affect her vision at all—the lenses appeared to be clear and nonprescriptive. "They're pretty good parents that way," Elizabeth remarked, putting the glasses back down. "They try to stay in touch with what me and my sister and brother are doing. They both work, and it would be easy to be too busy for that kind of thing—I guess they know they have to make an extra effort to make sure we have dinner together most nights, and do things on weekends and that kind of stuff."

Now it was Portia's turn to heave a wistful sigh. "I thought families like that only existed in the movies."

"There's nothing special about us—we're completely boring and ordinary," Elizabeth assured her. "Not like you. It's so exciting that you're following in your father's footsteps—Sir Montford must be very proud of you!"

Reaching for a jar of face cream, Portia twisted off the lid. "Oh, it's just grand. Maybe someday we'll have a chance to perform together—Shakespeare at the Globe, perhaps, or an American made-for-TV movie."

Portia had reverted back to her usual haughtiness so rapidly, Elizabeth couldn't pinpoint the moment of transition. She stared as Portia turned back to the mirror and began smoothing white face cream on her cheeks and forehead. The mask went back on; Portia became a different person before Elizabeth's very eyes. *Or did I imagine that momentary warmth and sympathy?* Elizabeth wondered, baffled and disappointed.

Elizabeth was just drifting off to sleep when Jessica slipped into the bedroom and dashed over to pounce on her sister's bed. "I'm home!" she whispered loudly.

"I noticed," Elizabeth whispered back.

A shadowy nightgowned figure sat up in the other top bunk. "How was your big date?" whispered Lina.

"Fantastic!" Jessica gushed.

She was so excited, she forgot to whisper. "Would you *please* be *quiet*?" Portia snapped. "Tomorrow is dress rehearsal—I need my beauty sleep."

Jessica had to clap a hand to her mouth to stifle

125

a giggle. In the dark, she could see Lina doing the same.

"Now that you've woken us all up," whispered Elizabeth, "let's go downstairs and raid the refrigerator. C'mon, Lina!"

A minute later, the three girls were tiptoeing down the dark stairs, Elizabeth and Lina in their nightgowns and Jessica still in the dress she'd worn for her date with Robert. They crossed the foyer holding their breath. When Jessica tripped on the rug in the hall outside of Mrs. Bates's apartment, all three of them burst into hysterical laughter.

"Ssh!" Elizabeth hissed. "If she catches us, we're doomed."

"No, listen." Lina held up a hand, her head tipped.

In the silence, Jessica could hear the distant sound of someone snoring. Another giggle tickled her throat. "She sounds like a snuffling old bear."

Lina grinned. "I don't think she heard us—how could she, making all that racket herself?"

In the kitchen, they scrounged up a loaf of homemade raisin bread, some cold roast chicken, and three ripe pears and then sat down at a table in the dark dining room to eat. "I don't know how I can be hungry," Jessica commented as she bit into a sweet, juicy pear. "Robert and I totally pigged out at this fabulous French place, Le Mouton Noir."

"That's one of the finest restaurants in London," said Lina. "He must really be trying to impress you."

"Lord Robert Pembroke doesn't have to *try* to

impress anybody," said Jessica. "For your information, it comes naturally."

Elizabeth snorted. "You mean, it comes with being a rich and pampered aristocrat!"

"Have it your way, Liz. But it just so happens that Robert has very kindly invited both of us for a weekend in the country at Pembroke Manor. He *even* said *you* could bring a date. *If* you can scrape one up."

"A weekend in the country—how delightful!" said Lina. "You should take him up on the offer, Elizabeth. Pembroke Manor is quite a showplace . . . or so I've heard."

"They have an ancestral castle and tons of land and a whole stable full of thoroughbred horses," Jessica confirmed. "Although maybe you wouldn't stoop to ride the horse of a rich and pampered aristocrat."

Elizabeth bit into a piece of raisin bread, smiling. "I'd consider it."

Jessica had a brilliant thought. "Why don't you bring Rene?" she suggested. "He's very sophisticated—I'm sure he'd pass muster with the Pembrokes."

"And that's all that matters," Elizabeth said dryly. "Well, to tell you the truth, I don't see me and Rene spending a weekend together anytime soon." She told Jessica and Lina about spacing out her dinner date with Rene, and his reaction when he saw her come in with Luke.

"Luke? That boring poet guy from work?" When Elizabeth's face turned red as a beet, Jessica pounced. "What happened? Did he kiss you?"

"Not really . . . well, sort of," Elizabeth confessed.

"Well, then, I suppose you could bring Luke," Jessica said. "I mean, Rene would be better . . . Luke's kind of a nobody. . . . You really should be nicer to Rene, Elizabeth."

"Thanks for the advice," Elizabeth said. "But I don't plan to bring Rene or Luke anywhere, least of all to Pembroke Manor. Why would I want to spend a weekend at the home of total strangers? And what about you? You hardly know this guy. What would Mom and Dad say?"

Jessica nibbled delicately on a roasted chicken wing. "I'll call them and ask them, but I'm sure they won't mind. Robert's parents will be there, naturally—we'll be chaperoned. And Robert's a perfect gentleman—it's not like he's some bum I picked up on the street. All you have to do is look at him to know what kind of person he is! The way he dresses, the way he speaks, his manners . . ."

"Being rich doesn't automatically make you a good person, any more than being poor makes you a bad person," Elizabeth pointed out. "If you ask me, Robert Pembroke sounds like a conceited, insufferable prig, and he had you wrapped around his finger in under ten seconds simply because he puts the word 'Lord' in front of his name."

Lina had been listening to this exchange with an amused smile. "Oh, Rob's not a bad sort," she interjected.

Both Jessica and Elizabeth shot Lina a look as if to ask, *How would you know?*

"What I mean is, he doesn't *appear* to be a bad sort," Lila amended. "He doesn't make it into the gossip columns nearly as often as *some* of the spoiled young gentry in this town."

Jessica flashed a triumphant smile. "See, Liz? Face it, you're just jealous. But I'll tell you one thing right now. Nothing, and I mean *nothing*, is going to keep me away from Pembroke Manor this weekend!"

Having polished off their midnight snack, the three girls tiptoed back upstairs. Lina made a detour to the bathroom and Jessica and Elizabeth crawled into their bunks. With Portia snoring softly, it seemed safe to whisper.

"Jess, do you think there's anything . . . funny about Lina?" Elizabeth asked.

Jessica hung over the edge of the bed and looked down at her sister. "What do you mean?"

"I mean . . ." Elizabeth couldn't really put her finger on what it was about her new friend that didn't seem quite right. Was it the eyeglasses? Something Lina had said? "Take the nightgown she's wearing tonight. With all that fancy lace—it must have been expensive."

"Just because you're poor doesn't mean you can't have a few nice things," Jessica pointed out, reluctant to mention the dress she and Emily had found in the back of the closet. "Maybe somebody gave it to her."

"Maybe."

"If you ask me, the only thing odd about Lina is

that she could be a knockout if she tried," remarked Jessica. "You don't have to have a lot of money to have style—it's almost like she goes out of her way to be dowdy."

"Hmm." Elizabeth plumped up her pillow and changed the subject. "I told Luke about how Dr. Neville died, Jessica, and about Lord Pembroke and the police chief being at the scene of the murder when Lucy was reporting it, and Lucy quitting because of a cover-up. And he thinks . . . Dr. Neville's murder, and Poo-Poo's . . . Luke thinks it might be the work of a werewolf."

"A werewolf?" Jessica burst out laughing. "Liz, I was just *kidding* when I said that. Honestly, I think all that poetry has addled both your brains!"

"Something very strange is going on," Elizabeth insisted, "and Lord Pembroke Senior knows what it is and he's making Henry Reeves and the police department hush up about it."

"The Pembrokes have nothing to do with the murder or any cover-up," Jessica declared hotly. "It's just a coincidence that Lord P. Senior owns the *Journal* and was friends with Dr. Neville—it doesn't make him guilty of anything. You're jumping to conclusions in the worst way, Liz, and I think it's very unfair."

"Well . . ." Her sister had a point. Still, Elizabeth wasn't quite ready to trust the Pembrokes. "Have you talked to Robert about the murder, and what—who—we saw at Dr. Neville's flat?"

"No," said Jessica. "It didn't come up tonight, either."

"Don't mention it, then. Not until we've had a chance to do more sleuthing and find out what's really going on at the *Journal*. It's possible that Lucy could be wrong, that things don't add up the way she thinks they do."

Suddenly, Jessica's eyes lit up, gleaming in the dark. "Remember what Lucy said to Tony, though, about this not being the first time, or something like that? Werewolf or not, maybe other murders have been covered up or played down!"

"That would explain why Lucy got so mad about this one," Elizabeth agreed.

"First thing tomorrow, then," Jessica proposed, "let's find out!"

Arriving at the *London Journal* offices half an hour early on Wednesday morning, the twins hurried straight to the research department. The large, cluttered room was unoccupied. "Good," said Elizabeth, sitting down at a microfiche machine. "I'd just as soon not have to explain to anybody what we're doing."

"You mean, you'd just as soon not have to lie," said Jessica.

Elizabeth grinned. "Right."

Jessica scanned the microfiche index. "They have copies of the *Journal* going back about a thousand years," she announced. "How far back should we look?"

"Let's start with recent issues—the last month, say. If we don't find anything, we can go back further."

With Jessica looking eagerly over her shoulder,

Elizabeth twirled the knob of the microfiche machine. Past issues of the *Journal* rolled across the screen, the print very tiny. After skimming a week's worth of "Crime Reporter" columns to no avail, Jessica suddenly cried out. "How 'bout that one: 'Man Found in Park, Dead of Multiple Stab Wounds?'"

"It's a pretty straightforward case, though," Elizabeth pointed out. "He was mugged and stabbed a bunch of times. It's horrible, but not mysterious. They lay the facts right out. We're looking for something that's *not* there, remember?"

"Right. Keep rolling."

They'd pored over three weeks of London crime when Elizabeth caught her breath sharply. "Take a look at this one," she commanded Jessica. "The blurb at the bottom of the page."

Jessica read the brief headline: "Nurse Dies on the Job." She nodded, her eyes moving quickly to the end of the short article. "It reminds me of the story they printed about Dr. Neville, the way it's so vague about how she actually died. They say it was a robbery, but did the attacker stab her, shoot her, bludgeon her?"

"It could definitely be another cover-up," Elizabeth asserted. "We have to talk to Lucy about it."

"Easier said than done," Jessica reminded her sister as they left the research department and headed toward Tony's office to get the day's assignment. "She quit, remember?"

"We'll just have to call or visit her at home. Maybe Tony knows where she lives."

"But what if they get mad?" said Jessica. "Tony

and Lucy, I mean. We'll have to tell them we were sneaking around at Dr. Neville's when we were supposed to be keeping out of trouble with Sergeant Bumpo!"

"I'm sure they'll overlook it—it's a pretty small crime compared to murder," Elizabeth reasoned. "Or to covering up a murder."

Rounding a corner, they nearly collided with Luke. "Good morning," he said, his cheeks turning faintly pink as he smiled at Elizabeth. "Where are you off to in such a rush?"

Elizabeth glanced at Jessica. "I think we should tell him. We may need his help."

Jessica shrugged. She was peeved with Luke for casting aspersions on the integrity of the Pembroke family, but in general he was bland and harmless enough. *If Liz wants to bring her little crush along for the ride, fine with me.* "Whatever."

"Tell me what?" asked Luke.

Elizabeth filled him in on their microfiche discovery. "You're onto something," he agreed, his blue eyes blazing. "And Lucy Friday may very well hold the key to the puzzle."

Brimming with purpose, the three charged over to Tony's desk. Elizabeth cleared her throat. "Tony, we need to talk to you about something important."

He raised his sandy eyebrows. "I'm all ears."

"It's about . . . Dr. Neville's murder," she explained.

Tony sat up in his chair. "What *about* Dr. Neville's murder?"

"Well, we know Lucy quit because Reeves didn't print her story of what really happened. And we know what really happened because . . . we were there."

Tony looked both puzzled and astonished. "You were *where?*"

"At Dr. Neville's townhouse," Elizabeth confessed.

"Looking in the window," Jessica elaborated.

"The girls saw the body," Luke offered.

"And we heard Lucy describe its . . . condition," Elizabeth finished.

Tony whistled. "And all that time, Lucy thought you were safe with our man Bumpo!"

Relieved that Tony didn't appear angry, Elizabeth forged ahead. "We also saw two men at the scene with Lucy—Lord Robert Pembroke, who owns this newspaper, and Andrew Thatcher, the London chief of police. So we think that maybe they were in on the decision to suppress the true facts of Dr. Neville's death. Now we need to find out *why* anyone would want to do that, and we think we've found a clue—a connection to another murder that took place about a month ago. We need to speak to Lucy."

Tony shook his head. "It all sounds a bit wiggy to me. But I know Lucy sincerely believes something is amiss here at the paper. She felt strongly enough about it to quit her post." Rising to his feet, he reached for his rumpled tweed jacket. "She'd want to hear what you have to say. Come along—I'll take you to her."

Tony had to press the doorbell at Lucy's flat

three times before they heard the sound of approaching footsteps. A bolt rattled and the door swung open.

Lucy gazed out, her hazel eyes widening. "Frank! Twins! Luke!" she exclaimed, startled. "What brings you here?"

"I'm just the chauffeur," Tony said. "The children have something urgent to discuss with you."

Lucy escorted them into her parlor, which was decorated with antiques and potted plants. When they were all seated, Elizabeth went straight to the point, talking fast. "We know you quit because Reeves didn't print your story about Dr. Neville, and we know what was in your story because we were at the scene, looking in the window, and saw the body and heard you speaking into your tape recorder. We did some research and came upon an article about a murdered nurse. Can you tell us if Nurse Handley's body was . . . mangled like Dr. Neville's?"

Lucy stared in disbelief at Elizabeth. "You picked up on the Handley case? You'll make darn good reporters." She drummed her fingers on the arm of her chair. "Yes," she said, after a long, pregnant pause. "Nurse Handley died in the same way that Dr. Neville did. She was savagely attacked—her throat was ripped open and she bled to death."

Elizabeth gasped, putting a hand to her own throat. Jessica and Luke both blanched, and even sensible Tony looked spooked.

"The crimes appeared very similar," Lucy continued. "Serial killers tend to have a distinctive signature, and for this one, it's the clawed, mutilated throat."

"Serial killers?" squeaked Jessica.

Lucy nodded. "A serial killer is on the loose. There's no question about it. I know the police and Scotland Yard have come to the same conclusion, but for some reason they're keeping quiet. They're dragging their feet . . . on *someone's* orders."

A stunned silence fell over the room. Goose bumps prickled up and down Elizabeth's arms. A serial killer . . . *Dr. Neville wasn't the only victim. There have been multiple killings, with more to come. Maybe Luke is right about the werewolf.* . . .

"They may be keeping quiet so as not to panic the public," Tony suggested reasonably.

Lucy's eyes flashed. "The public has a right to know! How else can people protect themselves?"

Elizabeth shivered, remembering Poo-Poo. Someone had killed him, too. Someone . . . or something . . . that might still have been lurking in the shadows when Elizabeth and Lina discovered the poor dog's body.

"Remember Lady Wimpole's missing Yorkie?" Elizabeth asked Lucy. "Did you read in yesterday's 'Crime Reporter' about how I stumbled across his body . . . dead, with his throat ripped out?"

Lucy's expression grew even darker. "It's a serial killer," she repeated. "And perhaps one of the most heinous ever to walk the night streets of London. Is there a method to how he—or she—chooses his victims, or does he simply lose control?"

For some reason, words Luke had uttered at

136

the wax museum suddenly flickered through Elizabeth's brain. *"We all have an animal side, Elizabeth. . . ."*

"Do you think Lord Pembroke, the owner of the *Journal*, could have anything to do with the cover-up?" wondered Luke.

Lucy pushed back her hair, looking thoughtful. "Hmm . . . the silver cigarette case," she murmured.

"The one Lord Pembroke was holding?" asked Elizabeth.

"It was found by the body," said Lucy, "and it was engraved with the intials R.H.P., the Lord's own initials—or those of his son."

Elizabeth and Luke exchanged a meaningful glance. "The only other idea we've had," she said, "is that Reeves may have played up the sensational Princess Eliana headlines to deflect notice from Dr. Neville's murder. What do you think about that?"

"I hadn't considered that angle, but it makes sense, especially if Reeves is trying to compete with the *Post*—"

Tony had been listening to the conversation with an anxious look on his face. Now he jumped up from his seat and cut Lucy off with a sharp gesture. "Friday, really," he reprimanded her. "Ought you to discuss confidential details of such sensitive cases with our teenaged summer interns? We don't know anything for sure. The cover-up is just speculation, and in all propriety we shouldn't presume—"

"Just speculation?" Lucy burst out. "All propriety? Balderdash, Frank. Don't you trust my judgment? Of course there's a cover-up, and Reeves and the police department are behind it, and perhaps Pembroke is behind *them*!"

Suddenly, her eyes narrowed suspiciously. "And what about *you*, Frank? You've been getting pretty tight with Reeves lately." Tears of anger and disappointment sprang into her eyes. "I thought you were— But you've always wanted my job, haven't you? You never thought a woman could handle it. Are you part of the cover-up, too, Frank? Did you see this coming, that I'd quit over it? Did Reeves promise you the crime desk if you took his side against me?"

"How dare you accuse me of such underhanded tactics!" Tony exploded. "I'm not taking Reeves's side—I'm not taking anyone's side! I'm merely attempting to be rational and objective in the interest of good journalism and basic human justice."

"In the interest of climbing the *London Journal* ladder and feathering your own nest, you mean!" Lucy countered hotly.

The twins and Luke gaped. "You're way out of line, Miss Friday," Tony said hoarsely.

"And so are you, Mr. Frank," she shouted. She pointed toward the door, her eyes shooting sparks. "Get out of my house this minute. I never want to see you again!"

Chapter 10

Jessica, Elizabeth, and Luke quickly said an embarrassed good-bye to Lucy, who was so agitated she didn't even seem to hear them. Hurrying out to the sidewalk, they looked in both directions, but Tony, and his car, had disappeared from sight.

"Looks like we're hoofing it back to work," Luke observed. "What a row *that* was!"

"Poor Lucy," said Elizabeth.

"Poor Tony!" said Jessica.

Slowly, the three began walking in the direction of the *London Journal* offices. "So, where do we go from here?" wondered Luke.

"I'm still totally confused," Elizabeth confessed. "The evidence points to the same person killing both Dr. Neville and Nurse Handley, but is there a connection between the victims or is the murderer's choice just random? Is it important that the silver cigarette case belonged to a Pembroke?

What motive could Lord Pembroke, Chief Thatcher, and Henry Reeves have for conspiring to suppress the facts of the case?"

"We have more questions than ever," Luke agreed.

"Well, *I* don't," Jessica piped in. "I don't think you can lump Lord Pembroke in with Thatcher and Reeves—there's just no way he has anything to do with a cover-up." Her blue-green eyes flashed indignantly. "I mean, really! The Pembrokes are one of the most prominent families in England—they're the *nobility*."

"That doesn't automatically put them above suspicion," argued Elizabeth.

"It does in my opinion," Jessica insisted. "You're barking up the wrong tree, Liz. If you want to find some crooks and killers, start looking in the lower classes."

Luke clenched his jaw. "The aristocracy manage, in their own fashion, to commit just as many crimes as the rest of us," he said stiffly. "And they probably get away with them more often."

"I think we can agree on one thing," Elizabeth intervened. "Two people and a dog have been brutally killed, and the newspapers and police department are hushing it up. Something nasty is going on." She looked at her sister, her eyes flashing a challenge. "So, are we going to crack this case together?"

Jessica nodded. "You bet. If only to prove that you're wrong about the Pembrokes!"

"I think that's enough scones," Lina said with a

laugh. "I count at least a dozen and half, and we're only five people!"

Elizabeth, Lina, Emily, David, and Gabriello were roaming the food courts at Harrod's, London's largest department store, buying sweets for a late-afternoon picnic tea in the park. "But there are so many different flavors, and they all sound so delicious," said Elizabeth. "Did we get any of these orange-currant scones?"

"Plain is fine for me," announced Emily, holding up a carton of Devonshire cream and a jar of jam. "I plan to drown mine in cream and jam, anyway!"

"And don't forget, we have cookies." David displayed a bulging paper sack. "This should tide us over until dinner."

After paying for their selections, the HIS group crossed the street and entered the cool green oasis of Hyde Park. Gabriello pulled a blanket from his rucksack and spread it out on the grass under a spreading oak tree. All five dropped down and reached for the bags of scones and cookies.

"This is the life," remarked Emily, topping a plump scone with a generous dollop of cream.

Elizabeth sighed rapturously, her eyes on an equestrian cantering past on the bridle trail. "I think London must be the most beautiful city in the world."

"Then you haven't been to Florence or Rome," said Gabriello with a wink.

"London's not so bad," David agreed in his soft Liverpudlian accent. He cast a shy glance in Lina's direction. "Though it's too big and fancy to have the charm of Liverpool, eh, Lina?"

She shrugged, not replying.

"It's funny, though, what people think about Liverpool." David shook his head, grinning. "There are two Americans in my program at the university, Zack and Kelly, and of course the only thing they'd ever heard about Liverpool is that the Beatles came from there. They asked me if I'd known John, Paul, Ringo, and George."

Elizabeth laughed. "Even though you weren't even *born* when the band was together in the sixties!"

"Right. I pointed that out. So, you know how there was a fifth Beatle, another drummer before Ringo? Well, just for a laugh, I told the Americans that my father had been the *sixth* Beatle—the drummer *before* the drummer before Ringo. I was joking, of course. But they actually fell for it. 'Ah, that's right, the legendary sixth Beatle,' Zack said." David mimicked a flat-voweled American twang. "'I always *wondered* who that was!'"

Elizabeth, Emily, and Gabriello burst out laughing. Lina's lips twitched as if she were trying hard not to smile.

"Not all Americans are so ridiculous," said Elizabeth. "But I'll admit I don't know much about Liverpool."

"You should visit," David urged her. "Shouldn't she, Lina?"

Lina shifted restlessly on the blanket. "Certainly, if she wants." Abruptly, she sprang to her feet. "Let's feed these extra scones to the ducks, shall we?"

Lina, Gabriello, and Emily strolled to a nearby pond, which sparkled like gold in the last rays of the sun. Elizabeth and David watched them toss crumbs to the birds that flocked over, clamoring loudly.

"I'm a bumbler, I am," David muttered after a moment, glancing shyly at Elizabeth out of the corner of his eye. "The harder I try to make her notice me, the more she turns and looks the other way."

It wasn't difficult for Elizabeth to guess that he was talking about Lina. "She does come across as a little . . . standoffish," she had to agree.

David pulled his knees up to his chin and sighed glumly. "The thing is, I really like her," he confided. "I'd like to ask her out. But just when I think I'm finally making a connection, she runs away like a frightened deer."

Elizabeth shook her head thoughtfully. "She's a puzzle. Because I get the impression she likes you, too, though she won't admit it. I guess . . ." Elizabeth offered the obvious explanation, even though it didn't quite satisfy her. "I guess she's just shy. It might take a while, but I bet you'll get through to her one of these days."

"Do you really think so?" David's eyes glowed with hope. "Do you think . . . do you think you could help me, Elizabeth? Put in a good word?"

Elizabeth smiled. David and Lina *would* make the sweetest couple. And helping along their romance might be a nice change from tracking down a serial killer. . . . "Sure. I'll put in a good word. We'll find a way to get you two together, just wait and see!"

•   •   •

143

"I can't believe Portia's already up and gone," said Lina on Thursday morning as she and the twins dressed for work. "She's slept late every day we've roomed together."

"Tonight's opening night, right?" Jessica grinned wickedly. "She probably went someplace else to get her beauty sleep, because we always make so much noise."

Sliding a headband into her hair, Elizabeth stepped over to her dressing table to see how it looked. Someone had propped an envelope on the table—Elizabeth recognized Portia's bold, flowery script. "Look, it's addressed to the three of us, from Portia!"

"What's in it?" asked Jessica.

"Poison, I bet, or explosives," kidded Lina.

Elizabeth opened the envelope and drew out a bunch of theater tickets. "Tickets to the opening-night performance of *A Common Man*," she said in disbelief. "Seven of them! *And* an invitation back-stage after the performance."

Lina blinked through her wire-rimmed glasses. "You're joshing!"

"Not at all. There's a note, too." Elizabeth read it out loud. "'Elizabeth, Jessica, and Lina, I'd be very pleased if you would attend my West End debut this evening, as my special guests. I'm en-closing tickets for Emily, Rene, David, and Gabriello as well. Wish me luck!'"

"She expects us to wish her luck, after the way she's treated us?" Jessica snorted. "Fat chance. 'Break a leg,' maybe—I wouldn't mind if she did!"

"What do you suppose she's up to?" Lina's brow furrowed with suspicion. "Maybe it's a trick— maybe the tickets are fake and we'll go to the theater only to be turned away."

"No, they're real," said Jessica. "She's showing off—she wants us to see what a big star she is so she can gloat endlessly."

"Either way, I say we boycott *A Common Man*," Lina declared. "I bet the others will agree."

Elizabeth studied Portia's note thoughtfully. There was something very unPortialike about it, something simple and sincere. "I don't think she's showing off or trying to trick us," Elizabeth disagreed. "Maybe the tickets are just a friendly, generous gesture."

"I doubt that," Jessica said disparagingly.

"We won't know unless we go to the play," Elizabeth concluded. "What harm will it do us to give Portia one last chance?"

Since the morning was sunny and beautiful, Jessica and Elizabeth decided to walk an extra half mile before getting on the tube. "There's a station near Buckingham Palace," Elizabeth recalled. "We can watch the changing of the queen's guard."

Despite the early hour, quite a few tourists had gathered to observe the pomp and circumstance of red-uniformed guards on shiny black horses parading in front of the royal residence. "Those hats kill me," said Jessica, pointing to one of the tall beaver hats. "And why don't they wear the chin straps under their chins where they belong?"

Elizabeth pondered other questions as the dignified guards trotted by. "A lot of people work awfully hard to safeguard the queen and her family," she mused. "How did anyone manage to get to Princess Eliana and steal her away?"

"I wonder if they'll ever find her." Jessica crossed her arms, shivering. "Maybe they won't find her until she's dead. Maybe the serial killer has gotten her!"

"Jess, you have the sickest imagination," Elizabeth exclaimed, but the same possibility, however unlikely, had occurred to her, too.

Jessica tossed a final, wistful glance over her shoulder at Buckingham Palace as they headed toward the tube station. "It must be amazing to live there," she said. "And to think we have a chance to visit someplace *almost* as cool—Pembroke Manor!"

"I told you the other night, I'm not interested in spending a weekend with the Pembrokes," Elizabeth reminded her sister.

"Please, Elizabeth?" Jessica wheedled. "It will be a blast, I swear. It could even be educational—you'll get to see another part of England, with lots of old historical stuff."

"I'd rather take a day trip to Oxford or Cambridge."

Jessica hung on Elizabeth's arm. "But Mom and Dad said I can only go if you go, too, and I'll just *die* if I don't go," she wailed melodramatically. "Robert said you could bring Luke, remember? Don't you want to spend some time with him, since you have such a crush on him? Please, please, *please*."

Elizabeth kept Jessica in suspense for a good long minute. "OK," she said at last. "I'll come, and I'll ask Luke. At least then I'd have someone normal to talk to."

"I knew you'd come around." Jessica gave her sister a hug. "You're going to just love the Pembrokes!"

Elizabeth doubted that, but she didn't say so. Jessica had hit on one tactic to get Elizabeth to change her mind about going to Pembroke Manor: her growing romantic interest in Luke Shepherd. But there was another, equally compelling reason for her decision.

I don't expect to love the Pembrokes, Elizabeth thought as she and Jessica boarded the tube, *but maybe I'll learn something about them that will help me solve the mystery of the murder cover-up!*

"We need a plan of action," Luke declared as he and Elizabeth huddled over cups of tea at his desk in the corner of the *Journal* offices. "If there's a cover-up taking place—and we both agree with Lucy that there is—we need to uncover it. But how?"

"Let's go over what we know and don't know," Elizabeth suggested, grabbing a pen and paper so she could make a list. "We know that Dr. Neville was murdered last Sunday night by someone—or something—that tore his throat out. Approximately twenty-four hours later, Lady Wimpole's dog was dispatched of in much the same manner. But it started a month ago, with the murder of Nurse Handley. We have three bodies."

"Both Nurse Handley's and Dr. Neville's deaths were downplayed in the *Journal*, apparently on the orders of Henry Reeves, the editor-in-chief," Luke contributed.

"We suspect, but we don't know for certain, that Lord Robert Pembroke, owner of the *Journal* and father of the guy my insane sister is currently dating, may have dictated Reeves's editorial decision. Pembroke was at the scene of the crime when Lucy went to report it, as was Andrew Thatcher, the London chief of police. To the best of our knowledge, Pembroke is acquainted with all the key players, dead and alive, except the nurse and Poo-Poo, of course."

"And there's that cigarette case. . . . Yes, he's the crucial link," Luke agreed. He raked a hand through his mop of glossy dark hair. "Now, what we *don't* know . . ."

Elizabeth ticked off the items on her fingers. "The identity of the murderer. The motives for the murders, and the link, if any, between the victims. The motive for the cover-up. Are Pembroke and Reeves and the police protecting someone? Do they have a suspect?"

"We've got a long way to go," Luke remarked, sitting back in his chair and folding his hands behind his neck.

Elizabeth sipped her tea. "A long way. But I've thought of a place we could start. Pembroke Manor."

Luke's dark eyebrows shot up. "Pembroke Manor?"

Elizabeth nodded. "Robert Junior invited Jessica up to the country for the weekend. I'm invited, too, and I can bring a date." Warmth flooded Elizabeth's cheeks, and she dropped her eyes, wondering if Luke would detect how nervous and excited she was at the thought of going off for a weekend with him. "Would you—would you like to come with us?"

"Yes."

Elizabeth glanced up in surprise at Luke's rapid response. There was a strangely intense and yet faraway look in his eyes, and suddenly she remembered what she'd said to Jessica a few nights ago: "How well do you know Robert Pembroke? Do you really want to spend a weekend in some remote, isolated place with a perfect stranger?"

I don't know Luke any better than Jessica knows Robert, Elizabeth thought, momentarily disconcerted. *How did we come to be so involved with this whole mystery . . . and with each other . . . in just three days?*

"Yes, I'll come with you," Luke repeated. He put a hand on Elizabeth's, and a warm, electric tingle shot up her arm. "Just think of the sleuthing possibilities!"

Elizabeth smiled. "Right. How better to learn about the Pembroke family, and their secrets, than by staying in their home?"

Chapter 11

"It's the weekend!" Jessica exulted as she, Elizabeth, and Luke dashed out of the *London Journal* office building late Thursday afternoon. "For us, anyway."

"Tony was really nice to give us tomorrow off so we can have an extra day at Pembroke Manor," said Elizabeth.

"It's the least he could do, seeing as how he's still making us tag after Sergeant Bumpo." Jessica rolled her eyes. "We thought we'd get a break, now that Reeves has put Tony in charge of the crime desk temporarily," she explained to Luke. "Maybe we'd get to tackle something hard-core. Real crime, you know? No such luck."

"Tony decided that we'd been doing such a good job covering Bumpo's beat, we should stick with it." Elizabeth laughed. "So off we went to look into what Jessica dubbed 'The Case of the Exploding Eggplant.'"

151

Luke grinned. "Sounds like something Holmes himself would have hesitated to take on."

"Can you walk partway home with us?" Elizabeth asked.

"Nothing would give me more pleasure," said Luke. "Shall we go by way of Piccadilly Circus and Carnaby Street? I bet you haven't been there yet."

As they strolled the tree-lined, sun-dappled streets, bombarded by a cheerful cacophony of city sounds, Jessica related their latest Bumpo misadventure. "It was probably the biggest case to challenge Scotland Yard in decades," she began solemnly. "A vendor at the farmer's market had complained that some of his produce was, er, exploding."

"Exploding," Luke repeated, one eyebrow lifting skeptically.

"First a melon." Jessica spread her arms. "Ka-bam. Then a bushel of tomatoes. Ker-plooey. It was a mess! And not too good for business—who wants to buy exploding veggies? Enter Sergeant Benjamin Bumpo, the pride of Scotland Yard."

Elizabeth giggled, remembering. "He looked so dapper and professional—you could tell his suit had just been pressed. And his hair—what's left of it—was combed oh so carefully over his bald spot. Every strand in place."

"We arrived at the scene just as he did," Jessica continued. "So, there's ol' Bumpo talking to McDivitt, the produce vendor, when all of a sudden, out of nowhere . . ."

"Ka-bam?" Luke guessed.

Jessica nodded. "A dozen heads . . . of lettuce

went flying. One shot right by Bumpo like a cannonball. You should have seen his expression!"

Elizabeth picked up the tale. "A few seconds later, on the other side of the cart, a big purple eggplant exploded. Bumpo went to investigate. And just as he was leaning over the bin . . ."

"Ker-plooey?" said Luke.

"Another eggplant detonated right in his face," Jessica confirmed. "Seeds and pulp spattered all over his nice suit, and a big slab of purple eggplant skin ended up draped on top of his head like a toupee. I have never, *ever* laughed so hard."

"Poor Bumpo." Elizabeth wiped tears of laughter from her eyes. "He should really ask for a desk job."

"Well, did he solve the crime?" asked Luke as they turned onto Carnaby Street.

"To his credit, he did," said Elizabeth. "It turned out another vendor at the farmer's market thought McDivitt was encroaching on his turf, and undercutting his prices to boot. He planted little firecrackers in the fruits and vegetables to try to scare McDivitt off."

"But he didn't reckon on Bumpo of the Yard," concluded Jessica.

They all laughed as they continued up Carnaby Street, window-shopping and people-watching. "I've never seen so much black leather," Elizabeth whispered. "And the hairdos!"

All three turned to stare after a young man with a foot-high, neon-green Mohawk. "His ear must have been pierced ten times," Jessica marveled.

She stopped to thumb through a rack of gauzy "grunge" dresses. "How 'bout it, Liz? Want to give Mom and Dad a scare, and arrive home wearing clothes like this and with our hair dyed five different colors?"

"And some studded leather accessories and skull-and-crossbone jewelry," Elizabeth suggested.

To Jessica's disappointment, Piccadilly Circus wasn't a circus at all. "It's just shops and cinemas," she observed.

"We use the word differently in Britain," Luke confirmed. "A circus is a big, open place where a bunch of streets intersect. There's usually a market of some kind. They do have street performers in Piccadilly, though. Look at the clown selling balloons!"

They browsed the stalls, Jessica buying a silk scarf and Elizabeth emptying her pockets of change to purchase a beautiful used leather-bound copy of *Wuthering Heights*. "We should probably head home, Jess," Elizabeth said after half an hour. "Don't forget, we're seeing Portia's play tonight."

"Just one more thing," Jessica begged. She dragged Elizabeth and Luke over to a stall draped with rainbow-colored curtains. "A gypsy fortune-teller. I want to get my palm read!"

"You don't really believe in that stuff, do you?" scoffed Elizabeth.

"Well, that depends." Jessica grinned. "If she tells me I'm going to marry a tall, dark-haired British nobleman with the initials R.H.P., I'll believe!"

The gypsy was an unbelievably ancient woman with a dried-apple face and a turban decorated with tiny silver-and-gold stars and planets. She gestured with one withered, clawlike hand and Jessica sat down in the chair next to her, Elizabeth and Luke standing at a polite distance.

"I want to know what my future holds," said Jessica, extending her hand with the palm facing up.

The gypsy took Jessica's hand, smoothing it flat. As she traced the lines with her own gnarled index finger, her lips moved in some kind of incantation. "What's she saying?" Elizabeth whispered to Luke.

"I can't tell," he whispered back.

Suddenly, the gypsy froze, her wrinkled cheeks growing pale as she stared down at Jessica's palm. "Beware the full moon," she croaked, closing Jessica's hand into a fist. "Beware the full moon."

"Is that all?" Jessica asked in surprise when the gypsy dropped her hand and took a step backward.

"Geez, what a rip-off," she muttered indignantly as she rejoined Luke and Elizabeth. "I thought she was going to tell me all about my future—what my career would be, who I'd marry, how many kids I'd have, stuff like that. 'Beware the full moon'—what kind of dumb fortune is that?"

Elizabeth and Luke exchanged a worried glance. "It's the same thing the bag lady said the day we arrived in London," Elizabeth reminded Jessica. "It's what the villagers said to the boys in *An American Werewolf in London*."

"I know, isn't it hysterical?" Jessica laughed. "Maybe it's the same old lady—she must have seen the movie!"

Somehow, Elizabeth couldn't bring herself to

laugh. Somehow, she couldn't see it as a harmless coincidence. She looked at Luke, and found her own apprehension mirrored in his somber eyes. *We're both thinking about the same thing*, she realized. *The murders . . . and the killer, still at large . . .*

"There's a full moon tomorrow night," Luke told the twins. "You know what that means. . . ."

At HIS, Elizabeth, Jessica, Emily, David, and Gabriello gobbled an early dinner before heading out to the theater.

"Too bad Rene isn't able to come tonight," remarked David. "He has an embassy function, as usual." He lowered his voice. "But where's . . ."

"Lina?" Elizabeth shook her head. "I don't know. Sometimes she gets tied up at the shelter—I'm sure she'll be here any minute. And I'll make sure you two sit next to each other during the play," she whispered with a conspiratorial wink.

When it was time to leave, however, Lina still hadn't appeared. "I'll just check upstairs," Elizabeth offered. "She may have come in while we were eating and gone to the room to change."

She did find Lina in their bedroom. But rather than getting ready to go out, Lina was just making herself comfortable in one of the easy chairs, an afghan wrapped around her knees and a book in her hand.

"Aren't you coming?" Elizabeth asked in surprise.

Lina shook her head. "Portia hasn't had one nice thing to say to me all this time we've shared a room. I had a long day and, frankly, I'd rather spend a pleasant, quiet evening reading than watch her strut about onstage."

"But David will be so disappointed!" Elizabeth exclaimed. Lina turned bright pink and Elizabeth pressed her point. "He's really hoping for a chance to get to know you better."

"He *mustn't* get to know me better!" Lina burst out.

"But I thought you liked him," said Elizabeth, puzzled. "And he likes you. Isn't that good?"

"Definitely not," Lina declared. "Don't you see, Elizabeth? I can't go out with David, and I can't attend opening night at a fashionable West End theater. I just *can't*."

"Why not?" asked Elizabeth, completely baffled.

"Don't you see?" Lina repeated. She stared at Elizabeth, saying again, "Don't you *see*?"

Elizabeth stared back at Lina. Speaking just now, Lina's voice had altered, her thick Liverpudlian accent giving way to more modulated, elegant tones. There was something different about her expression, too, something almost . . . regal.

Taking off her wire-rimmed glasses, Lina tossed back her cropped brown hair and lifted her delicate chin. "Look at me," she commanded Elizabeth. "Look closely."

Elizabeth did as she was told and suddenly felt a jolt of recognition. *The picture in the newspaper at the airport our first day!* she thought. The hair was shorter and darker, and the glasses were new, and of course the accent was a fake, but the face was the same. . . . "Princess Eliana!" Elizabeth gasped.

Eliana heaved a deep, tired sigh. "None other."

Elizabeth's knees buckled as if she'd been kicked from behind. She sank, breathless, into the other armchair. "But how . . . why . . . ? You ran away—you weren't kidnapped at all!"

"I ran away," Eliana confirmed.

"But why?" Elizabeth looked at Eliana's plain white blouse and drab gray sweater and then glanced around the spartan bedroom.

"I know what you're thinking," Eliana said. "Why would anyone give up life in a palace for this? Why would I go from my mother, the Queen of England, to crotchety old Mrs. Bates? From private tutors and charity balls to soup kitchens and homeless shelters?" She lifted her slender shoulders. "I was tired of living behind a fence, like a rare bird in a gilded cage, sheltered and pampered. I wanted to find out what my city was really like. And I wanted to give something back to the world, for once—I've never had to do anything for myself, much less for other people."

"How did you get away?" Elizabeth wondered.

"It was remarkably easy." Eliana laughed lightly, remembering. "I snuck into a bathroom on the main floor that no one ever uses, dyed and cut my hair, cleaned up the mess, donned my new uniform, and ducked in with a tour group passing through the palace. Then, *voilà*! Lina Smith was out on the streets of London, with hardly a penny to her name."

Elizabeth shook her head, impressed by Eliana's reckless boldness. "Weren't you scared?"

Eliana sat forward, her eyes shining. "I was exhilarated. For the first time in my life, I was free! I could go anywhere I wanted, do or say anything I wanted, live a normal life. I've learned so much, Elizabeth, I can't tell you. From people like you and Jess and Emily, from the people at the shelter, from everyone I've met. *Real* people."

"This explains a lot of things," Elizabeth exclaimed. "Your glasses, and your fancy nightgown. And that's why you've been brushing off David, because you're not really from Liverpool!"

"Right." Eliana smiled. "The poor dear fellow's homesick and wants nothing more than to chat about Liverpool. I've been so afraid he'd see through my masquerade. As for the opening night of Portia's play, remember when I was in such a rush to leave Mondo the other night?"

The puzzle pieces clicked. "We'd just spotted Princess Gloria, your big sister!"

Eliana nodded. "I can't risk bumping into her, or anyone else who might recognize me, and there are bound to be dozens of celebrities attending such an eagerly awaited premiere."

"But your sister, your family, the whole country . . . people are terribly worried about you," Elizabeth told Eliana. "You must be aware that there's a huge search on. They think you may have been kidnapped or killed! Maybe it's time for you to go back."

Eliana shook her head stubbornly. "It's too soon. There's still so much I want to discover! I couldn't do it, living in a palace with the paparazzi recording my every move. You just don't know how liberating it is to be Lina Smith! Besides," she added, "I've communicated with my family. They know I'm safe and not kidnapped. I don't understand why the newspapers are printing stories like that."

The two girls gazed at each other in silence. "So, what are you going to do about me, Elizabeth?" Eliana asked solemnly.

Elizabeth hesitated, her sense of duty dueling with sympathy and admiration for the young princess.

Seizing Elizabeth's hands, Eliana squeezed them tight. "Please," she begged. "Keep my secret. Let me be free for just a while longer."

For a long moment, Elizabeth looked deep into Eliana's sincere, pleading eyes. Then she nodded reluctantly. "I'll keep your secret, Eliana. I won't even tell my sister. But I'm warning you." Elizabeth couldn't help smiling. "David's not going to give up easily. He has a serious crush on you!"

Eliana threw her arms around Elizabeth. Elizabeth hugged her back. "Thank you, Elizabeth," the princess whispered, tears glimmering in her eyes. "Thank you, my true friend."

The last purple and orange glimmer of sunset was coloring the western sky as the twins, Gabriello, David, and Emily stepped out of their cab in front of the Ravensgate Theatre. A brightly lit marquee proclaimed opening night of *A Common Man*, starring British stage favorites Margaret Kent and Richard Winters.

A festive, elegantly dressed crowd filled the

lobby and spilled out onto the sidewalk. "The way Portia always talked, you'd have thought she was getting top billing," Emily said dryly as they made their way toward one of the ushers. "I bet she has a walk-on role with only one line."

"She probably plays a maid," Jessica said. "Or a cook. Wouldn't that be perfect?"

Handing them each a playbill, the usher showed them to their seats in the tenth row of the mezzanine. "They're great seats, anyway," remarked Elizabeth, sitting down in between Jessica and David. Tipping her head, she looked up at the glittering chandeliers and then over at the box seats festooned with rich velvet curtains. "I don't see how we can complain."

"Hullo, what's this?" Leafing through her playbill, Emily pointed to the cast of characters. "Portia's name isn't anywhere on here!"

Quickly, the others flipped to the same page. "'Peter Huntington is played by Richard Winters,'" read Jessica. "'Margaret Kent plays his wife, Genevra, and Penelope Abbott is their daughter, Isabel.' You're right, Em," she exclaimed. "Portia's not even down for any of the minor characters!"

Gabriello's dark eyebrows knotted in puzzlement. "Is this some kind of hoax?"

Just then the lights began to dim. Voices hushed and the last few people still standing in the aisles slipped hurriedly into their seats. "We'll just have to watch and see," Elizabeth whispered as the theater was plunged into darkness.

They held their breath as the red velvet curtain

slowly rose, revealing a tastefully decorated but not opulent drawing room. The figure of a man leaned against the mantel; a woman stood in the doorway, and a second woman reclined on a sofa.

Elizabeth's eyes took in the scene. She recognized the girl on the sofa just as Jessica's elbow jabbed into her side. "It's Portia!" Jessica hissed.

The play began with an argument between the "common man," Peter, his aristocratic and dissatisfied wife, and their spoiled, sharp-tongued daughter, Isabel . . . Portia.

Elizabeth watched, spellbound. Lounging, Isabel held a book at eye level, effectively blocking out her view of her father. She lowered the book only to address occasional disdainful remarks to her mother.

Every gesture and intonation was full of expression; the character was instantly full of life. "Portia's good—she's really good!" Elizabeth whispered to Jessica.

"She's fantastic," Jessica whispered back, "as much as I hate to admit it. But I still don't get it. Why does the program say Isabel is played by Penelope Abbott?"

"Maybe Portia is Penelope's understudy," Emily whispered from the other side of Jessica.

"Maybe," Elizabeth murmured, but she was dubious. That didn't make sense, either—the understudies' names were all listed, and Portia's wasn't among them.

Still puzzled, they sat back in their chairs to watch the gripping, fast-paced drama. As the minutes sped by, something peculiar happened. Elizabeth found herself anticipating some of Isabel's dry, sardonic lines; she could predict how the character would react in a given scene. *It's almost as if I've seen the play before*, she thought, bemused. *As if I knew Isabel . . .*

The play built up to a pre-intermission climax. Onstage, Isabel turned on her browbeaten father and blasted one of his humble suggestions with the scathing remark, "How quaint, Papa. Let's do."

How quaint . . . The little words echoed in Elizabeth's brain. Suddenly, she saw something, as clear as day.

"I figured it out!" she announced excitedly as soon as the curtain fell and the lights went up for intermission.

The applause died down and the audience poured out into the aisles, streaming toward the lobby. Elizabeth, Jessica, Emily, Gabriello, and David went out to the sidewalk for some fresh air.

"You figured out why Portia's name isn't in the playbill?" said David.

"No, something even more important," Elizabeth declared. "I've figured out Portia."

"How do you mean?" asked Emily.

"Didn't you notice?" Elizabeth prompted. "The first scene, when she was holding the book up so she wouldn't have to look at her father, and the scene where she was preparing for bed in an elaborate dressing gown, putting on eyeshades and earplugs to shut herself off from the world. Remember our first night at HIS, Jess?"

"Yeah, but—"

"And some of Isabel's lines," Elizabeth continued. "They were snotty things we've all heard *Portia* say around the dorm—nearly verbatim!"

David's eyes glinted with comprehension. "You're absolutely right. Portia is Isabel. Or should I say, Isabel is Portia?"

Elizabeth nodded eagerly. "She's been playing this part all along. Things she's said and done around the dorm—it's all been rehearsing. This isn't Portia's personality—it's Isabel's!"

Jessica and Emily both looked skeptical. "More likely, Portia just found the role she was born for," said Emily. "I never got the impression she didn't really mean it when she was being nasty to me!"

"We won't know until we go backstage after the play," Elizabeth conceded. *And perhaps meet the real Portia Albert for the first time!* she added to herself.

When the final curtain dropped, the standing-room-only crowd at Ravensgate Theatre leapt to their feet in an enthusiastic ovation. When Portia took her bow, dozens of bouquets rained down on the stage. Gathering an armful of flowers, she curtsied again and then darted behind the curtain.

Backstage pass in hand, the HIS crew hurried to congratulate their dormmate. They spotted Portia through an open dressing-room door, busy unpinning her hair.

Everyone but Elizabeth hung back. "I still don't trust her," Elizabeth heard Jessica murmur.

She walked forward alone, her hand extended. "Portia, you were—"

Before Elizabeth could finish her sentence, Portia unexpectedly flung both arms around her. "I did it!" she cried. "Oh, thank you so much for coming!"

Realizing they weren't going to get their heads bitten off, Jessica, Emily, David, and Gabriello pressed forward to offer their congratulations. "You were great, Portia," Jessica gushed.

"You stole the show," David confirmed.

"I predict rave reviews," said Gabriello, "and a long, successful run."

"Oh, thank you, you all," Portia said tearfully. She patted Emily's arm. "I really wasn't sure until I went onstage tonight. I wasn't sure I could pull it off."

"But you were born to it, said Elizabeth. "You're a natural."

Portia's smile was wistful. "Do you think so? Does it appear that way to you?"

"Of course," said Jessica. "You're Sir Montford Albert's daughter, after all!"

Portia sighed. "Yes. Yes, I am."

"So, what's the story?" Emily demanded. "Why isn't your name in the playbill?" She pointed at the door to the dressing room. "And who's Penelope Abbott?"

"Penelope Abbott is . . . me." Portia waved toward a stack of folding chairs. "Maybe we should all sit down!"

As Elizabeth, Jessica, David, Gabriello, and Emily listened eagerly, Portia launched into a surprising tale. "I know you assumed that my father was the reason I landed a role in a big new West End play," she began. "You probably assumed that he pushed me into acting, and cheered me on every step of the way. Well, it wasn't exactly like that."

She dropped her eyes, and suddenly Elizabeth recalled their conversation of a few nights ago. "In fact, it was the opposite," Portia continued quietly. "The first time I told him I wanted to be an actress, he yelled at me. When I acted in little plays at school, he'd refuse to come and watch. When he finally did see me perform, instead of praising me or just saying something vaguely encouraging, he ridiculed me in front of everyone, telling me I had no talent."

"That's horrible!" Emily declared, her eyes flashing.

"You poor thing," murmured Elizabeth, her heart aching with sympathy.

"I believed him," Portia went on. "He was my father, after all, and the greatest living actor in England. Who would know talent if he didn't? But no matter how many times he cut me down, I couldn't shake my desire to be an actress. It's in the blood."

"So you left Edinburgh and came to London," said Elizabeth.

Portia nodded. "I came to London to throw myself body and soul into acting—to prove myself to him, to prove him wrong. I had to get away from him in order to do that. I had to get out from under his shadow . . . and his name. That's why I auditioned for parts as Penelope Abbott. I didn't want anyone, including my father, to claim I'd gotten a role because of his fame and influence."

"Well, you proved yourself tonight," Emily told her. "You're going to be a big star. And that's not idle flattery," she added dryly. "Frankly, none of us would go out of our way to butter you up!"

"I've been a witch, haven't I? There was so much at stake . . . my performance had to be perfect, down to the last gesture. But maybe I took my immersion in the role of Isabel too far. I never meant to alienate you. I hope it's not too late . . ."

Portia gave them a winsome, hopeful smile. It was impossible not to smile back. "To be friends?" finished Elizabeth. "Of course it isn't."

"Friends." Beaming, Portia leaned forward to give Jessica's hand a firm shake. "I promise I won't put on any more airs back at the dorm."

"Which reminds me." Jessica hopped to her feet and they all followed suit. "We'd better get moving if we don't want Mrs. Bates to lock us out. *Her* wicked witch imitation isn't an act!"

Chapter 12

As they'd arranged when they parted the afternoon before, Luke met Elizabeth and Jessica in front of HIS at eight o'clock sharp Friday morning.

Hoisting her duffel bag, Jessica turned to wave good-bye to her friends. "See ya, Em. Bye, Portia and Lina. Be good, David and Gabe!"

Mrs. Bates bustled out the front door to give each girl a brisk hug. "You'll be in good hands with the Pembrokes, my dears, but telephone if you won't be home by curfew Sunday eve. I'll worry myself sick, otherwise."

"Will do," Elizabeth promised. "Bye, everybody!"

Portia blew a kiss. Lina smiled at Elizabeth, holding one finger to her lips in a silent "don't tell" signal. Beyond them, in the front hall, Elizabeth caught a glimpse of a tall, dark-haired boy. Stepping to the door, Rene looked out at Elizabeth. At the sight of her overnight bag, and

Luke, he frowned, then turned away again without so much as a wave.

Elizabeth sighed. Rene had been giving her the cold shoulder for days, but what could she do? She'd tried her best to smooth things over with him, but if he didn't want to be friends . . .

They took a cab to Victoria Station and hurried directly to the ticket counter. "Robert's meeting us in Pembroke Woods," Jessica told Elizabeth and Luke. "He expects us to catch the nine-fifteen train—it takes about two hours, making a few stops on the way."

The agent, a wizened old man, peered at them through the ticket window. "Destination?"

"Pembroke Woods," said Elizabeth, pulling out her wallet. "Three seats, please."

"One way or return?"

For an instant, she hesitated. A strange premonition flooded over her, chilling the blood in her veins. *What if something happens to us? What if we go to Pembroke Manor . . . and don't come back?*

Don't be ridiculous, Elizabeth chastised herself. "Return, please," she replied briskly.

Tickets in hand, the three rushed to track nine, where the northwestbound train was already boarding. Climbing into a non-smoking car, they stowed their luggage overhead and sat down, Elizabeth and Jessica sitting next to each other on one side, with Luke in the seat by the window facing Elizabeth's.

A few minutes later, the train shuddered and

began rolling forward. Soon they were roaring out of London into lush green English farmland. "A weekend in the boring, safe countryside—this is going to be great," remarked Jessica, slumping so she could put her feet up on the empty seat next to Luke. "Aren't you guys relieved to get out of the city, to leave all that scary serial killer stuff behind?"

Elizabeth stared out the window. Again, for no earthly reason, she felt goose bumps prickling the skin on her arms. *Were* they leaving the danger, the evil, behind in London? She pictured the face of the gypsy fortune-teller as the old woman examined Jessica's palm. The gypsy saw something there—something that made her blanch and stutter. *Beware the full moon. . . .*

The full moon will follow us, Elizabeth realized, her eyes on the cloud-streaked sky. *Tonight it will shine as brightly over the village of Pembroke Woods as over London. . . .*

While Jessica regaled Luke with stories about the Pembroke family—stories she'd already forced her sister to listen to at least twice—Elizabeth continued to gaze pensively out the train window. *What a week it's been, and our internships at the* Journal *have only just begun!* she thought. The action had been nonstop: Dr. Neville's murder, Poo-Poo's mangled corpse, Lucy quitting over the alleged cover-up, Tony and Lucy's fight, Reeves naming Tony temporary crime editor. *And Luke . . . my friendship with Luke—our talks, our walks . . .*

Even dorm life had been far from dull. She'd bumped into an old flame, Rene Glize, only to

171

have a trivial misunderstanding spoil their chance at renewed friendship. Plain, ordinary Lina Smith had turned out to be the missing Princess Eliana. *Both Lina and Portia aren't who they seemed to be at first,* Elizabeth mused. *Everybody has their secrets, I guess.*

She glanced at Luke, who was smiling politely at Jessica's story. There was a visible tension about his body, in the tautness of his shoulders and the wariness in his eyes. *He knows it's not as simple as Jessica thinks, this escaping into the country,* Elizabeth guessed. They were almost certain there was a Pembroke connection to the murder of Dr. Neville . . . and at that very moment, they were on their way to Pembroke Manor.

Everybody has their secrets. And some secrets are darker than others. . . .

"There he is!" Jessica squealed as the train screeched to a stop in the quaint, tiny village of Pembroke Woods. "See? The tall dark-haired guy in the white shirt and ascot standing by the cool car. Isn't he gorgeous?"

The "cool car" was a silver Jaguar convertible. Elizabeth and Luke gaped.

Jessica was already on her feet, struggling to get her duffel bag out of the luggage compartment. The instant the door opened, she leaped out onto the platform. "Robert, hi!" she called, waving energetically.

Elizabeth and Luke followed at a slower pace. "I feel out of my element," Luke muttered nervously, putting a hand to his throat to loosen his necktie. "How am I going to know what to say to these people?"

"Don't worry," said Elizabeth. "You're ten times smarter than Robert Pembroke—according to Jessica, he was kicked out of just about every boarding school in Great Britain. Just be yourself and you'll charm the pants off all of them."

Luke gave her hand a quick, grateful squeeze. "Thanks, Elizabeth."

Robert strode forward to meet Jessica, relieving her of her duffel bag at the same time that he bent to brush her cheek with a kiss. "It's so wonderful to see you here," he proclaimed, his blue eyes glinting. "I can't wait to show you around our little corner of heaven."

Jessica smiled up at him, fluttering her eyelashes and looking as if she might swoon. Elizabeth and Luke exchanged a glance, rolling their eyes.

Collecting her wits, Jessica turned to present her sister to Robert. "In case you couldn't guess, this is my twin sister, Elizabeth. Oh, and her friend, Luke Shepherd—he works at the *Journal*."

Robert took Elizabeth's hand, flashing her an ultra-white, ultra-charismatic smile. "What a pleasure this is, Elizabeth. Jessica told me you were twins, but I really didn't believe it until now—I simply couldn't conceive of there being another girl as pretty as she is."

Elizabeth smiled back stiffly, taking an instant dislike to Robert Pembroke and his overdone, insincere flattery.

Facing Luke, Robert shook his hand next.

"Glad you could join us, old chap," he said in jovial, lord-of-the-manor style. "We'll have to chat about the newspaper business. You can bring me up to speed on goings-on at the *Journal*—it's a little Pembroke family operation, you know, and I really should be more in tune."

Luke nodded, his eyes intent on the other young man's face, as if he might be able to penetrate Robert's innermost thoughts. In the brief moment that they stood that way, Elizabeth was struck by the contrast they made. Though both were tall and well-built, with dark hair, fair complexions, and classic English features, any resemblance was only skin deep. Where Luke's manner was pure, open, and unpretentious, Robert's was artificial, arrogant, and condescending. *What does Jessica see in him?* Elizabeth wondered.

Oh, yeah—that, she thought as Robert led them over to the Jaguar. *The title, the money, the car, the estate. How could I forget?*

Robert unlocked the trunk of the car and tossed in Jessica's bag. "Put your things in the boot and hop in."

Luke held the back door for Elizabeth while Robert held the front passenger side door for Jessica. As she belted herself in, Jessica turned to flash a deliriously happy smile at her sister. *Isn't this the life?* her expression seemed to say.

Elizabeth smiled back with as much warmth as she could muster. No matter what she personally might think of Robert Pembroke, the fact was that her sister was crazy about him. *It's not fair to spoil*

174

Jessica's fun, she reminded herself. Besides, why not keep a positive attitude? No matter how snobby the Pembrokes might be, it was exciting to be in a beautiful new place . . . and with Luke at her side.

The Jaguar's powerful engine purred to life and Robert steered into the left lane of the narrow cobbled street that ran through the center of the village. With one hand, he gestured to the gray fieldstone cottages that lined the street, dark green ivy curling up around the doorframes. "These weavers' cottages were built in the sixteenth century," he informed his passengers. "This has always been sheep country."

They rumbled over a little wooden bridge. In the clear, bubbling brook below, a pair of large white swans glided majestically. "This pair and their ancestors have been coming here to raise their cygnets for a century or more," Robert said. "Hence the name of the local tavern."

Elizabeth laughed when she saw the weathered wooden sign swinging in the breeze over the door of the inn. "The White Swan—how appropriate!"

Rounding a bend, they left the village behind. On one side of the road, white sheep dotted lush green fields; on the other, woods swept upward toward high, forbidding moors. Through the trees, on the bank of another creek, Elizabeth spotted a ruined stone tower. "Look! What's that?" she called up to Robert.

"Woodleigh Abbey," he called back. "Or what's left of it. It's been a ruin for centuries—since it was burned during the Reformation, to be exact. They say it's haunted by the ghosts of four monks who perished in the conflagration."

Looking back over her shoulder, Elizabeth thought she glimpsed a ghostly form flitting through the trees. *It's just your overactive imagination, silly,* she chided herself, suppressing a shiver.

"It's all so beautiful," Jessica exclaimed.

Robert waved a hand in a proud, proprietary gesture. "It's all ours," he said simply. "We Pembrokes live a charmed life—always have. The land has been in the family for countless generations, passed down in unbroken succession to the oldest son." He grinned at Jessica. "Lucky me."

Lucky you is right. Elizabeth darted a sympathetic glance at Luke, who sat stiff and tense, his hands folded on his knees and his eyes fixed on the back of Robert's head. *How come some people have so much, and others so little?* she wondered. *What did Robert Pembroke do to deserve all this?*

The Jaguar crested a hill and Jessica caught her breath. "Is *that* Pembroke Manor?" she gasped in wonder.

Robert smiled, clearly pleased by her delight and awe. "Home sweet home."

The manor was constructed from the same gray fieldstone as the houses in the village, but on a far more splendid scale. It was shaped like a "U," with two wings extending forward on either side of a courtyard the size of a football field. *I bet it has a hundred rooms!* Jessica thought. *Eat your heart out, Lila—this makes Fowler Crest look like a gate-keeper's cottage!*

"I've never seen anything so magnificent," Jessica gushed. "It looks like someplace a king or queen might live."

"They've stayed as guests, anyway," Robert said nonchalantly. "Queen Victoria and her consort came here to hunt, and, back in the fifteenth century, one of the King Henrys stopped through. We had Malcolm, Gloria, and the rest of the current royal brood five or six summers ago. Boy, were we a wild bunch!"

They coasted to a stop in the circular drive. Out of nowhere, a uniformed groundskeeper appeared. Robert popped the trunk and stepped out of the car, leaving the keys in the ignition. Another servant was already pulling the luggage from the trunk.

Taking Jessica's hand, Robert gestured to Elizabeth and Luke. "Follow me." He pushed open a dark oak door two times as tall as Jessica and they stepped into a hallway as lofty and solemn as a cathedral. Both the floor and walls were gray stone; the ceiling was of blackened beams.

Jessica pointed to a large, ancient tapestry draping one wall. It depicted a shield divided into four quadrants, each containing a different emblem. "What's that?" she asked Robert.

"The Pembroke family crest. See the 'P' and 'R' intertwined? That's for Pembroke and 'Rex,' King, indicating the fealty of the Pembrokes to the royal family. The sword represents our willingness to do battle for crown and country. The water is

177

Woodleigh Falls—a symbol of the streams that flow through our land, making it rich and fertile. And the wolf is, for some reason I've never been able to figure out, our patron saint." He grinned. "Kind of a funny choice, considering we've always raised sheep. Perhaps early Pembrokes chose the wolf to honor and placate him, to bribe him to leave their flocks alone."

Jessica gazed in fascination at the coat of arms. Elizabeth also stared at the wolf, her eyes wide.

"I'll give you the grand tour presently," Robert promised as they proceeded down the hall. He stopped at a wide doorway. "First let's make the introductions. Hullo, anyone home?"

The room beyond was wide and bright, with tall casement windows standing open to the summer breeze. A table was set for lunch, and a buffet table next to the wall held an array of covered silver dishes. Four people dressed in elegant summer weekend clothes lounged by the windows, cocktail glasses in their hands.

"Mother, I'd like to reintroduce you to Jessica Wakefield." Robert slipped an arm around Jessica's waist, gently propelling her forward. "The crack reporter for the *Journal*, remember? And Jessica's sister, Elizabeth, and their friend, Luke."

With the smallest and coolest of smiles, Lady Pembroke extended one paper-thin hand. Jessica shook it gingerly, not wanting to crush the birdlike bones. "It's nice to see you again, Lady Pembroke. I'm glad you got your mink back."

"And my father."

Lord Pembroke bowed over Jessica's hand, squeezing it warmly. Jessica smiled, feeling an immediate liking for this gallant, distinguished older version of Robert. "Thank you for inviting us, Lord Pembroke."

"It's our pleasure, my dear," he assured her. Taking Elizabeth's hand, he repeated the sentiment. Then he shook Luke's hand. "What did you say your name was, young man?"

"Luke." Luke gazed deeply into the older man's eyes. "Luke Shepherd."

Lord Pembroke gave a start; his fingers tightened around Luke's, and something flickered behind his eyes. *Surprise?* Jessica wondered. *Recognition?* "Luke Shepherd," he muttered.

"Do you know the name, sir?" Luke asked pleasantly. "Perhaps because I work at the *Journal*."

"Yes, that's it." Lord Pembroke's smile didn't quite reach his eyes. "Of course."

Liz should have brought Rene, Jessica thought, biting her lip. *Doesn't she see how common Luke is? Doesn't she realize he makes us look bad?*

Robert had turned to the other people in the room, a middle-aged man whom Jessica thought looked vaguely familiar and an attractive, young blond woman. "Joy and Andrew, how jolly to see you. I didn't realize you were joining us this weekend." With a flourish, Robert presented the pair to Jessica, Elizabeth, and Luke. "Our good family friend, Andrew Thatcher, and his fiancée, Joy Singleton."

That's how I know him—from that day at Dr.

179

Neville's, and the picture in the newspaper! Jessica thought, just as Elizabeth burst out, "Andrew Thatcher, the London chief of police?"

Andrew Thatcher smiled. "At your service."

Elizabeth and Luke exchanged a meaningful glance. Meanwhile, Joy Singleton shook Jessica's hand, giving her a friendly smile. "Robert Senior has promised us a ride this afternoon, and I'll make sure they put you on Cinnamon. She's my favorite mount—as gentle as a kitten and as comfortable as an easy chair."

Jessica smiled back, discreetly ogling Joy's butter-soft suede trousers, expensive casual silk shirt, and plentiful gold jewelry. "I'm not much of a rider—Cinnamon sounds perfect." *It all sounds perfect,* she thought blissfully. *It all looks perfect. It all is perfect.*

Robert rubbed his hands together. "I'm ravenous. What's for lunch?"

"Jessica appears to be having the time of her life," Luke observed to Elizabeth as they cantered along the bridle path a few horse-lengths behind the others.

"She is," Elizabeth agreed. Her sister was riding side-by-side with Robert. As Elizabeth watched, Robert leaned over to say something and Jessica tossed back her loose blond hair, laughing.

He's certainly treating her like a queen, Elizabeth conceded silently. *I can't fault him on that point.* Lord Pembroke Senior was also lavishing paternal attention on her, and Jessica had hit it off famously with the bubble-headed but pleasant Joy Singleton. "I don't think I've ever seen her fall so hard for a guy," Elizabeth remarked. "Although in this case, of course, it's not just the *guy*—she's infatuated with everything to do with the Pembrokes."

Abruptly, Luke reined in his horse, Nightwing. Sitting back in the saddle, Elizabeth slowed Lollipop, her mount, to a walk as well. "What is it?" she asked Luke.

Luke gestured to a trail that branched off from the main path and led into a grove of birch trees. "Let's go this way," he suggested. "I wouldn't mind sneaking away from the others."

If Elizabeth's cheeks hadn't already been flushed from the wind and sun, they would have turned pink at the thought of being alone with Luke in this enchanted place. "Let's," she agreed.

Dismounting, they led their horses to the verge of the wood, pausing to let Nightwing and Lollipop nibble at a clump of lush, tall grass.

A gust of wind swept down from the hills, stirring Elizabeth's hair and causing the grain in the fields to ripple like an ocean. Luke glanced back to where Jessica, Robert, Lord Pembroke Senior, Joy, and Andrew were just disappearing over the crest of a hill. "What do you think about Thatcher being here?" he asked Elizabeth.

Elizabeth tugged gently on Lollipop's reins. "It proves there's a close connection between him and Pembroke. Thatcher might very well put a muzzle on a police investigation at Pembroke's request."

181

"Right. And when we first arrived earlier, didn't Lord Pembroke Senior strike you as a bit . . . edgy?"

"As if he were guilty of something," Elizabeth agreed, "like covering up a murder."

"At the very least," she thought she heard Luke mutter. More loudly, he said, "Yes, it certainly looks like it's going to be an interesting weekend."

Leading the horses, they strolled into the grove of birches. Waving gently in the breeze, the trees cast a dappled pattern of sun and shadow upon the path. Elizabeth breathed deeply of the damp, ferny scent. "I'm glad Jessica talked me . . . us . . . into coming with her," she said, glancing at Luke with a shy smile.

He smiled back. "So am I. Here, let's tether the horses and explore."

Looping the reins around the branches of a tree, Luke reached for Elizabeth's hand. "Do you hear a stream?" he asked.

Cutting off the path, they waded through the ferns in the direction of the sound of running water, still holding hands. Elizabeth's heart pounded with anticipation . . . of precisely what, she wasn't sure. *Something, though,* she knew, her blood feeling hot in her veins. *Something is going to happen between us. . . .*

They came to the banks of the stream, and suddenly Luke stopped. Dropping Elizabeth's hand, he bent to examine a bushy plant growing under the birches. "What is it?" Elizabeth asked.

Luke ran a finger along the petals of one of the

strange, hooded white flowers. "Wolfsbane," he said somberly. His gaze locked onto Elizabeth's and a hot spark shot between them. "According to medieval lore, it blooms when it's time for the werewolf to come out."

Elizabeth had been about to pick one of the unusual flowers. Now she drew back her hand as if she'd been stung, her eyes shadowed with dread.

"It's all right." Luke stepped close to her, one arm wrapping protectively around her shoulders. Sliding the other hand into his trouser pocket, he pulled out a tarnished silver pendant on a chain. "See this symbol?"

Tentatively, Elizabeth touched the pendant. "It's a wolf's head, with a five-sided star."

"The pentagram is an ancient, magical symbol of immense power, did you know that? Here, the werewolf is inside it. It will contain and neutralize his power." Lifting his hands, Luke clasped the chain around Elizabeth's neck. "Wear this at all times, and it will protect you."

The pendant was cold against her bare skin . . . and yet, somehow, warm at the same time. *I can feel it,* she thought, staring up at Luke with wide, mesmerized eyes. *I can feel the power.*

"It will protect you," Luke repeated softly. His hands lingered on her neck; he tilted her face toward his. "And *I* will protect you."

Slowly, he bent his head to hers. A sudden, fierce hunger swept through Elizabeth's body and she went to him eagerly. At last, their lips met in the kiss they'd both been dreaming of all week long.

Chapter 13

"I really wish we'd made friends with Portia in time to borrow some of her clothes for this trip," Jessica said mournfully, twisting to examine herself in the full-length mirror. "This dress is OK in Sweet Valley, but somehow it doesn't seem right for a formal dinner at Pembroke Manor."

Elizabeth flung up her hands. Jessica had brought four dresses with her, and tried on every one of them twice. "We'll miss dinner altogether if you don't hurry and make up your mind. You could always just put on your nightgown and go straight to bed!"

Jessica sighed. Lila and Amy had helped her pick out the cherry-red, square-necked dress—it *was* the most elegant, grown-up dress she'd ever owned, and fancier than Elizabeth's sailor dress. "I guess with a single strand of pearls, it will do," she decided. "But I'm sure Joy will look a thousand times nicer."

"Probably," Elizabeth said without much sympathy. "She's the type who has a closet full of designer originals and spends all her time thinking about what outfit to put on next."

"Really, Liz, you're such a reverse snob," Jessica accused, slipping her feet into a pair of black patent leather sling-backs. "Joy's a perfectly nice person—you'd find that out if you gave her half a chance." She paused at the dressing table to spritz herself behind the ears and on the wrists with perfume, then breezed toward the door. "I'm ready!"

Luke and Robert, both wearing jackets and ties, were already standing in the entrance to the large, imposing dining room. "Look at that *table*," Jessica hissed to Elizabeth. "It's fifty feet long!"

"You need a bullhorn to ask for the butter," Elizabeth hissed back.

Just then, Lord and Lady Pembroke approached from the drawing room, walking arm-in-arm. Andrew Thatcher and Joy Singleton followed. *Joy's in* sequins, Jessica thought with envy and dismay. *And, wow, can she carry it off.*

Robert took Jessica's hand, slipping it through the crook of his arm. "May I have the honor?"

Jessica nodded, smiling up at him. With the last rays of sunset shooting like golden arrows through the windows, Robert looked more like a fairy tale prince than ever. As they walked into the dining room, she couldn't even feel the floor under her feet. Only Robert's arm kept her connected to earth. *This is how it will be,* she thought, *walking together down the aisle of the village church on our wedding day. . . .*

Robert pulled out a chair for Jessica. On the other side of the table, Luke did the same for Elizabeth. The instant all eight were seated, two uniformed maidservants materialized out of nowhere, one filling crystal goblets with ice water and the other placing flat, broad-rimmed bowls of creamy lobster bisque in front of each diner.

Jessica started to reach for a spoon and then shot a glance, half amused and half panicked, at her sister. *Two knives, three spoons, and four forks . . . what are we going to be eating here?* Out of the corner of her eye, she saw Lady Pembroke select a spoon and mirrored the choice.

"We had the nicest horseback ride this afternoon, Lady Pembroke," Jessica said, smiling at her hostess. "I wish you could have joined us."

Lady Pembroke laughed dryly. "I don't ride, my dear. But I'm glad you enjoyed your little tour of the property."

"We only saw half of it," Robert told his mother. "We'll have to ride out in the other direction tomorrow."

"Can we ride to Woodleigh Abbey?" Joy asked. "I'd love to explore the ruins."

"Didn't Andrew tell you about the ghosts?" Robert teased. "Even in broad daylight, Woodleigh can be a disconcerting place."

"Oh, I don't worry about such things when Andrew's along," said Joy, dimpling. "Do you really think the ghost of a meek old monk would stand up to the London chief of police?"

Robert laughed heartily. Lord Pembroke

chuckled. "Such fearlessness," he said. "Perhaps you should join the force yourself, Joy, my dear."

"I've considered it," Joy replied in a bantering tone.

"Or she could report for the *Journal*," Robert suggested, one eyebrow cocked ironically. "Uncovering the wicked truths of the world takes fearlessness, too."

"That it does," his father agreed. There was an unexpected note of seriousness in his voice, but it vanished as he turned to speak to Jessica. "I haven't heard, my dear, how you and your sister are finding your summer internships at the newspaper."

"Oh, we love it," Jessica declared, looking to Elizabeth for confirmation. "It's so exciting! Our very first case, at Dr.—"

Elizabeth shot her a warning look, and Jessica bit off the sentence. *We weren't supposed to be there. We're not supposed to know anything,* she reminded herself. "At Lady Wimpole's," she amended, toying with her soup spoon. "And then, of course, the mink thing at Pembroke Green, when I met Robert. It was quite a day. What I started to say is that we're very sorry about the death of your friend, Dr. Neville."

"Oh, yes, well . . ." Lord Pembroke exchanged a glance with Andrew Thatcher. Then his eyes darted to his son. Robert sipped his soup, oblivious.

Maybe I'm not even supposed to know they're friends. Jessica bit her lip. She couldn't remember—her mind had gone blank. *What can I say and what can't I?*

Elizabeth came to the rescue. "Robert told us

Dr. Neville was your best friend," she said softly. "We're truly sorry."

"Thank you, my dear," Lord Pembroke said gruffly. "It's quite a loss, quite a loss."

At that moment one of the servants, who'd been performing her duties in absolute silence, stepped to Lord Pembroke's side and cleared her throat timidly. "Excuse me, sir, but there's a visitor. Constable Pickering. He says . . . it's urgent business."

Dropping his crumpled cloth napkin on the table, Lord Pembroke rose to his feet. "Urgent? I can't imagine—well, bring him in, bring him in. We'll find out what's on his mind and offer him dinner."

Lady Pembroke frowned. "Really, darling. The local *constable*, for dinner?"

Lord Pembroke waved at her. "Hush, Henrietta."

The constable entered the dining room, his hat in his hands. Jessica and the others gaped at him, curious. *Something's wrong,* Jessica guessed instantly. *That man's as white as one of Woodleigh Abbey's ghosts!*

"I'm sorry to interrupt. Perhaps, Lord Pembroke . . ." Constable Pickering shot an uncomfortable glance at Lady Pembroke. "Perhaps we could have a word . . . alone."

"It's all right, Pickering," Lord Pembroke assured him somewhat impatiently. "Just tell us your news so we can get on with our meal."

With visible reluctance, the constable complied. "It's the sheep, sir."

Lord Pembroke's dark eyebrows shot up. "The sheep?"

"The flock in the northeast pasture. A villager out potshotting rabbits along your property line found them, just at sunset. Four of them."

"Found them . . . ?"

"Dead," Constable Pickering said flatly. "Their throats torn right out. Hard to say if it was the work of man or beast."

Lord Pembroke sat back down as if the wind had been knocked out of him. Somebody dropped a soup spoon with a clatter. Jessica stared at the constable and then ran her wide, horrified eyes around the table. All present had turned pale with shock and revulsion.

Jessica gripped the arms of her chair. The room was spinning around her; she knew she was on the verge of fainting. *Dead with their throats torn out,* she thought. *Just like Poo-Poo and the nurse and Dr. Neville . . .*

Understandably, the dinner party broke up early. No one much felt like playing cards or charades. "I'm sorry your first night at Pembroke Manor hasn't been more fun," Robert said to Jessica as they strolled through the manicured English gardens.

Jessica glanced up at the black sky. Shreds of tattered clouds raced along, momentarily obscuring the round, full moon. "Are—are you sure we're . . . safe out here?" she asked Robert, shivering in the jacket he'd lent her.

The manicured English gardens were set in the courtyard, surrounded on three sides by the house. "Safe as if you were tucked in your own bed," Robert promised. "The outside gate is locked. Besides . . ." He reached out, pulling her toward him. "I'm here with you, aren't I?"

Jessica wrapped her arms around Robert's waist and lifted her face to his. Robert bent his head and their mouths met in a deep, searching kiss. "Yes," Jessica whispered. "Oh, yes."

Robert hugged her tightly, his lips moving to her throat. "So, don't worry about the sheep." He nibbled lightly on her ear. "Most likely, it was just the work of local youths, out looking for trouble. The constable will get to the bottom of it in the morning."

Above, the wind pushed the clouds aside. Suddenly, the gardens were bathed in the pale, silver light of the full moon. *Maybe it was just local kids*, Jessica thought. *But maybe not. Maybe the danger isn't limited to London—maybe it followed us here.*

"Elizabeth and Luke think . . ."

"What?" Robert asked, kissing her cheek, her temple, her forehead.

She'd been about to tell him Elizabeth and Luke's werewolf theory. All at once, though, she realized how silly it would sound. *Elizabeth and Luke have gone completely off their rockers. There's no such thing as werewolves—any sane person knows that!* Anyway, who wanted to think about werewolves when Robert Pembroke, the richest, handsomest boy in all of England, was driving her crazy with kisses?

"Elizabeth and Luke think I'm incredibly lucky to have met you," Jessica murmured. "And on *that* topic, I agree with them one hundred percent."

Lord and Lady Pembroke and Andrew and Joy had retired upstairs, leaving Elizabeth and Luke alone in the parlor. They'd pulled the sofa close to the hearth, but despite a roaring fire, Elizabeth couldn't seem to get warm.

Outside, the wind howled relentlessly. Something tapped against the window, making them both jump.

"It's OK," Luke said soothingly. "It was just a tree branch."

He wrapped an arm around Elizabeth's shoulders and she pressed her head against him. "There's something out there," Elizabeth whispered. She could sense it lurking in the windy dark, encircling the manor like the evening mist. "Something terrible, something evil."

Luke touched her chin, then traced his finger down her throat to the pendant he'd given her that afternoon. "You're safe with this," he reminded her. "And with me. We're safe here, inside."

Suddenly, they heard a crashing sound. Elizabeth jumped from Luke's arms, her heart in her throat.

The wind had blown one of the casement windows open; it banged against the wall, the curtain fluttering. Leaping to her feet, Elizabeth raced to shut it. The cold air sliced through her clothes, carrying a scent of the wild moors. *The moors, where the werewolf roams, hunting for his next victim. . . .*

With both hands, she pushed against the window. Just then, she heard a wailing sound in the distance. Was it the call of a bird? A dog barking?

Luke stepped up behind her and wrapped his arms around her waist. Elizabeth leaned back against him, closing her eyes. "We're safe . . . inside," he repeated, his lips against her hair. "But don't venture out there, Elizabeth, even for a breath of fresh air. Keep your windows tightly shut."

"The slaughtered sheep," she whispered. "It was the werewolf, wasn't it?"

She felt him nod. "He's strong and hungry," said Luke. "Stay inside, Elizabeth. The moon is full—this is his night. The werewolf's night . . ."

Somewhere in the house, a clock struck midnight as Elizabeth padded down the hall in her nightgown and robe to Jessica's bedroom. *Why did the Pembrokes give us rooms so far apart?* she wondered, suddenly wishing she and Jessica were sharing a room.

Reaching the door, she tapped lightly. "Come in," Jessica called.

At the sound of her sister's voice, Elizabeth's knees buckled with relief. She pushed open the door.

Jessica was sitting at the dressing table, brushing out her hair. "What are you doing up, Liz?" she asked cheerfully.

"I knew you and Robert went for a walk in the gardens, and I just wanted to make sure you—you got back in safely," she stammered. "It's such a creepy night." *And I don't trust him*, she added silently to herself.

Like Elizabeth's, the room was darkly paneled, with heavy velvet curtains draping both the windows and the antique four-poster bed. Jessica had lit some candles, and in the flickering light, the portraits of long-gone Pembrokes hanging on the walls seemed almost to glow with life, to breathe.

Shivering, Elizabeth sat down on the edge of Jessica's bed, pulling the coverlet around her legs. "Did you have a nice walk?"

"Oh, it was wonderful," said Jessica, stars in her eyes. "Robert is . . . wonderful. Isn't he? And this house—isn't it awesome? Robert says it takes a full-time staff of *ten* people just to keep it running."

"Hmm," Elizabeth murmured.

"Wasn't the ride this afternoon fun? I just think the Pembrokes are so nice. And Joy is great, isn't she? So elegant and well-bred. Doesn't it seem silly to you now?"

"Doesn't what seem silly?" asked Elizabeth.

"Your conspiracy theory. Your werewolf theory." Jessica laughed. "Really, to think that all those random bad things are connected somehow, and that the Pembrokes have anything to do with it!"

"They *are* connected," Elizabeth insisted. "The facts haven't changed, Jessica."

Jessica waved her hairbrush dismissively. "You and your pale boyfriend are wrong about the Pembrokes, just plain wrong. Go to sleep, Liz. You were scaring each other with spook stories—I can tell. You'll come around and see things my way in the light of day."

There was no point arguing. "Good night, Jess," Elizabeth said, crossing to the door.

"Good night."

Back in her own room, Elizabeth sat down at the cherry writing desk. Opening a drawer, she found a neat stack of creamy stationery and some pens. "I don't feel the least bit tired," she reflected out loud. "I'll write a letter to Todd. I really have been neglecting my correspondence with him. . . ."

Taking a sheet of paper, she uncapped a pen and scrawled a line. "Dear Luke," she wrote.

Her mistake jumped out at her, stinging like a slap across the face. Elizabeth bit her lip, flooded with guilt. She could still feel Luke's passionate good-night kiss, searing her whole body like a flame.

Oh, Todd, I'm sorry. I just don't know what I'm doing. She crumpled the paper and tossed it into the wastebasket. Turning off the light switch, she ran across the cold wood floors and jumped into bed.

The sheets were like ice; Elizabeth tucked her feet up under her nightgown, shivering. Pulling the covers up to her chin, she stared out into the shadowy room with wide-awake eyes.

How will I ever be able to sleep? she wondered. Outside, the wind had picked up. The windows rattled; a draft made the curtains stir. And the full moon was shining right into the room. So bright, so revealing . . .

Elizabeth tossed in the big bed, her eyelids fluttering. She struggled to wake, to shake herself free of the nightmare, but in vain. She was captured by the dream, helpless.

In it, she ran through Pembroke Manor, searching for someone. First she flew into the dining room, only to find the table smashed, broken china and glass everywhere, and the white linen tablecloth spattered with blood.

Her heart pounding, she dashed into the parlor. The fire was dead; the windows flapped open in the wind.

Where is she? Elizabeth wondered, running, running.

Jessica's bedroom was empty, the velvet hangings ripped from the bed and the sheets tumbled. *The garden,* Elizabeth remembered. *They went for a walk in the garden. She's alone with him. . . .*

She burst out into the courtyard, and plunged into the maze constructed of tall, pruned hedges. She ran right and then left, left again, and then right . . . in circles . . . *I'll never reach her,* she thought, tears streaming from her eyes as she tried to claw her way through the hedge. *I'll never find my way out. . . .*

Suddenly, the hedges dissolved. Elizabeth found herself in a dim corridor, face-to-face with royal figures from the sixteenth century. They were silent and stiff and lifeless—*the wax museum!* she realized.

She knew she was almost there. Dashing forward, she rounded a corner. And there was her sister! "Jessica!" Elizabeth screamed.

But Jessica didn't hear; she turned and fled, her blond hair billowing. At that moment, a wax figure came to life and sprang after her. Elizabeth saw a glint of red eyes—a pointed snout and the flash of white fangs dripping with blood—an elongated, hairy, powerful body . . .

The werewolf. The werewolf was after Jessica!

Elizabeth ran, knowing she had to reach her sister before the werewolf did. She heard voices behind her—strangely enough, the voices of young Robert Pembroke and Rene Glize— but although they seemed to be calling to her, she didn't slow down. "Beware the full moon!" Rene shouted. "Beware the full moon!" Robert echoed.

Her eyelids felt as heavy as lead; Elizabeth lifted them with an effort.

The dim, gray light of a misty dawn filled the strange bedroom. Elizabeth blinked, disoriented. Then she remembered where she was: Pembroke Manor.

And she remembered her horrible dream—the reason her sleep had been fitful and unsatisfying.

Jessica, Elizabeth thought, pushing back her covers.

An immediate, instinctive fear for her sister's well-being seized Elizabeth's heart in a viselike grip. She knew Jessica wouldn't appreciate being awakened at the crack of dawn, especially after she'd stayed up so late, but Elizabeth just had to see her. She had to make sure she was all right.

In bare feet and with her nightgown flying, Elizabeth ran down the hall to Jessica's bedroom. The door was ajar; she burst through it.

As in her dream, one of the curtains that draped the four-poster bed had been ripped down. A body lay on top of the tumbled sheets, face-down, its blond hair swirling across the pillow.

The girl wasn't asleep. Her limbs were twisted at an unnatural angle, and she was too still . . . too still. And the blood . . .

The sheets were white no longer, but soaked with scarlet blood. Elizabeth couldn't see the face, the throat, but she knew . . . she knew. The scream exploded from the very center of her being, splitting her in two. "Jessica!"

She screamed again, and again, wordless shrieks of infinite agony. A few seconds later, Luke rushed into the room, still in pajamas, his dark hair tousled. Running straight to the bed, he took the pale wrist between his thumb and forefinger, feeling for a pulse. For a moment that seemed to last forever, he waited. Then he dropped the wrist, shaking his head.

Hastening back to Elizabeth's side, Luke

clasped her tightly in his arms. She buried her face against his chest, brokenhearted sobs wracking her body. Luke stroked her hair, whispering, "Ssh. Ssh."

But Elizabeth knew her tears would never end; her pain and sorrow could never be soothed. Her beloved twin sister was dead—*murdered*!

Don't miss Sweet Valley High No. 105, **A Date with a Werewolf,** *the second book in this thrilling three-part mini-series.*

A DATE WITH
A WEREWOLF

Written by
Kate William

Created by
FRANCINE PASCAL

BANTAM BOOKS
NEW YORK · TORONTO · LONDON · SYDNEY · AUCKLAND

In memory of Kelly Weil

Chapter 1

"She's dead! Jessica is dead!" Jessica Wakefield's identical twin sister, Elizabeth, sobbed wildly into the coarse knit of Luke Shepherd's sweater. Her new boyfriend's arms felt warm and safe around her—as they had the day before, when Luke had kissed her seriously for the first time. But Elizabeth could not be comforted. Behind her, on the bed of Jessica's room at Pembroke Manor, a body lay facedown on blood-soaked sheets—a girl with golden hair, exactly the same shade as Elizabeth's.

The sixteen-year-old twins had traveled to London for a summer internship at the *London Journal*. Not a week had gone by before Jessica's new boyfriend, Robert Pembroke, had invited them to spend a long weekend at his family's country manor. Jessica, of course, had been thrilled about the invitation, but Elizabeth had had misgivings from the start. And now, as Elizabeth stared at the blond-haired body on the

1

bed she wished they had never even left California.

"I knew Jessica was in danger!" Elizabeth cried, pounding her fists against Luke's hard chest. "I should have warned her. I should have warned her."

"Warned me about what?" said a familiar, sleepy voice. Elizabeth whirled, blue-green eyes wide. Jessica was standing in the doorway, yawning. Her hair was disheveled, and her eyes looked tired, and her satiny pink nightgown was wrinkled from sleep, but besides being unaccustomed to getting up at dawn on a Saturday, Jessica seemed like a perfectly healthy teenager.

"You're not dead!" Elizabeth cried, almost knocking her sister over with a bear hug.

"Then who *is*?" asked Luke.

"Dead? Why did you think I was—" Elizabeth felt her sister's body freeze as Jessica saw the bloody girl on the bed. "Oh, my—"

Before Jessica could react further, Andrew Thatcher, London's chief of police and another weekend guest at Pembroke Manor, pushed past the twins into the room. Behind him was Lord Pembroke himself, accompanied by Lady Pembroke, their son Robert, and several servants.

"We heard screams," Robert said, staring wildly at Jessica, his eyes full of concern. "Are you all right?"

The chief of police reached for the dead girl's shoulder and gently turned the body over. Then he cried out and stepped back, shaken. The murdered girl was Joy Singleton, his fiancée.

And her throat had been ripped open . . . *as if by a wild beast*.

2

The words roared into Elizabeth's mind, unbidden. She had first heard them on Monday morning, the twins' first day of work at the *London Journal*. As high-school interns, they would never have been allowed to cover such a grisly murder. But, wanting to be where the excitement was, Jessica and Elizabeth had rushed through their seemingly trivial missing-Yorkie assignment, sneaking off to the Essex Street murder scene.

Elizabeth would never forget the sight of Dr. Cameron Neville's body, lying facedown in a pool of blood that was slowly soaking into the floral-patterned carpet. And Elizabeth would never forget the clear, dispassionate voice of Lucy Friday, the *London Journal* crime desk editor: *"The victim's throat has been ripped open, as if by a wild beast."*

The doctor's murder wasn't the first one in London recently to fit that pattern. Elizabeth, Jessica, and Luke—an intern with the arts and literature section of the newspaper—had been doing some sleuthing into the bizarre incidents. And Luke, at least, was seriously convinced that they were the work of a werewolf.

And as if to add credence to the werewolf theory, some of the Pembrokes' sheep had been found with their throats ripped open—just hours before Joy's murder.

Elizabeth shuddered, remembering the flowering wolfsbane Luke had pointed out to her in a nearby grove Friday afternoon. According to Luke, who was an expert on werewolves, medieval legend said the wolfsbane bloomed only when a werewolf was hunting prey.

3

She reached beneath the collar of her flannel nightgown to finger the silver pendant that hung around her neck. Luke had given it to her. "It will protect you," he had said, clasping the chain around her neck. The pendant showed a five-pointed star—a pentagram—in a circle, with the image of a wolf in its center.

Normally, Elizabeth would have laughed at the notion of needing protection from werewolves. She had always been considered the rational, responsible twin, unlike her more impulsive sister, Jessica. But ideas that would have sounded ridiculous to Elizabeth under the bright California sun somehow seemed more reasonable when voiced through an English fog—especially when voiced by sensitive, handsome Luke. Elizabeth had known Luke for less than a week but she was falling fast for him, despite her feelings for her boyfriend, Todd Wilkins, back in California.

Besides, the evidence from the other victims did point to a murderer who was not quite . . . human.

Now, pleasant, if a little vapid, pretty Joy had been murdered in the same way. Elizabeth felt unsteady and was grateful for Luke's steadying hand on her elbow. Her mind was racing. *Joy had been murdered in Jessica's room*, she thought wildly, *in Jessica's bed.* In the dark, it would have been impossible for the murderer to tell one sleeping blonde from another. *Could Jessica have been the real target?*

Thatcher, visibly trying to collect himself, seemed to be thinking along similar lines. "Jessica," he asked in a strained voice, "Joy's room was across the hall from yours. Why was she sleeping in here instead?"

For once, Elizabeth noted, her sister didn't seem at all concerned about what she looked like. Tears streamed down Jessica's face, and her golden hair was tangled. Jessica had known Joy for only one day, but Elizabeth knew she had liked Thatcher's pretty, young fiancée. And the sight of that bloody bed would scare anyone.

Except for Robert Pembroke, Jr., it seemed. He was as disagreeable as ever, Elizabeth noticed. She scowled as the younger Lord Pembroke turned to two of the servants and began barking out orders.

"Alistair," he said to tall, thin Alistair Crane. "Call the constable right away. Set up extra chairs in the parlor, and be prepared to serve tea." He turned to the pretty, brown-haired cook. "Maria, put the water on, and assemble the other servants."

Then he placed a protective arm around Jessica's trembling shoulders, and Elizabeth pursed her lips at the sight. She couldn't stand Robert's arrogance and his aristocratic airs, and she hated the fact that he and Jessica had become so close. But Jessica gazed gratefully at him through her tears.

"Joy knocked on my door in the middle of the night," Jessica explained haltingly to the chief of police. "She asked me to switch rooms with her. She said she couldn't sleep with the full moon shining in her window."

Beware the full moon. The words came to Elizabeth's mind out of nowhere, and she remembered the scary old lady hissing them at Jessica the day the twins had arrived at their London dormi-

5

tory—HIS, or Housing for International Students. A few days later, a gypsy fortune-teller had given Jessica the same warning. *Beware the full moon.*

Jessica seemed calmer now, but as Elizabeth stared at her twin, she felt a wave of terror. *Jessica is in horrible danger.*

Emily Cartwright picked up Saturday morning's edition of the *London Journal*. "Here's another princess story!" she exclaimed to her friends Lina Smith and Portia Albert. "But that's a frightfully bad little photograph with it. All you can see is a blur of blond hair."

The three girls were huddled around the table in the kitchen of HIS. Breakfast wouldn't be served officially for another hour, but Emily and Lina were up early for a day of sight-seeing, and Portia had an early rehearsal for *A Common Man*, the play in which she was making her London stage debut. The girls were fixing themselves an early breakfast of toast and orange marmalade.

"I suppose it's because I'm Australian," Emily said, gesturing with the newspaper, "but I do not understand this all-consuming passion you Brits have for gossip about the royal family. I was addicted to it when I first got here, but now even *I'm* getting tired of it."

"Sometimes I don't understand it myself," Lina remarked, running her fingers through her short brown hair. "So, Portia, what time is your play rehears—"

"Listen to this morning's bit," Emily interrupted, pointing to a banner headline across the front page of

6

the newspaper. "'Witnesses Spot Princess in Tokyo! Two London residents were on holiday Thursday in Japan, where they claim to have seen Princess Eliana, missing since last week, in a Tokyo bathhouse.'"

"That's preposterous!" Portia exclaimed. "What would the youngest daughter of the Queen of England be doing in Tokyo?"

"Taking a bath, apparently," Lina said dryly.

"Does the article cite any evidence?" Portia asked in her elegant, cultured accent.

"No, that's the odd part," said Emily. "The article goes on to quote the police as saying the witnesses were probably mistaken. There's no proof at all! My internship may be with BBC television instead of a newspaper, but I know enough about newspapers to know this is shoddy journalism. What were the editors thinking, to run such a dicey story on page one?"

"I suppose they were thinking, 'This article will sell a lot of newspapers,'" Portia remarked.

Lina reached for the *Journal* and ruffled through it. "Here's an advertisement for your play, Portia!" she exclaimed in her charming Liverpudlian accent. "Listen to this: 'Young Penelope Abbott, playing the part of Isabelle, is the most exciting thing to hit the London stage since Felicity Kendall.' That's just super, Portia! I'm sorry I couldn't go with everyone on Thursday night. I can't wait to see it."

Emily laughed. "I'm not surprised about your rave reviews. You practiced the part of stuck-up Isabelle Huntington so diligently, twenty-four hours a day, that we all believed you were an insufferable snob! I've heard of dedication, but even an

7

actress has to be at leisure now and then."

"Once again, I do apologize," Portia said, with a formal bow. "I don't know how you all ever forgave me. I really got carried away."

Lina laughed. "We're just thankful you weren't rehearsing for the part of Jack the Ripper!"

"It's too bad you can't use your real name in the cast," Emily said. "Have you called your father in Scotland yet to tell him that you landed a role? I would think he'd be pleased that you want to follow in his footsteps. Maybe someday, you'll be as famous an actor as he is."

"No, I haven't told him," Portia said. "And I'm not sure I will. I told you—the venerable Sir Montford Albert disapproves of my ambition to be an actress. He claims it's too hard a life, and he's not certain I have the talent to make a go of it. That's why I haven't told him I got this role, and why I'm using the stage name Penelope Abbott. I had to learn what I'm capable of, on my own. I couldn't let my father's name influence people's reactions to my work."

"Sometimes you have to get away from your past before you can find out who you really are," Lina said thoughtfully. Emily stared at her curiously. She liked Lina a lot, but sometimes the girl from Liverpool said the oddest things.

Portia didn't seem to think it was odd. "Then I guess I've learned that I am an actress," she said. "I still don't know if I've any real talent, but I do know that it's all I've ever wanted to do. Now that I know what it's like to be onstage in a professional production, I want to act more than ever. I just hope I can someday con-

8

vince my father and make him proud of me."

"You will," Lina said staunchly.

"Well, speaking of being an actress," Portia said, rising from her chair, "I have to get to rehearsal."

"Break a leg," Emily called as she left the room. "That is the expression, isn't it?"

Emily had plenty of faith in Portia's talent. But she thought the conversation had become much too serious. "I miss the American twins," she said suddenly. "This place was much jollier with them around."

Lina smiled. "Yes, it certainly was."

Emily sighed jealously. "It's bad enough that Jess and Liz are gorgeous and nice. But within a few days of arriving in the country, Jessica snagged a real English nobleman! It's not fair!"

"Robert Pembroke *is* one of the most eligible guys in London," Lina admitted.

"And Elizabeth hooked up with that cute, sensitive Luke, from the *Journal*—not to mention the torch that Rene Glize is carrying for her! The best-looking boy at HIS! Who could have guessed that he knew the twins from their trip to France? And now he's here working for the French Embassy!

"Face it, Lina," she concluded, "coincidences like that only happen to people like Jessica and Elizabeth. They obviously lead charmed lives—unlike normal, everyday blokes like you and me."

Lina smiled enigmatically.

"Of course," Emily continued in her characteristic nonstop fashion, "it's a shame that Rene is jealous of Luke and has been giving Liz the cold shoulder all week."

"I know," Lina said. "Liz just wants to be friends with Rene, so he won't even talk to her."

Emily sighed. "Until Rene gets over Liz, he's no good as potential boyfriend material. So—except for Gabriello Moretti, who already has a girlfriend—it seems that the twins, between them, have tied up all the good-looking guys around!"

"Not all of them," Lina pointed out.

Emily smiled. "David Bartholomew, right?"

"Am I that transparent?" Lina blushed.

"You're so honest, Lina, that you couldn't keep a secret if your life depended on it. Everybody at HIS knows that you and David are crazy about each other. We're ready to take wagers on when you'll finally give in to all that passion and go out on a date. So when's it going to be?"

Lina blushed again. "Tonight," she said. "Liz finally convinced me that I should, as the Americans say, go for it."

"Liz would know," Emily says. "Look where she and her sister are right now—guests of Pembroke Manor! I bet they're having a fantastic time. . . ."

A half hour after Joy's body was found, Jessica sat next to Robert on an overstuffed sofa in the Pembrokes' parlor, drinking a cup of tea. Now that she was away from the bedroom and those bloody sheets, the murder hardly seemed real. She leaned against Robert's shoulder and put the gory scene out of her mind, concentrating instead on the excitement of being in the middle of a real English murder mystery—just like in an Agatha Christie book.

The sumptuous furnishings and aristocratic people around her were pretty exciting, too. Jessica thought of Lila Fowler, her best friend back home in California. Lila was the daughter of a millionaire, but even Lila wasn't related to royalty, like the Pembrokes. She would be green with envy when she heard about the people Jessica was hanging out with.

The Pembroke family, their staff, and the weekend guests were assembled in the parlor for questioning by the local authorities. Thin, regal Lady Pembroke was sitting, ramrod straight, on the edge of an upholstered chair. Even at this hour of the morning, Jessica marveled, she was perfectly coiffed and made up. Lord Pembroke was nervously pacing back and forth across the thick oriental carpeting.

But it was their son Robert to whom Jessica's thoughts kept returning. She loved his classy, English clothing and his handsome face. But she was even more impressed by his confident manner, and how he took command of every situation. At the murder scene earlier today, the others had stared at the body in shock. But Robert had known exactly what to do. He had set the servants in motion and instructed everyone to meet down here to wait for the authorities. Now she snuggled against his strong body, feeling safe and secure.

Elizabeth and Luke huddled together on a sofa that faced the one Jessica sat on. Elizabeth, as usual, held a small notebook in her hand. *Leave it to my twin*, Jessica thought. *She never can give those reporter's instincts a rest*. Elizabeth was scribbling wildly in her notebook, stopping only when she noticed the police constable's unfriendly glare.

Constable Sheila Atherton, a small, dark-haired woman in her mid-thirties, stood near the sofa, looming over Elizabeth in a way that made her look much larger than her short stature.

"You say that you and your sister are from a village called Sweet Valley, California?" she asked in a no-nonsense voice. Thunder crashed outside the window, punctuating the constable's question and whipping the light morning drizzle into a downpour.

Village? Jessica thought. *How very English.* Frequently, she found herself annoyed and mystified by the unfamiliar words she'd been hearing in England. British English and American English were very different languages, she was learning. But in this setting—the parlor of a British manor house—words like "village" seemed absolutely right. She would have to get Robert to teach her how to talk that way.

"That's right," Elizabeth answered the constable's question. "We're in London for a summer internship, and the Pembrokes invited us to spend the weekend here."

The constable drained her teacup and set it on the table with a loud clank. "Dawn was hardly a civilized hour to be roaming about the corridors this morning, Ms. Wakefield. How did you happen to discover the body?"

"I was worried that Jessica might be in danger," Elizabeth explained, "so I ran down the hall to her room and saw . . . the victim."

12

Lord Pembroke, still pacing, wheeled abruptly, nearly crashing into the tall, thin man who was carrying in a tea tray. Pembroke sat down quickly in a straight-backed chair as the servant righted the tray and carried it to the table in front of the constable. Jessica heard the silver serving pieces clinking together; the servant's hands were trembling. Apparently, the murder had set the whole household's nerves on edge.

The constable poured herself a second cup of tea. "But *why* were you worried, Ms. Wakefield? What would make you suddenly believe your sister was in danger?"

Elizabeth blushed. "It may sound silly, but I had a nightmare about it."

The constable raised her eyebrows.

"And when I woke up," Elizabeth continued staunchly, "I just knew there was something wrong."

Jessica spoke up helpfully. "It happens to us all the time. It's because we're identical twins."

"Oh, really?" the constable asked sarcastically, taking in the girls' identical heart-shaped faces, blue-green eyes, and slim, athletic figures. Even their California suntans were exactly the same shade, though they were starting to fade after a week in foggy England. "I hadn't noticed."

Thatcher rose from his chair, an imposing figure, even in his grief. "What did you do when you entered the room, Elizabeth?" he asked in a tightly controlled voice.

Constable Atherton cast the police chief a dark look. "With all due respect, sir, this is not London," she reminded him. "And we are out of your jurisdiction. *I* am conducting this investigation, if you don't mind."

Andrew turned his back on her and stared instead at the rain-soaked gardens outside the window.

Elizabeth glanced over at him, her eyes full of sympathy. Then she took a deep breath and spoke to the constable. "I walked into the room and saw . . . everything. . . . It was Jessica's bed, so I thought it was Jessica. I guess I started screaming. Then Luke came running in. A minute later, Jessica showed up."

The constable turned to Luke. "And why were *you* roaming the halls at sunrise, young man?"

"I wasn't," he said quietly. "I was having trouble sleeping. I heard Elizabeth scream, so I ran out of my room to find her."

Lord Pembroke spoke up suddenly. "I hardly see that this line of questioning is leading anywhere!" he said in his booming voice. "You don't honestly believe that this girl is the murderer, do you?"

"I admit it's unlikely," the constable replied evenly. "But everybody is a suspect." She glared at him thoughtfully. "And I do mean everybody."

Lord Pembroke seemed awfully nervous, Elizabeth noticed as the family patriarch sat down. Of course, anyone would be jumpy, after what had happened in Jessica's room that night. But Elizabeth thought his reaction seemed extreme—especially coming from a man so accustomed to affecting the cool, superior demeanor of the British aristocracy.

Elizabeth wrote a line in her notebook: *"Keep an eye on the elder Pembroke."*

14

She gazed around the room again, thankful that the constable seemed to be finished with her for now.

Everybody in the room was a suspect, the constable had said. So who else appeared to be hiding something? Elizabeth gazed thoughtfully at the servants. Tall, thin Alistair had seemed friendly and innocuous when she had met him the day before. She could hardly believe he was a killer. But she had noticed his hands shaking as he set down the tea tray. Why? Maybe he knew more than he was saying.

Alistair whispered something to Maria Finch, the Pembrokes' pretty, plump cook. She stared at the rich red carpeting, wringing her hands; Elizabeth was afraid the woman would burst into tears. Was Maria hiding something, as well? Elizabeth resolved to question the two servants herself, later.

"Alistair," a calm, commanding voice reproached suddenly. "You forgot the lemon." Elizabeth focused thoughtfully on young Robert Pembroke, who sat with his arm around Jessica.

Alistair bowed apologetically. "I beg your pardon, sir," he said. "I'll fetch it right away." He turned on his heel and disappeared through the double doors.

Elizabeth shook her head disapprovingly. Ever since she'd come to Pembroke Manor, she'd been annoyed by the way the Pembrokes treated the "lower" classes. She had never heard a "please" or a "thank you" out of Robert; he took it for granted that people would cater to his every whim. She hated his commanding tone and bossy manners.

15

Now, Elizabeth had to admit, Robert had a concerned expression on his face, especially when he looked at Jessica. But unlike his father and the servants, Robert didn't seem nervous. In fact, he looked particularly cool and regal. Somehow, he—like his parents—had found time in the last twenty minutes to dress fully; his cravat was expertly tied and his dark hair was combed. Robert was handsome, certainly. And Jessica was crazy about him. Still, Elizabeth couldn't stand his smug, superior way of looking down his nose at people. Of course, that didn't make him an animalistic murderer.

"We all have an animal side," she found herself writing in the notebook. For a moment, the sentence startled her, as if someone else had written it there. Then she remembered Luke using those words earlier in the week, as he and Elizabeth toured the eerie werewolf exhibit at the wax museum in London. *We all have an animal side.* As much as Elizabeth hated to admit it, she had to agree—especially after what had happened early Saturday morning.

Thank goodness for sweet, gentle Luke, Elizabeth thought, feeling the warmth of his fisherman's sweater against her shoulder. The young poet was becoming more important to her with every passing day, making it disturbingly easy to put out of her mind the image of Todd Wilkins, her boyfriend back in California.

In fact, to Elizabeth, sitting in the parlor of an English manor house the morning after a murder, California seemed like another planet altogether.

She was startled out of her thoughts by Constable

16

Atherton, who wheeled abruptly to face Jessica.

"A girl was murdered last night in the bed you were supposed to be sleeping in!" the constable reminded Jessica. "Tell me, Ms. Wakefield, who might want you dead?"

Jessica shrugged her shoulders comically. "Well, there's Lila Fowler, but she's still back in Sweet Valley. Other than her, I can't imagine!"

Elizabeth smiled. She could always count on Jessica to cover up her anxiety with a joke.

The constable's eyes narrowed. "This is a serious situation, Ms. Wakefield. Do you have any enemies?"

Jessica rolled her eyes, and Elizabeth realized she wasn't covering up her fear—she wasn't afraid at all. *She doesn't take any of this seriously,* Elizabeth realized with dismay. *She thinks she's the star of an Agatha Christie play.*

Jessica shrugged her shoulders. "I'm one of the most popular people in my town, and I hardly know anyone within about a million miles of here. Besides, I'm only six—" She stopped and glanced at Robert. "I'm only a teenager," she concluded.

Elizabeth sighed, realizing that Jessica must be pretending to Robert that she was older than sixteen. *Leave it to Jessica to be worried about keeping a rich, handsome twenty-year-old interested in her—even with a murderer on the loose.*

"Face it," Jessica said to the room full of people. "I couldn't have been the target. Nobody would want me dead. It was just a random murder, like that doctor who was killed in London last week, and the nurse before that."

17

The chief of police turned from the window and stared at Jessica curiously. Elizabeth held her breath. *Leave it to Jessica to open her big mouth!* Nobody was supposed to know that the girls had been at the Essex Street murder scene. And only someone who had been there—and seen the body— would make the connection between Dr. Neville's death and Joy Singleton's. And no information had been released about a connection to the death of a nurse the month before—despite the fact that the police must have noticed similarities between the cases. Somebody—or something—had ripped out the nurse's throat, too.

For some reason, *London Journal* editor Henry Reeves had not printed the details of the doctor's death. Lucy Friday had been crime desk editor at the time, and she had quit her job over the decision. Jessica and Elizabeth were determined to find out why Reeves—or the *Journal's* owner, Lord Pembroke himself—would cover up such important news. But now Jessica may have tipped their hands.

Andrew opened his mouth to question Jessica, but Lord Pembroke beat him to it. The older man jumped from his chair again, knocking it over with a clatter.

"What do you mean, Miss Wakefield?" Lord Pembroke asked sharply. "Why would you compare last night's slaying to the death of Cameron Neville?"

Jessica glanced apologetically at Elizabeth. Then she smiled at Lord Pembroke. "That's just what I meant," she explained sweetly. "Both were completely random incidents. There is no connection."

18

"Let's stick to the facts of the case at hand, please," the constable insisted. "Ms. Wakefield, at approximately what time did Ms. Singleton come to your room?"

Jessica shrugged. "Sorry, but keeping track of the time isn't one of my strong points," she said. "I don't even wear a watch in the daytime—let alone in the middle of the night."

The constable's expression was venomous. "Could you hazard a guess?"

Jessica shrugged again. "I don't know—two or three o'clock in the morning, I suppose."

The constable turned around slowly, staring, in turn, at every person in the room. "Was anyone else awake this morning between two o'clock and, shall we say, five o'clock?"

Elizabeth shook her head quickly and saw that most of the others did, too. But she noticed that Maria looked down at the floor, blushing as red as the expensive oriental carpet that covered it.

The constable noticed too. "Ms. Finch, may I remind you that this is an official police investigation? Were you awake at that time this morning?"

Maria nodded slowly, still looking down. "Yes, ma'am," she replied, barely above a whisper. Alistair had returned to the room a few minutes earlier, with a dish of lemon wedges for the tea. Now he stood beside Maria, and she clutched his arm tightly as she spoke.

"I'm always up and about early," Maria stammered, "to prepare the morning meal, you know." She paused, a frightened look on her face. "But I

19

didn't see a thing, ma'am. I swear it. I was mostly in the kitchen, anyways."

The constable glared at her suspiciously. "Very well," she said at last. "I suppose you can all go about your business, for now. But don't anyone leave the country without first notifying my office."

As the group began filing out of the parlor in the direction of the dining room, Luke leaned over to whisper in Elizabeth's ear. "Doesn't it seem odd to you that we're calmly preparing to eat brunch, just hours after a murder?"

Elizabeth nodded. "You know how these Pembrokes are caught up in tradition," she whispered back. "If the custom is to eat brunch on Saturdays, they certainly wouldn't let a little thing like a murder get in the way."

Out of the corner of her eye, she noticed Lord Pembroke tap Andrew Thatcher on the shoulder as if asking him to stay behind in the parlor.

"You go on with the rest," Elizabeth whispered to Luke. "I'll catch up with you in a minute."

Elizabeth turned back to the parlor and peered into the room, around the edge of the open door. The two men stood facing the window, their backs to her. Elizabeth felt a twinge of conscience about eavesdropping, but put it out of her mind as Lord Pembroke began to speak.

The older man patted Thatcher's shoulder in a paternal manner. "Just a little more time, Andrew," he said. "It's too good an opportunity to pass up—"

Thatcher whirled to face him. "But Joy—"

"You know how sorry I am about your young lady, Thatcher. But it doesn't change anything. This is still the chance of a lifetime. We only have to hold on a little longer."

Andrew turned back to the window and nodded, almost imperceptibly. Elizabeth had to strain to hear his next words. "All right, Robert. As you wish."

Lord Pembroke steered the younger man toward the door. Elizabeth darted behind it and scrunched her body against the wall, scribbling down everything they had said. Then she followed them down the hall, keeping what she hoped was a safe distance as she pretended to admire the paintings of stern-looking relatives who stared accusingly from the richly brocaded walls.

Constable Atherton met the two men at the end of the hallway. "Gentlemen," she said in a low voice. "I have been thinking about the comment young Ms. Wakefield made concerning the unfortunate incidents in London. You must be involved in that investigation, Chief Thatcher. Do you believe there is any connection?"

There was a pause before Andrew's voice answered. "No, Constable. I honestly do not believe there is a connection between the two deaths in London, or between those deaths and this one. There is no evidence to support such a link."

Elizabeth's eyes widened. As the threesome disappeared into the dining room, she struggled to copy down Thatcher's exact words, incredulous that the police would lie about the fact that three murders had been committed in exactly the same gruesome manner. *Four* murders, she corrected herself, thinking about poor Poo-Poo, the Yorkshire terrier. The story of Poo-Poo's disappearance had been the twins' first assignment for the *Journal*. The case had seemed insignificant at first, but it had taken on a chilling tone when Elizabeth found the little dog's lifeless body on a London street corner Monday night, its throat torn open.

Elizabeth scribbled one more line in her notebook: *"Who is Thatcher trying to protect?"*

Suddenly, a strong hand locked on Elizabeth's wrist. She jumped, slamming the notebook shut.

Lord Pembroke's voice sounded in her ear, calm, but with what Elizabeth thought was a note of menace. "I've seen you writing in that tablet of yours," he said. "Don't entertain any grand ideas about getting your byline in the paper with any of this. The young woman's death is of no interest in London. It's local news. That's all."

He dropped her wrist abruptly and glided to the other end of the room, not looking back.

Elizabeth flushed guiltily. She *had* been imagining her byline on page one of the *London Journal*— on an article that covered something more important than an exploding eggplant or a missing dog, which were the kinds of stories she'd been assigned all week. Of course, Pembroke owned the *Journal*. If he really was covering up information about the murders, her chances of exposing him in the newspaper were slim. Still, she was determined to learn the truth.

She turned back to her first page of notes and underlined a sentence: *"Keep an eye on the elder Pembroke."*

She studied him as he stood with Robert, Jessica, and an uncomfortable-looking Luke. *Poor, sensitive Luke!* He hated being around rich, snobby types even more than Elizabeth did, but he had come to spend the weekend here because Elizabeth had asked him to.

Now Luke was staring, eyes narrowed, at both Pembrokes, as Jessica carried on what appeared to be an animated monologue. The Pembrokes ignored Luke completely. Robert's eyes never left Jessica's face, and even Lord Pembroke seemed to relax, caught in the spell of Jessica's vivacity.

Elizabeth noticed that the dining room was decorated with safari trophies. From the wall over Jessica's head, a tiger's mouth gaped open, its dagger-like teeth glistening in the morning sunlight.

A sense of dark foreboding washed over Elizabeth, and she felt as if she were drowning. And again she heard Luke's words in her mind, so clearly that she almost turned to see if he was standing beside her, whispering in her ear:

We all have an animal side.

Chapter 2

"Thanks for the snack, Maria," Elizabeth said, sitting at the worktable in the huge kitchen of Pembroke Manor. "Your homemade cookies—I mean, *biscuits*—are first-rate."

"Oh, it's no bother at all, Miss Wakefield," the plump, pretty cook replied.

"I guess I wasn't feeling very hungry at brunch," Elizabeth said carefully, "after what happened this morning."

Maria turned away quickly, but not until after Elizabeth caught a frightened look in her brown eyes. Once again, she was certain that the cook knew more about Joy's murder than she had told the constable.

Alistair walked into the kitchen, carrying a dust rag, and Elizabeth noticed the familiar way he rested a hand on Maria's shoulder as he leaned over to whisper something in her ear. She smiled up at him gratefully, as if he'd offered words of encouragement.

Maria wasn't the only person who was grateful for Alistair's presence. Elizabeth wanted to question both of them, somewhere out of earshot of the Pembrokes. Now was her chance.

"Would you care for more biscuits—I mean, *cookies*—miss?" Maria asked.

"No, thank you, Maria. Actually, I wanted to talk with both of you for a moment. About last night."

Maria's face turned white, and Alistair began clasping and unclasping his hands.

"As I told the constable, miss," Maria said, "I was awake at the time, but I didn't see a thing near Miss Jessica's room."

Interesting, Elizabeth thought. *I didn't mention Jessica's room.* And Maria had implied to the constable that she'd been only in the kitchen that morning.

"I heard what you said to the constable," Elizabeth replied carefully. "I was just wondering if you'd remembered anything else since you talked to her."

Maria stared at the linoleum. "Not a thing, miss."

"I know what it's like to be awake, in the dark, when everyone else is asleep," Elizabeth began slowly. "Sometimes you hear noises, and they scare you, but you tell yourself it was only the house settling, or the wind rattling the gutters. Did either of you hear anything like that this morning?"

Alistair's hands were trembling again.

"Alistair, the constable never asked you directly. Were you awake at all between two and five this morning?"

He sat down limply at the worktable. "We would like to oblige you, miss," he said in a tense whisper, "but we mustn't. We could lose our positions if Lord Pembroke were to find out."

So that was it. They were terrified of their employer. The realization made Elizabeth even more determined to discover exactly what Pembroke's role was in all of this. *What was he hiding?* She knew she would have to proceed slowly with Alistair and Maria.

"Somebody is trying to cover up the facts of some murders here and in London," Elizabeth said. "I'm investigating to find out the truth. I won't tell anyone you spoke to me."

"You won't tell young Master Pembroke?" Maria asked.

"Maria, no!" Alistair begged. "It's too dangerous."

"Please, Alistair. A young woman is dead. If we can help Miss Wakefield find the killer—" She hesitated.

"Nobody will ever know you talked to me," Elizabeth assured her. "A good journalist never reveals her sources."

Maria swallowed hard and then began to speak haltingly. "The moon was full last night," she said, "and Alistair and I crept out for a romantic walk in the gardens, an hour before I was to begin the morning's work in the kitchen. Of course, we stayed quite close to the house, what with the poor sheep that were found dead, and all. We had just come inside, around about four o'clock, and were at the end of the upstairs corridor."

"We had come upstairs for clean table linens for the morning meal," Alistair interjected, drumming his fingers nervously on the wooden table. "We

27

planned to bring them down the servants' stairway at the end of the hall, and—"

"And somebody was in the hallway leaving Miss Jessica's room!" Maria blurted out.

Elizabeth felt the hair rise on the back of her neck. "Who was it?" she asked breathlessly.

"I heard footsteps in the hallway—" Alistair admitted.

"Alistair didn't see the person," Maria said. "Only me. He already had the stairway door open and was about to head down the steps. Of course, it was very dark," she added. "I really couldn't tell who it was in the corridor."

"Can you give me any information at all about the person you saw?" Elizabeth asked. "Hair color? Height? Clothing?"

Maria shook her head and refused to meet Elizabeth's gaze. Tears glistened in her dark eyes. Now more than ever, Elizabeth was sure Maria knew—or could guess at—the identity of the person in the hallway. But she was obviously too frightened to say more.

"It was very dark," Maria repeated.

"It's awfully early for it to be so dark." Jessica clasped Robert's hand tighter, as if she were frightened by the drifting English mist in the boxwood garden.

It was twilight on Saturday. Except for anguished Andrew Thatcher, who had driven back to London after brunch, the guests at Pembroke Manor had spent a quiet day indoors, recovering from the morning's horror and avoiding a torrential downpour that had finally stopped late in the afternoon.

Jessica wasn't really cold, but she shivered. Robert draped his strong arm around her shoulders, which is just what she had wanted him to do.

"We can go back inside, if you'd like," he said. "I know you've suffered a terrible shock. It's beastly of me to keep you out in this sort of weather."

"Oh, no!" Jessica said. "It feels good to get out in the fresh air after being cooped up inside with everyone all afternoon—even if it's so misty I can hardly see the garden! Besides, I feel perfectly safe, with you. I know you would never let anything hurt me."

Robert smiled down at her, and Jessica felt her knees turn to jelly. He was definitely the best-looking guy she had ever dated. And being fabulously wealthy—and part of the British aristocracy—didn't hurt. Despite the damp weather, Jessica suddenly felt warm under his gaze.

"You poor girl. You're still unsteady. I'm horribly sorry you've had to endure such trauma while a visitor at my home. I suppose it doesn't say much for the Pembroke hospitality."

"Oh, Robert. It's not your family's fault that such an awful thing happened to poor Joy. And just because it happened in my own bed doesn't mean I'm frightened or anything."

Of course, Jessica admitted to herself, she had been frightened at first. Now she felt completely recovered, but there was no reason to act like she was—not when he was being so attentive. Traumatic experiences had their uses.

"You are so brave, Jessica," he said, squeezing her hand. "I'm proud of you. Even *I* am feeling a bit troubled about the situation—a murder has taken place in my own home! But you are determined not to let it spoil everyone's weekend."

Jessica smiled shyly. "Robert, I want you to know how much I appreciate your invitation to visit your family's beautiful country home." She gestured around the garden, knowing that sculpted hedges and tasteful flower beds hid beneath the shroud of mist. "Despite what happened to Joy, I've had a great time this weekend—with you."

He frowned. "I'm just sorry it's about to end. Do you have to take the first train in the morning?"

"Well," Jessica pretended to hesitate, "Elizabeth *is* a real stickler when it comes to punctuality. . . ."

Robert grinned. "I've got an idea. Allow me to make it up to you for the horrendous weekend. I know this smashing restaurant in Windsor. It takes weeks for most people to get reservations, but the owner is a friend of my family's. I'll arrange a table for tonight. In the morning, you can sleep as long as you like, and I'll drive you back to London at your leisure. How does that sound?"

"Heavenly," Jessica declared, thinking of an evening alone with Robert—and his luxurious silver Jaguar convertible. "You know, I really could get used to this lifestyle, Robert. You always seem to get the best and the nicest of everything!"

Robert stared into her eyes. "You deserve nothing but the best and the nicest."

Then he leaned over and pressed his warm, soft lips against hers. A warm tingling spread through Jessica's body as she returned his slow, ardent kiss.

Afterward, she stood for a few minutes in Robert's arms, breathing the heady scent of his cologne and gazing over his shoulder at the wisps of fog that drifted across the yellow face of the moon.

Late that night, Elizabeth stood in the dark corridor outside the door of the room that Joy Singleton had died in. She looked down the long, dim hallway in both directions and then breathed a sigh of relief. It was empty.

The train for London would leave first thing in the morning, so this could be Elizabeth's last chance to search for clues. Robert and Jessica were out for a late dinner in nearby Cambridge. The Pembrokes and their servants had gone to bed, or were busy in other parts of the great house. Andrew Thatcher had returned to London that afternoon. And Luke was in his room, studying the werewolf lore that had always been a hobby for him, but had lately become an obsession.

Elizabeth felt a pang of guilt at investigating Joy's death without letting Luke know. After all, they were in this together. It wasn't that she wanted to keep secrets from him, exactly. But Luke was so convinced about his werewolf theory that Elizabeth was afraid he wouldn't keep an open mind about any clues they might discover.

"Of course," she said under her breath, "Luke may be right. It just might be a werewolf. But a good journalist has to consider every possibility."

She entered the room and quietly pulled the door shut behind her. "Clues," she said aloud. But where should she look for them?

31

The crime had taken place on the bed, of course. Elizabeth's heart began pounding as she approached it. The scene was there before her: the body that looked like Jessica's . . . the golden hair . . . the crimson blood that soaked into the sheets and dripped steadily into a small pool on the parquet floor.

She shook her head to clear it of the image. Of course, the bed was empty now, cold and bare of linens. The only sign that remained of the morning's crime was a round reddish-brown stain on the floor beside the bed.

Clearly, no clues were left on the bare mattress. She scanned the tastefully furnished room. An armoire stood in one corner, its doors wide open to reveal an empty interior. No doubt it had already been searched by the police. Of course, the police must have searched the entire room. But they might have missed something, Elizabeth told herself. Something important.

She traced what might be the murderer's footsteps. The killer must have entered through the door, walked across the rug to the bed, murdered Joy, and skulked out—to be seen by Maria Finch, who had been standing near the door to the servants' stairs at the far end of the hallway.

Elizabeth peered at the rug that covered much of the floor. There was no trace of the killer's having crossed it—not that Elizabeth had really expected to find any.

"What else in the room did the murderer touch?" she asked herself. Then she realized she was staring at the answer. The door.

Elizabeth inspected the shiny brass door handle. As expected, she found nothing. The constable's assistant had dusted it for fingerprints that morning, and the servants had polished it carefully afterward, to remove the powdery black dust.

"What's this?" she whispered, running her hand up and down the wooden door frame. Caught in a crack in the wood were some silky threads from some kind of dark-green fabric. At last, she had found some evidence.

But there was more. She pulled a small wad of a wiry material out of the crack. Chills raced up and down her spine as she realized what she was holding in her hand.

It was a piece of animal fur, with long, coarse hairs.

The applause was over; the curtain had closed on Saturday night's performance of *A Common Man*. But the biggest standing ovation yet was still ringing in Portia's ears as she stood backstage, tired but exhilarated.

She felt a small hand clasp her shoulder. "Great work, Penelope!" said tiny, dark-haired Adrian Rani, a cast member who was about Portia's age. "That was your best performance yet!"

After chatting for a moment, Adrian walked to the stage door, where a beaming middle-aged couple waited for her. Portia sighed as she watched Adrian embrace her parents.

"What's the sigh for, Portia—or should I say, Penelope?" asked a voice behind her.

"Rene!" Portia exclaimed, glad to see the tall, handsome French boy. "How did you like the performance?"

"The play was *tres bon*—excellent. And you were even better. I am pleased that I was finally able to see it. But why did you sigh so sadly?"

Portia smiled. "Oh, I do feel great about tonight's show. I just wish my parents could be here and feeling great about it, too. Without my father's support, even the standing ovations seem empty."

"So, invite your papa to tomorrow's show."

Portia bit her lip. "You know, my father is actually here in London at the moment. He arrived today from Scotland for a meeting with the Royal Shakespeare Company." Then she sighed and shook her head. "But it's not that easy, Rene. You know how he feels about my chances of making it as an actress."

"The important thing, Portia, is this: How do you feel about your chances of making it as an actress?"

"I don't know," Portia said, biting her lip. "Maybe my father's right. Anyone can get lucky in one little play. Perhaps I don't have enough talent to make a career of acting."

"And perhaps you do. Personally, I believe you must. Only an actress *par excellence* could have created the illusion that you created at HIS in the last few weeks. You portrayed Isabelle so well that we all—as Jessica would say—*hated your guts!* Only now can I truly understand why you were being such a royal pain in the neck." He laughed. "But after seeing you in action tonight, I think I can forgive you."

Portia blushed under her heavy stage makeup. "I know I was beastly to everyone, Rene. Playing a role is no excuse for that kind of behavior. I'm glad you can forgive me for it." She stared him straight in the eye. "But now can you forgive Liz, as well?"

Rene flinched. "Ah, Portia. Let's not bring that up. I loved Elizabeth. She was everything I could ever want in a girl, but she betrayed—"

"No, she didn't betray you," Portia protested. "You and Elizabeth didn't have a relationship when she started seeing Luke."

Rene forced a laugh. "Come now, Portia. Hasn't anyone ever told you it's presumptuous for a *Brit* to advise a *Frenchman* on matters of love?"

Portia shook her head. "Oh, no. You are absolutely not going to extract yourself from this conversation by trying to engage me in Franco-English sparring. I'm quite fond of Elizabeth. She was the only person who made an effort to befriend me at first—even while I was treating everyone so abominably." She folded her arms. "Rene, before the Wakefields arrived in London, you hadn't set eyes on Elizabeth in months. Isn't it a wee bit possible that you've fallen in love with a memory, rather than a real person?"

"She didn't allow me to get reacquainted with the real person!" Rene protested. "She had hardly stepped off the plane when she began keeping company with that . . . *poet*."

"You make 'poet' sound like a dirty word."

"I can't help it. I love her. I don't want to see her with another beau."

"If you love Liz, you should want her to be happy. And she seems happy with Luke. Don't spoil that for her."

"But she said she cared for me."

"She does," Portia assured him. "Your friendship is very important to Elizabeth right now. And who knows what might happen in the future? If you can't be her mate—I mean, *friend*—now, you'll lose her completely, forever."

Rene cocked his head. "I don't know, Portia. I'm not sure I could handle being 'mates' with Elizabeth—especially if I have to watch her swooning over Luke Shepherd's poetry. But I suppose you've given me something to think about."

"Good," Portia said. "Now, let's think about stopping somewhere for a bite to eat. I'll introduce you to the old English standby, fish and chips."

Rene grimaced. "Hasn't anyone ever told you it's presumptuous for a Brit to advise a Frenchman on matters of *food*?"

"How did Jessica enjoy her date last night with Little Lord Pembroke?" Luke asked Elizabeth, who sat beside him on the Sunday morning train back to London.

"I don't know," Elizabeth said. "She was still asleep when we left this morning. I suppose she had a wonderful time, but I'm worried about her. I don't think Robert Pembroke is the right kind of guy for her. I've heard he's led kind of a wild life. What do you know about him?"

Luke narrowed his eyes. "Quite a bit, actually. His father tries to quell the gossip, but the Pembrokes are the sort of people everyone adores talking about. Robert has been booted out of some of the finest

36

schools in Britain. He's known for his attendance at the wildest parties. And he drives that Jaguar of his like a bloody maniac. In addition, his picture is in the tabloids every fortnight or so with a different female companion hanging on to his arm or gazing adoringly into his wealthy, aristocratic eyes. What do girls like Jessica see in his type?"

"Jessica's never been a very good judge of character," Elizabeth admitted. "In fact, we never like the same people. She's not a bad person, Luke, but she gets carried away. She places too much importance on appearances."

Luke touched Elizabeth's cheek for a brief, exquisite moment. "And appearances, as we know, can be deceiving," he replied in the soft, lilting accent that made everything he said sound like poetry. "I'm glad you're so different from your twin sister—despite your identical appearances."

"And *I'm* glad that you're nothing like Robert Pembroke," Elizabeth asserted. Her cheek felt warm where Luke had touched it.

"In one area, Robert has me topped," Luke admitted. "He took his girlfriend out last night, while I remained cloistered in my room, reading about werewolf imagery in Native-American rites and rituals. I hope you weren't too lonely, on your own."

Elizabeth pulled an envelope out of her backpack, and handed it to him. "Actually, I was busy last night," she said, unable to conceal her excitement. "Look what I found in the door frame of the room where Joy was murdered."

Luke twisted the green threads in his fingers.

37

"Fibers from some sort of fabric—it looks like silk." His eyes widened. "And this is animal fur!"

Elizabeth nodded, feeling every bit like Nancy Drew. "When we find out where those green threads come from, we'll be much closer to identifying the murderer."

"And the fur proves that it's a werewolf!"

"It doesn't *necessarily prove* anything," Elizabeth argued, trying to remember that first and foremost she was a journalist. "We don't know for sure what that fur comes from."

"We most certainly do!" Luke insisted. "What else but a werewolf could have murdered Joy Singleton by ripping her throat open? Not to mention the London victims. The question is, who is the werewolf?"

"I'm still not sure I believe in werewolves, but I'm willing to accept the possibility."

"Are you familiar with the words of your American poet, Thoreau?" Luke asked. "'The moon now rises to her absolute rule. And the husbandman and the hunter acknowledge her as their mistress.' The werewolf is the ultimate hunter, Elizabeth. He can change shape whenever he's so moved, but when the full moon shines, he's at his greatest strength. And the full moon was shining on the night of Joy's death."

Elizabeth suppressed a shudder. "Well, whether the murderer is a werewolf or not, the constable said everyone is a suspect. So let's go over all the possibilities. Who could have killed Joy Singleton?"

Luke counted on his fingers. "Besides Joy, the only people at Pembroke Manor this weekend were you and me, Jessica, the three Pembrokes, the servants, and Andrew Thatcher. I guess we can safely say it wasn't you, me, or Jessica."

Elizabeth nodded. "Right. And I can't believe Thatcher could have killed Joy. He was in love with her."

"Agreed," Luke said. "That leaves the Pembrokes and the servants. You questioned Maria and Alistair. What's your opinion about them?"

"I don't think they're murderers," Elizabeth said thoughtfully. "But they were in the upstairs hallway around the time of the murder. And I'm sure they're hiding something. Maria saw someone—or something—in the hallway outside of the room where Joy was killed. She says she doesn't know who it was. I think she's lying."

"Interesting. What about Alistair?"

Elizabeth shook her head. "I don't believe he saw anything. I'm not sure if Maria told him who she thinks she saw, but I know he's afraid to let her talk about it."

"Who are they afraid of?"

"Pembroke," Elizabeth replied. "The elder Lord Pembroke, that is. They were terrified that he would find out they spoke with me."

"Pembroke again," Luke said. "And the only suspects we haven't eliminated are Lord Pembroke, Lady Pembroke, and Robert. It must be one of them."

"We can't accuse someone of murder based only on the process of elimination," Elizabeth reminded him. "The Pembrokes could be innocent. Maybe we're wrong about one of the other suspects. Maybe there was some other servant in the house that night. Or maybe someone we've never heard of broke into the house and murdered Joy."

"Do you honestly believe that, Liz?"

Elizabeth hesitated before shaking her head. "No. I guess I agree that the Pembrokes are our prime suspects. But we can't do anything about it until we have some firm evidence that implicates one of them."

"We'll find the evidence," Luke assured her. "Werewolves are expert killers. But they aren't terribly skilled at covering their tracks."

Chapter 3

"One Million Pounds for Missing Princess!" screamed the front page of Sunday's *London Journal*. Elizabeth and Luke saw the headline at a crowded newsstand in London, after they left Victoria Station that morning.

"Pembroke is at it again," Luke complained. He shoved through the crowd to pick up a copy of the newspaper, reaching past a teenage couple with stiff green hair and a middle-aged man walking a poodle. The dog began yelping loudly at Luke, straining at its leash.

"You'd better watch it, chap," the green-haired boy said, laughing at him. "That little yapper is out for your blood!"

Elizabeth shuddered at the word "blood," but Luke just cast the youth a dirty look and threw a few coins on the counter. Elizabeth could hear the sound of the poodle's frantic barking following them as she and Luke began walking along Victoria Street.

The train station had a connection to the tube, but Elizabeth and Luke had chosen to walk.

"It's hard to believe that a newspaper with the *Journal*'s sterling reputation would sensationalize this missing princess bit all over the front page, day after day," Luke said, handing her the newspaper. "You read it. I can't bear to."

"I thought Pembroke sunk to a new low yesterday," Elizabeth said, "with that fantasy about the Tokyo bathhouse. Next it'll be 'Missing Princess Abducted by Space Aliens.'"

She scanned the article. "At least today's story is true. The paper is putting up a huge reward for information leading to the return of Princess Eliana."

"It's just another excuse for Pembroke to cover up the really big story," Luke scoffed. "This front-page headline should be about Joy Singleton's murder."

"But why is he doing this?" Elizabeth asked. "He knows there's a murderer on the loose. Why would he endanger a whole city?"

"He's protecting somebody," Luke said. "And that's not surprising, with the suspect list narrowed down to just Pembroke, his wife, and Robert."

"We still can't prove that," Elizabeth reminded him.

"We will," Luke said, staring with interest at the article. "Actually, Pembroke may have done us a big favor with today's edition. A million pounds just might induce someone to turn in the missing princess." He rolled his eyes. "Unless, of course, she really has been kidnapped, or is in Japan, or has been abducted by space aliens."

"And if the princess is returned home soon, safe

and sound, Pembroke will lose his smoke screen!" Elizabeth said. "He won't have an excuse to bury the murder stories at the back of the newspaper anymore."

Luke stopped walking and faced Elizabeth. "And," he said, his voice rising with excitement, "people will realize that the *Journal* made up those stories about Tokyo and kidnapping. Pembroke's cover-up will be exposed."

Elizabeth shook her head. "It's a nice theory, Luke, but nobody's going to turn Lina in. Nobody else knows who—"

She gasped, realizing what she had said.

Luke's mouth dropped open. "Lina?" he asked loudly. He glanced around guiltily and then softened his voice. "Are you saying what I think you're saying?"

"Please, Luke. I'm the only one who knows, and I promised her I wouldn't tell a soul. I never should have opened my big mouth. You won't tell anyone, will you?"

Luke pulled her to a secluded bench a few meters off the sidewalk. "Elizabeth, are you telling me that your roommate, working-class Lina from Liverpool, is really the missing Princess Eliana—the youngest daughter of the queen of England?"

Elizabeth nodded, sick that she'd divulged Eliana's secret. "She's tired of being sheltered and elite. She wanted to meet real people and see what the real London is like, so she ran away from Buckingham Palace, moved into HIS, and found a job in a soup kitchen."

Luke leaned over and kissed her. "Elizabeth Wakefield, you are just full of surprises. All you have

43

to do now is write up an article about the princess's real whereabouts, and Pembroke's cover-up will be exposed. If Tony won't print it in the *Journal*, I'm sure an editor at some other newspaper in town would be happy to."

Elizabeth jumped up from the bench. "Luke! I can't betray Lina's confidence! Besides, exposing the cover-up wouldn't do much good right now—not until we're sure of exactly what Pembroke's covering up."

Luke sighed. "I guess you're right," he admitted. "And don't be alarmed. I won't reveal her royal highness's secret if you don't want me to. In fact, I admire the girl for what she's doing. But when we have enough evidence to go to the police, you may need to convince Lina—or Eliana—to turn herself in. After all, lives are at stake."

Elizabeth remembered the sight of Joy's body on the blood-spattered sheets of Jessica's bed. Her stomach gave a sickening lurch.

"Especially *Jessica's* life," she whispered.

"Welcome home," Eliana said to Elizabeth as the American girl walked into the dorm room at noon on Sunday. It felt good to put aside her fake Liverpudlian accent and speak instead in her natural, softer tones. Elizabeth was the only person she could truly be herself around.

Then Eliana laughed. "Home. It's strange how quickly I've come to think of this place as home."

Elizabeth glanced around the spacious but messy dorm room and raised her eyebrows.

"My mother would be horrified if she knew where

44

I was living," Lina continued. "Actually, I called her again this morning—from a pay phone across town, so she can't trace me. I was afraid that today's *Journal* article would upset her—a bounty on my head and all. So I called to tell her that I'm still all right, but that I can't bear the thought of going back to my old life yet. She's furious with me."

"I'm sure she's just concerned about your safety."

"That's for certain. Mum is so overprotective that it's like living with a prison warden!"

Elizabeth laughed. "With Buckingham Palace as the world's best-decorated prison."

"Did you see today's *Journal*, by the way? The going rate for a princess is now one million pounds."

"Don't worry about anyone trying to collect it," Elizabeth said reassuringly. "Your secret is safe with me." Then she looked away, blushing.

"Liz, what's wrong?"

Elizabeth sat down on the bottom bunk. "To tell you the truth, your secret isn't safe with me. I accidentally told Luke about you, just a half hour ago. I'm sorry, but it slipped out."

Eliana felt a stab of fear. "Is he going to turn me in?"

"No, of course not," Elizabeth said quickly. "You can trust Luke—and me, even though I haven't given you much reason to."

Eliana relaxed again. Elizabeth looked so miserable that she felt sorry for her. "It's all right, Liz. I know *you* trust Luke. That's good enough for me. Besides, I'm too happy today to let it bother me. And I owe it all to you."

Elizabeth looked at her expectantly, though

Eliana could see that her mind wasn't really on the conversation.

"David and I went out together last night and had a marvelous time!" Eliana bubbled. "You know, I've lived in London all my life, but I've missed so much of the city. David and I explored it together. We were real tourists—Westminster Abbey, St. Paul's Cathedral. We even dropped by Buckingham Palace to watch the changing of the guard! Of course, I wore my dark glasses for that."

Elizabeth smiled. "I'm glad you had a good time."

"It's amazing how much David and I have in common, Elizabeth. For one thing, our politics are exactly alike." She stared at her fingernails for a moment. "He'll hate me if he ever learns the truth about who I am. You know, we both despise the whole idea of royalty, the idea that some people were born to have power and wealth and position, just because they're descended from a line of interbred snobs. You have a much better system in America."

"We have problems in America, too," Elizabeth said absently.

Eliana crossed the room and sat beside her. "You sound as if you're a thousand miles away. What's the matter, Liz? Are you still upset about telling Luke my secret?"

Elizabeth shook her head. "No, Eliana. I'm fine."

Eliana clapped her hand to her mouth. "Oh, I almost forgot to tell you! Here's a bit of news to cheer you up. Rene was in here looking for you this morning. He has to attend an embassy function for most of the day, but he left you a message. He asked me to tell you he's sorry for acting, as he put it, 'like a spurned lover.' He wants to be friends now, and asked if you'll meet him for lunch tomorrow."

Elizabeth's blue-green eyes lit up. "That's wonderful, Eliana! I'll leave him a note accepting the invitation."

"Good. But you still haven't told me what's wrong, Elizabeth. Didn't you have a good time at Pembroke Manor?"

"No . . . I didn't," she said, getting up from the bunk. "Suddenly I'm starving. Will you excuse me if I go downstairs to raid the kitchen? I'll fill you in on what happened later."

Eliana watched the American girl thoughtfully as she headed out of the room. Elizabeth had seemed agitated for most of the week—ever since the night she and Eliana came across the mangled body of a Yorkshire terrier on a foggy London street. Elizabeth had recognized poor Poo-Poo as the subject of her missing dog story at the newspaper.

Eliana shivered at the memory of the Yorkie's body, the blood on its throat glistening crimson in the moonlight. She couldn't imagine what had happened at Pembroke Manor to further upset Elizabeth. But somehow, she knew it was related to Poo-Poo's bloody death.

Jessica walked into the kitchen of HIS Sunday afternoon and set her suitcase on the floor. She was surprised to see her sister at the table, reading the most recent issue of the *London Journal* and eating leftover chicken.

"I didn't know you were back!" Elizabeth began.

"Robert just dropped me off," Jessica explained. "I haven't even been upstairs yet. Is there any more of that fried chicken?"

"Help yourself."

Jessica poked the front page of Elizabeth's newspaper. "How about that million-dollar reward Robert's father is offering for the missing princess?" she asked. "The Pembrokes are just about the most generous people I've ever met."

"It's a million *pounds*," Liz corrected her.

Jessica rolled her eyes. "What difference does it make? A million is a million. Somebody's going to get rich by finding Eliana. Too bad it can't be us. Maybe we've been investigating the wrong news story. If you were a princess, where would you go?"

Instead of answering her question, Elizabeth changed the subject. "How was your dinner date with Robert last night?"

Jessica sighed dreamily. "You should have seen the restaurant, Liz. There were enough forks at my place setting to stock the whole silver department at Simpson's department store back home. We ate chateaubriand—that's steak, you know. And trifle—a scrumptious dessert with layers of fruit and custard and sponge cake and I don't know what else. There was candlelight and soft music and the world's best-looking waiters. It was the most elegant dinner I've ever had!"

"How nice," Elizabeth said without much enthusiasm.

"Robert is just amazing, Liz. He knows absolutely

everyone worth knowing in England. A member of parliament stopped by our table to say hello. *A member of parliament!*"

"It sounds like fun."

"Then why do you look as if you've just eaten a sour pickle?"

"Oh, don't mind me, Jessica. I'm still recovering from what happened this weekend."

"What's to recover from? It's over and done with. Of course, I feel awful about Joy. But there isn't anything we can do about it. She would want us to go on having a great time in England. And, Liz, I am having one heckuva great time! I haven't been this happy since before Sam died. I didn't think I would ever love another boy the way I loved Sam. But I do, Liz. I'm in love with Robert Pembroke. This is definitely the Big L!"

Elizabeth looked startled. "Are you sure it's Robert you're in love with, and not just the money and the celebrities and the expensive dinners?"

Jessica folded her arms impatiently. "Give me a little credit, Liz. I'm not *that* superficial. Robert is kind, generous, and a lot of fun. He really cares about me. Of course, having tons of money and being related to royalty is always a plus in a boyfriend. But you know I wouldn't date someone who was *naff*, or a real *narg*, just because he was rich."

"Naff? Narg? I had no idea you were bilingual."

"They're British words," Jessica said with an air of importance. "Robert taught them to me. Naff means uncool, and a narg is a nerd—like your friend Winston Egbert in Sweet Valley. In fact, most of your *mates* in Sweet Valley are nargs."

49

"*My* friend! Winston is *our* friend, and as for—"

"Oh, cool off, Liz. I'm only kidding," she lied. "The point is that I'm in love with Robert Pembroke and he's in love with me. My own twin sister should be happy for me."

"I'm happy that you're happy, Jess. But I think you're rushing into this. Isn't it awfully soon to be talking about love? I mean, you met Robert less than a week ago. There are probably a lot of things you don't know about him . . ."

Jessica jumped from her seat. "What did Robert ever do to you?" she yelled. "Why do you hate him so much?"

"I don't hate Robert. It's just that—"

"Besides, you've known Luke less than a week, too. Why is it all right for you to be serious about him, if it's not all right for me and Robert? You're only four minutes older than me, Liz. You have no right to tell me how to live my life!"

"But Jessica, I—"

"I don't have to stand here and listen to you criticize the guy I love," Jessica shouted. "I'm fed up with your bossy, holier-than-thou attitude!" She stormed out of the room.

Elizabeth pounded a fist into her open palm as she watched Jessica's retreating back. "Sometimes she makes me so mad—" she said aloud. Then she noticed Eliana hesitating in the doorway.

"I didn't mean to eavesdrop, Liz," Eliana began. "And I'll leave if you want me to. But are you all right? I was reading in the library and I couldn't help hearing—"

"It's OK," Elizabeth said. "You might as well come in. And I'm fine. I just get so angry with Jessica sometimes! I don't know why I bother trying to help her. All I get for it is yelled at. She's so absorbed in little Lord Robert that she won't pay attention to anyone else. But I don't trust Robert or his family. And what happened at Pembroke Manor this weekend certainly didn't increase my confidence. I just know they're hiding something."

"I'm still in the dark about just what happened this weekend," Eliana reminded her.

Elizabeth took a deep breath and described her discovery of Joy's body in Jessica's bed Saturday morning. "I'm not accusing Robert of being a murderer," she admitted. "At least, I don't think I am. But somebody who was in that house this weekend *is* a murderer, and the evidence seems to point to the Pembrokes."

She decided not to mention the werewolf connection just yet, realizing how crazy it would sound.

"Even aside from the murders, I don't think Robert Pembroke is the kind of guy my sister should be going out with. He has a terrible reputation, and I don't want to see her get hurt. After all, she hardly knows him, and now she's convinced that she's in love. Tell me honestly, Eliana," she concluded. "Was I out of line to caution her against jumping into this relationship so quickly?"

Eliana looked thoughtful. "No," she decided. "It's never out of line to be concerned about somebody you love. But in this case, I can tell you that you don't need to worry so much. I know Robert; in fact, the

Pembrokes are distant cousins of mine. Certainly, the family isn't everyone's cup of tea. They're much too— *aristocratic*." She smiled ironically.

"Robert's been a bit of a handful for his parents," Eliana continued, "but it's only with schoolboy pranks and that type of thing. He's not a bad sort. And I'm a hundred percent certain that he doesn't have it in him to be a killer. The worst injury Jessica could get from Robert is a broken heart, when he moves on to his next conquest."

Elizabeth sighed deeply. "I'm relieved to hear you say so, Eliana. I hope you're right. I do know that there's no real evidence for accusing him of murder."

"Of course there isn't," Eliana said. "And what possible motive would he have for murdering the young woman at Pembroke Manor?"

Elizabeth shook her head. "None that I can think of."

"Maybe you're overreacting to Jessica's relationship with Robert. It's only natural to want to protect your sister, but she's sixteen years old—old enough to make her own decisions."

"And old enough to make her own mistakes," Elizabeth pointed out. "But you're right. If Robert turns out to be a rat, Jessica will have to learn about it on her own—though I still plan to keep an eye on her."

Elizabeth fingered the newspaper on the table in front of her. "If you know Robert," she said thoughtfully, "then you know his father, as well. You, of all people, must have noticed the way the *Journal* is exploiting the missing princess story. What would

Pembroke have to gain from plastering you all over his newspaper?"

Eliana shrugged. "The coverage is annoying, but I don't question Lord Pembroke's interest in using his newspaper to help find me. As I said, we are cousins."

"All the same, it seems like there would be more important news to cover than this steady stream of princess stories. No offense."

Eliana laughed. "I suppose it must seem strange to an American, but to the British, anything dealing with the royal family—even idle gossip—*is* important news."

"Come on, Eliana. A kidnapping? A Tokyo bathhouse? Both of those stories were based entirely on hearsay."

"All right, so the *Journal* has gone a bit overboard. But I'm certain the stories are selling a lot of newspapers. Why do you think there's something sinister behind them?"

"Joy's murder was not the first one of its kind. You know about Dr. Neville and Poo-Poo. There was also a nurse, about a month ago. Every time, the newspaper had the information, but buried it toward the back of the paper, or refused to run the stories altogether. Doesn't it seem odd to you that the owner of the *Journal* was at a murder scene yesterday, yet there's no mention of it in today's newspaper? He's protecting somebody, Eliana. And I intend to find out who."

"Actually, it doesn't seem odd in the least," Eliana said, "not if you know Lord Pembroke. The man has a terrific fear of scandal. For instance, he had the courtroom closed to the public the last time Robert was arrested for traffic violations. And when Robert was kicked out of his most recent school, Lord Pembroke endowed a new wing for the school's library—in exchange for having the records say Robert transferred out of his own accord."

"So you think Lord Pembroke is using the princess stories to cover up something terrible Robert has done?"

"I didn't say that!" Eliana protested. "I'm just trying to explain that Lord Pembroke doesn't want to sully the family name—for instance, by allowing a newspaper article that says a body was found at Pembroke Manor. He may not be covering up the identity of the murderer, Liz. He could be more interested in covering up the location of the murder."

"I know what it's like to have your family's name dragged through the mud," Elizabeth admitted, biting her lip. "Not long ago, I was in court myself—Jessica's boyfriend was killed in an accident, and I was driving the car. The accident turned out to be someone else's fault. But I would have given anything for a news blackout up until that point!"

Eliana looked startled. "Oh, Liz! How awful that must have been for you. I had no idea. But maybe that experience will help you understand Pembroke's actions. I remember hearing that the Pembrokes were involved in some sort of scandal fifteen or twenty years ago. Since then, Lord Pembroke has been fanatical about keeping the family name clean."

"What kind of scandal?" Elizabeth asked.

"I don't remember. It must have happened a year

or two before I was born. But as a child, I heard of a deep, dark secret that was causing the Pembrokes great embarrassment."

Very interesting, Elizabeth mused, wondering if the old scandal was somehow tied in with the current goings-on. *Now if I could only find out what the big scandal was.*

Unfortunately, the Pembrokes were the only logical source of information on the old scandal. Jessica would have a fit if Elizabeth went anywhere near Robert; besides, Robert would have been a baby at the time. The elder Lord Pembroke was already suspicious of Elizabeth. That left only Robert's mother. Elizabeth decided she would have to question Lady Pembroke about the twenty-year-old scandal—and about the recent murders.

I'll get to the bottom of this mystery if it's the last thing I do!

Chapter 4

"What with Lucy gone and all, this is going to be a crazy week for me," Tony Frank told the twins early Monday morning. "And I'm sorry to say that supervising interns isn't terribly high on the priority list. You'll have some assignments, but I'm afraid you'll be on your own a lot, too. So plan to do a lot of sightseeing, or whatever it is that American teenagers do in London."

Jessica grinned, thinking this way she'd finally have time to hit the stores. *Will it be Harrods or Bond Street?*

Elizabeth, though, had a thoughtful look on her face.

"Tony," Elizabeth began, "you don't mind if I spend some of that extra time tracking down some stories on my own, do you?"

Jessica rolled her eyes. It was just like her narg of a sister to want to spend the week writing. Well, she was still mad at Elizabeth for criticizing Robert, and she wasn't going to waste a moment worrying about whether Elizabeth was having fun this week.

"Still thinking about that Pulitzer, Liz?" Tony replied. "Go right ahead. I like reporters who take the initiative. Just don't get in over your head. Leave the breaking news to the professionals. Well, I guess that's singular now," he said, referring to Lucy's absence.

"Do you think Lucy is gone for good, Tony?" Elizabeth asked, taking his cue.

"I'm afraid so, Elizabeth," Tony answered. "And I'm also afraid you're looking at the *London Journal*'s new crime desk editor."

"Congratulations!" Jessica said, happy for Tony's success but sorry that it meant she wouldn't be seeing any more of the grouchy but glamorous Friday. "That's more exciting than covering tea parties for the society desk."

"I've wanted this job all my life," Tony admitted. "Though I hate the idea that I'm here only because Lucy resigned."

"And I guess this isn't going to make her any more likely to want to make up with you," Jessica said sympathetically.

Tony's face fell. Jessica had known from the start that Tony was in love with Lucy, even though they spent most of their time together bickering, arguing, and just plain yelling at each other. Lucy had accused Tony of sensationalizing the princess story in order to get the crime desk job for himself. Now that Tony had the position, Jessica reflected, their chances for a reconciliation were zilch.

"It's too bad about Lucy," Elizabeth said. "She seemed difficult to get to know, but she's a first-rate journalist."

"You're right on both counts," Tony agreed. "I'm the first to admit that Lucy's really the best *man* for the crime desk job. It'll be tough to fill her court shoes."

Jessica stared at him. "Huh?"

"You know, *court* shoes." Tony laughed. "High-heeled pumps, in American."

Jessica sighed. "Why can't the English speak English, like regular people?"

"Because regular people are naffs and nargs," Elizabeth said, reminding Jessica that she'd been dropping a few Briticisms herself.

"Speaking of words," Tony said, laughing, "I've got an assignment I want you both to work on this morning." Jessica's visions of shopping dimmed. "In the last week you two have been assigned a number of disparate topics—everything but the kitchen sink, in fact. Today, we'll remedy that deficiency."

"That sounds ominous," Elizabeth said.

"We're calling this the Case of the Flying Sink," Tony continued. "It seems that a university student was walking down Tottenham Court Road, when he was hit on the head by a kitchen sink that came soaring through the air."

The twins groaned in unison. "Another Bumpo story!" they exclaimed. Sergeant Bumpo was the bungling Scotland Yard detective who always handled the most ridiculous cases.

I'd rather be shopping, Jessica thought ruefully.

"Well, I guess we'd better catch up with Bumpo," Elizabeth said with a sigh after Tony dismissed the twins. Jessica knew that Elizabeth was itching to show off her journalistic skills on the Case of the Werewolf Murders. *How could calm, reasonable Elizabeth have turned into such a basket case that she actually believes in werewolves?*

Jessica glanced up and saw the answer to her question: Luke. He had somehow convinced Elizabeth that a werewolf could be responsible for the deaths of Joy and the other victims.

Luke smiled warmly at Elizabeth. "Would you like to go to the cinema with me tonight, Liz? *The Howling* is playing at the Paradiso."

"That would be great," Elizabeth replied, smiling and actually sounding pleased at an invitation to watch a werewolf movie.

Jessica shook her head. The old Elizabeth thought horror movies were childish. Then Jessica remembered a snatch of an old Warren Zevon song and began singing tunelessly: "'Ow-ooooh! Werewolves of London! Ow-ooooh!'"

"Jessica!" Elizabeth protested.

Jessica folded her arms in front of her. "I can't believe this. You two are taking this goofy werewolf stuff too seriously."

"Don't make light of werewolves, Jessica," Luke said in a quiet voice. "They're very serious business."

Luke leaned over to kiss Elizabeth on the forehead. "I'll come by your dorm at eight," he said, then crossed the room and disappeared through the door, leaving Jessica shaking her head in disgust.

• • •

"So, Sergeant Bumpo, have you determined where the flying sink came from?" Elizabeth asked the short, round detective, trying to keep the impatience out of her voice.

"Certainly. It was dropped from the window of the sixth-floor flat."

Jessica grimaced. "Why would anyone try to kill a college student by dropping a kitchen sink on his head?"

"I have conducted an intensive investigation on that very point," Bumpo said in an important-sounding voice. "Fingerprints, interviews with witnesses, analysis of the forensic evidence—"

"And what did you discover?" Elizabeth interrupted. Bumpo loved using every investigative technique known to criminal science—and he loved talking about them even more. Usually, Elizabeth found him amusing, but today she was in a hurry to go question Lady Pembroke—if she could find an excuse to get away from Jessica.

"After serious examination of the evidence," Bumpo said, "I've determined that the young fellow was hit entirely by accident. It seems a carpenter in the sixth-floor flat was installing a new washbasin. The old one was rather heavy to tote down the stairs, and the lift wasn't working, so he dropped it out the window instead. Unfortunately, he failed to notice the poor chap walking past, below."

"So what's the condition of the, uh, victim?" Elizabeth asked.

"The fellow's doing splendidly—conscious and in

61

good spirits," the detective replied. "He's in hospital, of course, but it's only a slight concussion. Luckily, he's a jolly strapping youth—university football player, you know."

Jessica brightened. "Football player?"

Bumpo wiped a hand across the top of his head, as if to assure himself that his few wisps of hair still shielded his rather large bald spot. "I suppose that's *soccer* to you Americans, isn't it?"

Suddenly, Elizabeth knew how to get away from her sister. In love or not, Jessica never passed up a chance to meet a good-looking college boy.

"Jessica," Elizabeth said, "I think it's very important that we interview the victim. Would you mind heading over to the hospital to question him? I'll stay here and finish up with Sergeant Bumpo. Then I'm meeting Rene for lunch. I'll see you at the *Journal* later this afternoon, and we'll write up the story."

Jessica smiled gratefully, ignoring the fact that she was angry with Elizabeth. "I think you're absolutely right," she said. "I'll get over to the hospital right away."

After Jessica was gone, Elizabeth hurried through the rest of her discussion with Sergeant Bumpo and then took a taxi to the Pembrokes' fashionable Eaton Square home, Pembroke Green.

Ciao for now to the Case of the Flying Sink, she thought as she sank back into the cushy seat of the distinctive black Austin, London's standard taxi. As exciting as it was to work for a real, big-city newspaper, Elizabeth had been bitterly disappointed by the types of articles she was assigned to write. She knew

it was unrealistic to expect to cover a major story—
she *was* just a high-school intern. But she was sure
she could do it. Maybe her private investigation of
the werewolf murders would give her the chance.

As London flew past her window, Elizabeth imagined her byline on a page-one *Journal* exclusive,
"Murder Suspect Apprehended."

She smiled at the familiar daydream. Then she
gave a long sigh and forced herself to concentrate on
her upcoming interview with Lady Pembroke.

"What do the Pembrokes have to hide?" she
asked under her breath. Lady Pembroke might not
know about the *Journal*'s cover-up of the murders,
but she would certainly remember the scandal that
had rocked the family name fifteen or twenty years
earlier.

Whether she would tell Elizabeth—or rather,
Jessica—was another question entirely. Unclasping
her hair from its neat ponytail and stuffing the bar-
rette into her purse, Elizabeth began her transformation into Jessica, who usually wore her hair down.
Then she pulled out a lipstick and applied it liberally;
Elizabeth seldom wore makeup, but Jessica wouldn't
think of walking into the Pembrokes' town house
without it.

A few minutes later, "Jessica" sat in a sumptuously
furnished parlor with Lady Pembroke. A butler hov-
ered nearby, waiting to refill their teacups—and glaring suspiciously at Elizabeth.

*Why didn't I put more thought into my clothes
today?* she silently chastised herself, looking down at
her simple navy skirt and white blouse. Lady

Pembroke, of course, was dressed impeccably, in a cream-colored silk suit and a strand of pearls. Not surprising, considering this was a woman who owned at least one mink coat that was worth roughly as much as a four-year college education in the States.

"Thanks for seeing me on the spur of the moment like this, Lady Pembroke," she said with exactly the right amount of Jessica's bounce in her voice. "I was in the neighborhood, and had just a few questions to go over with you, about your missing mink coat."

Lady Pembroke looked down her long, thin nose. "I thought we had exhausted the topic when you and that dreadful Sergeant Bumpo interviewed me last week," she said. "But go ahead, if you must. Especially if it will help recover my mink."

"As I understand it," Elizabeth said carefully, "you checked your mink while you were having tea at Browns. When you went to claim it afterward, you were given a chinchilla instead."

"A simply *wretched* chinchilla," Lady Pembroke emphasized.

Elizabeth stifled an urge to roll her eyes. Instead, she pretended to write in her reporter's notebook. "I suppose you were having tea with your husband, Lord Pembroke?"

"No, I was not," Lady Pembroke replied, narrowing her eyes.

"Then you were alone."

"Miss Wakefield, a woman of breeding never dines alone in public. I was with friends, of course—as I said in my statement to the detective. But I fail to see what difference it makes who my companions were."

Elizabeth smiled, hoping she looked friendlier than she felt. "I was just wondering if there were any other witnesses to the, uh, crime. But you're right; I can get that information from Sergeant Bumpo's report. So I won't waste any more of your time on it."

Lady Pembroke sniffed. "See that you don't. But I am gratified that somebody at the newspaper is taking this case seriously. My husband certainly isn't. And that horrible little Scotland Yard detective seemed to think the disappearance of my mink was a simple misunderstanding. I, for one, am convinced that a crime has taken place."

"I'm sure you're right, Lady Pembroke," Elizabeth agreed. Then she decided to press her advantage. "You know, a thorough newspaper article has a way of bringing a crime like this out into the open. The more information I have, the easier it will be for the police to recover your mink. For instance, does anyone have a reason to hold a grudge against you or your family? Even an incident that took place a very long time ago—like twenty years ago—could cause somebody to perpetrate a crime like this, for revenge."

Lady Pembroke's perfectly manicured fingers gripped her teacup tighter, her long, pink fingernails clinking against the fine bone china. When she stood up, her eyes were flashing, and Elizabeth realized she had gone too far.

"I have no idea what you are alluding to," Lady Pembroke said in a furious but perfectly controlled voice. "I understand that my son thinks quite highly of you, but I find you to be a boorish, ill-bred young woman. This interview is over."

* * *

"So this is the newsroom," Emily said, coming up behind Jessica, who sat at a computer on Monday afternoon, typing the day's Bumpo article with two fingers. "Are you ready to go out for tea?"

Jessica grimaced. "Not until I finish this stupid story for the evening edition."

"Another exploding aubergine? Or was it a turnip this time?"

"Ha, ha. Very funny," Jessica said. "But this happens to be an important article. A college student was injured in a major accident this morning. It was, uh, water-related."

"Oh, really? A boating accident? That does sound important. Let me see—"

Jessica tried to block Emily's view of the computer screen, but she was too slow.

Emily burst out laughing. "A kitchen sink fell on his head? I've heard of it raining cats and dogs, but never plumbing fixtures!"

Jessica laughed in spite of herself. "What a waste of a perfectly good morning. The guy who got clobbered by it wasn't even good-looking—tons of acne, and no neck!"

"Speaking of good-looking, wasn't Elizabeth having lunch with Rene today? How did that go?"

Jessica raised her eyebrows. "Apparently, it's going well. My deadbeat sister hasn't come back. That's why I'm stuck writing this story."

"Elizabeth hasn't returned? Do you suppose she finally gave in and decided that she loves Rene, after all?"

"A few weeks ago, I'd have said you were crazy.

But Elizabeth has really gone off the deep end since she's been here." She shook her head. "Nobody back home would believe it if they heard *I* was sitting in a stuffy newspaper office, writing an article that Elizabeth promised to do, while *she's* out with a great-looking French guy. It's as if she's turned into *me!*"

"What's so unusual about Elizabeth having a date?" Emily asked. "I thought she had a rather handsome boyfriend at home."

"That's just the point. She's usually boringly loyal to Todd. If she can forget all about him to have a fling with Luke, maybe she'd go out with Rene, too! I never thought I'd say this about my sister, but I've got to hand it to her—juggling three boys at once! As I said, she's sounding more and more like *me*."

"Are you still mad at her for what she said yesterday?"

"I guess I'll get over it," Jessica said. "I wish she'd give Robert a chance. But she really thinks she's looking out for me. Liz can be kind of a mother hen. She's four minutes older than I am, and she thinks that gives her the right to boss me around!"

The phone rang. Jessica picked it up to hear Robert's voice, inviting her to dinner at Pembroke Green that night with him and his mother.

"My father won't be present, of course," Robert told her. "He's still at the manor house, taking care of some business. But I was hoping to bring you and Mother together to help you two become *reacquainted*. From what Mother said, I take it your interview with her at the house today was less than successful."

"Interview? What interview?"

"You know, the one this morning about her missing mink coat. She told me you came by to follow up on it for your newspaper story."

Jessica's eyes widened as realization swept over her. *Elizabeth went to Pembroke Green today, disguised as me!* Jessica's forgiveness faded, replaced by rage. "Oh," she said in a quiet, strained voice. "That interview."

"She seems rather upset with you, in fact," Robert continued. "I'm sure it was all a misunderstanding. She said you were asking a lot of personal questions, but I know you were just doing your job. Don't worry too much about it, Jessica. Mother can be rather difficult to get along with. But I'd like to give the two of you a chance to become friends. How about if I pick you up around six o'clock?"

"That would be fine, Robert." Jessica hung up the phone and sat quietly, her hand still clenching the receiver.

"What is it, Jess?" Emily asked. "You look upset."

"She's done it now," Jessica said in a barely controlled voice. "She's convinced that Robert's no good. She'll go to any lengths to find dirt on him. But this time, she's gone too far. And she's going to pay for it."

"Jessica, who are you talking about?" Emily asked. "What happened?"

"I think I'm finally going to have a major story to report on for the *Journal*," Jessica announced. "American Teenager Murders Twin Sister."

"My visit to Pembroke Green was disastrous,"

Elizabeth confided to Rene as they strolled through Regent's Park after lunch Monday. "Lady Pembroke practically had me thrown out of the house. I'm sure she hates me."

"Except that she thinks it is Jessica she hates," the French boy supplied.

"That's right. And Jessica will be furious when she finds out."

Rene chuckled. "Can you blame her?"

"On one hand, I hope I didn't wreck Jessica's relationship with Robert's family. But on the other hand, anything that pushes Jessica away from the Pembrokes can't be all that bad. I'm still convinced that there's something sinister going on with that family."

"Did you learn anything else of importance from Lady Pembroke?"

"Not really," Elizabeth said. "Except that she practically sneers every time she mentions her husband's name. There's no love lost between those two! You know, I didn't notice it over the weekend, but now that I think about it, they hardly said a word to each other the whole time I was at Pembroke Manor."

"A loveless marriage? Could that—how do you say, *shed some light* on the other avenues you are investigating?"

"I don't know. I keep wondering about the big scandal. Apparently something awful happened nearly twenty years ago that caused the Pembroke name to be dragged through the mud. Maybe whatever it was turned Lord and Lady Pembroke against each other. Of course," she admitted, "that's pure speculation."

"Perhaps Jessica has heard something about this scandal, in the time she has spent with the Pembrokes."

Elizabeth shook her head. "I doubt they would bring up a topic that apparently caused them so much embarrassment. And I'm certainly not going to mention it to her. She wouldn't believe anything bad about the Pembrokes anyway. She thinks they're perfect. Whatever Jessica says, I believe that Lord Pembroke knows more than he's saying about the murders of Joy Singleton and Cameron Neville. It's possible that he's the murderer himself—or that Robert or Lady Pembroke is."

"From what you've said of the lady, it sounds as if she could freeze her victims to death with a single glance. But seriously, Elizabeth, I am worried about you. This investigation is beginning to sound dangerous."

Elizabeth was touched by his concern, but she thought it was unwarranted. "Don't worry about me, Rene. I'm perfectly safe."

"Elizabeth, you have seen two mutilated bodies— three, if you include the small terrier. You've been warned to cease your inquiries into the deaths, by a man whom you admit could be the murderer—a wealthy, powerful man who's accustomed to having his every wish obeyed. How can you say you are in no danger?"

"Rene, I was at Pembroke Manor Saturday night, too. But it was Jessica's room the murderer chose, and Joy who was killed. Nobody has threatened my safety. I don't think—"

She stopped when she noticed Rene looking at her curiously.

70

"What's that silver pendant you're clutching so tightly, Liz?" he asked. "On the chain around your neck?"

Elizabeth blushed and let go of the necklace. "It's, um, a pentagram."

"A pentagram? Isn't that a talisman for use against werewolves?" He inspected the pendant. "Elizabeth, where did you get this?"

Elizabeth sighed. "From Luke," she said, watching Rene's face.

Rene grimaced. "Not Luke again."

"Please, Rene. Don't be upset."

Rene forced a smile. "I am trying not to be," he said. "But this is an odd gift from a beau, is it not?"

Elizabeth took a deep breath and looked him straight in the eye. "I wasn't going to tell you, Rene, because it sounds so crazy. But Luke and I believe the murderer could be a werewolf."

"Now you are jesting with me."

"No, I'm not. Look at the evidence, Rene. The bodies were found with their throats ripped out! That doesn't sound like your normal, everyday serial killer. And I found some animal fur at the scene of Joy's murder."

"Even if werewolves did exist, I thought they hunted only when the moon was full," Rene objected.

"That's not true," Elizabeth said. "Luke has been studying werewolves for years. He says they can change their shape any time they want to—though they're at their greatest strength under the full moon."

Rene just shook his head.

Elizabeth blushed again, realizing how farfetched

the theory sounded. "I see what you mean," she said haltingly. "Our evidence is pretty sketchy. And from your perspective, the idea must sound irrational."

"Completely," Rene said. "Certainly, the murders were grisly, but humans have been known to kill in horrible ways. And the animal hair could have come from a family pet—or perhaps from one of Lady Pembroke's furs."

Elizabeth sighed, knowing that Rene was right. Luke, with his love of romantic horror fiction and his lifelong interest in werewolf lore, had *wanted* the murderer to be a werewolf, so he had convinced himself that it was true. And Elizabeth, caught up in the excitement of falling in love and of having a real mystery to solve, had gone right along with him.

She glanced at Rene, walking beside her. He was practical, reasonable, and totally objective—so different from romantic, sensitive Luke. She was in love with Luke, but she resolved to be more like Rene. She would never find out what the Pembrokes were hiding if she kept allowing herself to be carried away by fantasies.

"Okay," she admitted. "There are no werewolves."

And for the first time in days, she truly believed it.

Chapter 5

Jessica was standing with her back to the door when Elizabeth walked into the girls' room at HIS Monday evening.

"Do you think this dress makes me look fat?" Jessica chirped, modeling an elegant white sheath for Lina and Portia. Of course, Elizabeth knew, Jessica realized the dress looked stunning on her.

Jessica turned, posing for her friends. Then she caught sight of Elizabeth in the doorway, and her expression turned to poison.

"The dress looks terrific," Elizabeth said, ignoring the thunderclouds in Jessica's eyes. "And that gold jewelry is perfect with it. Are you going somewhere special tonight?"

"When I want your opinion, I'll ask for it," Jessica said acidly. "But don't hold your breath."

Lina and Portia glanced hesitantly from twin to twin, looked at each other, and silently left the room.

Elizabeth took a deep breath. "Jessica, I—"

"How could you do such a thing?" Jessica stormed. "I can't believe you would pretend to be me, just so you could spy on my boyfriend and turn his mother against me."

"It wasn't like that, Jessica, I swear! I wasn't trying to turn Lady Pembroke against you. I just needed some information—"

"Right. And now you're going to tell me it was all in the name of journalistic integrity. Darn you, Liz! You've hated my relationship with Robert from the start—you just want me to break up with him. What's the problem? Are you jealous that I'm dating a nobleman and you're not? Stringing along three guys isn't enough for you, is that it? Now you want Robert, too!"

Elizabeth was mortified that Jessica could have mistaken her motives so badly. "Jessica, you know that's not true—"

"Don't tell me what I know! One thing's for sure—I don't know *you* anymore. The sister I know wouldn't pretend to be me and bother my boyfriend's mother with a lot of rude questions! What gives you the right to pry into Robert's life?"

"Jessica, you've got to believe me. I'm not investigating Robert. This has nothing to do with your relationship with him. A killer is on the loose! My investigation of why Lord Pembroke is covering up the murder stories in the newspaper may lead to the murderer!"

Jessica's voice was laden with sarcasm. "Oh, I remember. That's the same investigation where you discovered a ferocious werewolf, stalking the streets of London, hunting its next victim! England will certainly sleep easier tonight, knowing you and Luke the kook are on the job! Face it, Liz—you two are out of control. Covering murders is way out of your league. Maybe you should stick to homicidal kitchen sinks."

"Jessica," Elizabeth said, trying to keep her voice even, "I'm sorry I upset Robert's mother. But the Pembrokes are hiding something important about the murders."

"The Pembrokes have nothing to do with the deaths, and you don't have a shred of evidence that proves otherwise! Well, I'm not going to take the rap for your obnoxious questions. How do you think Lady Pembroke will respond when she hears who really interviewed her this morning?"

Elizabeth grabbed Jessica by the shoulders and stared at her wildly. "Please, Jessica," she said, aghast. "You absolutely cannot tell the Pembrokes the truth about the interview today. If you do, you'll tip off Lord Pembroke that I'm investigating him, and you'll blow any chance I have of discovering who the murderer is!"

To Elizabeth's surprise, her sister burst into tears. "You've ruined everything!" she screamed. "I love Robert! I wanted so badly to fit in with his family, but now his mother hates me! The worst part about it is that I can't even tell her it was you at Pembroke Green today. If I do, she'll think I come from a family of complete flakes! Why couldn't you mind your own business for a change? I never want to speak to you again!"

Jessica ran out of the room, slamming the door behind her. Elizabeth sighed. But she couldn't spend time worrying about Jessica's anger. The important thing right now was to find the murderer, even if it meant rattling any skeletons that hid in the Pembroke closet.

It wasn't me! Jessica wanted to scream at dinner Monday night. *I didn't ask you all those obnoxious questions! It was my evil twin, Elizabeth!*

Instead, she took another bite of the perfectly prepared pheasant, and wished she could savor the sumptuous meal. Unfortunately, under Lady Pembroke's icy glare everything she ate tasted like sawdust.

"So, Jessica," Lady Pembroke began in a cold, hard voice. "Are you enjoying your work as a reporter? Your interview style is rather—unsubtle. I had heard that Americans prize directness. In England we favor a more moderate approach."

"Please, Mother," Robert interjected. "It's a reporter's business to ask a lot of questions."

Jessica smiled gratefully at him, but Lady Pembroke raised her eyebrows, obviously unimpressed.

It's hard to defend myself when I don't know what I'm defending, Jessica thought. Unfortunately, she still wasn't sure exactly what Elizabeth had asked that morning. Maybe she could get Lady Pembroke to tell her.

"I am so sorry if some of my questions were too personal," Jessica said, hating herself for taking the blame for Elizabeth's blundering. "But I'm still very

76

new at this reporting thing, and I was feeling nervous, interviewing someone of your, uh, stature. Maybe you could help me improve my skills. Can you tell me just which questions were, um, inappropriate?"

Lady Pembroke sniffed, as if the unfortunate questions had left an odor that still wafted through the halls of Pembroke Green. "*All* of your questions were inappropriate, young lady."

"Mother—" Robert protested.

"In particular," Lady Pembroke amended quickly, with a glance in Robert's direction, "the question about Pembroke family history was in exceedingly poor taste. And the identity of my dining companion was entirely irrelevant to my stolen mink."

Jessica was mystified. *Family history? Dining companion?* She couldn't believe her sister had seen fit to conduct a background check on one of the oldest, most respected families in England—all because she was afraid Robert wasn't good enough to date Jessica. Who did Elizabeth think she was? The Pembrokes were related to the royal family! What would Elizabeth look for next—character references?

Robert took Jessica's hand and his mother's, and squeezed them both heartily. "It's marvelous that you two have managed to clear the air so quickly, and can now go on to become friends," he said hopefully.

Lady Pembroke made a noise that sounded like "Humph."

She hates me, Jessica told herself. *Elizabeth has destroyed my chances of ever fitting in with Robert's family.*

"I apologize for my mother," Robert said later, as

he escorted Jessica outside to his silver Jaguar convertible for the drive back to HIS. "But don't worry. In time, she'll come to love you as much as I do."

"I wouldn't bet on it," Jessica said glumly. "Eliz— I mean, *I've* made her so mad that she'll never forgive me."

"That isn't true," Robert insisted, gently brushing a stray lock of golden hair out of her eyes. "But even if it were, it wouldn't matter. I don't need my mother's permission to be in love with you."

Robert was definitely the most wonderful boy in the whole world.

"You said Tony Frank wants you to adopt a relaxed attitude toward the *Journal* this week," he said. "Why don't you take Wednesday off and spend it with me? We'll take the Jag and go for a drive in the country—with the top down if the weather holds. Have you been to Stonehenge yet?"

Jessica raised her eyebrows. "Isn't it just a bunch of old rocks?"

"Oh, no," Robert explained, staring intently into her eyes. "It's much more than that. It's you and me, Jessica—all alone in the countryside—with nothing around us but lonely fields and the open road."

Robert's hands slid to Jessica's back. When his full, warm lips met hers, she felt tremors radiating through her whole body.

After they kissed, Robert held her at arm's length. "So, do we have a date?" he asked. "Do you want to go to Stonehenge with me on Wednesday?"

Jessica smiled dreamily. "I'm *dying* to."

•　　•　　•

"Humans are our prey," said a gnarled, unshaven man. The werewolves, all in human form, were slowly circling Karen White, the television reporter.

A raven-haired woman panted at the reporter, her face twisted into a hungry, toothy leer. "She's ours now."

Elizabeth jumped as something hairy touched her arm. Then she realized it was only the sheepskin cuff of Luke's jacket, as he reached for a handful of popcorn. Normally, horror movies left Elizabeth unaffected—she would be too busy analyzing the plot deficiencies to be terrified by the special effects. But that Monday night at the Paradiso, *The Howling* didn't seem so farfetched.

Karen had been sent to a colony in the woods to recover from an attack by a serial killer. But the other patients there were werewolves, and their plan was to infiltrate society.

For an instant, Elizabeth had a mental image of Pembroke Manor as the colony.

Robert Pembroke glided toward her, his fangs dripping with blood. . . . But it wasn't Elizabeth he was approaching; the blondes had switched beds. It was Jessica, and she smiled serenely and offered him her throat. . . .

Elizabeth shook her head to clear the daydream and tried to concentrate instead on the more ridiculous elements of the film's plot. *This is a stupid movie*, she told herself. *There's no such thing as werewolves.* But other images kept crowding into her brain.

She saw Dr. Neville's body lying on floral carpeting in a pool of blood, murdered *as if by a wild beast*. She saw the jewels sparkling in the moonlight from Poo-Poo's crimson-stained dog collar. She saw Luke, bending over a low shrub covered with hooded flowers—wolfsbane, he'd said, which blooms only when the werewolf is stalking its prey. She thought of the Pembrokes' sheep, mutilated. Then Elizabeth remembered the scrap of fur, caught in the door frame, and the full moon streaming through the casement window of Joy's bedroom at Pembroke Manor. *Beware the full moon*.

Last, Elizabeth saw Joy's body, lying still and cold, as the blood from the gash in her throat dripped slowly into a puddle on the floor beneath the bed.

The bed that was supposed to have been Jessica's.

"We should never try to deny the beast, the animal in us," the doctor in *The Howling* had advised.

We all have an animal side, Luke had said.

Karen White had an animal side. She returned from the colony. But she had been bitten and so was destined to become an animal herself. Elizabeth watched, mesmerized, while Karen transformed into a wolf while anchoring the evening news.

The reporter's body began to tremble. "Now, I'm going to show you something to make you believe," she said to the camera. She rose painfully from her seat and arched her neck, her eyes gleaming with an eerie light. Her anguished cry turned into a howl as hair began to transform her face and neck. Her teeth elongated into fangs, but a very human tear spilled from the corner of one eye.

By the time Karen's friend shot her, mercifully, with a silver bullet in the heart, Elizabeth's doubts about werewolves were also laid to rest. She clutched her pentagram pendant as if it were a security blanket.

"Werewolves do exist," she whispered under her breath. "And one of them is stalking its prey in London."

Chapter 6

"The Slaughtered Lamb," Elizabeth said, looking across her coffee cup at Luke as they sat in a pub after the movie Monday night. "Last week, I thought it was a quaint name for a pub." She shuddered. "Now I'm not so sure—after what happened Saturday night to the sheep at Pembroke Manor."

Luke shook his head sadly. "We can't dwell on that, Elizabeth. We must concentrate on proving that the Pembrokes are guilty."

"But guilty of *what*?" Elizabeth asked. "We still don't know who the murderer is—all we know for sure is that Lord Pembroke is hiding something."

"He's hiding the fact that one of the Pembrokes is a murderer," Luke said, "and a werewolf."

Elizabeth gripped the pentagram pendant that hung around her neck. "You've finally convinced me about the murderer being a werewolf. There isn't any other explanation that fits the evidence we've found.

But we can't prove that one of the Pembrokes is the murderer."

"Then we must get the proof," Luke said quietly. "And we must do it quickly. Lord Pembroke is already suspicious."

Elizabeth nodded. "He's the key to all of this. But, Luke, he hates me. He'll never agree to an interview."

"Maybe not with you," Luke said. "But he seems to be rather fond of your sister."

A smile spread across Elizabeth's face. "Yes, he is; isn't he?"

"The only catch is that Pembroke is still out at Pembroke Manor, in the country," Luke reminded her. "You'll have to come up with an excuse for going there."

Elizabeth shrugged. "The mink-coat story worked for getting into Pembroke Green today. I'll tell him I have a few more questions about the incident, for a follow-up article."

"That may sound a little *lame*—as you Americans say," Luke said. "A restaurant coat checker swapping a chinchilla for a mink is not exactly the fall of the Berlin Wall. He might not believe you're writing another article on it. Do you think you can pull it off?"

"I'm sure *I* couldn't," Elizabeth said. "But Jessica can. I'll pour on the Jessica-charm that's broken the hearts of a hundred teenage boys. He'll talk."

Late that night, Eliana leaned back into a comfortable old leather chair in the library at HIS, and smiled at Elizabeth. "Mrs. Bates looked a bit disappointed when David and I squeaked through the door at the same time as you—about two seconds before curfew!"

Elizabeth laughed. "I suppose our dorm mother was looking forward to locking the three of us out of the house for the night, as soon as the clock struck eleven. She certainly loves throwing the rule book at people!"

"She'll still have a chance to exercise her pitching arm tonight," Eliana said, checking her watch. "It's now eleven thirty—a half hour past curfew. And your twin is still out with Robert. Aren't they a little late, for just having dinner at his house?"

"Maybe Robert took her somewhere afterward—probably to make up for his mother curdling the food with those wicked stares of hers. You know, Eliana, I'm sure I've ruined Jessica's chances with Robert's mother. I did a rotten job of interviewing her this morning. But it's not all my fault. Lady Pembroke seems like a totally disagreeable person."

Eliana wrinkled her nose. "She would not be my first choice for a dinner companion," she admitted. "But I wonder if Mrs. Bates will make good on her threat to lock Jessica out for being late."

"No way," Elizabeth said, shaking her head. "You know her weakness for the upper class. She's always willing to look the other way—if Jessica is out with Little Lord Pembroke. Not like you and me, who are dating commoners!"

Eliana laughed. "The only thing I'm looking forward to about ending my charade is the look on Mrs. Bates's face when she discovers the truth—that working-class Lina from Liverpool is really Princess Eliana, the queen's daughter, from Buckingham Palace!"

"What about when David finds out the truth?"

Eliana looked at the floor. "I don't even want to think about it," she said evenly, squashing down the feeling of panic that rose within her every time she thought about it. "Things are going so well for us, Elizabeth. I've never had a beau like David. Most of the boys I date are more interested in having people see us together than in getting to know me."

"How terrible," Elizabeth said. "I never thought about it that way. Of course, appearances aren't important to David."

"No, they're not. David likes me for myself. And he cares about things that are really important. For instance, he has no classes tomorrow, so he's coming with me to work, to help out in the soup kitchen."

"That's wonderful," Elizabeth said. "You both deserve to be happy."

"So do you, Liz. But you seem so preoccupied lately. I suppose it's all this business with the murders. You don't still believe Robert or someone in his family is a killer, do you?"

"I don't know what to believe." Elizabeth sighed, nervously gripping a silver pendant that hung on a chain around her neck.

Eliana wondered if Elizabeth had deeper fears about the murders—fears she was keeping secret.

"I know Lord Pembroke is related to you," Elizabeth continued, "but I also know he has arranged for the police department to help him hide the truth. I suspect that Pembroke knows who the werew—uh, *murderer* is—if he's not guilty himself."

86

Eliana gasped. "Surely you don't think Lord Pembroke is a crazed killer!"

"No, somehow I don't," Elizabeth said. "He doesn't seem like the type. But I'm determined to find out for sure. I have to learn the true identity of the murderer. Will you help me?"

Eliana squirmed uncomfortably. "I don't know, Elizabeth. As I said, the Pembrokes are my cousins—"

"Oh, I'm not asking you to dig up any dirt on them," Elizabeth assured her. "I plan to travel to Pembroke Manor tomorrow, disguised as Jessica, to see if I can get some information about the newspaper cover-up. I want to know what Pembroke is hiding under all those stories. I guess you saw the latest fantasy, in today's paper—'Did Missing Princess Elope with Palace Guard?'"

Eliana burst into laughter, but quickly stopped when she saw the frown on Elizabeth's face. "But, Liz, what if Lord Pembroke mentions to Robert that 'Jessica' came to see him, and Robert mentions it to Jess?"

Elizabeth shrugged. "It's worth the risk. When I find absolute proof that something is criminally wrong at Pembroke Manor, Jessica will have to forgive me. And I intend to find proof."

"So what do you need from me?"

"An alibi," Elizabeth said. "I'll tell Pembroke I'm working on another article about his wife's mink. But what can I tell the people at HIS and the newspaper?"

"Make up another article to work on," Eliana suggested. "There must be something of interest to report on in the vicinity of Pembroke Manor. Then all you'll need is a last-minute excuse for staying in the country overnight. I can help you by running interference here at the dorm—especially with Mrs. Bates."

Elizabeth clapped her hands together. "Ostriches!"

"As you Americans say—*come again?*"

"From the train window on my way back to London, I noticed a field with *ostriches* in it. I've heard there's quite a market for them in some parts of the world—the hide, the eggs, and even the meat. I'll ask Tony if I can interview the farmer who's raising them."

"Not bad. It's weird enough to catch an editor's interest, but minor enough so that he won't send a more senior reporter. I think you've got yourself an assignment."

Elizabeth let out a long, sad sigh.

"What's wrong?"

"Nothing. I just wish I could cover a real story—something more important than ostriches, mink coat swaps, or exploding eggplants—I mean, *aubergines.*"

"Something like 'Serial Killer Arrested'?"

"Yes," Elizabeth said with a sudden gleam in her blue-green eyes. "Something exactly like that."

A shaft of morning sunlight pushed through a crack in the heavy velvet curtains early Tuesday, intensifying the murky shadows and bright patches of light in the library of Pembroke Manor.

In the shadows in one corner of the room, the elder Lord Robert Pembroke sat at his heavy mahogany desk. He sighed heavily, absentmindedly stroking a cigarette case that gleamed silver in his hand. The grandfather clock in the parlor tolled seven sonorous times.

Pembroke exhaled loudly. "Seven o'clock in the bloody morning," he said in a slow whisper that was almost a moan. It was a full hour before his usual time for rising, but he had been awake since four, watching the light of dawn infiltrate the dark room. Usually, Pembroke slept easily—the sleep of a man who is secure in his wealthy, powerful, eminently stable existence. But that morning, he realized he had hardly slept in three days—not since Saturday's dreadful awakening, when one of the American girls had discovered the body of Thatcher's lovely fiancée.

The young lady's death was a horrible tragedy. Poor Thatcher had been a mere shell of himself since Saturday morning. Pembroke empathized completely with his friend, the chief of police; Pembroke had also lost the love of his life—a beautiful young woman with startlingly clear blue eyes and a lilting laugh. But that was long ago. He had moved on in his life, and Thatcher would, as well.

"We only have to hold out a little longer," he had told Thatcher on Saturday.

Pembroke sighed at the memory. On Saturday, he had still harbored hope.

Those hopes had begun a month earlier, at the murder scene of that unfortunate nurse back in London. By chance, Pembroke had accompanied Thatcher to lunch that day, and so was present when the chief of police inspected the murder scene.

The evidence had confused Thatcher—a gash in the throat, as if the woman had been mauled by a beast. But Pembroke understood immediately. Werewolves were his lifelong passion. He had spent hours poring over dusty volumes and faded court proceedings from medieval werewolf trials. He had recognized the signs instantly. Nurse Dolores Handley had been murdered by a werewolf.

A real werewolf! Pembroke had dreamed all his life of studying one—in person, as it were—and learning all there was to know about it.

Besides, an authentic werewolf for Pembroke's trophy collection would have been the culmination of a lifetime of exotic game hunting and the crown on his years of study of werewolf lore. It would have brought him fame and fortune—not only in his native England, but around the world. Sales of the *Journal* would skyrocket with the articles he'd print. And the name of Robert Pembroke, Sr., would be on the lips of every journalist and every enthusiast of the hunt, on every continent of the globe. It would be a far cry from the last time the Pembroke name had been the subject of major news stories, almost twenty years earlier.

Pembroke had begged Thatcher to help him suppress the evidence of the nurse's murder, to keep every fortune hunter in Europe from converging on the city. He didn't want his private werewolf hunt to escalate into a contest for amateurs.

Then came the murder of Dr. Cameron Neville. Pembroke had been deeply distressed to see the body of his oldest and dearest friend, sprawled on the carpeting of the doctor's Essex Street residence. Certainly, the torn clothing, the bits of fur scattered about the murder scene, and the telltale wound in Neville's neck had sickened Pembroke. But they had also reinforced his original theory: A werewolf was on the prowl in London. As he stood over the doctor's body, Pembroke had resolved once again to find the murderous beast. The slaying of his friend had turned his werewolf hunt into a personal mission.

At that point, he had known for sure that he would prevail in the end. Werewolves were notoriously messy about their business of killing. All Pembroke had to do was follow the clues, anticipate the beast's next actions, and watch and wait.

But it was at the scene of Neville's murder that Pembroke's fears had started. As he turned away from the body, he had noticed the silver cigarette case gleaming like moonlight on the floor.

When he recognized the distinctive silver case, Pembroke felt as if his own heart had been torn out. Finally, he had some evidence of who the werewolf could be. But the evidence pointed in a direction he did not want to investigate. Nothing could make him believe that the cigarette case's owner was a murderer—much less a werewolf.

The case could have been stolen, he had told himself. Perhaps its owner had visited Neville before the murder, despite testimony from Neville's housekeeper that the doctor had entertained no visitors.

Then, on Saturday, Joy Singleton was found dead. Pembroke still didn't believe what the cigarette case seemed to reveal about the identity of the werewolf. But he knew that others would believe it—especially after he found fragments of a fabric he recognized,

91

stuck in the door frame of the room where the were-wolf had struck. The evidence was overwhelming.

Suddenly, hiding the details of the mysterious deaths was no longer a matter of adding a new trophy to his collection. A cover-up was vital to protecting his family. The last scandal had made him the subject of derision throughout London. He had spent more than a decade rebuilding his reputation. He wasn't going to lose that reputation now.

Even more important was protecting the person who would be implicated by the evidence: the owner of the silver case.

Suddenly, a finger of shimmering sunlight jabbed through the curtains of the still-dark library. It seized the cigarette case Pembroke still turned in his hand, staining its surface a deep crimson.

Pembroke dropped the case as if it were on fire—the cigarette case that belonged to his son, Robert.

The grandfather clock in the parlor had just chimed nine o'clock when the phone rang on Pembroke's desk, startling him out of a fitful doze. Other newspaper executives insulated themselves behind armies of secretaries. Pembroke prided himself on being accessible; the *Journal*'s editors knew they could ring him up directly in his library at Pembroke Manor.

He opened his mouth to yell at editor Reeves about the latest ridiculous story concerning the Princess Eliana—*eloped with a palace guard, indeed!* Of course, Pembroke had told the editors to play up the princess story to deflect attention from the recent deaths, but the sight of that sort of fiction in his newspaper made him positively ill.

"Hello, Lord Pembroke!" exclaimed a breathless, youthful voice at the other end of the line.

For the first time in days, a genuine smile sprang to Pembroke's face. The caller could be no one but Robert's young ladyfriend, Jessica Wakefield.

"I have a few itsy-bitsy questions for you about that mink coat of Lady Pembroke's—for a follow-up article in the newspaper, of course," Jessica said brightly. "Would you mind if I dropped by Pembroke Manor this afternoon to talk to you about it?"

Pembroke chuckled to himself, flattered. The girl was charmingly transparent. The mink swap was hardly worth one newspaper article, let alone two. Obviously, the pretty young intern was paying special attention to it because it involved him. After all, along with being the owner of the newspaper she worked at, he was her beau's father. Eager to be in his good graces, she erroneously assumed that he cared about his petty wife and her blasted mink.

In addition, the girl was probably eager for an excuse to revisit Pembroke Manor. He remembered the way Jessica's eyes had gobbled up its luxurious furnishings, like the eyes of a penniless child in a sweet shop.

"I wouldn't mind at all, child," he told her. "Glad to have you anytime. In fact, you should plan to stay for supper, and to spend the night as well. We've plenty of room, and Lord knows we could use some cheer around here!"

Then his eyes narrowed as suspicions rose in his mind. "You will be alone, won't you, dear?" he asked.

"That is to say, you don't plan to bring that twin sister of yours, do you?"

"Oh, no," Jessica assured him. "I'm working on this story all by myself."

Thank goodness, he thought, as Jessica chatted on about her internship.

It was remarkable that a guileless girl like Jessica could have an identical twin who was so nosy and suspicious, Pembroke thought. Elizabeth was the Wakefield he had to watch out for. She spent entirely too much time peering into dark corners with those big blue-green eyes, and scribbling endlessly in that little notebook of hers. It was no wonder she had hooked up with young Mr. Shepherd. Pembroke's lips tightened into a thin, hard line at the thought of the boy. The young poet made him unspeakably uncomfortable. Every time he looked at Luke, he felt battered by the accusations in the boy's brilliant blue eyes. Elizabeth's choice of Luke as a companion made her doubly suspect in Pembroke's book.

"Lord Pembroke?" Jessica asked uncertainly.

"I'm sorry, dear," he said, grateful that he was speaking to charming Jessica rather than her nosy sister. "What were you saying?"

"I just asked if Lady Pembroke has said anything about me to you. I'm afraid I was a little too assertive when I interviewed her yesterday. She may be a bit upset with me."

"Don't worry yourself," he assured her. "Lady Pembroke hasn't breathed a word to me." He didn't mention the fact that he and his wife had barely spoken to each other in years—seventeen years, to be exact. "And I'm sure you acted quite properly," he added. "A good reporter must be aggressive." *But don't tell your sister I said that.*

An uncharacteristic wave of sentiment swept over Pembroke, sparked by the girl's cheerful innocence and her fondness for his unfortunate son.

"Miss Wakefield—no, *Jessica*," he began. "I owe you a debt of gratitude, my dear. And a Pembroke always pays his debts."

"I don't understand."

No, of course she wouldn't. The changes she had wrought in Robert had come about naturally, just from being near her sweet influence.

"Jessica, you must realize that you're very different from other young ladies Robert has courted in the past. You wouldn't like them—a pretentious, stuffy, empty-headed lot. What I'm trying to say is that Robert has been quite a handful to discipline, at times. He's never been a bad youth, just rambunctious—untamed. But since he's been courting you, I've noticed a change. My son has more direction than he did even a short while ago. He's more responsible. And I'm certain that he's happier than he's ever been. I owe all of that to you."

The girl seemed at a loss for words.

"Jessica," Pembroke concluded soberly, "I want you to know that Robert loves you very much. Please remember that—no matter what happens."

Elizabeth paid the taxi driver and began walking up the long driveway to Pembroke manor through a misty rain.

Convincing Tony to let her cover the ostrich story had been easy. Eliana was right—ostriches were weird enough to catch his interest, but minor enough so that he didn't want to send a more senior reporter. Of course, Jessica had glowered at both of them as Tony told Elizabeth to go ahead with it. Jessica had been aching for a chance to return to Pembroke Manor; she must have realized that this story would put Elizabeth right in the neighborhood. Elizabeth felt bad about sticking her sister with today's Bumpo cases, but she knew that her investigation was more important than Jessica's jealousy.

Elizabeth sighed, thinking of what Lord Pembroke had said on the phone that morning. He had sounded so different from his usual overbearing self. He had been vulnerable—grateful, even. In other words, he had sounded like a normal, concerned father. And he thought Jessica was helping his son. For a moment, Elizabeth wondered if she and Luke were wrong about Robert and his family. But she didn't want to have sympathy for the Pembrokes; that could get in the way of her investigation.

She forced herself to remember Joy Singleton's body in Jessica's bed, and knew she had to find proof of the murderer's identity. *Even if it turns out to be the young Robert Pembroke*, she thought, remembering his father's words. Especially if it turned out to be Robert.

Elizabeth cleared the crest of the hill, and the front of stately Pembroke Manor rose into sight. Elizabeth gasped. Red lights flashed through the rain, from an ambulance that waited in front of the mansion's grand entranceway. Uniformed police officers and medical personnel rushed around the ambulance, while servants huddled together on the front portico, watching.

"Jessica," Lord Pembroke said in a distracted voice as he caught sight of Elizabeth. "In all the commotion, I quite forgot you would be arriving. You're welcome to stay, of course. But there's been an unfortunate incident. I'm not certain when I may be able to speak with you."

"What's happened?" Elizabeth asked.

Instead of answering, Pembroke placed a hand on her shoulder. Elizabeth was surprised to feel it trembling.

"Jessica," he said. "See that you don't mention today's, er, event to anyone at the newspaper—including that sister of yours. It is the subject of a police investigation, so any publicity at this time would be inappropriate." He spoke quietly, but his voice held a note of thinly disguised panic.

"Oh, you can count on me," Elizabeth assured him. "But I will stay, if you don't mind. Can you tell me what's—"

Before she finished speaking, Pembroke had turned away, satisfied, and was hurrying toward Constable Atherton, who was awaiting him near the ambulance with her arms folded impatiently in front of her.

Elizabeth approached the house and skirted the row of parked police cars. As she neared the clustered servants, she saw that most of them were weeping. "What in the world is going on?" she asked under her breath. "And is it related to the deaths of Joy and the others?"

She quickly decided on a course of action. After she learned what had just happened, she would slip inside the manor house and search for clues about the werewolf's identity and the Pembrokes' part in the murders.

Two servants passed close to where Elizabeth stood behind a hedge. ". . . found murdered this morning," she heard one of them say, before the couple moved out of earshot.

"Who was found murdered?" Elizabeth asked herself, out loud.

A moment later, she had her answer. Alistair, the tall, thin butler who had served tea on the morning of Joy's death, was led, sobbing, out of the house. Behind him, two paramedics carried a stretcher bearing what Elizabeth knew was a sheet-covered corpse. The constable lifted the sheet, and Elizabeth gasped.

On the stretcher lay the body of the Pembrokes' pretty, brown-haired cook, Maria Finch. Even from a distance, Elizabeth could see on her throat a bright red gash.

Chapter 7

Eliana took a dripping saucepan from David on Tuesday afternoon and began rubbing it with her dish towel.

"Working at the shelter's soup kitchen with you today has been just super, Lina," David said, plunging his hands back into the soapy water. "So many people are less fortunate than we are. Nothing can compare to the feeling of knowing you've helped people who are down on their luck."

Eliana grinned. As she had told Elizabeth the night before, David was different from any boy she had ever dated. She tried to imagine self-centered Harry Camden, the prime minister's nephew, rolling up his cuff-linked sleeves to scrub pots in a soup kitchen. The image wouldn't come.

"I feel the same way about working with the poor," Eliana said, taking a large skillet from him. "Someday, I'd like to do something for them that's bigger than this—something that would make a real difference in people's lives."

David nodded solemnly. "The need is there, certainly. I served lunch to a woman with a broken arm. And to a man with cataracts. And to a little boy who couldn't stop coughing. Do these people have any means of receiving free medical services?"

"Not in this neighborhood," Eliana said with a sigh. "The nearest clinic is more than a dozen blocks away. I remember an announcement, at the opening ceremonies for this shelter, that a clinic was being planned, as well. But the funding fell through."

"That's a shame!" David said. Eliana felt a warm rush of love at the sincerity in his voice. "You know, Lina, if I had a lot of money, I would use it to fund the facilities for proper medical treatment for these people. And then instead of studying literature, I would put myself through medical school, so I could administer the treatment myself."

Then he looked at her curiously. "But Lina," he said, confused, "did you just say you were at the opening ceremonies for this shelter? That was several years ago. I thought this was your first visit to London."

Eliana chastised herself for the slip. Her mother considered her too young to be the royal family's representative at such events as the ribbon-cutting ceremony at the city's new homeless shelter—though it was one of the few royal duties she would have relished. But in this case, she had accompanied her older sister, Gloria, who despised such events. Of course, she couldn't let David know she had been there.

"Oh, I wasn't actually there!" she said breezily, keeping her eyes on the soup tureen she was drying. "One of the managers here told me about the ceremony. I would have been back in Liverpool at the time of it, of course."

"Ahh, Liverpool," David said, looking almost satisfied with her explanation. "I used to help out occasionally at a shelter there. Perhaps you know of it—it's not far from the Lime Street station—"

"Oh, I'm certain that I don't know it," Eliana interrupted. "My mother is quite overprotective. She would never allow me to work in this sort of place at home. That's one of the reasons I left, really." *At least, I'm not lying to him about that much.*

David's handsome face took on a thoughtful expression. "It's unfortunate that your mother feels that way," he said. "Helping people who are in need is just about the most important thing in the world. That's why I'd like to use my skills someday to treat the illnesses of the poor and the homeless."

Eliana looked at him admiringly. "The other young people I know who aspire to medical school are planning to specialize in diseases of the rich. What an empty life that would be."

"Most people think I'm insane!" David replied bitterly. "They tell me how much more money I could make in a specialty like plastic surgery." He gazed deep into her eyes. "But not you, Lina. That's what I love about you. You're so down-to-earth."

Eliana's breath caught at the word *love*. David hadn't exactly said he loved her, but he had come close. Part of her longed to hear him use those words, and then to repeat them back to him. On the other hand, the very thought of it sent her into a panic. Was she leading David on? Did she have any right to become this close to a boy she knew would hate her when he learned the truth about her?

David began to place his hands on her shoulders as though he was about to kiss her on the lips. Then he remembered the soapy dishwater that dripped from his fingers, and stopped, laughing. He leaned over to kiss her lightly on the forehead, holding his wet hands away from her.

"We're almost finished here," he said. "What do you say we spend the rest of the day sight-seeing together? Have you been to the Portobello Road flea market? We ought to make use of the free afternoon. Two working-class blokes from Liverpool don't often get the chance to explore the big city."

Elizabeth stood in Robert's room at Pembroke Manor on Tuesday afternoon, feeling guilty about prowling around his bedroom. *Maybe I should have just stayed in London,* she thought.

Elizabeth sighed, impatient with her own indecision. She had been thinking in circles all day—ever since the phone call to Lord Pembroke that morning. His gratitude toward Jessica made her feel reluctant sympathy toward the father and son. Maybe she was totally off base, suspecting them of murder. But then she remembered the odd way Lord Pembroke had ended their telephone conversation.

"I want you to know that Robert loves you very

much," he had said. *"Please remember that—no matter what happens."*

No matter what happens? "What does that mean?" she asked herself aloud, for the tenth time that day. "Does it mean that Lord Pembroke is protecting his son? Is young Robert Pembroke a serial murderer—and a werewolf?"

She felt a prickling along her spine and was grateful that Jessica was not planning to see Robert that day. *And after today, I might have enough evidence to keep her from seeing him ever again.*

The scene that had taken place in front of the mansion a half hour earlier played back in Elizabeth's mind. Most of all, she remembered the sight of Alistair's slender shoulders shaking with anguished sobs as Maria's body was brought out of the house. The recollection of the cook's body helped Elizabeth steel herself for prying into Robert's belongings. She had to know, beyond any doubt, if he had killed Maria and the other victims.

As Elizabeth prepared to search the room for clues, the question she had tried to banish from her mind suddenly shoved its way to the forefront. Was Maria dead because of Elizabeth's investigation? Had somebody discovered that the servants had spoken to her? Perhaps the werewolf had seen Maria at the end of the upstairs corridor, just after the murder. Or perhaps Robert—or whoever the murderer was—had been outside the kitchen door, listening to every word of Elizabeth's interrogation of the servants. Was it her fault that Maria was dead?

She shook her head. "I won't think about that

right now," she whispered. "The most important thing now is to prove who the murderer is. If it's Robert Pembroke, something in this room ought to tell me that."

She started poking around Robert's spacious bedroom, unsure of exactly what she was searching for. But when she opened the door to the enormous walk-in closet, Elizabeth gasped. She finally had her proof.

Hanging inside the closet door was a paisley-patterned silk bathrobe, in hunter green—with a small tear on one shoulder.

With trembling hands, Elizabeth removed the envelope from her backpack and pulled out the threads she had taken from the doorway at the murder scene. The bathrobe was a perfect match. Robert Pembroke had been in the room where Joy Singleton was murdered!

Elizabeth jumped at the sound of approaching footsteps. She shoved Robert's bathrobe into her backpack to study later, and ran out into the hallway, seconds before a white-haired chambermaid appeared.

"May I help you?" the maid asked in a distracted voice. Elizabeth saw tearstains on her face, and knew she was grieving for the murdered cook. "It's Miss Jessica Wakefield, isn't it?"

"That's right," Elizabeth said, trying to control her excited breathing. She smiled tentatively, showing the dimple in her left cheek. "I'm afraid I'm lost in this big house," she said solemnly. "Can you direct me to, uh, the library?"

The library was the first thing that popped into

Elizabeth's head, and she wanted to kick herself as soon as she said it. Nobody who knew Jessica would believe she was searching for a library.

Elizabeth let out a sigh of relief as the maid gave her directions. *Of course, nobody here knows Jessica well enough to be suspicious of a statement like that.*

When Elizabeth pushed open the double doors to the library, she gazed admiringly at the huge, well-stocked room. She closed the doors behind her carefully and began wandering around the ceiling-high shelves, reading the titles. As always, Elizabeth was fascinated by books.

Like every room at Pembroke Manor, the Pembroke library was richly decorated in a style Elizabeth thought of as very English. This room had a masculine look, with a big mahogany desk in one corner and accents of burgundy leather everywhere. Grouped on the desk and arranged on one wall was a collection of formal family portraits in gilt-edged wood frames.

She stood for a moment in front of the wall of portraits. The largest was a studio photograph of Robert, standing in the full riding attire that Jessica had described from her first meeting with him. He looked just as he always did to Elizabeth—handsome, smug, and self-important.

But the books were what held Elizabeth's attention. She pulled out a copy of *Wuthering Heights*—a first edition, she was sure—and lovingly fingered its well-dusted leather spine. Then she pushed it back onto the shelf, forcing herself to remember her mission. She began looking for clues.

When she saw Robert Louis Stevenson's *The Strange Case of Dr. Jekyll and Mr. Hyde,* Elizabeth forgot her resolve once more. She had started to read the book last week at HIS and hadn't had a chance to get back to it since. Well, Pembroke had told her to make herself at home. Perhaps he wouldn't mind if she borrowed it for the evening, to read in bed. She reached up and began to pull the book from the shelf.

Elizabeth heard a loud click. She whirled guiltily, and her eyes widened with astonishment. A leather-covered panel in the wall had sprung open. Pulling out the volume had triggered a secret door!

"Even the walls here aren't what they seem," she whispered breathlessly.

Then Elizabeth pushed open the secret door and walked slowly into the small, dark room.

Jessica sighed dramatically. "But what's wrong with my sentence?" she asked, jabbing at Tuesday's Bumpo story on her computer screen. "It says 'the man who was arrested stole a single shoe from each of seventeen women!' What right do you have to make me change it?"

"Don't be angry at me," Luke said. "You know Tony asked me to help you with your article, in Elizabeth's absence. Actually, I think you've done a fine job, except that you can't say the man stole the shoes, because you don't know that for sure."

"Yes, I do," Jessica said. "I heard him tell Sergeant Bumpo he likes clogs the best—with platform heels. Face it, the guy is loony tunes. Even

Sergeant Bumpo says he's definitely the thief."

"He probably is," Luke conceded. "Nonetheless, you can't say so in the newspaper before he's been convicted of the crime. Until then, you have to say he's *suspected* of stealing the shoes."

Jessica sighed again. Life wasn't fair. She should be out in the country, covering a story within dropping-in distance of Pembroke Manor. And Elizabeth should be sitting here, listening to Luke tell her what's wrong with her article.

Of course, she admitted to herself, if Elizabeth had written it, there probably wouldn't be anything wrong with it. Jessica knew that writing wasn't her greatest talent. Still, it was humiliating to be told she needed a tutor. Besides, she was still mad at Elizabeth for hating Robert, so by extension, she was mad at her sister's boyfriend, too.

Jessica's only consolation was the knowledge that Elizabeth would get stuck with the Bumpo stories tomorrow, while Jessica and Robert drove out to Stonehenge, alone, in his silver convertible. She'd like to see the look on Elizabeth's face tomorrow, when she realized Jessica wasn't going to accompany her to the newspaper. She hoped Bumpo would dig up something particularly trivial and ridiculous to be reported on in Wednesday's *Journal*.

"I trust Robert has been showing you some of the high points of our fair country," Luke said after Jessica had sent the computer file to be printed. Jessica was surprised by his amiable tone.

"Yes," she boasted. "As a matter of fact, we're driving into the countryside tomorrow, to visit

Stonehenge—just the two of us, alone in the country!"

"You seem to have become very close to Robert in a short time," Luke said.

Jessica smiled, thinking of Robert. "Yes, I have," she answered happily. "I haven't felt this way about anyone in a long time. Consider me officially in love!"

"And does Robert return your feelings?" Luke asked, looking at her intently.

Jessica nodded. "Of course he does." Then she wrinkled her forehead. "Elizabeth didn't ask you to give me a big-brotherly talk about why I shouldn't love Robert, did she?"

Luke laughed, but his eyes looked troubled. He absentmindedly pulled a silver key chain from his pocket and began drumming it on the desk. "No—though I have to admit that the Pembrokes are not my favorite family."

Jessica bristled.

"Don't be upset, Jessica. I promise not to get big brotherly."

Jessica stared at him for a moment, until she was satisfied that he was telling the truth. Then she noticed his key chain and pointed to it. "Hey, that looks just like that weird necklace you gave Elizabeth. Do you really believe that werewolf stuff, or are you just putting my sister on?"

Luke laughed, then said, "I've been studying werewolves for a long time, Jessica. My mother was sort of an enthusiast; she got me interested when I was a small child. And after all these years of study, I've reached the conclusion that werewolves really do exist."

He gazed at her intently, and even Jessica had to admit that his startlingly blue eyes had a sexy, almost hypnotic quality. Then Luke recited in a solemn voice:

> "Through darkened wood he runs alone;
> White teeth gleam like sharpened bone.
> Wolfsbane bloom is softly kissed
> By moonlight drifting through the mist.
> By day he wishes no one ill;
> At night he hungers for the kill."

Jessica felt a shiver run down her spine, as if she ought to be looking over her shoulder. "Did you write that?"

Luke smiled, looking perfectly normal again. "Well, yes," he admitted. "But I'm still working on it, really. Do you like it?"

Jessica hesitated, uncertain. "It's kind of spooky."

"Good. It's supposed to be."

Suddenly, Jessica thought she knew what Luke was up to. She shook her finger at him. "I get it! You're trying to scare my sister so you can play the big, strong boyfriend. Well, you don't have to worry about me. I won't tell her your secret; I'm not even speaking to her."

"No, Jessica. It's not like that—"

"I don't know why Elizabeth is such a wimp all of a sudden," Jessica continued, "but I don't scare so easily. You poets are too weird. I'm just glad I'm dating a *normal* guy."

Chapter 8

Elizabeth groped for a light switch and stared around her. The secret room was a small, book-lined study.

Animal skins and heads adorned the walls, as in the dining room. But the dining-room animals were from African safaris. The animals in this room were wolves, leering down at her with their teeth bared.

"The wolves' den!" she whispered, spooked.

The room was stuffy, but Elizabeth shivered.

She caught sight of some of the titles of the leather-bound books, and her mouth dropped open. It seemed that every book in the room had something to do with werewolves. She suppressed a shudder. "Lord Pembroke must be some kind of werewolf fanatic," she whispered, more because of the eeriness of the room than out of a fear of being discovered. "How creepy!"

Then she remembered that Luke was also a serious student of werewolf lore. But, she told herself loyally, there was nothing creepy about Luke's fascination with the subject—not like Lord Pembroke's obsession. Collecting werewolf books and wolf heads and hiding them in a secret room was downright weird.

Still, Elizabeth had to admit that Luke would love this place. She couldn't wait to tell him about it.

For a moment, Elizabeth considered calling him. She eyed the telephone that sat on a small, cluttered desk in the center of the room. Then she shook her head. Her time for searching for clues was too limited to spend it talking on the phone; she would tell Luke later. But she did notice that the phone number was not the one she had used to call Pembroke that morning. The werewolf room was so secret it even had its own telephone number. She wondered if that was to keep people from picking up other extensions in the house and hearing Pembroke's private conversations.

Elizabeth turned to the crowded bookshelves and scanned the titles. Unlike the well-kept volumes in Lord Pembroke's main library, most of the books in the werewolf room were blanketed with a layer of dust. Obviously, not even the servants knew about this room.

Elizabeth selected a beautifully bound volume, a sixteenth-century French work called *Discours de la Lycanthropie*. "Discourses on Lycanthropy," she translated aloud. Before coming to England, she had never heard of lycanthropy. Now, she knew the term was used both for the study of werewolves and for the delusion that a person has turned into a wolf. The book fell open in Elizabeth's hands. She blew the fine powder from the title page and read an inscription written in graceful, elongated script: "To Robert. With all my love, Annabelle."

The inscription was dated twenty years earlier, so Elizabeth knew the words had been written to the elder Lord Pembroke, rather than his son. "But who is Annabelle?" she asked aloud. The inscription sounded as if it had been written by a lover—but certainly Lord and Lady Pembroke had been married at the time; Robert was twenty years old.

But Lady Pembroke's first name was not Annabelle.

Elizabeth's imagination began to race. Had Lord Pembroke and Annabelle had a tragic love affair, twenty years earlier? Was that the scandal Eliana had mentioned? And where was Annabelle now?

For a moment, Elizabeth felt a twinge of sympathy for Lord Pembroke, but she pushed it aside, chastising herself for being too sentimental. She was here to solve a mystery and capture a killer, not to moon over a twenty-year-old romance.

Elizabeth stared thoughtfully at the inscription. "Could Annabelle be the key to the mystery?" she asked herself aloud.

Elizabeth didn't know, but she was determined to find the answers.

"Earth to Lina and David!" Emily called, waving her hand between her two friends' faces, as a group of HIS residents sat on the front steps of the dormitory Tuesday evening. "Stop gazing longingly into each other's eyes for a moment, will you? We have serious business to discuss."

Eliana and David both blushed.

"You're both about as red as that double-decker bus that just passed by!" Gabriello Moretti said gleefully, pretending to play a cadence with a pair of imaginary drumsticks. "I suppose that means you had a pleasant afternoon." He winked at Rene.

Eliana blushed again. "So, Emily, what's this important business we have to discuss?"

"We must determine what we're going to do tonight, of course. I'm as bored as a kangaroo in a body cast. How about it, Jessica? You're always a good one for ideas."

Jessica shrugged her shoulders. "I don't know."

"Where's Elizabeth tonight?" David asked.

Ooops, Emily thought. *Bad subject.*

Jessica grimaced. "Miss Newspaper Reporter is out in the countryside for the evening, covering the story of the century: 'Farmer Raises Flamingos.'"

"Ostriches," Eliana corrected.

Jessica stared at her. "How did you know about that? Tony didn't approve the story until today."

Eliana shrugged innocently. "Elizabeth told me last night that she was going to ask Tony if she could write about them."

"Whatever," Jessica said airily. Then Jessica bit her lip sadly, and Emily realized that Jessica missed her twin sister, despite their argument.

"And I suppose Portia has a performance of *A Common Man* tonight," Rene said.

"That's right," Eliana said. "So what shall the rest

114

of us do with ourselves tonight? I don't think we want to sit here on the steps all evening, complaining about how bored we are."

Emily snapped her fingers. "I have an idea! I've heard about a posh comedy club in Soho. The admission's supposed to be a little pricey, but it'll be worth it. The place is called Comic-kazi."

"That won't work," Eliana said offhandedly. "Comic-kazi is closed on Tuesdays."

Emily stared at her, surprised that Lina would be so familiar with the fashionable London club. This wasn't the first time the working-class girl from Liverpool had revealed a surprising knowledge of London society. Emily noticed that David looked at Lina, too, his face full of anxiety.

"How did you know that, Lina?" Emily asked.

Eliana blushed again. "I suppose I must've read about it somewhere."

"Is anyone in the mood for a film?" Rene asked.

"I don't think so," Jessica said glumly.

"There aren't many good movies out that I haven't seen," Emily said.

"I've got it!" Gabriello said. "A friend of mine is in a band that's playing at the Pink Zebra tonight."

"The Pink Zebra?" David said. "Sounds trendy!"

Emily grinned. "It is! I've read about it in one of the tabloids—it's where the fashionable crowd goes when they feel a need for punking out!"

Even Jessica seemed to brighten.

But Eliana shifted uncomfortably on the concrete step. "I hope you have a wonderful time," she said, yawning. "But I think I'll bow out and get to bed early. I'm a bit tired all of a sudden."

Eliana jumped up from the step and disappeared into the dorm.

"What's with her?" Emily asked. "Just a few minutes ago, she was as eager to go out as any of us."

David sighed and shook his head. "I don't know," he said, almost in a whisper. "Sometimes I don't understand Lina at all."

Elizabeth leaned over Lord Pembroke's ornately carved mahogany desk early on Wednesday morning. Her search of the library and werewolf room had been interrupted the day before when a servant came to dust the library. Elizabeth had barely made it out of the hidden room in time.

She resolved to be more careful today. Elizabeth hadn't seen Lord Pembroke since her arrival the day before; she hoped he was still in bed that morning. Certainly, Maria's murder had made Pembroke forget all about the interview he was supposed to have with "Jessica" today. But that was fine with Elizabeth. She thought she had a better chance of finding something useful if she could manage some uninterrupted time for sleuthing around Pembroke Manor.

So far, Elizabeth's trip had been successful. The green robe was circumstantial evidence, but it did implicate Robert for Joy's murder. And the werewolf room was interesting, though Elizabeth wasn't sure how Lord Pembroke's obsession with werewolves tied in to the murders. What did it mean? Had Lord Pembroke known all along that his son was a werewolf? Was his study of lycanthropy an effort to understand more about Robert's condition? No, she decided. The date on Annabelle's gift book proved that Pembroke had been interested in werewolves at least since the time of Robert's birth. So what did it all mean?

Elizabeth sighed. Despite her discoveries, she still hadn't even found solid proof that the younger Robert Pembroke was a werewolf and a murderer. But time was running out; her train would leave for London in a few hours.

"Annabelle," she said aloud, thinking of the inscription on the werewolf book. "I don't know why, but I know she's important to all of this."

Elizabeth slowly opened the top drawer of Pembroke's desk and immediately saw what she was looking for—an address book.

"Annabelle," she said again, thumbing through the pages as quickly as she could. "Why couldn't Annabelle have signed her last name on her inscription, too?"

She laid the address book back in the drawer and sighed heavily. Of the entries that listed first names, not a single one mentioned an Annabelle. Then she turned and scrutinized the shelves until she saw what looked like a college yearbook. From the date on the spine, she guessed it was Pembroke's yearbook.

"Oxford," she said. "Naturally."

She flipped through the pages until she found his photograph.

"Lettered in crew and polo," she read. "Debating Society, Dramatics Society, Hunt Club."

Not much help there. Elizabeth leafed through the back section of the book, where several pages had

117

been left blank for signatures. She scanned the pages for the elegant, elongated handwriting she had memorized from the inscription in the werewolf book. There was no Annabelle.

"I guess I'll try the wolves' den one last time," she said under her breath, reaching for the copy of *Jekyll and Hyde* that she now knew would trigger the secret door.

As her fingers grazed the volume, Elizabeth froze. She could hear Lord Pembroke's voice, just outside the library doors.

Elizabeth dove under the mahogany desk as Pembroke strolled into the room, followed by Andrew Thatcher. Then she clapped her hand over her mouth in consternation—the secret door had clicked open and was standing slightly ajar. If Pembroke or Thatcher noticed it, they would surely discover her.

"Yesterday's murder was the last straw," Thatcher said after he had closed the double doors behind them. Elizabeth noticed that the police chief looked thinner and more haggard than just a couple days earlier; Joy's death was apparently taking its toll on him. "I know we agreed that the killer would be apprehended more quickly if we kept it out of the newspapers. And that due to your expertise you would, in a sense, carry on your own investigation." He ran his hand through his dark hair, making it stand on end. "But I can't risk any more lives, Robert. We have to bring this monster in. My detectives at Scotland Yard are breathing down my neck. They suspect that you know more than you're telling—and I think so, too."

Pembroke began pacing. Elizabeth held her breath as he approached the secret door; she let it out, relieved, as he passed by the door without stopping.

"Just a little more time, Andrew," Pembroke pleaded. "We've known each other since boyhood—trust me for a few more days. You know that we're onto something big here, but we can't afford to play our hand too early."

"We can't afford to wait!" Thatcher yelled. "Four people have died! How many more will it take? I know you have evidence of who it is—"

"But Andrew," Pembroke argued.

"Don't try to deny it," Thatcher said. "I've gone along with you until now, but no longer. I don't care how long we've been friends. Robert, I have to know what you know. Tell me who the evidence points to, and hand over any clues you have—regardless of who they implicate."

Pembroke shook his head nervously. "I don't think that's a good idea. The evidence I've found is misleading. It points to an innocent man!"

What evidence can he have? Elizabeth wondered, thinking of the large portrait of Robert on the wall. *Does Lord Pembroke suspect Robert, too?* Then she cringed as he passed near the partially open door to the werewolf room.

"That's what police investigations are for," Thatcher said. "You just hand over the evidence, and let us decide if it warrants an arrest. Don't worry. We'll have to be bloody sure of the evidence before we accuse a man of being a werewolf!"

Elizabeth's eyes widened. Pembroke and Thatcher

119

had known all along about the werewolf!

"But if I have all the evidence," Thatcher continued, "I can put out a warrant for the suspect's arrest. Then we can question him and arrive at the truth of the matter."

Pembroke sat down heavily in the desk chair, and Thatcher took over the pacing. Beneath the desk, Elizabeth scooted as far away from his knees as she could get, plastering her body against the opposite side. For a moment, Pembroke sat with his elbows on the mahogany surface, cradling his forehead in his hands.

"All right," he said reluctantly, his voice muffled. "I'll turn over the evidence. But not right now. Let me talk to him first." He hesitated. "Perhaps I can coax him to quietly turn himself in for questioning—although, as I told you, I'm certain he's innocent."

He pushed the chair out from the desk and turned to Thatcher. The police chief stopped pacing and stood with his arms folded—directly in front of the door to the werewolf room.

Elizabeth stiffened, willing the police chief not to turn around and see that the leather-covered panel was slightly open.

"I'll allow you until ten o'clock tonight to give me the evidence," Thatcher said. "But that's it! If you can convince your friend to turn himself in, then perhaps the law will go easier on him. But if you even think about changing your mind, Robert, remember that I can subpoena you to turn over any evidence you've found."

Pembroke nodded wordlessly.

"Our friendship is important to me, Robert," Thatcher said. "But you know I could lose my job if anyone finds out I've been allowing you to withhold evidence."

"I understand, Andrew. And I appreciate your co-operation. You're a good friend."

Thatcher strode across the room to the double doors of the library and then turned to face Pembroke again. "Do me a favor, Robert," he said. "Tell Reeves to ease up on the princess hype. It's making us look like we're not doing our job!"

After the police chief had left, Lord Pembroke stood in front of Robert's portrait. "The evidence must be wrong," he said in a determined voice. "My son is not a killer—or a werewolf! I refuse to believe it. I'll clear your name, Robert," he vowed, eyes fierce with determination. "I promise I will."

Lord Pembroke stared up at his son's portrait, slowly shaking his head. Robert was innocent. Of that, he had no doubt.

Perhaps he was misinterpreting the evidence he'd found—the cigarette case from the Essex Street murder site and the green threads from Robert's silk bathrobe. Or perhaps someone else had planted the evidence, in order to frame his son. But who would do such a thing? And why?

The only thing he knew for sure was that he couldn't let the police arrest his son. Robert was no murderer. And Pembroke had promised himself years earlier that he would never let another scandal rock the Pembroke family name.

"I must warn Robert before I talk to Thatcher,"

he decided aloud. "He must disappear for a bit—allow me time to find the real werewolf."

He reached across the desk for the telephone, but then changed his mind. For this call, he needed the complete privacy of his hidden room, with its separate phone line. It would never do for a bumbling servant to happen upon him at an inopportune point in the conversation. *Too many people are investigating this case already,* he told himself, thinking about Jessica Wakefield's nosy sister scribbling in that notebook of hers. He would make the call from his secret study.

Pembroke reached for *The Strange Case of Dr. Jekyll and Mr. Hyde* to trigger the hidden door. Then he froze. The leather-covered panel was already open.

"That's odd," he said aloud, fighting down a feeling of panic. "I'm certain I didn't leave that door ajar." But nobody else even knew of the existence of the wolf den—not even his wife. "Annabelle is the only other soul who ever knew about this room, and that was years ago."

He stood in the doorway and gazed around his private study. Nothing seemed to have been disturbed. In fact, he felt the same rush of emotion that always engulfed him upon entering the secret room—an odd mixture of security, mystery, and passion. He and Annabelle had spent so many happy hours there, examining old documents and discovering new theories.

But the concerns of the present were too disturbing to allow more than a moment of nostalgia.

Somebody else had discovered his room. Perhaps one of the servants had pulled out *Jekyll and Hyde* while dusting, he told himself. He would have to investigate—after he called Robert.

He closed the hidden door carefully behind him as he walked into the little room.

Lord Pembroke had another mystery on his hands.

As soon as Lord Pembroke disappeared into the secret study, Elizabeth jumped out from under the mahogany desk and raced from the library. She leaped up the stairs, two at a time, to reach the telephone in the hallway outside her room. The information she had just overheard couldn't wait; she had to call Luke right away and fill him in on everything she had learned. It was lucky that the telephone Lord Pembroke was using in the werewolf den was on a separate line.

Elizabeth tapped her foot impatiently as the phone rang repeatedly on Luke's desk at the *Journal*.

"Rats!" she said aloud. "Where could he be?"

She dialed Tony's number instead.

"I'm not completely certain where Luke is this morning, Liz," Tony replied to her urgent question. "Out and about on an arts and entertainment scoop, no doubt. I've actually been able to get a lot of work done, with you and Luke out on your various stories, and Jessica spending the day with that young nobleman of hers—"

Elizabeth broke out in a cold sweat. *"Jessica is where?"*

"I assumed you knew," Tony said. "She took a holiday today to spend some time with the young Lord Pembroke. She didn't mention where they would be going."

Elizabeth's hands were trembling as she replaced the telephone receiver. Jessica was alone all day with a killer—and probably a werewolf!

Elizabeth knew she had to return to London immediately. She had to find Jessica—before it was too late.

Chapter 9

"They think you're the werewolf," Lord Pembroke told his son over the phone Wednesday morning. "I know you're not, of course, but soon the situation will be out of my control."

Robert's voice over the phone sounded impatient and a bit smug. "I didn't think anything was out of the control of the Pembroke family. Besides, the police have no proof against me."

"They will, soon," Pembroke replied ominously. "Thatcher has threatened to subpoena me if I don't tell him everything I know by ten o'clock tonight."

"I believe you're overreacting, Father."

"Overreacting? You don't seem to understand, Robert. The police will believe you are a serial killer and a werewolf. They'll put out a warrant for your arrest. And the newspapers will have a field day. There will be a horrible scandal, even if they determine there isn't enough evidence to bring you to trial."

"And what would you have me do, Father?"

"We can't let Thatcher's people bring you in for questioning. I must clear your name."

"How do you propose to do that?"

"I probably know more about werewolves than any living person in England. If anyone can track down the real werewolf, I can. Until then, I want you to disappear for a few days. Get out of town this morning—now!"

"I'm afraid that's not possible. I have plans for this morning. I'm—"

"Change your plans," Pembroke interrupted. "I'll get word to you when it's safe to return."

"All right, Father, if you insist. But I can't depart immediately, Father. I'd planned to meet somebody shortly—and our appointment is even more crucial, now that I know the police will be after me soon. I'll leave town as soon as I've finished."

Jessica jumped into the passenger seat of Robert's silver Jaguar.

"Why's the top up?" she asked, after kissing him good morning. "The London weather is actually co-operating, for a change. What's the use of having a convertible if you can't take advantage of a little good weather?"

"How are you this morning, Jessica?" Robert asked formally.

Jessica looked at Robert curiously. He seemed awfully distracted. His eyes hadn't even lingered on the outfit she'd chosen especially for the occasion—a short, breezy dress that showed off her shoulders and exactly matched the turquoise color of her eyes.

Well, Jessica knew the cure for a distracted boyfriend. A little bit of bright chatter would cheer him up right away—especially when combined with the prospect of spending the day together out in the country, just the two of them. She was confident that he would notice her outfit in no time.

"I'm so relieved to have the day off from that boring newspaper!" Jessica exclaimed. "Yesterday's story, the Case of the Clog Robber, just about did me in. You don't know how much I've been looking forward to our trip to Stonehenge today!"

Robert sighed, keeping his eyes focused on the road ahead of him. "I'm afraid there's been a change of plans," he said. "Let's go to the Connaught, shall we? I'll fill you in over breakfast."

Jessica felt her heart sinking. She rode the rest of the way in silence.

Jessica poked her fork at the uneaten eggs Benedict on her plate. She couldn't believe that Robert was canceling their date—and that he was leaving town.

"But where are you going?" she asked. "How long will you be gone?"

"I don't know," Robert said, reaching across the table to take her hand. "But you'll have to look out for yourself until I return. Unfortunately, I may not be able to contact you."

"Why not?"

Robert ignored her question. "Don't worry. As soon as I get back, I'll find you."

"Get back from where?"

"I can't tell you that. Just promise me you'll be careful while I'm away."

Jessica looked into his eyes and saw an intensity there that frightened her. "Robert, none of this makes any sense! It's bad enough that my sister's turned into a basket case. Now you're getting all paranoid on me, too!"

Robert shook his head. "It's not like that, Jessica. But I can't go into the particulars."

"Are you in some kind of trouble? Let me help you!"

"There's nothing you can do," he told her. "Just promise me you'll be careful!"

Jessica shrugged, unable to resist his intense gaze. "All right, Robert. I'll be careful." *Is everyone in England crazy?* she wondered, remembering a snatch of an old song about mad dogs and Englishmen.

Robert glanced at his expensive watch. "I'm in a terrible hurry, Jessica. Here's enough money to pay the breakfast bill and to take a cab anywhere in the city that you want to go. If anyone asks, tell them you didn't see me this morning."

He tossed a few notes on the table in front of her, and kissed her with an urgency that was disturbing—almost frightening.

Then Jessica watched sadly as Robert—the only guy she'd loved since Sam's untimely death—hurried away from her.

●　　○　　●

Elizabeth practically leapt off the train as soon as it pulled into Victoria Station.

"The customary procedure, miss," said an amused porter, "is to wait until the train has stopped before disembarking."

Elizabeth barely heard him as she ran toward a bank of telephones, all of which were in use. She shifted anxiously from one foot to the other as she waited for one of the callers to finish up.

My sister is in terrible danger! she wanted to scream. *Please let me use the phone.*

Elizabeth blamed herself. It was true that she had tried to warn her sister about the Pembrokes; Jessica wouldn't pay attention. But she should have tried harder.

She wished she had been able to get hold of Luke at the *Journal* that morning. Maybe he was back from his assignment by now. *Maybe he's seen Jessica—or knows where Robert was taking her!*

"Thank goodness for Luke," Elizabeth said under her breath. "I could never handle this alone."

A minute later, she was on the phone with Tony at the newspaper.

"Sorry, Liz. Luke isn't back yet. How are your ostrich friends?"

"Huh?"

"You know, the ostriches. The story you traveled all that distance for."

"Oh, fine, Tony. What about Jessica? Have you heard anything from her?"

"Well, no, Liz. But she's on a date with her beau. I

129

hardly. would expect her to check in with me. Is something wrong? You sound rather distraught."

After she hung up the phone, Elizabeth stood for a moment with her hand on the receiver, contemplating her next move.

"The police!" she said aloud. Her sister was with a murderer. Obviously, she should call the police. She lifted the receiver, but quickly dropped it. Andrew Thatcher was the only person on the police force who would believe her story, and he hadn't returned to London yet.

She could just imagine herself saying to anyone else on the police force: "Excuse me, Officer, but I need your help. My sister's in terrible danger. You see, she has this date with a werewolf."

No, the police weren't an option. With Luke unreachable, she would have to rescue Jessica all by herself. But first, she had to find her.

"When the going gets tough, the tough go shopping," Jessica said aloud, standing in front of Harrods as her taxicab pulled away from the curb.

She still couldn't believe Robert had canceled their excursion to Stonehenge; she had been eager to spend some time alone with him, far away from the distractions of the city and the prying eyes of her nosy sister.

Even more disturbing was Robert's evasiveness. Why was he leaving town so suddenly? Where was he going? And why couldn't he answer any of her questions?

For a moment, she wondered if Robert could be some sort of secret agent, on a dangerous mission. "Nah," she decided, dismissing the notion almost as soon as it occurred to her. The idea appealed to her sense of adventure, but it was almost as farfetched as Elizabeth's fears about werewolves. At least one Wakefield had to hang on to her senses.

To make matters worse, the clear sky of early morning was now shrouded in gray storm clouds. It looked as if it would rain again, after all.

Well, Jessica had always prided herself on her resourcefulness. She hadn't had a minute to hit Harrods since she'd arrived in London—thanks to her stupid internship at the *Journal*. Now was her chance. And Robert had made the opportunity even more tempting, by leaving her with a little money to spare after she had covered the restaurant bill and cab fare.

Jessica pushed open the door of Harrods solemnly, as if she were entering a temple. She sighed, feeling lonely for the first time since she'd arrived in England. *Lila Fowler, where are you when I need you?*

Immediately, Jessica was drawn, as if by a magnet, to a department full of high-class European fashions. A black-and-white culotte set beckoned from the rack.

If shopping wouldn't cheer her up, nothing would.

"I'm looking for a sixteen-year-old blond girl—" Elizabeth began frantically, speaking with a street vendor that afternoon, just outside of Kensington Gardens.

"Aren't we all?" the college-age boy replied with a sardonic grin.

"She looks just like me."

The vendor took in her size-six figure and long golden hair. "This is sounding better and better," he said with a wink.

Elizabeth stifled the urge to slap him. Instead, she turned and ran into the gardens.

Ever since Elizabeth had gotten off the train at Victoria Station, she had been racking her brain to think of places Jessica wanted to see in London but hadn't been to yet. Where in London would Robert and Jessica go on their date?

Elizabeth's first stop had been Bond Street, to see if her sister was window-shopping at any of the high-class stores. Jessica and Robert could even be doing some real shopping, Elizabeth realized, remembering the size of Robert's family fortune. Jessica would be thrilled to bring back a souvenir worthy of anything Lila Fowler owned. But the store clerks Elizabeth spoke to hadn't seen Jessica and Robert. If Jessica had succumbed to her addiction for buying clothes she couldn't afford, she hadn't done it on Bond Street.

Now Elizabeth was in the biggest park in the city—and a park with a palace in it, to boot. And, Elizabeth realized, it was a perfect place for a romantic stroll. She hurried along the garden path, peering down the long rows of sculpted shrubberies that branched off to both sides. It was a weekday, so the gardens weren't crowded. She could just imagine Jessica and Robert walking hand in hand between the manicured hedges, in a secluded part of the park— *when suddenly Robert turned to Jessica, and blood dripped from his fangs. . . .*

"Stop it!" Elizabeth said to herself, aloud. A woman pushing a baby stroller looked at her curiously and steered a wide path around her.

Elizabeth took a deep breath and wrenched her mind away from dramatic images of Jessica in danger. "I have to be calm and objective," she told herself under her breath.

She wished Luke were there, but she had called the newspaper again, from Bond Street, and he still hadn't returned from his assignment. She would try again soon, but for now she was still on her own for finding Jessica—if it wasn't already too late.

She noticed Kensington Palace up ahead and remembered how eager Jessica had been to visit it. Several members of the royal family were living in Kensington Palace, but parts of it were open for tours. Elizabeth was sure the royals wouldn't hang out with the tourists, but it would be just like Jessica to expect to see a princess or two—or better yet, a prince.

Elizabeth allowed herself a moment of irony: *Won't Jessica be surprised to learn she's been sharing a room with a real, live princess all this time?*

She prayed that her sister would live long enough to hear all about it.

"You look as if you're attempting to buy out the

whole store!" a young salesclerk exclaimed as Jessica lugged her shopping bags to a checkout counter in Harrods, clutching a lovely silk scarf that would go perfectly with the chic purple minidress she'd bought a few minutes earlier.

"I guess I am on a serious power-shopping binge," Jessica replied. "I'm trying to drown my troubles in store receipts."

Once again, she handed the clerk the credit card the twins' parents had given them for this trip—in case of emergency. If this wasn't an emergency, Jessica didn't know what was. Within the first half hour, she'd spent the rest of the money Robert had left. Since then, she'd been working on the credit card and hoping she hadn't reached its limit.

Besides buying overpriced European clothes, Jessica reflected while the clerk rang up the scarf, her only consolation was that Elizabeth must be back in town by now. *Maybe she's getting stuck with the latest Bumpo scoop, while I have the day off!*

Jessica's attention was caught by a display of Italian shoes. She sighed, knowing she was probably about to pay twice as much money as she would ever consider spending on a pair of shoes back home. But the medium-height heels with the violet panels of lizard-look leather would be perfect with her new minidress.

Suddenly, Jessica felt a prickling at the back of her neck. She had the distinct feeling that someone was watching her. For an instant, she plainly heard Robert's voice: *"Promise me you'll be careful."*

Jessica turned slowly, pretending to be engrossed in the shoe display, while she peered out of the corner of her eye. Nobody was there.

"It was just some nosy salesperson, spying on me," she speculated under her breath. "It's because I'm an American teenager trying on everything in the store."

Suddenly, Jessica was swept by a wave of depression. Even the shopping binge—usually one of her favorite activities—was leaving her feeling strangely empty.

She reviewed her mental list of whom she was mad at. She was ticked off at Elizabeth for interfering with her relationship with Robert. She was ticked off at Tony Frank for not letting her work on exciting, glamorous stories at the *Journal*. She was ticked off at the nasty English weather that stayed gray and rainy practically all the time. And she was ticked off at her parents for not being rich enough so that she could actually afford all this stuff she was buying.

Most of all, Jessica was ticked off at Robert for standing her up that morning and not explaining why. Nobody did that to Jessica Wakefield and got away with it. But Robert was getting away with it—and that made her ticked off with herself, for loving him so much that she would let him do this to her.

"He's hiding something from me," Jessica whispered. "And I don't like it one bit."

"What do you do when someone you care about is hiding something from you?" David asked Portia as the two walked toward HIS Wednesday afternoon. He was obviously trying to keep his voice sounding casual, but Portia could tell he was quite upset.

The two teenagers had run into each other on their way home. David was finished with classes for the day. Portia had come from a matinee performance of *A Common Man* and had several hours to rest before the evening show.

"When you love somebody, you're supposed to be honest with them," David continued. "But Lina is hiding something from me, and I don't know what it is. She claims to be from Liverpool, but she changes the subject every time I bring it up, as if she's ashamed of it. And sometimes she says the oddest things—as if she's lived a very different life from the one I would imagine. There's something strange in her past, Portia, but she won't confide in me at all. Maybe she doesn't really care about me, after all."

"Sometimes people keep secrets from one another because they do care," Portia said slowly. She was talking about Lina, but it was her father's image that popped into her mind. "If Lina is hiding something, maybe it's because she's afraid you wouldn't approve if you knew the truth." *Just like my father wouldn't approve if he knew I was appearing in a play.*

"But it would be better to know the truth!" David argued. "If you really love someone, then finding out their secrets wouldn't change that."

"Wouldn't that depend on the secret?" Portia asked.

David walked silently for a few yards. "I suppose so," he said. "But I think I deserve to know what Lina is hiding from me—no matter what it does to our relationship. She can't go on being dishonest with me, or the relationship doesn't stand a chance, anyhow!"

"If Lina is hiding something important, then I suspect she can't go on that way much longer," Portia said, realizing she was speaking about herself, as well. "A person can't hide behind a lie forever. The truth has a way of coming out eventually."

"So why doesn't she just tell me herself?"

"Perhaps she wants to tell you, but doesn't know how to broach the subject."

"Well, she'd better find a way," David said, pausing as they reached the front steps of the dormitory. "I love Lina, but I don't know how much longer I can continue in a relationship that's based on dishonesty."

"If you really love her, you should try to be patient with her," Portia urged. "But I suppose you're right. She can't hide from you forever—just as I can't hide from my father forever. I don't know if I've been of any help with your problem, David, but you've certainly helped me with mine. I've decided to find a way to tell Sir Montford Albert who Penelope Abbott really is. And I'm going to do it soon—while my father is in town this week. But I haven't the foggiest idea how."

The Knightsbridge tube station seemed strangely quiet as Jessica descended deeper and deeper underground. Of course, it wasn't yet rush hour, but Jessica was still surprised at the lack of activity on a Wednesday afternoon.

She maneuvered her bulky Harrods packages through the turnstiles. As she glanced down at the well-stuffed shopping bags, she felt a twinge of guilt about her high-priced shopping overdose.

"No way," she said under her breath. "I refuse to feel guilty about shopping. Robert abandoned me this morning. I deserved to have a fun day."

Then she sighed miserably, realizing that her day of shopping hadn't been the least bit fun.

Jessica walked along the yellow-tiled corridors to the train platform, listening to the echo of her footsteps through the dim, empty station. The platform was deserted. Jessica suppressed a shudder; the shadowy stillness made it easy to imagine that she was buried alive.

The silence seemed to wait, holding its breath. Jessica held her breath, too.

If I were skittish, she thought, *I'd call this eerie.* Elizabeth would probably call it eerie. But Elizabeth had turned into a paranoid chicken, after hearing a few of Luke's werewolf stories. Jessica was not paranoid. She forced herself to breathe normally, refusing to be scared by the fact that it was utterly silent in the cold, damp underground. Dead silent.

Suddenly, Jessica froze. A strange noise was coming out of the dark tunnel. It was a heavy, panting sound—definitely not the subway train.

And it was coming faster.

Jessica's eyes widened. She certainly wasn't going to wait around on the deserted platform to see if it was coming for her. She took off, running full speed down the platform, with her shopping bags bumping uncomfortably around her legs. She had to get away from the panting—away from something that was coming, faster and faster, out of the shadows. In a panic, she realized that the creature was rapidly catching up with her. She couldn't outrun it.

The panting was directly behind her. Jessica felt the creature's hot breath on the back of her neck.

Then she tripped and fell to the cold, tile floor.

Chapter 10

As Elizabeth raced through the door of the newspaper office on Wednesday afternoon, she plowed straight into Tony Frank, on his way out of the building in a rush.

"Sorry, Tony," she said breathlessly, as she helped him retrieve the notebook and tape recorder he'd dropped when she ran into him. "But I'm glad I caught you. I have to talk to you! It's urgent!"

"Not now, Elizabeth," he said brusquely. "Henry Reeves just informed me that a body was found at Pembroke Manor yesterday morning—there's no telling why the police didn't release the information yesterday. Not to mention Lord Pembroke himself. But I must head out there now to investigate."

Elizabeth opened her mouth to tell him Jessica's life was in danger, but Tony kept talking, in a frantic tumble of words.

"It's a nasty business, all right," he said. "Henry

heard a rumor that the dead woman might be Princess Eliana. So, as you can imagine, I've no time for a chat. Henry insisted that I write up a story, based on that rumor, so I have. But it would never do to run it in tonight's edition until it's substantiated. And nobody is willing to tell me anything over the phone."

He pushed past her and was about to rush out of the building, but Elizabeth's next words brought him to a halt.

"It's not the princess!"

Elizabeth's voice held such certainty that Tony turned to stare at her.

"It's not the princess," Elizabeth said again, feeling tears of frustration in her eyes. She was frantic about Jessica, and Tony was the only person she could turn to.

"I don't understand," he said. "How do you know it's not the princess?"

Elizabeth almost blurted out the whole story: *Because the princess is living in my dorm room and working in a soup kitchen.* But she stopped herself in time to keep Eliana's secret safe.

Elizabeth took a deep breath. "I was at Pembroke Manor yesterday morning when the body was carried out of the house. The dead woman is definitely not Princess Eliana. It's Maria Finch, the Pembrokes' cook. Please don't go, Tony. I've got to talk to you right now. It's about that murder, and another murder that could take place today if we don't stop it!"

Tony stared at Elizabeth for a moment, taking in her wide eyes and tense posture.

"All right," he said quietly, leading her back into

142

his office. "Let's hear what you have to say."

Jessica sprawled, facedown, on the cold floor of the subway platform, her fingers clenched around the handles of her forgotten shopping bags. Directly above her, something snarled; to Jessica, the noise seemed to echo off the vaulted ceilings, filling the deserted tunnels with terror and loathing.

Jessica tried to move, but her limbs wouldn't obey—as if she were paralyzed by fear in a nightmare that was terrifyingly real. The floor felt as cold as a tomb.

Something hairy brushed against the back of Jessica's arm. She stifled a scream. It was Elizabeth's werewolf. It had to be.

Jessica began to tremble. Hot breath seemed to singe the hairs on the back of her neck as the creature leaned over her. The panting filled her ears, like a sky full of thunder.

Then Jessica heard something else. Loud voices bounced off the walls of the corridors, coming closer. The heavy panting quieted to a low rumble, as if her attacker had stopped to listen.

"It's as if the firm were giving executives free lobotomies as a fringe benefit!" a man's voice boomed from a nearby corridor. A woman's voice responded: "Before they made her a vice president, Wanda was as reasonable as any of us—"

Then the hairy creature was gone. Through the pounding of her own pulse, Jessica vaguely heard it running away, down the empty platform.

For a moment, Jessica was too scared to move.

Then she picked herself and her shopping bags off the floor and dusted off her clothes. She was still alive. It hadn't gotten her.

Jessica stared around her wildly as she fought to catch her breath. Nobody, and no thing, was in sight. The hairy creature must have been swallowed up by the murkiness of the train tunnel.

She jumped at a harsh burst of laughter coming from behind her. But it was only a group of business-people in long raincoats, emerging onto the other end of the platform from the yellow-tiled corridor. The booming voice came from a tall man in a black bowler hat, who was loudly regaling the others with another anecdote about the new executive, Wanda.

Jessica wanted to ask the group for help, but she knew that her story would sound preposterous: "A big hairy thing attacked me on the tube platform. It must be the werewolf my sister's been looking for."

Instead, she shook her head and sighed loudly. Under her breath, she thanked the man with the bowler hat and the booming voice, for showing up when he did. He would never know it, but he had just saved her life.

Jessica's feud with her sister suddenly seemed unimportant. "I'll go to the newspaper office," she decided in a whisper, praying that Elizabeth and Luke would be there. "They're the werewolf hunters. They'll know what to do."

But the tube station was giving Jessica the creeps, after her encounter with her hairy assailant. She didn't think she could bear to wait there on the plat-form for the train; she would take a taxi instead.

Besides, it would be faster. She clumsily shifted a shopping bag from one hand to the other, to check her purse for the cab fare.

"Darn!" she said aloud, causing the man in the bowler hat to turn for a moment to look at her. Not only had her shopping spree topped the credit limit on her card, but it had also taken every last pence in her wallet.

Jessica had no choice now; she would have to wait for the subway. She edged closer to the cluster of people in raincoats, not daring to peer again into the depths of the murky train tunnel where she knew the hairy creature had disappeared.

But when she turned away from the tunnel, Jessica was gripped by terror. She imagined she still heard the panting behind her, and felt a pair of savage eyes boring hungrily into her back.

"You know, David really cares about you," Portia said to Eliana as the two girls sat down to tea in the dining room of HIS on Wednesday. "But he's upset. He thinks you don't trust him."

"I do trust David," Eliana said. "At least, I think I do."

"It's none of my business, Lina, but I hate to see a nice fellow like David get hurt. Besides, I think you love him, too. When you feel that way about someone, you should be honest with him."

Eliana's eyes glistened with sudden tears. "But what if David stops loving me when he knows what I really am?"

Portia was mystified. *What terrible secret can*

sweet, simple Lina be hiding? "David's not like that, Lina," she said gently. "You have to trust in his love for you, and let him know the truth—whatever it is."

"I could say the same thing about you and your father," Eliana reminded her.

Portia sighed. "My father doesn't care about the real me. He's made up his mind that I shouldn't be an actress, and that's that. He's so overprotective. I wish he would let me try myself, so I can succeed or fail on my own merits."

Eliana nodded her head. "I know what that's like. My mother is the *queen* of overprotection." She smiled enigmatically. "She barely lets me out of the pa—*house!*"

"That seems a bit extreme," Portia agreed.

"I guess it started when I was a baby," Eliana explained. "I was sick a lot, and I almost died once. So Mum's always been rather protective of me. To make matters worse, Glor—my older sister was kind of a swinger at my age. I suppose Mum's afraid I would be the same way if given the chance, even though my sister and I are nothing alike. I just wish she would trust me to make my own decisions."

Mrs. Bates bustled into the room. "Can I freshen your tea, Portia dear?" she asked, hovering over her.

"No, thank you, Mrs. Bates," Portia told her politely, annoyed at the interruption.

"I'll have some—" Eliana began, but the dorm mother didn't seem to hear her.

"Tell me, Portia, have you heard from your father lately? Did I tell you I saw him last year in *King Lear?*"

"Yes, you did, as a matter of fact—" Portia began, but the dorm mother kept talking.

"Sir Montford Albert! Now there's a fine figure of a man! Portia, dear, can I get you anything else to eat? I've got some lovely crumpets in the kitchen."

"No, thank you," Portia said, rolling her eyes at Eliana.

As soon as the door closed behind Mrs. Bates, Portia exploded. "I hate that!" she exclaimed. "Why do people treat you differently when they know you're 'upper class,' whatever that means? You know, that's one of the things I like about being Penelope Abbott. I want people to judge me by my actions, not my lineage." She sighed. "You don't know how lucky you are to be a normal person. But I guess that's hard for you to understand."

Eliana was staring at her intensely. "No, it's not," she said fervently. "I know exactly what you're talking about!" Then she softened her tone. "I mean, I notice the way Mrs. Bates and people like her act around you."

"I wish I didn't come from a famous family."

"But Portia," Eliana began slowly, as if she was just coming to a new realization. "Your lineage is part of you, too. More and more, I see that you can't hide who you really are. A person who really cares should accept you for the real you—all of you."

"So, are you going to trust David with the real you?"

"Yes," Eliana decided. Then she smiled, a little wistfully. "As soon as I can get up the nerve. Are you going to trust your father with the real Penelope Abbott?"

"Yes," Portia said, suddenly knowing exactly how to tell her father the truth about her. "And I'm going to do it today. I'm sending him tickets to tonight's performance of *A Common Man*. He's already judged me as his daughter. Now I want him to judge me as an actress."

Tony ushered Elizabeth into his office that afternoon and closed the door.

Elizabeth whirled to face him. "Has Jessica called in since the last time I talked to you?"

Tony shook his head impatiently. "You said you had urgent information about the murder, Liz! Do we have to waste time discussing your sister's social calendar?"

Elizabeth began pacing across the small office, terrified that Tony wouldn't believe her story. "This is about the murder," she said, her voice rising. "I think Jessica might be the next victim. We have to find her!"

"Whoa! Let's start at the beginning, shall we? Tell me what you know about the murder, and why you think Jessica is in danger. But first, stop that infernal pacing! You're making me dizzy."

Elizabeth perched nervously on the edge of his desk and told him about her investigation, beginning with eavesdropping outside the window of Cameron Neville's house more than a week earlier, and ending with Lord Pembroke's conversation in the library that morning.

A few minutes after she started, Luke walked into the office, looking for her. Elizabeth pecked him on the cheek gratefully, feeling her confidence returning. She filled him in on everything she had seen and heard since their last conversation—with the exception of the mysterious Annabelle, who had signed Lord Pembroke's book, "With all my love." Elizabeth still had no evidence that Annabelle was connected to the murders, except her own gut feeling. She decided she would tell Luke about the inscription later, when Tony wasn't around.

"Well, I can't say that I believe the murderer is an actual werewolf," Tony said at last. "Though I know that the elder Lord Pembroke has been a bit of a werewolf hobbyist for years. But it does sound as if you could make a murder case against young Robert Pembroke—if he's still in town. But, Liz, I still don't understand about the cook's murder yesterday. You say Pembroke was there. Why didn't he inform the newspaper? Did he actually believe we wouldn't find out?"

"I don't know what he believed. But he seemed panicky when they carried the body out yesterday— as if he wasn't thinking straight. And he specifically warned me not to tell anyone at the *Journal* about the murder."

Tony stared at her curiously. "So why are you telling me now? How do you know I'm not in league with Pembroke to cover up the murder stories?" He looked down at his shoes. "Lucy Friday seems to believe I am."

Elizabeth shrugged. "I know we can trust you," she said. "Besides, I'm afraid for Jessica. I never would have stayed at Pembroke Manor if I'd known she was spending the day alone with Robert. He's a werewolf and a serial murderer! If anything happens to Jessica, it will be all my fault!"

Luke put a hand on her shoulder. "Nonsense, Liz. Until you overheard Pembroke and Thatcher this morning, you had no solid evidence that Robert could be dangerous. You can't blame yourself."

"Actually," Tony said, "I'd like to bring this to Lucy. She's angry at me, of course, but I'm sure we can put our squabbles aside for something this important. She was certain that the newspaper was intentionally covering up the earlier murders. And she's a more experienced investigator than any of us. I'd like to hear her take on what you've just told me."

"More talking?" Elizabeth asked, jumping from her seat. "Why are we wasting time talking? We've got to find Jessica!"

As she spoke, the door behind her opened.

"You've found her," Jessica announced from the doorway.

Elizabeth whirled in time to see an unwieldy load of shopping bags thud to the floor around her sister.

"Thank goodness you're all right, Jessica!" she exclaimed. "I thought you were in danger. I—"

Suddenly, she noticed her sister's sweat-streaked face and disheveled hair. Jessica's bare-shouldered turquoise dress was smudged with dirt. But the most disturbing thing of all was the terrified look in Jessica's blue-green eyes.

"You were right, Liz," Jessica began breathlessly. "It's after me! It attacked me in the Knightsbridge tube station. It chased me from behind. It was getting closer. Then I fell flat on my face, and I could feel it leaning over me."

"*What* attacked you?" Tony asked, disturbed.

Jessica shook her head. "I'm not sure. It was big— at least, it was bigger than me. And it made an awful kind of panting, growling, snarly noise."

She shuddered visibly. "I was wrong, Liz," she said. "I never dreamed I'd be saying this, but I am starting to believe in werewolves. Whatever attacked me was pretty hairy."

Chapter 11

Jessica settled gratefully into the overstuffed couch in Lucy's flat. It was only midafternoon Wednesday, but it had been a long, terrible day, and Jessica was exhausted.

Lucy rolled the green silk threads between her fingers. "So you found these in the door frame of the room where Joy Singleton was killed?"

Elizabeth nodded. "With the piece of fur."

"Do you know where the threads come from?"

Elizabeth nodded again, more nervously this time. She glanced over at Jessica, bit her lip, and unfolded a large piece of fabric from her backpack—the green paisley silk bathrobe.

Jessica gasped. "That belongs to Robert! What are you doing with it?"

"It looks like an exact match for the pieces of fiber I found in the door frame," Elizabeth explained, handing the robe to Lucy.

"Where did you get Robert's robe?" Jessica asked suspiciously.

"I took it from his closet at Pembroke Manor last night. I was—"

Jessica jumped up from the couch. "What were you doing at Pembroke Manor last night? And why were you snooping through Robert's stuff? I swear, Elizabeth, just because you don't like Robert is no reason—"

"Please, Jessica," Lucy interrupted, smoothly but forcefully. "I'd like to hear what Elizabeth has to say."

Jessica scowled at Elizabeth, but sat down quietly. When Lucy spoke in that commanding tone, it was hard not to obey. Besides, Lucy was one of the few people here whom Jessica had sincere respect for. Lucy wasn't afraid of anything.

"We all know that the newspaper has been covering up details of the recent murders, and that there are some similarities between the deaths," Elizabeth began. "Luke and I had narrowed down the possible murder suspects to three people: Lord Pembroke, Lady Pembroke, and the younger Robert Pembroke—"

Jessica opened her mouth to protest, but closed it when Lucy raised a warning hand.

"So I went to Pembroke Manor yesterday to find evidence that would implicate one of them," Elizabeth continued.

"I thought you were writing about ostriches!" Jessica interrupted.

"The ostriches were a ruse," Elizabeth admitted. "I only used them as an excuse to get out of town."

Lucy looked perplexed. "What is this about ostriches?"

Tony waved his hand. "Never mind that part right now. It's not important."

"Have you found any other evidence of young Robert's guilt?" Lucy asked.

Jessica tried to speak again, but Elizabeth cut her off.

"Yes," she said. "And I know Lord Pembroke has evidence of it, as well. I overheard a conversation between Pembroke and Andrew Thatcher. Thatcher knows Pembroke is protecting somebody. Apparently, Thatcher let him get away with it up until now, but Thatcher said the latest murder was the last straw. He gave Pembroke until ten o'clock tonight to tell him who the murderer is, or he'll subpoena him."

"So you never actually heard Robert's father say that Robert is a murderer!" Jessica said triumphantly.

"Actually, I did. Well, sort of. After Thatcher left, Robert's father said that the evidence he's found clearly implicates Robert, but that he doesn't believe it. He decided to call Robert and tell him to get out of town."

Jessica felt the color drain from her face. That explained Robert's sudden flight from London, and his evasiveness at breakfast that morning.

"That doesn't mean anything!" Jessica cried. "It doesn't prove that Robert is a murderer—much less a werewolf!"

Lucy raised her eyebrows. "A werewolf? You kids think the murderer is a werewolf? What kind of a cockamamie story is that?"

"It's true," Luke said quietly, his blue eyes blazing. "And it's not just us who think so. Even Pembroke and Thatcher believe it, if what Elizabeth heard this morning is any indication."

Elizabeth shrugged. "I know it sounds crazy, but look at the evidence. The victims' throats were ripped out, 'as if by a wild beast.' You said it yourself, Lucy. And I found fur on the door frame of the room where Joy was killed."

"The fur could have come from a number of animals," Tony pointed out.

"And even if it is from a werewolf, you can't prove it's Robert!" Jessica added.

"Well, I don't believe in werewolves," Lucy said thoughtfully. "But as journalists, we do have to consider every possibility. If this alleged werewolf is Robert, and he was wearing the green bathrobe on the night of Joy's murder, then we would, *theoretically*, find traces of fur on the robe. Fur that matches what you found in the door."

"Forensic studies should be able to tell us if the fur does come from a wolf," Tony said. "If we can find a police investigator who will examine the evidence for us, without tipping off Thatcher."

"I don't know about that, Tony," Lucy said. "Perhaps our best course of action now is to go to Thatcher with what we know."

"It's your call, Lucy," Tony said. "But Thatcher must have a lot of loyalty to Pembroke to have gone along with him this long. How do we know he won't bring anything we tell him straight to Pembroke Manor?"

Lucy frowned. "I suppose you're right. But that will complicate our chances of obtaining a forensic study of the evidence."

"Bumpo!" Elizabeth said suddenly. Everyone turned to stare at her. "Sergeant Bumpo loves doing forensic studies. And he's been thrilled to have Jessica and me covering his stories—nobody else ever acted as if they were important. He'll do it if we ask him to."

Tony nodded. "Good. I doubt a forensic study will prove that the murderer is a werewolf, but it could turn up other clues that could prove young Robert's guilt." He glanced at Jessica. "Or innocence," he added quickly. "I am glad to see that we're getting more out of your intern assignments than stories about exploding vegetables and murderous kitchen sinks."

Lucy raised her eyebrows again. "Murderous *what*?"

"Never mind," Tony said. "It's not important."

"Did Pembroke cite any other evidence for believing that the murderer is a werewolf?" Lucy asked.

"Nothing he said out loud," Elizabeth admitted. "But he and Thatcher both seemed convinced on that point."

Lucy crossed her arms in front of her and began pacing the living room. "As I said, I'm skeptical about this werewolf business. But I knew all along that Lord Pembroke was trying to hide something. I just didn't know what it was. Now, thanks to you, Elizabeth, it's clear. The evidence does seem to point to the conclusion that Robert Pembroke, the younger, is a murderer."

"No way!" Jessica protested. "I know him better than any of you do. Robert could never kill anybody—and he's not a werewolf!"

"But how else can you explain the threads from

his bathrobe, found at the scene of Joy's murder?" Elizabeth asked.

"What's so sinister about that?" Jessica asked. "It's his house, after all! Maybe he was in that room the day before."

Elizabeth shook her head. "I'm sorry if it upsets you, Jess, but you have to face the truth. Robert may be guilty of murder."

"Your life is in danger, Jessica," Luke warned her. "If you hadn't switched beds with Joy, you would have been murdered last weekend at Pembroke Manor. And you said yourself that someone attacked you in the tube station today."

Lucy turned to her, surprised. "Somebody attacked you?"

Jessica described the incident on the subway platform. Then she scowled at Elizabeth. "But it wasn't Robert!" she concluded. "Robert wouldn't hurt me—he loves me! I bet not one of you has come up with a motive for why he would kill me or those other people."

Tony and Lucy exchanged embarrassed glances.

"I'm afraid you've got us there," Lucy admitted. "Except that the murders clearly indicate a psychotic mind at work. Perhaps he doesn't even know he's doing it. I don't know, Jessica. I'm not a psychologist. But the evidence against Robert seems solid enough to warrant an arrest. And perhaps further investigations will reveal a motive."

Jessica shook her head. "No, they won't. Because he didn't have one. He didn't kill those other people, and he didn't try to murder me today. Besides,

Robert and I were supposed to spend today together, alone in the country. If he wanted to kill me, that would have been the perfect chance. But he didn't. In fact, he canceled our date at the last minute."

"Only because he had to leave town before Thatcher arrested him," Luke pointed out.

"No, no, *no!*" Jessica cried, her voice rising. "Wouldn't you leave town if you heard someone was about to arrest you for murders you didn't commit?"

Elizabeth laid a hand on her sister's shoulder. "But, Jess, who else but Robert could have been there in the tube station today? Everybody else thought you were out with him. Robert was the only person who knew you'd be alone. You've got to be careful, Jessica. You're in a lot of danger."

That was what Robert had said, Jessica remembered suddenly: *Promise me you'll be careful.*

"You're wrong about Robert," Jessica insisted. "I can't believe that he's any threat to me. But maybe you're right about the rest. Maybe I really am in danger."

With a shudder, she remembered the empty tube platform, the sound of heavy panting, and the brush of coarse hair against her bare arm.

"That's quite a painting!" David said on Wednesday afternoon, at the church of Notre Dame de France, on Leicester Square. The interior of the chapel was a little dim, so Eliana pulled off the sunglasses she'd become accustomed to wearing almost everywhere. Then she looked up at the cartoonlike mural, and smiled warmly when she felt David take her hand.

"It's a Cocteau, isn't it?" Eliana asked. "I've always been impressed with the way he combined surrealism with whimsy."

David looked at her with a mixture of admiration and curiosity. "How did you become such an expert, Lina? I wasn't aware that you knew about art."

Eliana smiled nonchalantly. "Oh, I've picked up a bit. I'm a voracious reader, you know."

She chastised herself for not being more careful. Expertise in art history didn't fit in with the image she'd built for herself. Why couldn't she keep her mouth shut? David already suspected that she was hiding something from him. All week, she'd been evasive whenever he'd mentioned Liverpool. And she kept slipping up—making remarks that were natural from a princess, but inappropriate from a working-class girl of sixteen.

Eliana sighed. The closer she felt to David, the more upsetting it was becoming to continue her charade.

"That's it," she decided under her breath, still pretending to be engrossed in the mural. "Portia has chosen tonight to tell her father the truth about herself. That's when I'll tell David the truth about me."

"Did you say something?" David asked.

Eliana blushed. "Oh, um, I was just noticing Judas up there on the mural—what an odd depiction!"

David laughed. "It certainly is. He looks a bit like the creature from the Black Lagoon!"

As they left the church a few minutes later, still

hand in hand, they passed an unusually crowded newsstand.

"Must be the evening edition of the *London Journal*," David said, dropping her hand to move close enough to buy a paper. "People seem frightfully excited over it."

Eliana held her breath as an inexplicable feeling of dread overwhelmed her.

"Look at the size of this headline!" David said a minute later. "Is this a newspaper or a billboard? Listen to this: 'Is Princess Eliana Dead?' Honestly, you would think that—"

Then he held up the newspaper and shook it open. Eliana saw with a sinking heart that an enormous photograph of Princess Eliana gazed serenely from its front page.

David's eyes widened and he did a double take. He turned slowly to look at Eliana. Then he examined the photograph again. Luckily, nobody else in the crowd was paying any attention to the two teenagers.

Eliana was afraid she was about to burst into tears. She wished fervently that she'd remembered to put her sunglasses back on when they left the church. She was sure that David recognized her.

I can't believe this is happening!

"David, I—" Eliana stammered. But she couldn't bear the look of shock and disappointment on his face. She had lied to him. And the real Lina—Princess Eliana, the daughter of the queen—was somebody a boy like David could never fall in love with.

Eliana shook her head helplessly, unable to meet his eyes. Then she spun on her heel and fled.

Lucy Friday wasn't the easiest person to get along with, Elizabeth decided. She could be brusque and overbearing, and was quick to judge people. But from the way Tony was smiling at Lucy, Elizabeth knew he loved her despite her aggressiveness—or maybe because of it.

"I have to admit, Lucy," he said as he held open the door to the *Journal* office. "It's great to have you back at the office, even if it is only for a visit."

Elizabeth, Jessica, and Luke passed by Tony through the open door, but Lucy stood outside with her arms folded. Elizabeth suppressed a chuckle. Lucy wanted it to be perfectly clear that she could get along without Tony's help—for opening a door, or for anything else. She had been certain that Tony was involved in the cover-up of the murder stories, in order to get the job of crime editor for himself. Now, at least, she seemed to realize that he was as perplexed by the cover-up as she was.

Jessica nudged Elizabeth's arm, and Elizabeth realized her sister had been thinking along the same lines.

"If nothing else," Jessica whispered, "at least this crummy murder mystery has brought Lucy and Tony back together again!"

Elizabeth smiled and nodded, somehow sure that things would work out this time between the two editors. But even more important was Lucy's role in the murder investigation. With an experienced journalist like Lucy helping, Elizabeth was sure they would have a solid case against Robert Pembroke in no time.

Elizabeth's hopes on both counts were quickly dashed.

When the little group filed into Tony's office, Lucy pounced immediately on the brand-new edition of the *Journal*, waiting on Tony's desk.

Lucy's beautiful brown eyes filled with suspicion as she read the lead headline. "That's seventy-two-point type!" she said incredulously, scanning the first few paragraphs of the article. "This is total rubbish. It says the body found at Pembroke Manor yesterday morning was the princess."

"I can't believe Reeves printed that!" Tony yelled. "He knew it was an unsubstantiated rumor. He was supposed to hold the story until I checked out the details at Pembroke Manor. What was he thinking of?"

Lucy spun toward him, furious. "Don't play innocent with me, Tony Frank! That's your byline, not Reeves's. You knew bloody well that this story was running in tonight's edition. Don't try to blame Reeves!"

Elizabeth shifted uncomfortably from one foot to the other. "Actually, he didn't know," she said, trying to help. "Mr. Reeves had Tony write up the story, but wasn't supposed to run it until—"

Lucy silenced her with a glance. "Save your breath, Elizabeth. I'm sick and tired of hearing people make excuses for this two-faced yellow journalist. You know, Tony, I used to think you had integrity, but the last couple weeks have shown me that *you're* the scandalmonger, not Reeves. You're more interested in selling newspapers than you are in printing the truth. And then you have the unmitigated gall to pretend you're on the side of journalistic integrity."

"But Lucy, that's not—" Tony began.

"Well, I've had it with you!" she lashed out. "And I've had it with this newspaper. Don't ever call me again!"

Lucy stalked out the door, slamming it behind her with a crash that rumbled through the office like an earthquake. When the reverberation died away, the room seemed utterly still and empty without her.

"Well, I guess that's that," Tony said in a thin, quiet voice. "She's gone."

Chapter 12

Portia stood in the wings a half hour before the curtain was due to go up on Wednesday night's performance of *A Common Man*. Around her, crew members arranged lights and fumbled with pieces of scenery, while the cast hurried about in various stages of dress.

Portia, already in costume, stood apart from the others. She pounced on Jessica as soon as the American girl returned to the backstage area.

"Did you see my parents out there?" she asked. "Did they come?"

"I saw them all right," Jessica said. "They're out in the lobby where all the ticket holders are milling around waiting for the play to start."

Portia sighed thankfully. "I was frightfully worried that they wouldn't show."

"I could've found your folks even without the photo you showed me," Jessica said. "Jeepers, Mrs.

165

Bates wasn't kidding when she said your father was famous! Everybody in the place was hounding him for his autograph. All I had to do was follow the crowd!"

"Thanks again for coming along to provide moral support tonight," Portia said. Then she smiled conspiratorially. "Not to mention spying services."

"No problem! I love the theater, especially from this side of the stage. Besides, I was desperate to get away from my overprotective sister. Elizabeth has become a real pain in the neck."

"But doesn't she have some cause to worry?" Portia asked. "She told me someone attacked you in the subway today. Do you have any idea who it was? It didn't sound like a simple mugging."

Jessica shook her head. "I don't know who it was," she said. "But you're right—it wasn't a simple mugging." She sighed. "It's too long a story to go into now, Portia. Besides, I really don't want to think about it." She smiled mischievously. "And I'm surprised you haven't asked what I heard your father talking about in the lobby a few minutes ago."

Portia stiffened. "I didn't realize you were close enough to hear anything! What did he say, Jessica? He hasn't figured out that Penelope Abbott is really me, has he?"

"No, I'm sure he hasn't," Jessica said. Then she turned to watch as a tall, well-muscled young actor strutted by, wearing only the bottom half of his costume.

Portia gritted her teeth with impatience. "Jessica! What did my father say?" she screeched.

Jessica grinned. "Sorry. I heard your father say

he's heard a lot about this Penelope Abbott. He was glad to receive the tickets to come see her in action tonight. He has no idea who sent them, but that didn't seem to bother him."

"It wouldn't," Portia explained. "Theater people send him tickets to plays all the time. They're always anxious for his opinion on actors or directors or scripts."

"They're not the only ones who are anxious," Jessica said, taking in her nervous eyes and tense posture. "Relax, Portia, he'll love your performance."

"But what if he doesn't?" Portia asked.

"He will," Jessica said confidently. "What an exciting profession!" she exclaimed, looking as if she were drinking in the backstage atmosphere. "I always wanted to act. You know, I was Lady Macbeth in a production this year. And before that, I was in *Splendor in the Grass*. Everyone said I had a lot of talent. . . ."

Portia's thoughts wandered from the American girl's words. She was sure Jessica could be a terrific actress, if she ever settled down long enough to apply herself to one thing. But that didn't sound like Jessica. *Making a career out of acting takes constant work—constant attention. You have to devote your whole life to the craft.*

But that was all Portia had ever wanted.

Except for her father's blessing. When she first left home, Portia had convinced herself that she didn't need his permission to follow her dream. But she knew now that she would never be completely happy as an actress, unless she had his approval.

"I just hope he likes my performance tonight,"

she whispered desperately, interrupting Jessica's cheerful chatter. "He just has to!"

Elizabeth finished her narration of the day's events Wednesday night and sat down on her bed, watching to see Eliana's reaction.

"Your evidence sounds quite convincing," Eliana said, a startled look on her face, "especially the conversation you overheard between Lord Pembroke and the chief of police. But Robert Pembroke—a serial killer?"

"Even his father admits that the evidence points to him," Elizabeth said. "Of course, he's in denial about it. He doesn't want to believe that his son has committed such horrible acts."

She shuddered, remembering the blood-soaked sheets on Joy Singleton's bed.

"We'll have more details in the morning," Elizabeth continued. "I stopped by Scotland Yard this evening and dropped off the animal fur, the silk threads, and the green bathrobe with Sergeant Bumpo. He's happy to have an excuse to use his high-tech analysis lab. He'll call me tomorrow with the results."

"And have you figured out who the Annabelle person is?" Eliana asked.

"No. But she obviously loved Pembroke, a long time ago. Pembroke said she knew about the secret room—years ago. I was going to talk to Luke about her today, to see if he could speculate on her identity, but I forgot to mention it to him."

"I don't know how I could have been so wrong

about Robert," Eliana said. "He and I have never been friends, exactly, but I have known him all my life. He's always seemed a bit wild—but never dangerous!"

"The worst part about it is that I can't convince my sister that Robert's trying to kill her. She refuses to believe that he's really a werewolf."

"Actually, Liz, I'm with Jessica on that point," Eliana said. "Nothing you say can make me believe in werewolves, although I know that Lord Pembroke has been quite fascinated by them for many years. Apparently he's even persuaded Thatcher that the murderer is a werewolf."

"After what happened in the tube station today," Elizabeth said, "even Jessica is willing to admit that werewolves exist. But she's still sure that Robert is innocent. Eliana, I'm worried about her. Robert has killed four people! Jessica is in terrible danger until he's safely in custody."

"Where is Jessica tonight?" Eliana asked.

Elizabeth sighed. "She went to the theater with Portia. I suppose she'll be all right, in a public place like that. I made her promise she wouldn't go anywhere alone. Still, I wish she were here tonight, safe and sound in her upper bunk. Speaking of going out, Eliana, why are you sitting around here with *me* tonight? I thought you were spending this evening with David."

Eliana shook her head and tried, unsuccessfully, to blink back her tears. "Not anymore," she said. "And probably never again—now that he knows the truth about me."

Elizabeth gasped. "Oh, Eliana, I'm sorry! I didn't

know you were going to tell him this afternoon."

"I wasn't," Eliana said. "I didn't. I had decided to tell him tonight. But then that newspaper of yours came out with my photograph plastered across its front page. David picked it up as I was standing right there next to him, and . . ."

"And he couldn't help but notice the resemblance," Elizabeth finished for her. "I'm sorry, Eliana. I was hoping he would take the news better than that. What did he say when he realized you're a princess?"

"I don't know. I didn't tarry long enough to hear his reaction." She bit her lip. "Ah, Liz, I feel so foolish. Running away was fun for a while, but it didn't accomplish anything except bring grief to my family and David. And provide an excuse for Lord Pembroke to push the spate of mysterious deaths off of page one of the *Journal*."

"You can't blame yourself for Pembroke's actions," Elizabeth assured her. "And if David really loves you, your family's royal status shouldn't matter to him."

Eliana shook her head. "Even if the fact that I'm a princess doesn't make any difference to David," she said, "the fact that I hid it from him will. As much as I love him, it's over. David will probably never speak to me again. I just wish there was some way I could make it up to him."

"Maybe there is," Elizabeth said thoughtfully. "You can't go on hiding forever. Sooner or later, you're going to have to come forward—"

"It has to be sooner," Eliana realized with a sigh. "If I come out of hiding now, at least something good can come out of all this. We can prove that Pembroke was trying to cover up the stories about the murder, and get people to focus their attention on the real news story in London—the fact that four people have died horribly."

Eliana jumped off the bed and stood in the center of the room for a moment before coming to a decision. "Liz, I'm going to turn myself in."

Elizabeth grinned. "No, you aren't," she said. "*David* is going to turn you in."

"I don't understand," Eliana began. Then her eyes widened. "Oh, yes, I do understand! If David is the one to turn me in, then *he'll* get the million pounds of prize money that the newspaper has put up. With that he can endow the clinic he wants to start at the homeless shelter—and send himself to medical school so he can work in it! Elizabeth, you're a genius! After what I've done to him, I don't expect that David will ever love me again. But this way, I'll feel as if I've done something to compensate for the ghastly way I've treated him."

Suddenly, the door burst open, and David himself walked in. He stopped, flustered, when he realized Eliana was standing in the center of the room as if she'd been expecting him.

Elizabeth realized David hadn't seen her at all, as she sat on the lower bunk bed in the corner of the room. She opened her mouth to announce her presence, but David began speaking before she had the chance.

"Lina, or should I say Eliana," he stammered, beginning a speech that had obviously been rehearsed. "I loved you as a pauper. I'll love you just as much as a princess—if you'll have me."

Eliana's smile lit the room, and Elizabeth thought she looked as radiant as a princess should. "I will, David," she answered, smiling shyly, "under one condition."

Jessica stood backstage, listening to the echoes of the biggest standing ovation she'd ever heard—and imagining that she, rather than Portia, was the object of everyone's admiration.

But Portia certainly deserved the applause. Her performance as Isabelle Huntington that night had been remarkable.

After the curtain came down, Portia tackled her with a bear hug. "I'm so excited, Jessica! The entire cast was absolutely perfect tonight." Then her face fell. "But he's not back here, Jessica. The other cast members' families have made it backstage, but I don't see my father anywhere. He would come to see me if he liked my performance. He must have hated it!"

"Whoa, Portia!" Jessica said. "I've never seen you so keyed up. Give him a chance. The final curtain just came down. At this very moment, he's probably shoving his way through hordes of autograph seekers to get to you."

A pretty, waiflike actress tapped Portia on the shoulder. Jessica recognized her as Adrian Rani, who'd had a small part in the play. "Did you hear the news, Penelope? You'll never guess who was in the audience tonight—Sir Montford Albert, the Shakespearean actor!"

Portia managed a weak smile. "Oh, really?"

"He's been my absolute favorite actor for years!"

Adrian confided. Suddenly, her mouth dropped open and she pointed across the room. "Oh, Penelope, he's here! Montford Albert has come backstage! I'm going closer to see if someone will introduce me to him."

She scurried off, leaving Jessica and Portia staring across the cluttered space to the tall, distinguished actor who was scanning the room.

Suddenly, he saw the person he was searching for. When his eyes locked with Portia's, Jessica felt as if an electric current passed between the two. The other actors must have noticed it, too; the room fell silent. As he moved across the floor, the cast parted before him like the Red Sea.

Then, Sir Montford Albert wrapped Portia in a huge bear hug, while the other actors looked on, astonished.

Jessica was the only one close enough to hear his whispered apology.

"I am so proud of you, darling," he said. "Can you ever forgive me for the beastly way I've treated you?"

Portia nodded eagerly, tears sparkling in her eyes.

"Way to go, Penelope!" yelled an enthusiastic young cast member.

At the mention of Portia's alias, Sir Albert looked up, realization dawning in his eyes.

"I think I understand what you've done, Portia," he said in a low voice. "And I know why you did it. But it won't be necessary anymore."

When he turned to the crowd, Sir Montford Albert was beaming. "Ladies and gentlemen," he announced grandly. "I'd like to introduce Portia Albert—my daughter, the actress!"

•   •   •

173

Lord Robert Pembroke was pacing again. It was eight steps across the gleaming parquet floor of his study at Pembroke Green, and eight steps back.

He had been fighting a wave of panic all day—ever since his telephone conversation with Robert that morning, when he urged his son to flee. He'd been unable to sit still since then—unable to eat or work or even to read his own newspaper. He'd made the trip into London, and locked himself in this infernal room, where he had reviewed the evidence over and over again, trying to find a flaw in the story it told. Now he was pacing.

He hated this room. In fact, he hated the entire house. Pembroke Green was his wife's domain; city living had never appealed to Lord Pembroke. He much preferred the open countryside. On his ancestral land at Pembroke Manor, he had a feeling of stability—of his place in time's continuum.

But now that continuum was about to come to a screeching, skidding, sickening halt, right at the foot of his heir and only son, Robert.

He consulted his watch for the third time in the last two minutes. His stomach lurched. It was exactly ten o'clock.

Somewhere in the distance, the doorbell rang. The sound was muted, but Pembroke's anxiety and the room's stillness magnified it into a harsh jangling. He pulled out a linen handkerchief and mopped the sweat that was running in rivulets down his face.

"Confound you, Andrew!" he said when Thatcher walked into the room a minute later. "Right on time, aren't you? You're like a vulture, diving in for the kill."

174

"An interesting choice of analogy, Robert," said the chief of police. "You have information for me, I presume?"

Pembroke stared at him wildly. "I'll tell you what the evidence reveals—though I still don't believe it, myself. But you must promise me that you won't release it to the media just yet."

Thatcher pounded his fist on the desk. "I'm not making any promises this time until I see the evidence, investigate it, and question the suspect. Don't you understand, Robert? Four people have been murdered! If I had followed my conscience after Joy's murder—" He stopped, shaking his head sadly.

"If I hadn't listened to you then," the police chief continued in a soft voice, not looking at Pembroke, "Maria Finch might still be alive today. No matter what the evidence says, Robert, her blood is also on my hands—and yours."

Thatcher turned to the older man, and Pembroke saw that his handsome face was hard, his mouth set in a grim line.

"Now, Robert, are you going to tell me what you know?"

The two men stared at each other for a full minute, but it seemed like an hour to Pembroke. Finally, he lowered his eyes, defeated. Then he reached for the top drawer of his desk, where he'd lovingly placed a handful of green threads, a clump of fur, and a silver cigarette case.

Chapter 13

Jessica practically stumbled over a scruffy-looking homeless man sitting on the sidewalk outside the *Journal* building Thursday morning, his face covered by a floppy old hat.

As she entered the newsroom, Jessica nearly stumbled again—this time over a row of rickety folding chairs that were stacked against the wall. In fact, she realized, the entire room was in chaos. A massive desk appeared out of nowhere and bumped toward her rapidly—carried, she saw, by two men in coveralls. Jessica scrunched against the wall to keep from being mowed down.

"What's going on here?" she called after them.

"We were told to move the desks out of the way to set up seats for a press conference, miss," one of the workers said in a cockney accent.

"A press conference about what?"

The man shook his head. "I sure as blazes don't

know, miss. I just move furniture."

The workers moved on. Jessica bit her lip, suddenly afraid. The only really big scoop she knew of was that the police would be looking for Robert soon. Could that be the topic of the press conference? Was her innocent boyfriend's name about to dragged through the mud?

She considered the possibility for a moment but rejected it. The *Journal* wouldn't hold a press conference on a murder investigation; the police department would do it. At least, she hoped so.

Then Jessica caught sight of Luke as he ducked under a huge boom microphone that a woman was setting up outside the door of Tony's office. She scrambled over to him. "What's the press conference for?"

Luke smiled sheepishly. "Sorry, Jessica, but your sister and Tony have sworn me to secrecy."

"Elizabeth knows about all this?" Jessica asked, gesturing around at the confusion. "I wondered why she was already gone when I woke up. But come on, Luke. Liz couldn't have meant *me* when she asked you not to tell anybody. Liz and I are identical twins. Telling me something is just like telling her!"

"Valiant attempt, Jessica, but Elizabeth specifically warned me not to say anything to you. I believe she mentioned something about 'a mouth the size of Westminster Abbey.'"

Jessica scowled. "Thanks a lot. Well, I see her near the copying machine, talking to Tony. Maybe I can wheedle it out of them."

She began striding across the room to confront

her sister. Then she remembered what Luke had said, and opted for a more subtle approach. She slipped behind a pair of desks that were stacked one behind the other and trained a practiced ear on her sister's conversation with the editor.

"Thanks for calling me last night with the big news," Tony said, "and for helping me arrange this press conference on such short notice."

Elizabeth smiled. "And thank *you* for letting me write a really big story—finally."

"It was an excellent article," Tony said. Then he smiled mischievously. "I suppose you've already prepared your acceptance speech for your first Pulitzer."

Elizabeth blushed, and Jessica knew she'd been dreaming of exactly that.

"What about the people back in the press room?" Elizabeth asked. "Certainly, they'll see the story when they print the newspaper. Can you trust them to keep it under wraps?"

"They're all sworn to secrecy," Tony replied. "In fact, they're printing the special edition right now. It'll be off the presses in time for the ten A.M. conference."

Jessica wished she had taken the time to flirt with some of the guys in the press room; maybe they would have told her the big secret.

"Will our special guests be here in time?" Tony asked.

"No problem there," Liz says. "What about Pembroke?"

"He'll be here, and I asked him to bring Thatcher, as well. I told Pembroke the gist of today's announcement, but not the details. I assume he's too distracted with his own problems to be angry at me for taking the liberty of setting all this up. If he's upset, I could be joining Lucy on the dole. That reminds me—did you call her? Is she coming?"

"It was a hard sell, Tony, but I think so. She's still angry with you, but I appealed to her journalist's sense of curiosity."

Tony rushed off to supervise the placement of the chairs, and Jessica leapt out from behind the desks.

"What was that all about?" she demanded. "What press conference? What article?"

Elizabeth gave her a smug, infuriating smile. "You'll know soon enough."

Elizabeth chuckled to herself as she saw Jessica's infuriated expression. Jessica had never been a patient person. Now she would just have to wait for the press conference to start, like everyone else.

Reporters from other newspapers were beginning to arrive. All they had been told was that Lord Pembroke had a major announcement to make. Now they were milling around the room, asking questions of one another and speculating about the answers. Elizabeth noticed Lucy, standing alone, and realized she was carefully avoiding Tony, though she had been too curious to stay away.

"Oh, well," Elizabeth thought. "At least she's here."

Jessica pointed toward the door. "Television cameras!" she exclaimed. "Does my hair look all right?"

"It looks fine, Jessica, as usual. But it won't matter. The BBC television people are not here to take pictures of you."

"You never know," Jessica said. "But look, there's Emily with the crew. *Some* media groups let their student interns come along on the big stories."

Emily caught sight of the twins and hurried over to them, dodging a radio crew on the way. Luke joined them a moment later.

"What's the big scoop?" Emily asked excitedly. "Do you *Journal* insiders have any inside information?"

Jessica scowled. "You know how much of an insider I am. If it doesn't deal with exploding vegetables, clog robbers, or falling kitchen sinks, I'm left in the dark. Elizabeth and Luke are in on the secret. Elizabeth even wrote the big exclusive in the special edition of the newspaper that's coming out today. But she's taken a vow of silence."

"Some of the BBC reporters think it's about the princess," Emily said. "Have they found her?"

Elizabeth shrugged, but kept her mouth shut.

"No way," Jessica said, with a speculative glance at her sister. "Liz couldn't have kept something that big from me."

"Here's Lord Pembroke now!" Emily said.

Lord Pembroke walked hurriedly into the room, followed by Andrew Thatcher. The men were obviously together, but there was a coldness between them that aroused Elizabeth's curiosity. And Thatcher's eyes looked blazing mad.

Luke took her arm and drew her aside from the others. "Do you suppose Pembroke told Thatcher about Robert at ten o'clock last night, as scheduled?" he whispered.

Elizabeth cast another glance across the room at

181

the two men. "My guess is yes. But Thatcher looks mad. I bet he's figured out that Pembroke told Robert to leave town."

"We've got every journalist in town assembled here," Luke pointed out. "I wonder if Thatcher will take advantage of the opportunity to announce a warrant for Little Lord Pembroke's arrest."

Elizabeth bit her lip. "I hope not, for Jessica's sake. I was counting on today's revelation to help people see that the *Journal* has been hiding the murders. But I'd rather see Robert brought in quietly."

"Any word from Bumpo on the forensic studies?"

"Not yet."

Elizabeth felt a tap on her shoulder. "Didn't anyone ever tell you it's impolite to whisper?" Jessica demanded. "Besides, something's happening over there." She pointed. "Isn't that yesterday evening's paper Pembroke is reading? He looks mad!"

Lord Pembroke folded the newspaper in a quick, jerking movement. Then he glared around the room. "Find Reeves!" he yelled to a terrified reporter. "I want him in my office, now!"

Then he stalked across the floor, ignoring the questions of a half-dozen journalists, and disappeared into his corner office.

A buzz of speculation arose from the gathered reporters. A moment later, Reeves emerged from his own office and strolled over to Pembroke's, a jaunty swing in his walk.

Elizabeth looked at Jessica, and both twins nodded. Then they motioned for Luke and Emily to follow as they slipped behind a row of stacked desks and

182

picked their way, unseen, to a spot near Pembroke's door.

Lucy Friday obviously had the same idea. She was already standing near the door when Elizabeth led the others around the stacked desks. Lucy put a finger to her lips as the teenagers approached.

Reeves's proud voice filtered through the door. "Lord Pembroke, sir, I knew you would be pleased with this week's circulation figures. Yesterday's edition sold more papers than anything since the royal wedding. The princess death story really did the trick! Tony Frank didn't want to print it without more research. But I wasn't about to let him dictate editorial policy. The man's a neophyte—has no business sense at all! I went right ahead against his objections."

Lucy gasped, her face filled with shame and hope.

Pembroke cleared his throat. "I'll see that you get exactly what you deserve," he said in a voice so low that Elizabeth had to strain her ears to catch his words.

Reeves didn't seem to notice the forbidding tone in Pembroke's voice. "And today's special edition, sir, should top even yesterday's sales! I know you haven't seen the article yet, but believe me—it will be the scoop of the century!"

"And as I understand it, Tony Frank and his staff were responsible for the news we will reveal today."

"Er, yes sir," Reeves said, sounding confused. "But only under my direction, of course."

"Of course."

"Actually, sir, I would recommend replacing Mr.

Frank immediately. The man obviously can't handle his new responsibilities."

Pembroke's response was calm, but held a note of rage. "It is *you* who will be replaced," he said. "For knowingly printing an unsubstantiated rumor, your employment is hereby terminated."

"But, sir," Reeves stammered, "it was you who told me to play up the princess story instead of focusing on the murders, to find new angles—"

"What murders?" Emily mouthed to Jessica. Jessica shook her head, listening. These Americans, Emily thought, certainly had a taste for the morbid.

"I never told you to print lies!" Pembroke said, his voice rising. "Choosing to print one story over another is a simple matter of editorial judgment. But choosing to print a story that is not true is blatantly irresponsible. There is no room in my newspaper for lies! See that your belongings are out of the building by the end of the day."

The newsroom was electric with excitement as everyone prepared for the press conference to begin. Emily could feel it pulsing around her, in the hurried movements of the reporters and in their eager conversations. She fidgeted in her front-row seat between Jessica and Luke, and then turned to see if all the seats behind them were full.

"It's standing room only," she remarked.

"How about a hint, Liz?" Jessica pleaded, craning her neck to see her sister, who was seated past Luke. "Just give me a teensy-weensy little hint of what this is all about."

Elizabeth refused, and Jessica slumped in her seat, her arms folded across her chest. Emily knew she hated feeling left out.

"Cheer up, Jessica," she said. "There's a lot you can tell me. Who's the good-looking young man in front of the room, the one who seems so nervous?"

Jessica yawned. "Oh, that's just Tony Frank, my boss. Officially this may be Pembroke's press conference, but from what I gather, Tony's running the show. He's kind of a wimp, but he's a nice enough guy."

"Your friend Lucy can't seem to keep her eyes off him."

Jessica smiled. "You're right. I hadn't noticed. We've been trying to get those two back together all week. I'm glad it's finally working."

"What was Mr. Reeves saying earlier about covering up some murders? Nobody else even seemed surprised. I know a young woman was killed at Pembroke Manor last week. Have there been other murders as well? Does Lord Pembroke know who committed them?"

Jessica gasped. "No!" she said, loud enough so that several heads turned. "He doesn't know anything about who killed those people," she whispered. "The evidence is wrong!"

Emily was perplexed, but didn't want to provoke Jessica further.

Then Tony stepped up to the microphone, and the room quieted instantly.

"We've all been regaled for the last week or two with information and speculation about the disap-

185

pearance of the queen's youngest daughter, Princess Eliana—"

A murmur rose from the crowd of reporters. Behind her, Emily recognized the frantic scratching of pens on notepaper and the furious clicking of keys on laptop computers. Had the missing princess been found?

"Lord Pembroke has an important presentation to make in a few minutes, but first I'd like to introduce somebody."

"That's Tony's office door he's pointing to," Jessica whispered. "Do you think he's got the princess in there?"

Emily held her breath as the door opened. Then she let it out, surprised and disappointed. David Bartholomew stepped out of the office, grinning nervously.

"What in the world is David the Bookworm doing here?" Jessica whispered as David and Tony conferred in low voices for a moment.

Emily shook her head, mystified. "I can't imagine a shy fellow like him speaking to all these reporters," she whispered back. Elizabeth and Luke, she noticed, didn't seem the least bit surprised.

Tony grasped the microphone again. "This young man is Mr. David Bartholomew, and he has a very important announcement to make."

David's voice was shaky when he began speaking. "I met somebody a couple weeks ago who seemed quite extraordinary. But I didn't realize just how extraordinary until yesterday evening, when I saw her photograph on the front page of the *London Journal*.

Ladies and gentlemen, allow me to present the Princess Eliana."

Tony unfurled a newspaper that Emily realized was a copy of the *Journal's* hot-off-the-presses special edition. A huge headline blazed across the top of the page: "Eliana Is Found: University Student Turns in Missing Princess."

Then Eliana herself stepped out of Tony's office, looking quite regal in a white silk dress, with her hair piled on top of her head. But her hair was brown, instead of blond. . . .

Emily nearly fell off her seat. *The princess was Lina Smith!*

Jessica, next to Emily, was opening and closing her mouth like a guppy. Only Elizabeth sat calmly, not the least bit surprised.

"We've been living with a real, honest-to-goodness princess," Jessica blurted out, "and we didn't even know it!"

Tony's assistant passed out copies of the special edition as Lina (*Eliana*, Emily reminded herself) held a whispered conversation with Tony, David, and Lord Pembroke, who had joined them at the front of the room.

"Congratulations, Liz!" Emily said, impressed with Elizabeth's first page-one byline in the *Journal.* Elizabeth was beaming. Then Tony's assistant leaned in to whisper something to her. She jumped up and walked quickly to the corner of the room, where Emily saw her taking a phone call.

"What was so frightfully urgent that she couldn't wait until after the press conference?"

Emily whispered to Jessica, who shrugged.

"Thank you all for your concern in the last few weeks," Eliana said into the microphone.

"As you can see, the rumors of my death have been greatly exaggerated," she continued. The reporters laughed, but Emily thought that Lord Pembroke looked uncomfortable. "I have not been to Japan. And I most assuredly did not elope with a member of the palace guard."

"What happened to the Liverpudlian accent?" Emily whispered to Jessica.

"She's so poised and polished," Jessica marveled, "like . . . a princess!"

"In reality," the princess continued, "I behaved a bit badly, and I apologize for any grief I may have caused my family and anyone else." She smiled at David. "I ran away from the palace because I felt the need to escape the royal lifestyle. I wanted to learn what life is like in the real London. And thanks to a few special new friends, I have learned a lot—a lot more than I ever dreamed, actually.

"I spoke with my mother, the queen, last night, and I have agreed to return to my family today. But there will be some changes. I will no longer be cloistered in the palace; I will be free to associate with whomever I please." She glanced warmly at David. "But the most important change is that I will begin using my position to help people."

Emily heard a murmur of skepticism from the reporters behind her. The princess apparently heard it, too. Eliana thought for a moment. Then she removed the microphone from its stand and moved closer to the crowd, speaking more casually.

"On my way here today, I saw a homeless man, only half a block from this building. He was crouched on the sidewalk, his clothing old and torn. A large hat obscured his face, as if he were ashamed to be seen. That man, and others like him, represent the real London. A few weeks ago, I barely knew of the existence of that London. But since then, I've been disguised as a Liverpudlian named Lina." She smiled and fingered her brown-dyed hair.

"Lina obtained a position, working in a London soup kitchen. In that soup kitchen, Lina has seen sights that Eliana would never have been exposed to. Lina has met hungry, sick people—many of them children—with no place to live and few places to turn. Now that I know about that London, I want to use my position to change it. I plan to work for the poor, providing publicity and fund-raising efforts to homeless shelters, soup kitchens, and similar facilities throughout the city."

This time, the murmurs Emily heard behind her were of admiration.

"As you all know, Lord Pembroke, the owner of the *London Journal* and a distant relation of mine, has generously offered the sum of one million pounds for my return. In a few minutes he will present a check for that amount to David Bartholomew. Before he does, I'd like to tell you what David plans to do with that money, because I'm sure he's too modest to tell you himself."

David blushed bright red.

"David plans to donate that money to a London

homeless shelter, to go toward a clinic where the poor can receive free medical treatment. The royal family will make up the rest from my personal trust fund, and has agreed to put David through medical school—on the condition that he agree to head up that clinic as chief physician, after his graduation."

As the audience applauded wildly, Emily sighed, watching Eliana and David gaze into each other's eyes. "Don't you just love happy endings?" she whispered to Jessica.

Jessica sighed, too, but she sounded wistful. Emily remembered that Robert had disappeared the day before.

"Any word from Robert?" Emily asked her, as the reporters began questioning Eliana and David.

Jessica shook her head and blinked rapidly, as if she was trying not to cry.

"I'm sorry," Emily said. "I guess you must miss him a lot."

"I do," Jessica whispered back. "I love Robert, and he loves me!" She cast a venomous glare at Elizabeth, who had just returned to her seat. "I just wish some people would mind their own business, and stop spreading terrible stories about him."

Elizabeth had a stricken look in her eyes. "I'm so sorry to have to tell you this, Jessica," she whispered, motioning Luke and Lucy to gather closer, as well. "That was Sergeant Bumpo on the phone, with the results of the forensic study."

"Bumpo?" Emily asked, amused. "Isn't he the funny little chap who handles Scotland Yard's lost dog cases?"

For some reason, the others looked terribly serious. Dead serious.

"The silk threads definitely came from Robert's robe," Elizabeth said. "And the analysis also showed traces of fur on the robe—the same fur that was found in the doorway."

Jessica's face lost all color. "Somebody planted it there," she whispered. "I know they did."

"That's not all," Elizabeth continued. She took a deep breath and turned to Luke. "Bumpo hasn't completed the analysis of the fur, but he's certain of one thing—*it definitely came from a wolf!*"

"I don't understand any of this," Emily said. "What's going on?"

Luke shook his head at her. "It's a long story," he said. "And this is no place for a lengthy explanation."

"I'd better fill Tony in on the results," Lucy said quickly, rising from her seat. From the warm light in her eyes, Emily guessed that discussing the evidence wasn't the only thing Lucy had on her mind.

Suddenly, a reporter from another newspaper jumped to her feet and pointed with her pencil at Andrew Thatcher, who had been standing off to one side.

"Chief Thatcher," she asked loudly, "you have been searching for the missing princess for two weeks, with no luck. Why is it that the entire London police department could not find one missing girl— while two teenage tourists were able to break the story?"

Thatcher stalked to the microphone, annoyed.

."Hasn't the media wasted enough time on this story?" he asked, staring at the reporters in disgust. "With all due respect to the princess and the royal family, there is a situation afoot in London that is exceedingly more momentous."

The room quieted. At Emily's side, Jessica was absolutely still, her face still ashen.

"My department has a suspect in the murder of Joy Singleton," Thatcher announced. "And that suspect is also wanted for questioning concerning the deaths of Dr. Cameron Neville, Nurse Dolores Handley, and Maria Finch, a cook at Pembroke Manor. The victims all bled to death, from wounds on their throats—rather like the mauling of a large animal. The police will make the arrest"—he cast a dark glare at Lord Pembroke—"as soon as the suspect can be located."

"Murder?" Emily whispered to Jessica. "The newspaper said the doctor died of natural causes! And what's this about a cook. . . ."

She stopped when she saw that the American girl wasn't paying any attention to her. Instead, Jessica was staring at Thatcher, shaking her head as if she were pleading with him. Remarkably, Lord Pembroke had adopted exactly the same posture. Emily had no idea what was happening.

Thatcher stared grimly at Pembroke and shook his own head almost imperceptibly. Then Pembroke sighed and walked, with a heavy tread, out of the building.

After watching him leave, Thatcher took a deep breath and made his final announcement, in a voice that revealed a mixture of determination and regret, but mostly just exhaustion.

"A warrant has been filed for the arrest of Sir Robert Pembroke, Jr."

Jessica felt as if she were plunging into a deep, black pit. The chief of the London police department was standing in front of her, calmly telling a group of reporters that the boy she loved was a psychotic killer. At least he hadn't mentioned the werewolf theory.

"Lord Pembroke is cooperating with the police in every way," Thatcher said in response to a reporter's question, "though he firmly believes that his son is innocent."

Jessica caught a sarcastic glance between Elizabeth and Luke.

"If he thinks his son is innocent, then why did he skedaddle out of here?" another reporter demanded.

"Lord Pembroke is understandably distraught. But he has assured me that he does not know his son's whereabouts at the present time."

Elizabeth reached over to lay a hand on Jessica's arm. Suddenly, Jessica's despair turned to fury.

"This is all your fault!" she hissed, knowing her voice was covered by the chaos that had followed Thatcher's announcement. Some reporters were rushing to the phones to call their offices, others were shouting questions at Thatcher, and a third group had torn out of the room, in pursuit of Pembroke.

Jessica focused her rage on her sister. "That's what you were being so secretive about last night. You must have called Thatcher with your so-called

193

evidence against Robert—even after we agreed nobody would go to the police with it!"

Elizabeth shook her head. "No, Jessica. I didn't call the police. I was being secretive about the princess story. It was Tony I called last night, to set up this press conference. I didn't know Thatcher would make this announcement."

"Yes, you did, because you told him to!"

"Calm down, Jessica," Elizabeth urged. "It must have been Lord Pembroke himself who told the police about the evidence. Remember Thatcher's ultimatum—he wanted the truth by ten o'clock last night."

Jessica jumped from her seat. "It's not the truth!" she cried. "And Lord Pembroke never would have turned over evidence about his son. But you would! You've hated Robert all along!"

"Yes, that is correct," she heard Thatcher saying calmly. "We have established a connection between a total of four deaths, and we now believe them all to be murders—violent, grisly murders."

Suddenly, Jessica saw the body of Dr. Neville, sprawled on the floor in a pool of blood that stained the floral carpeting. She saw Joy's blond head, looking so much like her own, in the midst of crimson-spattered sheets. And she felt coarse hair scrape against her arm, while the sound of heavy panting echoed through the deserted subway station.

Robert was not the murderer—or a werewolf. But somebody in London was. And until he was found, Jessica knew that her own life was in danger. Suddenly she felt more vulnerable than she had ever felt in her life. Without Robert here to protect her, she would have to rely on herself. Somebody bumped one of the bright television lights, and its reflection caught Jessica's eye, flashing off the anti-werewolf pendant that hung around Elizabeth's neck. A shiver skated down her spine, but Jessica thought about Robert's strong arms and warm kisses, and she swallowed her fear.

"I love Robert," Jessica said aloud, though nobody was listening to her. She straightened her shoulders and looked around her with a new, grim resolve. "And I'll do whatever is necessary to clear his name."

BEWARE THE WOLFMAN

Written by
Kate William

Created by
FRANCINE PASCAL

BANTAM BOOKS
NEW YORK · TORONTO · LONDON · SYDNEY · AUCKLAND

To John Stewart Carmen

Chapter 1

Sixteen-year-old Elizabeth Wakefield passed a platter of warm breakfast scones to her Housing for International Students roommate, aspiring young actress Portia Albert. After choosing a plump raisin scone, Portia passed the platter along to freckled, auburn-haired Emily Cartwright.

"I wonder what Lina's having for breakfast this morning?" mused Emily as she added a scone to her plate, already piled high with farm-style bacon, eggs over easy, and juicy broiled tomatoes.

Elizabeth's blue-green eyes crinkled in a smile. "You mean Eliana. Princess Eliana."

"She's probably having the same thing we are," Portia guessed. "Only, she's eating her eggs with a silver fork from a solid-gold dish."

The three girls laughed merrily. "I don't think snooty old Mrs. Bates will ever recover from learning that the Queen of England's daughter was living in her dormitory," said Elizabeth, pushing back a long strand of golden blond hair. "And the whole time, she'd been looking down her nose at her, thinking Lina was just a poor working-class girl from Liverpool!"

"She practically fainted when she saw the special edition of the *London Journal* with your article," Emily agreed. "Her fat old face turned white and then purple and then green. If there hadn't been a chair right behind her, she would have fallen flat on the floor."

"Maybe Mrs. Bates will learn a lesson," Portia speculated, filling her cup with steaming hot tea. "In the future, I wager she won't be so quick to play favorites based on whether she thinks one of her boarders is well born or well connected!"

Emily nodded, her green eyes twinkling mischievously. "Now, if I can only convince her I'm the runaway daughter of the Queen of Australia . . . !"

Elizabeth shook her head, smiling. The story really was like a fairy tale. When Elizabeth and her twin sister, Jessica, arrived at HIS a few weeks earlier, their home for the time they'd spend as interns at a London newspaper, the housemother, Mrs. Bates, had assigned them to a room with Portia Albert and Lina Smith. Elizabeth had struck up a friendship with Lina immediately, admiring the sweet, plainspoken girl with mousy brown hair and wire-rimmed glasses who was devoting her summer to helping at a homeless shelter and soup kitchen.

From the start, though, there had been something a bit puzzling, a bit off, about Lina. "Remember when you found that fancy cocktail dress in the back of the closet?" Elizabeth asked Emily. "And Lina had such elegant nightgowns—not at all what you'd think a girl from a poor family would wear."

"And you noticed that her glasses had clear lenses," said Emily.

Portia tossed her glossy raven hair. "And we all noticed that she had a mad crush on David Bartholomew but for some mysterious reason wouldn't do anything about it."

Emily grinned. "Plus, it always seemed funny to me that Lina should know more high-society gossip than me, seeing as how I've been known to spend every spare moment reading about the royals in the tabloids!"

"When she told me who she really was, that night before we went to the opening of your play," Elizabeth said to Portia, "I almost pulled a Mrs. Bates and fainted dead away. It was the hardest secret I ever had to keep."

"Especially with huge headlines in the paper every day," said Portia. "Her disappearance was the biggest news to hit London in ages."

"All's well that ends well," Elizabeth concluded. "She's back with her family at Buckingham Palace, but she's determined to stay in touch with the real world and the causes she cares about. She and David fell in love and they don't care in the least that their backgrounds are so different. And finally, when David received the one-million-pound reward for finding the princess, he turned right around and donated it to the homeless shelter!"

Portia stirred a spoonful of sugar into her tea. "It's absolutely the most romantic story, like something from a play."

"Maybe it will be a play," said Emily. "It could be your next stage role, Porsh!"

Lina's not the only one who surprised us, thought Elizabeth, digging into her bacon and eggs. Portia wasn't the girl they'd all thought her to be, either. The daughter of the incomparable Shakespearean actor Sir Montford Albert, who directed a theater company in Edinburgh, Scotland, Portia had come to London to launch her own acting career. Right away, she'd landed a role in a new West End play . . . on the basis of her famous name rather than on her talent, her fellow HIS residents had assumed. There wasn't much incentive to give Portia the benefit of the doubt; she was arrogant and pretentious and cold as ice, disdaining to socialize the least little bit with the other teenagers at HIS.

Then, the day of her opening night, she left complimentary tickets for us, Elizabeth remembered. Elizabeth had managed to talk Jessica, Emily, David, and Gabriello into giving Portia one last chance. At the theater, they'd been astounded to discover that Portia was performing under an alias: Penelope Abbott. Not only that, but the personality of Isabelle in *A Common Man* was uncannily like Portia's own personality . . . or what they'd all assumed was her personality.

"You fooled us, too, Portia," Elizabeth said out loud. "We thought Isabelle Huntington was the real you!"

Portia smiled ruefully. "I wanted so much to prove myself to the world . . . and to my father. The only way I knew to really excel in my art was to immerse myself one hundred percent in the role. I'm only glad you were willing to forgive me for practicing my lines on you!"

"I almost didn't," Emily teased. "You were a real pain in the derriere, Portia Albert!"

Portia flashed an endearing smile and patted Emily's arm. "But we're friends now, aren't we? That's why I told my father I don't want to move into the fancy flat he found for me on the other side of town."

"What fancy flat?" asked Elizabeth.

"After seeing the play the other night and realizing not only am I serious about becoming an actress, but I may actually be good at it, he's suddenly behind me heart and soul and pocketbook. You saw the flowers upstairs?"

"How could I miss them?" Elizabeth laughed. "That bouquet is bigger than I am!"

"It came with a card from my parents," Portia explained, "offering to rent me a place of my own, so I could have more privacy than here at the dorm."

Elizabeth's face fell. The third-floor bedroom already seemed empty with Lina gone. "You're not leaving, too, are you?"

Portia shook her head firmly. "I told them I'm happy where I am—I'm happy sharing digs with all of you. Your friendship helps keep me going, gets me up on that stage every night. No, I'm not budging." She grinned. "You're stuck with me!"

"I'm glad," Elizabeth said. "Because—"

Just then, the dining-room door swung open. David Bartholomew and Gabriello Moretti sprinted in, each waving a couple of newspapers. "Wait until you see these headlines," David called. "They're even bigger than the ones about the missing Princess!"

Elizabeth's heart sank. She already knew what the headlines would say. *If only I could wake up one morning and find it's all been a dream,* she thought, forcing herself to look at the newspapers the boys tossed on the table. *A terrible, terrible dream.*

The *London Journal* was uppermost, its lead story titled, "Young Lord Pembroke Suspect in Murder Case." The sensational *London Daily Post* used all capital letters for added drama: "WERE-WOLF STALKS LONDON BY NIGHT!" A three-inch-high headline in yet another newspaper asked, "Little Lord Pembroke: Werewolf?"

Elizabeth pushed the newspapers away, and her plate as well. Her appetite had vanished. "It's almost worse than not knowing who the killer was, to have it turn out to be him."

Emily clucked her tongue sadly. "Your poor, poor sister."

"Well, the man's innocent until proven guilty, isn't he?" said David, pulling up a chair.

"Yes," Portia agreed. "But is there really any doubt?"

Her expression grim, Elizabeth shook her head. "I wish there was still room for doubt—I'd give anything to believe the murderer wasn't Robert Pembroke." *The boy my sister's fallen in love with* . . . "But the evidence all points in his direction. His own father admits as much."

As her eye was drawn back to the newspaper headlines, Elizabeth's thoughts returned to the beginning of it all. Their very first day at the *Journal*, she and Jessica had taken it upon themselves to sneak over to the scene of a major crime. A prominent London physician had been brutally murdered and, spying through a window, the twins had seen his corpse. His throat had been ripped open, as if by a wild beast.

After that, events began to snowball. *Journal* editor-in-chief Henry Reeves drastically cut and altered crime editor Lucy Friday's article about Dr.

7

Neville's murder. Lucy in turn accused Reeves of conspiring in a cover-up with the *Journal*'s owner, Lord Robert Pembroke, and the London chief of police, and then quit her position. More bodies began to turn up, all killed in the same savage manner. And one of the victims was murdered in the very bed Jessica was supposed to be sleeping in at Pembroke Manor. . . .

Elizabeth shuddered, remembering the previous weekend. Jessica had been invited to the Pembrokes' country estate by Lord Pembroke's son and heir, Robert, and she'd talked Elizabeth and Elizabeth's friend from work, Luke Shepherd, into going with her. For Elizabeth and Luke, it was a chance to investigate the Pembroke family—to find out if there was any truth to Lucy Friday's theory that the Pembrokes had something to hide.

It was the night of the full moon, Elizabeth recalled. And the local constable came by the manor to tell Lord Pembroke that some sheep had been found on his property, slaughtered. Luke was sure it was a werewolf, and then she'd had that horrible dream. . . .

She'd dreamed that Jessica was being pursued by a werewolf, and she herself could only watch helplessly. When she woke the next morning and ran to her sister's room, it looked for a minute as if the dream had become reality. A girl with blond hair lay on the bed in a pool of blood . . . dead.

It turned out that Jessica had switched rooms

with another guest—the victim was actually Joy Singleton, fiancée of London police chief Andrew Thatcher. Soon the local police were on the case, but Elizabeth had decided to do some sleuthing on her own. Returning to Pembroke Manor, she'd discovered a hidden room filled with books about werewolves—Lord Pembroke had a passionate, perhaps obsessive, interest in the subject.

She'd also overheard a bone-chilling conversation between Lord Pembroke Senior and Thatcher. It turned out Pembroke had been hiding something—he'd been using his personal influence over Thatcher to stall the police investigation of the killings so he could gather clues and capture the werewolf himself. But with another dead body at Pembroke Manor, that of the Pembroke Manor cook, Thatcher finally persuaded Lord Pembroke to turn his evidence over to the police . . . and announce at a press conference that his own son, Robert Junior, was the number one suspect.

"We'd better put these away in case Jessica—" Emily began.

She didn't get a chance to finish her sentence. At that moment, Jessica herself entered the dining room.

Before Emily and the others could shove the newspapers under the table, Jessica charged over and snatched one of them up. Two spots of angry pink blossomed in her cheeks as she scanned the headline.

"Are you happy, Liz?" Jessica demanded, flinging the paper at her sister. "Are you pleased with what you've done?"

An awkward silence fell over the dining room. "I haven't done anything," Elizabeth said quietly.

"Oh, no?" Jessica put her hands on her hips, her eyes shooting sparks. "You and all your snooping around at Pembroke Manor. You wouldn't rest until you'd pinned this on Robert and his family. And then you and Luke forced your absurd, demented werewolf theory on everybody!"

"We didn't force any theory on anyone," Elizabeth protested. "The press jumped to their own conclusions, given the evidence."

"Well, they're wrong. You're all wrong! Robert Pembroke isn't a killer, much less a werewolf. You've ruined an innocent man's life, Elizabeth," Jessica cried passionately, "and you've ruined my life, too!"

At this, Elizabeth lost what grasp she had left on her temper. She jumped to her feet to stand face-to-face with her sister. "I've ruined your life? I'm trying to save your life, you idiot!" she shouted. "I can't believe how deluded you are!"

"I'm deluded, says the girl who believes in werewolves. I'm deluded!"

"Yes, you are," Elizabeth snapped. "All the evidence points to Robert. He had the opportunity to commit the murders. His cigarette case was found near Dr. Neville's body—threads from his bathrobe turned up on the door frame of your room at Pembroke Manor. And now he's skipped town, disappeared without a trace. If that doesn't prove he's guilty, nothing does, and if you weren't so blinded by his money and title, you'd see what everybody else sees."

"He didn't do it," Jessica insisted stubbornly.

Elizabeth's hands clenched into fists. She resisted the urge to grab her sister and shake her hard. "How can you defend him, Jess, when he tried to kill you, too, first at Pembroke Manor and then again the other day in the tube station?"

"It wasn't Robert who attacked me!" Jessica cried. "How many times do I have to say that? You're not even listening to me. The case is closed in your opinion. Robert is your idea of the perfect villain, isn't he? You disliked him on principle from the beginning."

"I did not," protested Elizabeth.

"You did, too. You're the worst kind of reverse snob, Liz. Because he's rich, you just assumed Robert was selfish and shallow and utterly without morals. Well, I'll tell you something that may shock you," Jessica said, in her most bitterly sarcastic tone. "Having money doesn't make a person bad, any more than people without money are automatically saints."

Elizabeth's eyes flashed indignantly at this disparaging allusion to Luke. "Don't even think about trying to drag Luke down to Robert's level. He's as good as they come, but then, you wouldn't know that. You've never given him the time of day because his name isn't *Lord* Shepherd."

"Luke may be as good as they come, but he's also a nut, if you ask me," countered Jessica. "You're both nuts. And you're lousy reporters. You think you're hot stuff, though, don't you, Liz? Getting your byline on that front-page article about Princess Eliana. Boy, it must have been tough to crack that case, seeing as how Lina came right out and told you who she really was! You'll have to work a lot harder to prove Robert's guilty, because the evidence you keep harping on is totally inconclusive and you couldn't come up with a motive if your life depended on it."

With that, Jessica dropped into a chair, folding her arms across her chest. Elizabeth stared down at her sister. Her mouth opened and closed—she was still seething—but she'd run out of arguments. As usual, she'd gotten nowhere fast trying to reason with Jessica.

What's the point of wasting my breath? Elizabeth wondered, grabbing her shoulder bag. *She doesn't want my help—she doesn't deserve my help.*

"See ya, Emily, Portia, David, Gabriello," said Elizabeth. Pointedly ignoring her sister, Elizabeth spun on her heel and stomped off. *I'm not waiting for her,* she decided. *I'm not riding to work with her. In fact, I'm not speaking to her ever again!*

• • • •

Jessica glared after her sister, her eyes narrowed into angry slits. *This is it,* she fumed silently. *This is really it, once and for all. I'm not speaking to that girl again for as long as I live!*

It wasn't the first time the twins had knocked heads about something. Their faces and figures might be identical, but their minds definitely were not. Over the course of sixteen action-packed years, they'd fought over toys, clothes, boys, friends, the phone, the car. *We usually fight because Miss Goody Two-Shoes is too stuffy and serious and responsible to see anybody else's point of view,* Jessica thought. Everything blew over eventually . . . when Elizabeth would finally lighten up and see reason. But Jessica had a feeling this fight wasn't going to blow over. It was the worst one ever.

David and Gabriello, both summer students at London University, hoisted their backpacks and waved good-bye. Jessica watched the boys go, her anger slowly draining away. With a heavy sigh, she slumped forward, her elbows on the table and her head in her hands.

She'd just woken up, but she felt as if she'd already run a marathon—because she knew what an uphill battle she faced. *How can I prove Robert's innocent after everything that's happened?* Jessica wondered bleakly. *Everyone assumes his father tipped him off and he skipped town to save his skin. Where is he?* Tears smarted in her eyes as she remembered Robert's sudden departure, his air of

13

mystery as he said good-bye to her two days ago. *Why didn't he tell me what was going on? Why did he leave me, alone and in the dark?*

On the other side of the table, Emily cleared her throat. "You probably won't want to hear this, Jessica," she began.

Jessica lifted her head. "Then don't say it," she advised coolly. "If you want to make accusations against Robert, go talk to Elizabeth."

"It's not that at all," Emily insisted, putting a hand on her friend's arm. "I just think you should be careful. I'm worried about you."

"Liz is right about that, at least," Portia agreed. "Someone *did* try to kill you. If you hadn't switched rooms with Joy Singleton . . ."

"It wasn't Robert," Jessica repeated. She sounded like a broken record, but she didn't care. She'd keep saying it until someone believed her. "It wasn't Robert. I know him. He loves me."

Her friends nodded sympathetically, but Jessica could tell they weren't convinced. Their doubts were written all over their faces. *They're thinking maybe I know him, but not well enough. They're thinking evidence is evidence.*

It was true, she and Robert had only been dating for a few weeks. All Jessica really had to go on was a gut instinct, but it was a strong one. *He's a good person, no matter what Liz says. Sure, he was wild as a kid, getting kicked out of school and stuff like that, but that hardly makes him homicidal ma-*

14

niac material. If he'd wanted to harm her, he'd had plenty of chances. Far from threatening her, though, the last time she saw him, Robert had been concerned about nothing but her safety.

No, Jessica was willing to stake her life that Robert Pembroke was not the werewolf of London. Which meant somebody else was. . . .

"I'm glad it's the weekend," Luke Shepherd said to Elizabeth as they strolled through the park down the street from HIS late Friday afternoon. "I'm ready for a few days off, aren't you?"

Turning up the collar of her jacket, Elizabeth nodded. "Things have been crazier than ever at the *Journal* since Reeves got the boot."

"What a turnaround on Lord Pembroke's part," Luke remarked. "One minute, he's masterminding a cover-up of the murders, the next he's publicly backing the police search for his son and firing Reeves for obeying his orders."

"It was one thing to play down the Neville murder, but Reeves went too far when he took it upon himself to print an unsubstantiated story about the princess," Elizabeth reminded Luke. "Lord Pembroke didn't order him to do that. Reeves just got carried away trying to compete with the *London Daily Post.* Too bad, too. He sabotaged a long, distinguished career."

"Well, one thing's for certain," said Luke, wrapping an arm around Elizabeth's shoulders. "There hasn't been a dull moment since you started your internship!"

"There hasn't," she agreed wholeheartedly. Because not only had she gotten caught up on the hunt for a savage serial killer, but she'd fallen head over heels for an adorable English boy.

Elizabeth looked up at Luke and he smiled down at her. In the misty gray dusk, with his fair skin, dark hair, lake-blue eyes, and rosy lips, he looked more than ever like the romantic hero of a nineteenth-century novel. Elizabeth's heart did a somersault. She hadn't come to London looking for a boyfriend—she had one at home, and she'd intended to be faithful to him. But she couldn't help the way Luke made her feel. They had so much in common—a love of literature and history—so much to talk about. And when he put his arms around her, the rest of the world—including Todd Wilkins back in Sweet Valley, California—disappeared.

It was a typical gray, drizzly London evening, but Luke's embrace warmed Elizabeth like a fire. They kissed and then continued strolling, hand in hand.

"I didn't see Jessica around the office much today," Luke remarked. "How is she handling all this?"

"She's not," Elizabeth said, frowning. "We had a total blowup this morning about it. She just won't let go of Robert."

16

"Are you two on the outs?"

"That's a nice way of putting it. I'm so frustrated with her! But I'm worried, too," Elizabeth confessed. "She's madly in love with him—she's obsessed. I know she's going to look for him. And I'm afraid she might actually find him."

"Or he might find her," said Luke.

"Right. So that's why I think we should try to track Robert down ourselves," Elizabeth proposed. "If we could help bring him safely into custody—"

Luke halted, gripping Elizabeth's arms with both hands. A gust of wind stirred the wet leaves overhead, showering them both with raindrops. "I don't want you taking any more risks," he told her with uncharacteristic sternness. "The police department and Scotland Yard are in charge of the case now. Promise me you won't strike off on your own and put yourself in danger."

Luke folded her in a protective hug. Elizabeth rested her head against his chest. "I promise," she said, feeling guilty about the fib. Because despite Luke's misgivings, she was determined. She couldn't just stand by and do nothing. *I've got to find Robert*, she thought, staring past Luke's shoulder at a homeless man in a shabby brown coat and cap, poking around in the leaves with a stick. *Jessica won't be safe until he's behind bars*.

Stepping back slightly, Luke placed a hand under Elizabeth's chin and lifted her face to his. "I'm serious about this, Liz," he said. "With Robert

17

named as the chief suspect and on the run, both you and Jessica need to be more careful than ever. Robert knows you helped turn up the evidence against him—he could seek revenge."

Elizabeth thought about Maria Finch, formerly the cook at Pembroke Manor, and shivered. Maria had seen something the night of Joy Singleton's murder, but before she could cast any light on the case, she, too, had been murdered. Silenced. Her throat torn open.

"I'm . . . I'm afraid," Elizabeth whispered.

Luke ran a finger gently down the side of her face to her throat. "I know you are." He touched the pendant she wore around her neck. "Remember when I gave this to you?"

Elizabeth nodded. The antique silver pendant was etched with the image of a wolf enclosed in a pentagram. Luke had given it to her as they strolled through the woods near Pembroke Manor. He thought there might be danger because they had seen wolfsbane in bloom and there was going to be a full moon. And he was right.

"I told you it would protect you," said Luke, "neutralize the werewolf's power, and it will if you continue to wear it night and day. But the danger is growing fiercer all the time."

He reached into his pocket and then pressed something cold and metallic into Elizabeth's palm. She opened her fingers, exclaiming, "A silver bullet!"

"One of the few weapons that can destroy a werewolf," Luke confirmed.

Elizabeth and Luke had held many conversations about werewolves. His mother, who died when he was young, had imbued him with a passionate interest in folklore; because of his poetic nature, he seemed to respond to the legends as reality rather than myth. From the beginning, Luke had been convinced that the string of barbaric murders was the work of a werewolf.

Jessica's sarcastic comments darted through Elizabeth's brain. *Absurd, demented, deluded* . . . She knew she should be skeptical, but not for the first time, she felt herself falling under the spell of Luke's convictions. An icy chill swept through her body even as she forced a laugh. "What good is a silver bullet without a gun?"

"Carry it in your pocket," Luke insisted. "He'll know that you have it, that you have the power to destroy him. Keep it with you. Just trust me."

Elizabeth looked up into Luke's anxious, sincere eyes and nodded. She did trust him, implicitly.

In all the strange, swirling mist of violence—of terror, mystery, and suspicion—she was certain of only one thing: her feelings for Luke Shepherd and his feelings for her. *He's been with me every step of the way,* she thought, slipping the silver bullet into her pocket and then throwing her arms around Luke. *He'll see me through this. He'll protect me.*

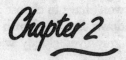

Chapter 2

Waking up Saturday morning, Elizabeth was glad to look out the window by her bed and see the rain had cleared.

"What a wonderful day to visit Buckingham Palace," said Portia, who was sitting at her dressing table brushing her long, dark hair. "I can't tell you how envious I am!"

Elizabeth hopped out of bed, stretching her arms over her head. "I wish you could come with us."

"If I didn't have a matinee performance, it would be jolly," Portia agreed. She winked. "Be sure to give my regards to the queen."

Out of the corner of her eye, Elizabeth saw Jessica roll over in the top bunk and pull a pillow over her head. Portia pointed to Jessica, mouthing the words, "Is she going?"

Elizabeth shrugged. "I have no idea," she whis-

21

pered. "We're not speaking to each other."

Portia clucked her tongue. "Not speaking? Why, Liz, you oughtn't let one little row—"

"It wasn't a little row," Elizabeth interrupted, loud enough for her sister to hear. "It's probably best if you don't get involved, Portia," she advised. "That way, you won't have to choose sides."

Portia put down her hairbrush and gazed at Elizabeth, her gray eyes cloudy with concern. "I just don't like to see—"

Elizabeth cut Portia off again. "I'm going to take a shower," she said, grabbing her bathrobe and breezing toward the door. "Have a nice day."

An hour later, as she and David sped to the royal residence in the car Eliana had sent for them, Elizabeth thought back to the scene earlier that morning. *I was kind of rude to Portia,* she thought ruefully. *It's not her fault she's caught in the middle—she just wants to make peace.*

Elizabeth pictured her sister, burrowing under the bedclothes like a crab in the sand, and she felt another pang. *Should I have called a truce? If Jess were going to the palace with me, at least I'd know she was staying out of trouble. . . .*

David had been looking out the car window in silence. Now he turned to Elizabeth. "My palms are sweating," he confessed. "I don't know if I have the nerve to date a princess."

"It's pretty daunting," Elizabeth commiserated.

"Meeting your girlfriend's mother . . . the Queen of England!"

"What if . . . what if her, Eliana's, feelings have changed?" David ran a hand through his straw-colored hair and then tugged nervously at the collar of his shirt. "I haven't seen her since she moved back home a couple of days ago. What if it doesn't make sense to her anymore, hanging out with an ordinary bloke like me?"

Elizabeth patted David's knee. "She'll feel exactly the same way she did when she was Lina Smith, working at the soup kitchen and sleeping in the bunk above Portia," Elizabeth promised. "She doesn't care about artificial social distinctions. That's why she ran away from home in the first place—to escape, to experience the real world, to establish an identity for herself apart from the royal family."

David smiled. "She's really something, isn't she?"

"She's one in a million. And she's wild about you."

"I'm still nervous about meeting the queen."

"No kidding." Elizabeth laughed. "I'm terrified!"

David grew even more jittery five minutes later, when a palace guard waved them through the gate. "We're having tea with the queen," he muttered, pink spots of excitement rising in his fair cheeks. "Every single citizen of England dreams of doing that, and it's happening to me, David Bartholomew!"

Elizabeth clasped her hands in her lap, her own

23

eyes bright with anticipation. What a story to tell her friends back home! Tea with the queen would definitely be the highlight of their day with Eliana. At the same time . . .

Elizabeth resisted an impulse to ask the driver to turn around and take her back to HIS. *Tea with the queen—is that really important?* she thought guiltily. *How can I goof off like this when people are dying . . . when my own sister might be next?* Sure, it would be fun and unforgettable to visit Princess Eliana at Buckingham Palace. Elizabeth bit her lip. *But I should be looking for Robert. I should be out there trying to solve this mystery.*

"Do you want to help me with my lines or not?" Portia asked somewhat peevishly.

It was late Saturday afternoon, and the two girls were sitting in Portia's dressing room backstage at the Ravensgate Theatre. For lack of anything else to do, Jessica had dropped by to gab with Portia in between the matinee and evening performances of *A Common Man*.

Now Jessica heaved a sigh, frowning at her copy of the script of Portia's play. "Sorry. I'm just a little distracted."

Portia arched one slender, sardonic eyebrow. "Really? I hadn't noticed."

"Let's try it again," Jessica offered. "From the beginning of the scene, when you come in from the garden."

Portia closed her script. "Actually, I think I'd like to leave it for now. I may change an inflection—a gesture—a little something, just to keep it from feeling stale. But not tonight."

Tossing down the script, Jessica glanced at the clock on the wall. It was four thirty—teatime. At that very moment, Elizabeth was probably perched on a velvet chair, sipping from a delicate china cup, her pinkie finger lifted, making conversation with the Queen of England.

It should have been me, Jessica thought petulantly. *What does Liz know or care about the royal family?* But she'd vowed not to be in the same room as her sister . . . and that included throne rooms.

"You're not doing anyone any good by moping, you know," Portia said as she leaned close to the mirror to touch up her mascara. "Do something productive."

Crossing her arms, Jessica pushed out her lower lip in a classic pout. "Like what?"

"Use your noodle," Portia suggested bluntly. "Do you want to help clear Robert's name so he can come out of hiding or not?"

Jessica sighed. Clear Robert's name . . . come out of hiding . . . It all sounded so dire and melodramatic. How on earth had they gotten into this predicament?

The *London Journal* internship had started out so fabulously. Her very first day on the job, she was sent to write up a story at Pembroke Green, the elegant London residence of the landed-gentry Pembroke family, distant relatives of the Windsors. She'd met Lord and Lady Pembroke's aristocratic only son, Robert, and he'd taken her to tea . . . and then dinner . . . and then dancing. He'd swept her off her feet, just like in a fairy tale. Jessica had found her Prince Charming.

Visiting the Pembrokes' country estate was supposed to be the most romantic and incredible experience of my life, she reflected morosely. Instead, Luke and Elizabeth and some insane murderer had turned it into a werewolf festival. Now the whole city of London was up in arms . . . and the love of her life was public enemy number one.

Portia tipped her head to one side, thoughtful eyes resting on Jessica's face. "Or maybe you're ready to write off Robert Pembroke," Portia speculated. "Maybe your feelings for him don't run deep enough to warrant unshaking loyalty in the face of the crimes he's being charged with."

"No," Jessica said forcefully. "I'm not writing him off. Sure, I could. Easily. And I would if Elizabeth were right and all I ever cared about was Robert's money and title. But we're in love. My feelings are real. And Robert's innocent."

Portia clapped. "Bravo!"

Jessica smiled ruefully. "What a speech, huh?"

"Now all you have to do is translate that passion into action."

Jessica thought about Elizabeth, taking the investigation into her own hands, snooping around Pembroke Manor scribbling notes and interviewing people. "Liz isn't the only one who can play Nancy Drew," Jessica declared. "If Robert isn't the killer, then someone else is—and it's time Jessica Wakefield, private eye, got to the bottom of things. So, how do I start?"

"How about at the beginning?"

"And in the beginning, there was a body." Jessica nodded thoughtfully. "And another body, and another . . ."

Her shoulder bag was slung over the back of a director's chair, and now Jessica reached into it to grab the small spiral notebook she used at work. Whipping it open to a blank page, she quickly jotted down a list of names. "Nurse Handley, who was attacked at the hospital where she works," she said out loud. "Dr. Neville, killed in his home, which was also his office. And Dr. Neville, by the way, was a close family friend of the Pembrokes. Poo-Poo, Lady Wimpole's Yorkshire terrier. Police chief Thatcher's girlfriend, Joy Singleton—me, almost. Maria Finch, the Pembroke Manor cook."

Portia shuddered. "Somebody's leaving a very bloody trail."

"If it's a trail, it's a pretty crooked one." Jessica tapped her pencil, the wheels in her brain churning. "There must be a thread connecting these victims—a thread that leads back to the killer. But what is it?"

• • •

"How was the concert?" Portia asked Gabriello on Sunday morning as the HIS residents yawned over brunch.

"That's right," said Elizabeth. "The music students at the university summer program put on a performance last night. I almost forgot."

"It went well," Gabriello replied. "But you should really ask Jessica and Emily. They came to cheer me on."

"He played first violin and he was fabulous," Emily raved.

"I didn't think classical music could be so exciting," Jessica admitted. "It was almost as cool as a rock concert."

"What about you?" Emily turned to Elizabeth and David. "I was so mad that the BBC made me work yesterday. How was the princess? How was the palace?"

As David launched into a glowing report of their visit with Eliana, Elizabeth peeped at her sister out of the corner of her eye. Munching a bowl of muesli, Jessica feigned disinterest, but Elizabeth could tell she was dying for details.

"You wouldn't believe the furniture," David gushed, "and the art. Old Master paintings and sculpture and tapestries all over the place. And Eliana's apartment . . . her closet alone is the size of this dining room. She must have a thousand formal gowns."

"Really?" Spoon in hand, Jessica stared at David with round, curious eyes. "What did they look like?"

"I'm the wrong one to ask," said David. "Fashion isn't exactly my bag. Maybe Elizabeth could describe some of them."

Elizabeth glanced coolly at Jessica. Jessica narrowed her eyes. "I guess I'm not that interested after all," Jessica said with a sniff.

Emily hurried to change the subject. "Speaking of fashion, anyone up for a shopping expedition this afternoon?"

"I am," said Jessica.

"Grand. I know you've got a performance, Portia. How 'bout you, Liz?"

Shopping had never been Elizabeth's favorite activity. *And I'm certainly not going if she is,* Elizabeth thought. *Nice try, Em.* Besides, even though Sunday was supposed to be a day of rest and recreation, Elizabeth had serious plans. She had to make up for lost time. "Luke and I are going to the British Museum," she fibbed. "Thanks, anyway."

As Emily and Jessica discussed which stores to target, Elizabeth mentally mapped out her own agenda. *A shopping expedition—perfect!* she thought. *That should keep her out of the way while I do some sleuthing.*

As soon as she and Emily rounded the block

29

and were out of sight of HIS, Jessica stopped dead in her tracks. She looked both ways to make sure the coast was clear. She didn't want Elizabeth to witness this change in direction and catch on to her scheme.

"What is it?" said Emily, peering nervously into the dense green of the park. "Do you see . . . something?"

"The werewolf?" Jessica laughed. "No, but this is as far as I'm going. I only said yes to the shopping idea to get Elizabeth off my trail. I've got some detective work to do."

"Oh." Emily's face crumpled with disappointment. Then anxiety took its place. "Are you sure it's safe to go off alone?"

"I'll be fine," Jessica assured her. "Just don't tell anyone where I'm going, OK?"

"Where *are* you going?" Emily called as Jessica hurried off.

"See ya!" Jessica yelled back, ignoring her friend's question.

At the corner, Jessica hopped onto a red double-decker bus heading across town. Ten minutes later, she disembarked at Essex Street. She hadn't ventured near the scene of Dr. Neville's murder since the morning she and Elizabeth spied the address in Lucy Friday's datebook and took it upon themselves to investigate. An icy shiver ran up Jessica's spine now as she recalled walking down the tree-lined street . . . sneaking into the cordoned-off yard . . . hiding in the rhododendron bushes . . . looking through the picture window. . . .

"Brr." Jessica forced herself to walk at a brisk, no-nonsense pace, but her teeth were chattering. "Good thing there's no reason to be scared anymore. The bloody corpse won't still be lying on the parlor floor!"

It was a typical cool gray London afternoon, with the ever-present threat of rain. Essex Street appeared deserted. As Jessica approached Dr. Neville's property, she slowed her steps. The gate wasn't blocked by a stern London bobby as on the last occasion, but it was fastened with a giant padlock. Beyond the gate, Jessica could see that the windows of the flat were tightly shuttered. *How on earth am I going to get in there?* she wondered. *And why do I want to get in there?*

She answered her own question. *Because if Robert isn't the werewolf, someone else is, and the best way to clear Robert's name is to unearth the real killer. So, who are my top suspects?*

In her mind, she ran over the list of people who'd been present at Pembroke Manor when Joy Singleton was murdered. *Robert, Lord and Lady Pembroke, Andrew Thatcher, me, Liz, Luke, the servants.* She scratched Elizabeth, Robert, and herself off the list. That left Robert's parents, Joy's fiancé the police chief, Luke, and the Pembroke Manor servants. *Or an outsider,* Jessica conceded with a sigh. *Face it, it could have been just about anyone. Which brings us back to the victims. If I*

*can just find that thread that connects them . . .
and it's not the thread from Robert's paisley silk
bathrobe, no matter what Liz thinks!*

Doubling back along the sidewalk, Jessica
slipped into a narrow alleyway, following it to its
end. On the right, an old brick wall stood between
her and what should be Dr. Neville's backyard.
Good thing I wore sneakers and jeans, Jessica
thought as she climbed the wall, feeling for finger-
and toeholds in the crumbling brick.

Swinging her legs over the top, she dropped
down into the damp, overgrown grass. What a lucky
break! The back windows of the townhouse weren't
shuttered. It took only a minute to jimmy one open
with the knife she'd slipped into her purse that
morning at brunch. Pushing the window up, Jessica
scrambled onto the sill and jumped inside.

She was in the dead man's kitchen. As she
glanced around the dim room, another shiver tickled her spine, lifting the hair on the back of her
neck. The table in the breakfast nook was set with
china and silver; a kettle stood on the stove, as if
about to whistle. *Dr. Neville didn't make it to breakfast that morning,* Jessica thought grimly. *Ugh.*

Wandering down the hallway, she peered into
each room. She passed a formal dining room, a film
of dust on the dark mahogany table; the patients'
waiting room, old magazines still fanned out on the
coffee table; an examining room, with instruments
and supplies displayed in a glass-fronted case; the

front parlor where the body had been found.

Goose bumps prickled Jessica's arms. She stared at the bare wood floor where at one point a carpet had been . . . a carpet that ended up permanently stained with blood. Outside, the wind stirred the shrubs, causing a branch to tap against the window . . . the very same window she and Elizabeth had gazed through. Jessica jumped. It sounded like a ghostly finger, scratching. . . .

Hurrying away from the parlor, she came to the doctor's study. At the sight of the ornate desk and three tall walnut filing cabinets, her heartbeat quickened. She didn't know exactly what kind of clue she was looking for, but maybe she'd find it here.

The cabinets had four drawers, all stuffed with papers. "Research and journal articles," Jessica muttered, running a finger along the file tabs in the top drawer of the first cabinet. She pulled out the next drawer, and the next. "Accounting and tax stuff—blech."

The second cabinet was more promising. "Patient files!" Jessica's eyes lit up. "This could be it."

She rifled through the folders, searching for anything that might constitute a clue. Not surprisingly, there were files for all the Pembrokes—Neville had been the family physician. "No Handley, though," Jessica observed out loud. "And no Wimpole." She swallowed a nervous giggle. Not that she'd expected to find a file for Poo-Poo—Neville wasn't a vet, after all!

She examined the name on each folder, making her way through the alphabet. Salisbury, Bernard. Sarton, Kendall. Sarton, Meredith. Scofield, Edna. Shafly, Sir Thomas. S., Annabelle.

Jessica paused, frowning at the folder. "S., Annabelle?" she said. "How come Annabelle only gets an initial?" All the other files were headed by the patient's full name.

Curious, Jessica pulled out Annabelle S.'s folder. When she opened it, a single sheet of paper fluttered out onto the floor. Bending, Jessica picked it up. It was a medical chart, mostly blank. The word "deceased" was stamped in red on the top and someone—Dr. Neville, Jessica assumed—had scrawled a brief notation: "cause of death: pneumonia."

Weird, Jessica thought. *How come there are no other charts or forms? Shouldn't there be more stuff about a patient Dr. Neville had treated for what turned out to be a fatal case of pneumonia? How old was Annabelle; where did she live? And what happened to her last name?*

It was mysterious, but probably not connected to the murders, Jessica decided. After all, according to the date on the chart, the woman had died nearly nine years ago. Annabelle S., whoever she was, was ancient history.

Jessica was about to replace the file when she heard something. What was that? She stood perfectly still, her ears pricked and her blood turning

34

to ice in her veins. She heard it again, coming from the far end of the hall. A shutter rattling in the wind? Or a footstep?

Her heart in her throat, Jessica pushed the cabinet drawer shut. Sticking the Annabelle S. file in her shoulder bag, she leapt toward the door and then dashed on tiptoes down the hallway away from the scary noise.

Reaching the kitchen, she saw with relief that she'd left the window open. As she dove through it and landed on the damp earth below, Jessica was pretty sure she'd never been so glad to breathe the cold, misty London air.

The shuttered French doors opening out into Dr. Neville's side yard hadn't been too difficult to pry apart, using the tools she'd brought with her. Easing one of the doors open, Elizabeth stepped cautiously into the stale, musty air of the deserted apartment.

The dining room, she thought, taking another tentative step forward. The parquet floor creaked beneath her feet and she froze. What was that?

She thought she heard a distant creaking sound somewhere else on the ground floor of the house, like an echo of her own footsteps. Elizabeth listened, her heart thumping wildly. Silence.

"You're imagining things," she whispered to herself. "Nobody lives here anymore, and there's no such thing as ghosts."

However, on the off chance that she was wrong and the house was haunted by the unfortunate Dr. Neville and his gory throat, Elizabeth decided to make her tour as brief as possible.

I'm looking for a clue, something that might lead me to Robert, she reminded herself as she scurried down the hall past the doctor's waiting and examining rooms. *Maybe I can find out something about Neville, something that would have given Robert a reason to kill him.*

At the door to the doctor's study, Elizabeth paused, taking a moment to let her pulse slow and her thoughts untangle. As her eyes moved around the room, coming to rest on a row of filing cabinets, she had a peculiar sensation—like déjà vu, or the kind of tingle she got when her identical-twin intuition kicked in and she could almost feel her mind melding with Jessica's. The atmosphere of the room seemed charged with energy. *It's almost as if I've been here before,* Elizabeth thought, hugging herself to ward off a sudden chill. *But I haven't.*

She strode over to the file cabinets. The deceased physician's records were orderly and for the most part uninteresting. What was it about Neville, about Neville and Robert Pembroke Junior? Elizabeth wondered. Preposterous scenarios presented themselves as she flipped through the alphabetized patient files. Maybe Robert was a drug addict and came here to steal from Neville's pharmaceutical supply and Neville caught him at it and there was a scuffle. Maybe Robert knew something about Neville, or Neville knew something about Robert, or . . .

Spotting the Pembroke family files, Elizabeth plucked out Robert Junior's. It was fat; Neville had probably treated Robert since babyhood. "I'll take it home with me," Elizabeth murmured to herself. "Maybe a careful reading will turn up something useful."

Shutting the file cabinet drawer, she turned to the doctor's desk. A dark-green blotter, an old-fashioned brass pen-and-ink stand, and a small stack of monogrammed stationery stood at the ready, as if Dr. Neville might come in at any moment and sit down to jot a letter. Or make a phone call, Elizabeth thought, reaching for the Rolodex.

She thumbed through the cards. "Parker, Pease, Pembroke, Pitcairn," Elizabeth recited. "Player's Racquet Club, Plum's Pastry Shop, Portnoy, Price."

"Price!" she repeated, gaping at the card. "'Mildred Price, Pembroke nanny.'"

She nearly laughed as the inspiration struck. *I bet there's a lightbulb shining over my head, like in a comic strip! Yep, this could be it*, Elizabeth thought triumphantly. Little Bobby's old nanny. Where would you go if you were a spoiled young English lord deprived of hearth and home? Why, back to your doting nanny, of course!

Grabbing a pen and a piece of Dr. Neville's stationery, Elizabeth began to scribble down the nanny's address in Pelham. M-I-L-D-R-E-D P-R-I-C-E, she printed. Then her hand jerked and the pen skidded across the paper.

Something had startled her—a creak that sounded loud in the silent, empty flat. *Old houses make noises all by themselves*, Elizabeth reminded herself. *They shift and settle*. She stood perfectly still listening. Another creak, closer this time.

Old houses might shift and settle, but nevertheless Elizabeth had a sudden, overpowering feeling that someone . . . or something . . . was making the noise. She wasn't alone in Dr. Neville's apartment.

Leaving the half-written note, she ripped the card with Mildred Price's address from the Rolodex file and stuck it in her pocket. Racing to the doorway, she peered down the gloomy hall. Off to the right, Elizabeth heard another creak, sounding ominously like a foostep this time.

I don't believe in ghosts, I don't believe in ghosts, she chanted silently to herself as she dashed off to the left, heading at top speed for the dining room. Slipping back out into the side yard, she closed and shuttered the French door, and then leaned back against it for a moment, breathing hard.

Ghosts or no ghosts, she couldn't get out of that house fast enough . . . and she hoped she never had reason to come back again.

• • •

The intruder prowled along the dim back hall of Dr. Neville's flat, his shoulders hunched, the muscles in his arms and legs tense. His breath came in ragged, painful gasps; tumultuous, unbearable emotions acted on his body like a whip, driving him, driving him mad. . . .

At the entrance to Dr. Neville's study, he paused. Clawing the door frame, he sniffed the air. Instantly, he recognized the scent of the two girls who had been there before him. A roar of outrage rumbled in his chest. He knew what brought them there. *They're looking for me.* . . .

Thoughts of the girls, and the hazy, nightmarish memory of what he'd done to Dr. Neville in that very house, lashed him into a frenzy. Leaping across the room, he yanked open the drawers of the file cabinet, one after another, frantically searching. *It's not here*, he realized at last, knocking over a cabinet in his haste and fury. *It's not here—they took it*.

An irresistible urge to destroy something, to rip it to pieces, swept over him, and a howl tore at his throat. Just as he raised an arm to sweep everything off the top of the desk, a scrap of paper caught his eye. He froze, staring at the name written there: Mildred Price.

Instantly, his fury dissolved and a look of cunning gleamed in his bloodshot eyes. *Nanny Millie*, he thought, crumpling the paper in his fist and stealing out of the room.

Chapter 3

Elizabeth checked her watch as she strode quickly away from Dr. Neville's. *Shoot,* she thought, seeing the time. She wanted to go to Pelham to talk with Mildred Price, but she'd made a date with Rene Glize to have tea. *It's already four—I'd better go straight to the restaurant,* she decided. *I can't stand him up again, after how he reacted last time!*

When Elizabeth and Jessica moved in at Housing for International Students, they'd been surprised and delighted to discover that Rene Glize, the young Frenchman they'd met on an exchange program to Cannes, was spending the summer in London and living at HIS, too. While she was in France, Elizabeth and Rene developed a special friendship bordering on romance, and meeting again in London, she'd felt immediately that the spark of attraction was still there. Clearly,

41

Rene thought so, too, and he'd rearranged his busy schedule at the French embassy so he would have time to take Elizabeth out to dinner.

But then she'd met Luke. The day of her dinner date with Rene, Elizabeth and Luke spent the afternoon sightseeing, and as afternoon melted into evening . . . and she grew increasingly captivated by Luke . . . she completely forgot about Rene. Offended and jealous, Rene had been cool to her for a week afterward, but he'd finally relented and they'd both agreed that the best course was just to be good friends.

It was always nice to hang out with Rene; still, as she rode the double-decker bus, Elizabeth could feel the Rolodex card burning a hole in her pocket. *The nanny will just have to wait until tomorrow,* she realized, swallowing her disappointment.

Rene was already seated at a table for two when Elizabeth arrived at the Parkview restaurant a few blocks from HIS. He stood up to pull out her chair. "I know it's terribly rude, but I had a cup of tea without you," he confessed. "This nasty English weather cuts right through to the bones. It is different from summer on the Riviera!"

Elizabeth laughed. "Tell me about it. Winter in southern California isn't this cold and damp!"

Rene filled Elizabeth's teacup. When a plate of fresh-baked scones and tiny tea sandwiches had been placed before them, he reached across the table to touch Elizabeth's hand. "I've been so busy at the embassy, we haven't had a chance to talk in days," he said. "I think about you all the time, though, and I worry about you. Ever since that horrible weekend you spent in the country, when the young woman was murdered in the very next room. . . ."

"So much has happened since then!" Elizabeth exclaimed. "You heard that young Lord Pembroke is the prime suspect?"

"Of course. No one talks of anything else."

"Well, this is how it came about. I was suspicious of Lord Pembroke Senior—I could tell he was hiding something, protecting somebody. So I went back to Pembroke Manor posing as Jessica. It turned out to be the very same day the cook, Maria—the one who'd gotten a glimpse of Joy Singleton's killer—was found murdered."

"You went back to Pembroke Manor?" Rene's dark eyebrows met in an anxious frown. "Why would you take such a risk?"

"I wanted to find out the truth about the Pembroke family. I wanted to learn their secrets."

"And you found . . . ?"

"All sorts of interesting things!" said Elizabeth. "When I was going through books in the library, I accidentally triggered a secret door that led into a little, hidden room full of books about werewolves and mounted animal heads and other creepy, superstitious things."

Rene gasped. "What does it mean?"

"I guess it means that the Pembrokes have a history of interest in werewolves. Pretty suggestive, considering the nature of the murders, wouldn't you say?"

"Umm," Rene agreed.

"Next I went upstairs to the room where Joy was murdered. I found a patch of fur and some dark-green silk threads snagged on the door frame—threads that turned out to be from Robert's bathrobe!"

"He went to the room that night—it was him!"

"It sure looks like it," agreed Elizabeth. "Right after that, I overheard Lord Pembroke speaking with Police Chief Thatcher and conceding that there was no other conclusion to reach. He realized he couldn't go on shielding his son—it would only lead to more bloodshed."

"But he must have warned Robert that the police were going to come after him, because Robert disappeared into thin air," said Rene.

"Right. And now he's out there somewhere. Someone attacked Jessica in the tube the other day, and I'm almost certain it was Robert. She doesn't want to believe she's in danger from him, though. That's why I'm going after Robert myself."

"I don't like you being so involved in this. I don't like it one bit. Until the killer is behind bars, you're not safe for one minute. Leave London, Elizabeth," Rene urged. "Go home to Sweet Valley."

A thrill of fear rippled through Elizabeth's body, but she dismissed Rene's earnest suggestion.

"We're only halfway through our internships at the *Journal*," she pointed out. "I don't know when I'll have another opportunity like this—I can't just throw it away."

"Then if nothing else, go to France and spend a few days with my mother," Rene persisted. He took Elizabeth's hand, squeezing it for emphasis. "She'd love to have you."

"You're sweet to be so concerned, but I'll be fine," Elizabeth assured him. She pressed his fingers, and then withdrew her hand. "Really." *Because I have Luke watching over me. . . .* "I'm not worried for myself, only for Jessica. After all, she's the one who's had two close calls at the hands—or should we say, paws?—of the wolfman!"

Rene's warnings were still ringing in Elizabeth's ears as she returned to HIS half an hour later. *Until the killer is behind bars, you're not safe . . . leave London . . . go home . .* It was a chill, rainy dusk; Elizabeth found herself looking over her shoulder as she passed the park. *Why did I insist that I didn't mind walking home alone?* she wondered, wishing she'd taken Rene up on his offer to escort her to the dorm before heading into town for an embassy function. *I could've let him do that much for me.*

With a surge of relief, she reached the gate at HIS and ran up the steps. With lights twinkling at every window, the brick Georgian boardinghouse looked cozy and warm. *With Mrs. Bates keeping us under lock and key, we couldn't be safer,* Elizabeth thought as she took the stairs to the third floor two at a time.

The bedroom she and Jessica shared with Portia, and formerly Lina as well, was empty. Dropping her jacket and purse on a chair, Elizabeth spotted a folded note card on her dressing table. "Liz," Portia had written in her distinctive, flowery script, "I've gone with Jessica, Emily, and Gabriello to hear G's friend Basil's band. Join us at the Star Twenty Club if you like. Love, P."

Elizabeth felt a pang of regret. Lunar Landscape was a fun dance band—the gang had seen them play before. *But maybe it's just as well I wasn't around when they headed out,* she thought, tossing the note in the wastebasket. *It would've been awkward, since Jessica and I aren't talking. . . .*

Anyway, she had work to do. Curling up in one of the easy chairs, she opened up Robert's medical file. She went through it page by page, reading every single word. There were records of Robert's childhood vaccines and annual checkups, charts relating to a tonsillectomy at age eight, and write-ups of visits over the years for strep throat, the flu, a broken arm after a fall from a horse, stitches in his knee, the flu again.

What a letdown, Elizabeth thought, closing the folder with a sigh. Robert had been a typically healthy, if somewhat accident-prone, boy. The file revealed nothing.

Tucking up her legs, she hugged her knees. The room seemed too quiet; she was lonely for someone to talk to. *If only Lina were still around,* Elizabeth thought. *Maybe I'll call Luke, just to chat.* She got to her feet, only to remember that she didn't have Luke's home telephone number. *Funny he never gave it to me. . . .* But maybe not; because they saw each other every day at the *Journal,* she really had no need for it. And besides, she'd gotten the distinct impression that Luke's home life with his widowed father was far from happy. *He just doesn't want to open that up to me. That's OK—he's entitled.*

Elizabeth sighed heavily, thinking about how easy it would be to pick up the phone and call one of her friends if she were home in Sweet Valley. Enid or Penny or Olivia or DeeDee . . . or Todd.

Crossing the room, Elizabeth opened her top dresser drawer. After hiding the medical file under a pile of clothes, she took out her most recent letter from Todd. Returning to the chair, she sat down again, wrapping one of Mrs. Bates's crocheted afghans around her legs.

The letter was newsy and affectionate. Todd hadn't known anything about the werewolf killings when he wrote it; neither had he known, and he still didn't, that she'd met another boy.

As she reread the letter, losing herself in memories of Sweet Valley and Todd, Elizabeth gradually pushed all thoughts of Luke and Rene and the newspaper and the Pembrokes and the murders from her mind. She laughed at his humorous account of a pool party at Ken Matthews', and sniffled when he wrote of haunting the mailbox in hopes of receiving a letter or postcard from England.

A painful feeling of homesickness rushed over her. Suddenly, Elizabeth found herself missing the bright stucco houses on Calico Drive, the warm southern California sunshine. She missed the beach and the ocean, and her parents, and her older brother, Steven, and his girlfriend, Billy, and Prince Albert, the family's golden retriever. *And Todd*, Elizabeth thought, her heart aching. *I miss Todd*.

It was the first time since she'd been in London that she'd really and truly felt that. There'd been so many distractions, so much excitement, and developing a wild crush on Luke Shepherd hadn't left her much time to think about Todd. But as a soft London rain pattered against the windows, Elizabeth realized something, felt something deep in her heart. *England is a foreign land. No matter how crazy I am about Luke, we're from different worlds. He could never replace Todd.*

Still, on a cold, gray, lonely night like this, Elizabeth would have been happy to feel Luke's strong arms wrapping around her. She grew warm just thinking about their first passionate kiss, in the woods of the Pembroke estate. The first of many such kisses . . .

"Under the circumstances, I'm pretty lucky to

have him," Elizabeth said out loud, fingering the silver pendant. "Because of him, I'm never really alone."

Unclasping the pendant, Elizabeth studied its strange, mystical markings: the head of a sharp-fanged wolf in a five-pointed star. Turning it over, she noticed for the first time that the initial "A" was engraved on the back. *Luke never told me where this came from—I wonder if it belonged to his mother?*

She knew how much Luke still missed the mother who had died when he was only eight years old, knew he still mourned. It was a sign of how much Elizabeth meant to him that Luke had entrusted the precious necklace to her.

Maybe it is magical, Elizabeth thought. *Nothing bad has happened to me since I've been wearing it. But do I really need it, when I have Luke to protect me? Isn't it selfish to keep it to myself when Jessica is so much more vulnerable?*

The shoulder bag Jessica carried to work was slung over the post of their bunk bed. Unzipping the inside pocket, Elizabeth tucked the pendant underneath a powder compact and a couple of lipsticks. It seemed like a small, insignificant gesture compared to the threat that loomed over them. Maybe it wouldn't help . . . but it couldn't hurt.

"The band is hot tonight," Emily raved, joining Jessica on the sidelines of the dance floor at the

Star Twenty Club, an underage juice bar. "How come you're not out there?"

Jessica shrugged. "There's nobody to dance with."

Emily laughed. "Are you joking? This place is crawling with gorgeous guys. Don't tell me none of them have approached you."

Jessica shrugged again. "I guess I'm just not in the mood."

"Well, let's sit down for a minute, then," suggested Emily. "Here comes Portia now."

After buying soft drinks at the bar, the three girls retreated to a relatively quiet corner. "What's on your mind?" Portia asked Jessica.

Jessica sighed. "What do you think?"

"Robert." Portia gave Jessica's hand a sympathetic pat. "I know this is tough on you. You must really miss him."

"I do," Jessica confessed, her eyes smarting with unshed tears. "But I'm taking your advice— I'm not just sitting around." Quickly, she related her afternoon adventure at Dr. Neville's boarded-up flat. "It was kind of a random search," she admitted, "seeing as how I had no idea what I was looking for. And the place was so creepy—I was practically jumping out of my skin the entire time. The only thing I came out with was this file. . . ."

She told the other girls about the Annabelle S. file, currently hidden under her mattress at HIS. Emily and Portia were intrigued. "It's so mysterious," exclaimed Emily. "Who could she have been?"

Portia rubbed her hands together. "I'm sure there's something illicit about it," she declared enthusiastically. "There are all sorts of old books and movies with titles like 'The True Story of Madame D.' They're usually pretty racy—the person's identity is hidden because she's having an adulterous affair or something like that."

"An affair?" Jessica wrinkled her nose. "With old Dr. Neville? He must have been sixty."

"Well, he wasn't always sixty," Portia pointed out, "and didn't you say it was an old file?"

"That's right," said Emily. "Annabelle S. died years ago—maybe they had a clandestine romance when they were young."

"Or maybe Annabelle S. had an affair with someone else, but Dr. Neville knew about it and was protecting him," suggested Portia.

Jessica nodded slowly, thinking back to the morning after Dr. Neville's murder when she and Elizabeth peeked through the window and saw the police chief and Lord Pembroke standing over the body. "Robert told me that Neville was his father's best friend," said Jessica. "Maybe the file will turn out to be helpful after all. Maybe there's some connection between the Pembrokes and Annabelle S.!"

"Let's pick up the pace," suggested Gabriello. "It's nearly eleven—curfew. We don't want Mrs. Bates to lock us out."

The four teenagers trudged quickly along the deserted street. Fog blanketed the city; the mist-shrouded streetlights offered little illumination. "Whose idea was it to walk, anyway?" muttered Emily. "We can't see two feet in front of our noses. What if we get lost?"

"We won't get lost," Portia assured her. "The club is only six blocks from HIS—it would have been silly to take a taxi. Don't be such a scaredy-cat!"

We won't get lost . . . don't be such a scaredy-cat. . . . Her hands pushed deep in the pockets of her jacket, Jessica walked as fast as she could. She repeated the words silently to herself, trying to feel as fearless as Portia sounded. *We won't get lost . . . don't be such a scaredy-cat. . . .*

"This reminds me of Lina and Elizabeth's story, the night we all went to hear the band at Mondo and those two left early and walked home alone," said Emily, her teeth chattering. "Remember? They got lost in the fog and stumbled upon the body of that dead dog."

Jessica's skin crawled. The werewolf got Poo-Poo that night. And he'd be out on a night like this. . . .

From the start, Jessica had laughed off Elizabeth's werewolf warnings, accusing her sister of having an out-of-control hyperactive imagination. But the attack in the tube station was still fresh in Jessica's mind. She vividly recalled the ominous sound of footsteps behind her, something panting loudly, a hairy arm brushing against hers. . . .

Jessica glanced apprehensively over her shoulder. The mist swirled all around them, thick and ghostly-white and impenetrable. *Someone—something—could be following us right now, but we wouldn't even know it.* She thought about the spooky noises she'd heard that afternoon in Dr. Neville's supposedly empty apartment and her heart galloped. *Following us . . . following me.*

She stepped closer to Gabriello, taking comfort in his rangy, athletic physique and confident stride. *There's safety in numbers . . . isn't there? The werewolf wouldn't attack four people at once . . . would he?*

"Winchester Street!" Emily cried with audible relief as they came to an intersection. "We're almost home."

Her friends hadn't wanted to admit they'd been scared, so no one could admit how glad they were to see the lights of HIS. But as they practically sprinted up the front steps, just as Mrs. Bates was peering out into the dark prior to bolting the front door, Jessica could tell she wasn't the only one whose heart was hammering.

"It's five minutes past eleven," Mrs. Bates informed them in a chiding tone. "You're right lucky my evening telly program ran late. Now hustle inside, the lot of you!"

Jessica and the others piled into the warm, brightly lit front hallway. Suddenly, Portia, Emily, and Gabriello were all smiling and chattering again, relief oozing out of their very pores. As Mrs. Bates double-bolted the door, Jessica leaned against the wall, taking deep breaths to calm her racing pulse. She couldn't wait to crawl into bed—she wished she could go to sleep for a week.

How many more nights like this? she wondered, not sure she could endure many more. *How many more scary, lonely nights? Will the police catch the werewolf before he strikes again? Will Robert ever come back to me?*

Chapter 4

After finishing breakfast on Monday morning, Elizabeth and Emily carried their dishes to the HIS kitchen. "Ready to go?" Emily asked. "I'll walk out with you."

"Actually . . ." Elizabeth glanced back into the dining room, which was fast emptying out. Portia had just come down for her morning coffee, still rumpled and sleepy, but everyone else had eaten and was leaving for work or school. *Everyone but Jessica*, Elizabeth noticed. *She's oversleeping, for a change.* "I think I might have another cup of tea. You go on ahead."

"Right-o," Emily said cheerfully. "See you tonight!"

Elizabeth loitered by the buffet table, looking from her wristwatch to the teapot and back again. *Should I run upstairs and wake her?* she wondered. As annoyed as she was with her sister, Elizabeth didn't like the idea of Jessica taking the tube to work by herself. *Come to think of it, I don't want to go alone, either!*

At the same time . . . Elizabeth picked up a clean teacup, then put it down again. *If I wait for her, I'll just be late myself. Jessica is responsible for getting herself up and out of here—I'm not her alarm clock.*

Waving good-bye to Portia, Elizabeth headed into the foyer and out the door. Overhead, the morning sun fought to break through a bank of low, iron-gray clouds. A cool breeze fingered Elizabeth's hair as she stepped through the HIS gate onto the sidewalk.

Her eyes fixed straight ahead, Elizabeth walked quickly down the street toward the tube station. After a block, she came abreast of the park where she and Luke had walked together . . . and kissed . . . Friday evening.

Usually, she and Jessica were part of a steady stream of people walking to work, but this morning, Elizabeth found she had the sidewalk to herself. *I'm glad I'm out in the open and it's daylight,* she thought, stepping up her pace. *I just hope there are more people in the tube station. I don't want to be alone there, like Jessica the other day . . . like Jessica . . . like Jessica. . . .*

Suddenly, the hair on the back of Elizabeth's neck stood on end. She felt electrified, as if she'd just stuck her finger in a light socket. She felt naked, exposed. She felt a pair of eyes staring at her, staring hard.

Someone's following me, she realized, the certainty hitting her with the force of a lightning bolt. *The pendant. Oh, why did I take off the pendant?*

She stopped in her tracks, her breath coming fast. Slowly, she pivoted on one heel to look back, afraid of what she might see . . . of what she might not see.

A tall, dark-haired young man in a dark suit and sunglasses was walking nearly a block behind her. When she stopped and turned, he veered abruptly off to the side, striding quickly into the wooded park, his face turned away from her. Once again, the sidewalk was deserted.

Elizabeth hunched her shoulders, shivering. From a distance, and with the shadows of the trees, she hadn't been able to tell if it was anyone she knew. Robert Pembroke had dark hair, but for that matter, so did lots of people, including Rene and Luke. She stood for a moment, waiting to see if the man would reappear. When he didn't, she darted across the intersection and continued on the other side of the street.

Just somebody going to work, taking a shortcut through the park, she told herself. *It wasn't the wolfman. Did it look like the wolfman? Hardly!*

Still berating herself for being paranoid, Elizabeth reached the entrance to the underground train station. She walked right by it, joining the queue at the bus stop instead. *It's not as fast,* she figured. *I'll have to switch buses and then walk a few extra blocks.* But this morning, that suited Elizabeth just fine. *There's no way I'm taking the tube!*

Jessica sat up in bed, rubbing her eyes. "I hate getting up for work. I hate Mondays," she groaned. She especially hated getting up this morning, because she'd barely slept a wink—she'd tossed and turned restlessly all night.

It must be late, she thought, gazing tiredly around the empty bedroom. Even Portia was out of bed. Jessica focused on the clock and grimaced. *It is late. It's really late!*

For a moment, Jessica felt a brief pang for the old days at home in Sweet Valley. *Liz would always wake me up when I overslept on schooldays,* she remembered nostalgically. *She'd yell, or throw something at me—she'd threaten to take the Jeep and leave me behind.*

With a sigh, Jessica hopped out of bed. Reaching into the closet, she grabbed the first shirt and skirt her hands touched. She didn't care how she looked; she didn't even care if her outfit matched.

She dressed quickly. Leaving her bed rumpled, she stuck her arms in the sleeves of her navy blazer and ran down the hall, stopping in the bathroom to brush her teeth and splash water on her face.

"Ugh," she muttered, staring at her pale face in the mirror. "You need makeup in a major way, Wakefield."

But there really wasn't time. Hurrying downstairs, Jessica bypassed the dining room, with its tempting smell of fresh-baked scones, and headed straight out to the sidewalk.

Halfway to the tube station, she reached for her wallet to buy a piece of fruit from a sidewalk vendor and made a discovery. "Darn!" she exclaimed, stomping her foot in aggravation. "I left my dumb bag with my dumb wallet and mini-corder and notebook back at the dumb dorm. Grrr!"

Wheeling, she jogged back toward HIS. *It's starting out to be another great day,* she thought sarcastically. *I look hideous, I feel worse, I'm late for work. Oh, yeah, and the whole United Kingdom thinks my boyfriend is a werewolf.*

Inside the dorm, she took the stairs to the top floor three at a time. *That's funny,* she thought as she approached her room. The door was slightly ajar—she usually closed it. *But then, if I could forget my purse, I could forget that, too.*

Reaching the end of the hallway, she stepped into her room and then froze, her eyes widening. "Somebody's been here," she gasped. "Robert. Robert was here!"

She clutched the back of a chair, her knees turning to butter. Since she left just a short time ago, Robert had been in her room, she was sure of it. She could smell his cologne, just a faint wisp of it, teasing her senses; she could feel the magnetism of his presence. "And my bed—someone made my bed."

She rushed over to touch the neatly smoothed coverlet on her bunk. "He was here," she repeated, her eyes lighting up. "He came to see me!"

Joy and love and hope flooded Jessica's heart, like the morning sun bursting through the clouds after a stormy night. Robert hadn't forsaken her, hadn't forgotten her; he'd risked his freedom to come to her. He'd been right there, where she stood, and only moments before—he must have left right before she returned.

Her shoulder bag was draped over the bunk post. Grabbing it, Jessica tore back down the hallway and downstairs. Her heart pounding, she flung open the door and raced to the gate, eagerly looking both ways. "Robert!" she cried.

He'd been there, but now he was gone. The streets were empty; there was no one in sight but a bedraggled, stubble-faced homeless man in a patched brown coat with a battered felt hat pulled down low on his forehead, poking around in a trash can with a stick.

Jessica stared at the homeless man, her eyes welling up with tears. Her hopes had soared so high; now the disappointment struck her like a blow. "Robert," she whispered, sinking down onto the curb. "Robert."

The tears spilled from her eyes, pouring down both cheeks. Sitting on the curb with her arms wrapped around her knees, Jessica buried her head and sobbed.

Striding into the busy offices of the *London Journal*, Elizabeth waved at the people she knew, calling hello. "Good morning, Rebecca. Hi, Arthur. Hi, Zena. Hello—"

Halfway across the newsroom, Elizabeth skidded to a stop abreast of the editor-in-chief's office. The massive, walnut desk had been empty for a few days, since the firing of Henry Reeves, but now someone was sitting there.

Elizabeth blinked in disbelief at the lovely, chestnut-haired woman. "Lucy? Is that you?"

Lucy Friday waved carelessly at the new brass nameplate on the door. "It's me," she confirmed, pushing her tortoiseshell glasses up on her aristocratic nose. "I'm back."

Elizabeth gaped at the nameplate. "Lucy Friday, editor-in-chief!" she read out loud. "But how—when—" She stuttered to a stop.

Lucy laughed. "Close your mouth, Elizabeth," she advised cheerfully. "You look like a fish on a hook. That's better. Now, turn around and toddle on back to the newsroom. I'm about to call my first staff meeting—you shouldn't miss it."

Clapping her hands and whistling, Lucy soon had the entire *London Journal* staff assembled.

Across the newsroom, Elizabeth spotted Luke and his boss, Martha, the arts editor. She waved at Luke and at her own boss, Tony Frank, who'd been promoted from society editor to take over the crime desk vacated by Lucy.

"This will be short and sweet," Lucy promised, leaning back against a desk with her slender ankles crossed. "You already know me, so I don't have to introduce myself, and you know my style. Well, my style," she said with a smile, "is now the style of the whole newspaper. In a few words: high-energy, nononsense. Aim high and get the job done. Now, we've all been concerned about competition lately. This is the bottom line on that subject. The *London Journal* is a newspaper, not a scandal sheet. We will not compete with the *London Daily Post* by imitating the *London Daily Post*. We will compete with them—and we will outsell them—by presenting more real news in greater depth. Got that?"

Her reply was an enthusiastic standing ovation. "One last thing before we all get back to work," Lucy said. "I need your cooperation on the werewolf murder case. If any of you becomes privy to any information, come to me immediately. Serial killers often make contact with the press, even develop a dialogue with an individual reporter— they're crying out for attention. The smallest tidbit could lead to a big breakthrough for Scotland Yard, so let's keep our eyes open and our ears peeled. Thanks for your time."

The meeting broke up. As Elizabeth followed Tony back to his desk, she saw to her surprise that Lucy was doing the same thing. Elizabeth hung back, letting the editor-in-chief approach the crime desk first. "Frank," Lucy said, rapping briskly on the wall of his cubicle. "May I have a word?"

Tony grinned. "A word? You may have ten thousand words, Miss Friday. Talk all day, if you'd like. Your voice is music to my ears."

"Cut the baloney," Lucy advised. "I'm here on business, Frank."

"Er, of course. I understand that now—you're in charge, and—can't joke around like we used to—"

"Like *you* used to," Lucy corrected. "This is the deal, Frank. You're free to joke all you want on your own time. But I'm not giving anything away here. Reeves made you the temporary crime editor and the assignment's still temporary. I want to see for myself what you can do."

Tony raised his sandy-blond eyebrows. "You mean, I'm on trial?"

"Let's just say that if someone better comes along, you may find yourself back on the society page." Lucy tipped her head thoughtfully. "Now, I like that Adam Silver who covers crime for the *Daily Post*. He's one of their better people—a real go-getter."

Tony frowned. "Silver's nothing but an ambulance chaser."

"And a darned good one," said Lucy. "He never gets caught flat-footed."

With that, Lucy sailed off. Elizabeth stared after her and then turned back to Tony. She expected him to be crestfallen. Instead, Tony tipped back in his chair with his feet on the desk, a broad grin wreathing his face. "I say, isn't it fitting? Isn't it grand? Just like a Hollywood movie. Noble, high-minded Lucy resigns her post as crime editor to protest Reeves suppressing the facts about Dr. Neville's gruesome murder. She's ready to sacrifice her career rather than be party to a cover-up. We investigative reporters take a pledge," he told Elizabeth, lifting one hand dramatically, "to tell the whole truth and nothing but the truth!"

"I remember all that," said Elizabeth. "But how did Lucy get to be the new editor-in-chief?"

"Well, it turns out our gal Friday was right, of course, and the *Journal's* owner, Lord Pembroke himself, was behind the decision to downplay the murders. He was protecting his son, we now know. But he never authorized Reeves to print lies. Reeves went too far, printing the unsubstantiated rumor about Princess Eliana's corpse turning up. In his misguided effort to one-up the *Daily Post*, he disgraced the *Journal* and himself."

"Yeah, yeah, I was here for that part, too," Elizabeth exclaimed somewhat impatiently.

"Well, the rest is simple. Pembroke fired Reeves, and he hired back Lucy in his place."

"What a vindication for Lucy!"

"Isn't it capital for her?" Tony agreed. "Though

now she's the big cheese, she's less likely than ever to give me the time of day." He sighed regretfully. "But what a stroke of genius on Pembroke's part! He's been worried about competition from the *Daily Post*? Why, under the stewardship of Lucy Friday, the *London Journal* will . . ."

Elizabeth suspected Tony's rhapsodic monologue could go on all day. Leaving Tony droning on to himself, she ducked out to visit Luke.

The arts and entertainment staff had desks in the far corner of the newsroom, around a bend in the hallway. "So, what's your opinion of our new editor-in-chief?" Luke asked, rising to give Elizabeth a quick hug.

Elizabeth blushed, glad there was no one else around to see them. "I think it's great. You should see Tony—he's delirious."

"He had her on a pretty lofty pedestal before," Luke remarked. "Now he'll probably place her so high, she'll be lost in the clouds."

"He has the hugest crush on her," Elizabeth agreed. "And for all her hands-off attitude, I think Lucy's hot for him, too. They just don't seem to get it. It's obvious to everybody else they're meant for each other—why can't they figure it out?"

"People can be pretty dense when it comes to matters of the heart. As for those two, I think they're too busy pretending the only thing they care about is getting the story," guessed Luke. "Reporters are supposed to be cynical and hard-nosed and detached, not sentimental and romantic." He put his arms around her again and nuzzled her neck. "Lucky for me, I'm a poet. I'm not afraid to follow my feelings, wherever they might lead me."

Elizabeth closed her eyes, melting as Luke kissed her throat, then her cheeks, then her lips. "Umm," she murmured. "But Lucy and Tony might have a point. This isn't necessarily the best way to get in the mood to write up the latest London crime story!"

Luke chuckled. Stepping back, he held her at arm's length, his blue eyes twinkling. "Sorry. I got carried away. It seems to happen all the time when I'm around you."

Elizabeth smiled, a tiny dimple creasing her left cheek. "Good thing we work at opposite ends of the newsroom."

At that moment, Luke's gaze dropped from Elizabeth's face to her neck, and his smile faded. "Elizabeth!" Reaching out, he touched her bare skin with one fingertip. "The pendant. You're not wearing it."

Elizabeth put a hand to her throat, remembering how naked and vulnerable she'd felt on her way to work, when she thought someone was following her. *I can't tell Luke about that—he'd only worry more.* "I gave it to Jessica," she explained, her tone carefree and light. "She needs it more than I do."

Luke frowned. "But you could be in danger,

too, Elizabeth—no less than Jessica. The only reason I'm able to sleep at night is knowing you're wearing the pendant—that you're shielded, safe."

"You take such good care of me yourself," said Elizabeth. "The pendant can't do nearly as much for me."

Luke folded her in his arms, resting his chin on top of her head. "I'm trying to take care of you. I'm trying."

Elizabeth pressed her face against his firm chest. She wondered if Jessica had found the pendant in her shoulder bag yet—if she was wearing it. "That reminds me," she said out loud. She knew it was painful for Luke to talk about his mother, but she was too curious not to ask. "When I took off the necklace, I noticed the letter 'A' etched on the back. Was that your mother's initial?"

"Yes." Luke's breath was soft and warm on her hair, his tone sad. "Her name was Ann. The pendant belonged to her. As I've mentioned, she was fascinated with werewolf lore."

"It's a very special keepsake, then. Jessica will take good care of it, don't worry."

At that moment, they heard footsteps pounding down the hall in their direction. They jumped apart guiltily just as Tony Frank careened around the corner.

Tony's sandy hair stood on end and his eyes glittered. *Something's up*, Elizabeth guessed, her pulse accelerating.

"There you are, Liz!" Tony exclaimed. "I just got a call about a murder in Pelham. Details are sketchy, but it could be the werewolf again. Here's our chance to prove ourselves to the boss. Let's hop to!"

A *murder in Pelham!* Elizabeth thought, adrenaline coursing through her veins. She climbed into the roomy backseat of the taxi and Tony followed suit after barking the address at the driver. "And make it fast!" Elizabeth heard her boss holler.

The cabbie dove into the driver's seat and gunned the engine. The big black Austin shot out into traffic. "Pelham," Elizabeth said, turning to Tony. "That's where the Pembrokes' old nanny lives!"

"Hmm." Tony looked up from the notebook he'd been flipping through energetically. "What, the Pembrokes' nanny, you say? Do we have any interest in her?"

"Possibly." Elizabeth hesitated for an instant, and then confessed that she'd broken into Dr. Neville's flat the previous afternoon. "Who could know the family members better than someone who lived with them for years?" Elizabeth asked. "The nanny may have information about Robert's whereabouts—she may even have seen him!"

"True. True!" Tony declared.

"I was planning to visit her at some point today. So, as long as we're in the neighborhood anyway . . ."

"We can swing by her house on the way back from this case," Tony proposed. "You're right, Liz—the nanny could be a good lead." His eyes twinkled. "Of course, I can't officially approve of your methods, but off the record: jolly good work!"

The cabbie continued to speed through town, weaving expertly in and out of traffic. At the outskirts of the city, the traffic thinned. The taxi roared along so fast, it almost overshot the turn. "Whoa, here's our road!" Tony shouted.

The driver slammed on the brakes and yanked the steering wheel. Tires squealing, they swung onto a side street.

Elizabeth glanced at the road sign, and then did a double take. "Bishop Street," she squeaked in surprise.

"Umm, yes," Tony mumbled, once again poring over the notes he'd taken when the call about the murder came through to the paper.

Bishop Street . . . Elizabeth's heart began to thump madly in her chest. According to the Rolodex card she'd filched from Dr. Neville's office, Mildred Price, the Pembrokes' former nanny, lived on Bishop Street. *It's a coincidence—just a coincidence,* Elizabeth told herself. But suddenly her mouth was dry as dust.

Elizabeth looked at the houses passing by, her eyes searching for street numbers. Eighteen, twenty-two, twenty-nine . . . "T–T–Tony," she stuttered, a feeling of dread tying her tongue in a knot.

"Where are we going? Where did the murder take place?"

At that moment, the cabbie braked in front of an ivy-covered cobblestone cottage. An ambulance was parked just ahead; two police cars flanked the ambulance, lights flashing and sirens wailing.

Elizabeth knew what Tony was going to say before he said it. "Thirty-seven Bishop Street," he told her, reaching for the door handle. "And here we are!"

The Rolodex card was tucked inside Elizabeth's wallet, but now she saw it as clearly as if she held it in front of her eyes. "Mildred Price, 37 Bishop Street, Pelham . . ."

A van from a local television station tore down the road, pulling over next to the taxi. As Tony and Elizabeth hurried toward the cottage gate, Tony gestured toward a beat-up green Triumph sports car parked in front of the house next door. "What did I tell you about ambulance chasing? It's Silver," he said wryly. "Can't say the *London Daily Post* doesn't know how to sniff out a story!"

The TV reporters, Adam Silver, and a police officer were talking to a young woman standing on the front lawn. Another police officer helped the ambulance crew wheel a gurney down the walk.

The blood drained from Elizabeth's face. She witnessed it all as if from a distance; the roaring in her ears deafened her. *No,* she thought. *Not her, too. Not her.*

But she'd seen the name on the picket fence. Price, #37.

"It's the nanny, Mildred Price," Elizabeth whispered.

Tony gaped at her, and then at the sheet-draped corpse on the gurney. "The nanny? Mildred Price was the Pembrokes' nanny?" Tony waved to Adam Silver of the *Daily Post*. "Silver, have they confirmed the identity of the victim?"

The *Daily Post*'s crackerjack crime reporter stepped to Tony's side. "Yep, it's the old woman, Mrs. Price—she lived here alone." Silver's icy gray eyes glittered in much the same way Tony's had when he'd come to Elizabeth in the office to sweep her off to investigate. *It's a story,* she thought dully. *To them, it's just a good story.*

"Foul play, no doubt about it," Silver continued. "I caught a glimpse of the body before they covered it."

Elizabeth stared at the still, white-shrouded form being lifted into the back of the ambulance.

"Her throat was horribly mangled," related Silver. "Ripped right open. Beastly."

Beastly . . . "The werewolf," Elizabeth gasped.

Chapter 5

"The werewolf," repeated Adam Silver, his eyes fixed on Elizabeth's pale, shocked face. "It certainly looks like it, doesn't it? The brutally torn throat seems to be our serial killer's personal signature. But why this victim? Why a harmless white-haired old widow lady?"

Turning away from the *Daily Post* reporter, Elizabeth choked back a sob. Silver paced off again to badger a policeman for more information.

Tony stepped closer to Elizabeth and put a hand on her shoulder. "Are you all right?" he asked gently.

Elizabeth shook her head. The tears she'd been fighting to hold back squeezed out. "Robert was here," she cried, wiping her damp cheek on her sleeve. "He did stop by to see his old nanny—to kill her. If only I'd come straight over here yesterday! I could have talked to her. I could have warned her. She might still be alive, instead of . . . instead of . . ."

Another sob wracked Elizabeth's body. "It's silly to blame yourself," insisted Tony. His grip on her shoulder tightening, he gave her a little shake. "If Robert was bent on knocking her off, he'd have found a way, no matter what. And chances are, old Mrs. Price wouldn't have believed you, anyway. She wouldn't have believed that her dear little boy could intend her or anyone else any harm."

Elizabeth nodded, trying to find comfort in Tony's reasoning. Tony turned on his heel to watch as Adam Silver hopped into his Triumph and roared off in a cloud of exhaust. A grim smile twisted his lips. "He thinks he has the scoop," Tony said with satisfaction. "He doesn't know the Pembroke connection, though—we've got him there! Lucy'll be proud of us."

Elizabeth took a tissue from her purse and blew her nose. "Robert Pembroke is the killer, isn't he?" she said quietly. "This clinches it."

"He's incriminated more than ever," Tony agreed.

Elizabeth tried to picture Robert in a murderous rage, attacking an innocent old woman who loved him—whom he himself had once loved. *I guess to a killer, no one is sacred. No one is safe. So, what about Jessica?* Elizabeth thought. *Will the pendant help her if Robert goes after her next?*

"He has to be stopped," she said out loud. "But how? What if the police can't catch him? Where will the bloodshed end?"

"Here's the research you wanted about the airline merger," Jessica said, stepping into Lucy Friday's new office and waving a fat manila folder.

"Jessica, you're a whiz," Lucy declared, taking the folder and glancing quickly at its contents. "I thought you'd need all day to get this together."

Jessica shrugged. "It's a trick I learned at school. When you have work to do, do it fast. Then you can go to the beach or the mall."

Lucy laughed. "I like your style, Wakefield. Fast is fine with me, as long as you also do your work well."

"I was pretty thorough," Jessica promised.

"Super." Lucy dropped the folder onto her desk and sat back down. "Well, I suppose now I have to turn you back over to Frank."

Jessica thought she detected a note of reluctance in Lucy's matter-of-fact voice. *Go for it*, she commanded herself. "Lucy, I mean, Miss Friday, I mean Miss Editor-in-Chief . . ."

Lucy waved away Jessica's fumbling attempts at propriety. "Lucy will do."

"Lucy, Tony's off on some story with Elizabeth and I—" Jessica gestured to the manila folder. "I'd rather do stuff for you," she announced boldly. "In your new job, you'll probably need a lot of extra help. You should definitely have your own summer intern. Can I be it?"

Lucy drummed her fingers on the desk, a thoughtful smile on her lips. "My own intern, eh? It would be handy having one." She narrowed her eyes at Jessica. "But I thought you and your sister were inseparable. A package deal, Tony told me on your first day here. If you work for me, this won't be as fun for you—you won't see much of Elizabeth."

"That's the way I want it," Jessica confessed. "Liz and I aren't getting along these days. In fact, we're not speaking to each other, which makes it kind of hard to work together. I don't want to be around her, but if Tony's my boss I can't avoid her."

Lucy continued to drum her fingers, pondering the proposal. Jessica held her breath. "Well, Wakefield," Lucy said at last, "I can't say I blame you for wanting a change from that society editor in crime editor's clothing. Frank is a lightweight. You'll learn more from me."

Jessica's eyes lit up. "You mean I can be your intern?"

"I'll be glad to have your help," Lucy assented.

"That's great," Jessica gushed, sitting down across the desk from the editor-in-chief, her new boss. "Oh, you've made my day!"

"But I have some advice for you."

"What's that?"

"Ordinarily, I wouldn't stick my nose into a colleague's personal business. I feel strongly that we should keep our private lives private—in other words, out of the office. But since you brought it up . . . it's no good fighting with your sister, Wakefield."

"She started it," Jessica protested. "She's being impossible. And cruel." Tears stung her eyes, but she blinked them back, refusing to cry in front of Lucy. "She wants Robert to be found guilty. She won't admit that the evidence could point in a whole bunch of different directions. She doesn't care about my feelings at all."

Reaching across the desk, Lucy placed her hand briefly on Jessica's. "No doubt about it, young Rob Pembroke is in a tough spot. It's dreadful for you if you care about him. But you two girls mustn't feud. Take it from me—I know. I have a sister of my own who's just as hardheaded and stubborn as I am, but even when we have a row, I never forget that she's my best friend."

"Elizabeth isn't my friend," Jessica insisted. "Not anymore."

"Blood is thicker than water," Lucy countered. "We'll find a way to patch things up between the two of you. In the meantime, let's check the storyboard, shall we?"

Jessica trooped after Lucy, her lips pressed together in a tight line. *Lucy thinks she's made up her mind, but I made my mind up first.* Jessica intended to work like a dog as Lucy's intern: run any errand, research any story, do anything Lucy asked her. Anything, that is, but kiss and make up with Elizabeth.

When the gurney was loaded into the ambulance, the attendant pulled the doors shut. As Elizabeth and Tony watched, the ambulance driver hit the gas, speeding off down Bishop Street with the siren blaring.

"Let's get some details, Elizabeth," said Tony. "I want to talk to the person who found the body."

They walked up the flagstone path to the front door of the cottage. Colorful flower beds bordered the path, and neatly pruned rosebushes laden with fragrant blossoms clustered under the cottage's front windows. Elizabeth sniffled, imagining the kindly old woman tending her garden in days past. *Poor old Mrs. Price. Who will give her flowers such loving care now?*

After examining Tony's press card, the police officer standing at the door waved them in, pointing to a small parlor off the front hall. "The victim's granddaughter is in there, Dolores Price," the officer said. "She's the one who discovered the body and called us over."

A young woman in her early twenties with curly auburn hair and a tear-streaked face sat on an overstuffed sofa, staring at the telephone on the end table. When Tony cleared his throat, she looked up with glazed eyes. "I have to phone the

78

rest of the family . . . her friends," Dolores stammered tearfully. "Oh, I just can't bear to!"

Elizabeth sat down next to Dolores and patted her arm helplessly. Tony took a notebook and pen from his jacket pocket. "Miss Price, I know you're upset—very understandably so. You have our sincere sympathy, and our apologies for intruding on your grief like this. But would you take a few minutes to speak with us?"

Dolores nodded. "Poor Gran," she whispered. "There's nothing I can do for her now but tell her story."

"According to the police, you found the body," stated Tony. Unobtrusively, Elizabeth removed her mini-corder from her purse and pushed the record button.

"That's right," said Dolores. "I live on the other side of town, not too far from here. I come by—" She caught herself, pain shadowing her face. "I came by nearly every day for a chat. Gran had lots of friends, but I knew it could be lonely for her, living alone as she did. This morning, I stopped at the farmer's market first and picked out some lovely fruit and vegetables for her." Dolores dabbed at her eyes with an embroidered handkerchief. "Strawberries and wax beans and baby carrots, her favorites."

Tony prodded her gently. "So, you entered the cottage . . ."

"Gran always left the door open. It is—at least,

I used to think it was—a safe, friendly neighborhood," continued Dolores. "This morning, Gran wasn't in the kitchen or the yard, so I called upstairs for her. I thought it strange she didn't answer, so I went up to see. I've always fretted that she might fall and break a hip or some such thing, and she'd have no way of getting help." Dolores buried her face in her hands. "I never imagined, in my darkest dreams . . ."

"She was in her bedroom?" Tony asked.

Dolores struggled to recover her composure. Elizabeth's heart went out to her. "In the sitting room adjoining her bedroom," Dolores replied at last. "On the floor. She was dressed, wearing a skirt and sweater, stockings and shoes. The police said she'd been dead for— He—he must have come last evening, before she got ready for bed."

Tony glanced sharply at Elizabeth. She nodded to indicate that she'd noted Dolores's use of the pronoun "he."

"Poor Gran." Dolores shook her head. "She never had a chance against someone so brutal, so strong. . . ."

"And the fatal wound . . . was to the throat," Tony ventured.

"If she hadn't been inside her own home, I would have thought an animal had attacked her," said Dolores. "She was so ravaged . . . so bloody."

Elizabeth swallowed, fighting a wave of dizzying nausea. Tony made a note in his book. "Do you know if your grandmother had any guests last night—anyone over for supper, for example?" he asked. "Was anyone staying with her?"

"Not last night, but . . ." Dolores stopped, visibly wrestling with violent emotions. Sorrow? Elizabeth wondered. Anger? Fear?

"But what?" prompted Tony, sitting forward, his expression intense.

"Last week for a night or two . . . Robert Pembroke was here."

Elizabeth gasped. "I was right!" she burst out.

Dolores glanced at Elizabeth, startled. "He was here, Granny's old charge. She gave the best years of her life to that family, and Robert came to her in his hour of need. He came to her, and of course she took him in. All my life, I heard nothing but wonderful things about young Rob Pembroke. Gran just doted on him."

"He only stayed with her for a night or two?" asked Tony.

"He left Friday when the newspapers came out with the werewolf murders, and about how he was wanted. Gran told him she didn't believe any of it. It didn't matter to her if there was a big manhunt for him, he could stay as long as he needed to. But he said he didn't want to involve her, his own dear Nanny Millie. That's what she told me happened, and she swore me to secrecy." Dolores's eyes flashed with anger through their tears. "But there's no reason to keep the secret now, is there? Young Lord Pembroke

81

isn't worth protecting. He's a criminal, a monster. He left, but then he came back last night—I'd bet my life on it. He came back and killed my grandmother!"

"Don't have enough cash on me for another cab ride—we'll have to take the bus," Tony told Elizabeth as they trudged down Bishop Street after concluding their interview with Dolores Price. "The bobby said there's a stop about half a mile this way. Are you up for a walk?"

"I don't mind it at all," said Elizabeth. "I need the fresh air. That was horrible in there."

"It really was," Tony agreed. "That poor, trusting old woman. What a gruesome end to a peaceful, blameless life! I feel a bit disgusted with myself, rushing out like this to record every last detail. What she was wearing when she died, her favorite fruits and vegetables, for God's sake. We're a flock of vultures, we reporters."

"You're just doing your job," Elizabeth assured him. "You were very kind to Dolores. And you heard her—she wants the story told. She wants her grandmother's murderer caught."

Tony pushed his hands deep in his trouser pockets and whistled thoughtfully through his teeth. "Why did he do it, though?" he wondered aloud. "How could he do it?"

Elizabeth shook her head. She recalled Dolores's words. *He's a criminal, a monster.* . . . "I really don't know."

Just ahead, they caught sight of the wooden bus kiosk. A bus had just pulled away from the curb. A solitary person walked away from them down the sidewalk. As they drew somewhat closer, Elizabeth's eyes widened in surprise. "Rene!" she called. "Rene, is that you?"

The young man in the dark suit turned, startled. "Why, Elizabeth," Rene said, his cheeks flushing slightly. "Fancy running into you out here!"

"Tony and I were investigating a story. What brings you to Pelham in the middle of a workday?"

"Oh, I, well—I rode the bus out to pay a call on a friend of my mother's," Rene explained. He waved vaguely over his shoulder. "She lives . . . that way."

"I thought you were always so busy at the embassy." Elizabeth smiled. "I can't believe they let you get away."

"Yes, well, a fellow deserves a lunch break every now and then," said Rene, his own smile somewhat stiff. "I'll see you at the dorm later."

Nodding good-bye, Rene hurried off. Elizabeth and Tony stepped under the bus shelter. "Just now— Did my friend seem . . . odd to you?" Elizabeth asked Tony.

"Odd? That a chap would spend his lunch hour visiting a friend of his mum's?" Tony shrugged. "Not particularly, no."

Elizabeth dismissed Rene from her thoughts. The conversation she and Tony had been engaged in was infinitely more pressing. Elizabeth tossed

Tony's question back at him. "Why do you think he did it? Why kill Mildred Price?"

Tony jingled the loose change in his pocket. "Because the werewolf . . . Robert Pembroke . . . is more desperate than ever," he theorized grimly. "He must have confided in Nanny Millie, or perhaps he only suspected that she'd guessed the truth about him. Then, fearing that she'd turn him in to the authorities, he silenced her."

It was coldly, perfectly logical. Elizabeth shuddered. "He has no mercy."

"None." Tony fixed a somber gaze on Elizabeth. "And that's why you mustn't pull any more stunts like yesterday's break-in at Neville's," he ordered. "I know you're hot to break open this case, and I am, too, but I can't let you investigate on your own. It's far too dangerous. Promise me, Elizabeth. If you must go out on a limb, take someone with you—me, or your young man Luke, or Jessica."

"I promise," Elizabeth said reluctantly. "I'll be careful. But I'm not likely to enlist Jessica's help. She still won't acknowledge that Robert's guilty— even this won't convince her, I bet." Elizabeth grew riled just thinking about it. "For some insane reason, she's blaming everything bad that's happened on me. In case you haven't picked up on it, we're not speaking to each other."

"This is no time for petty sibling quarrels," Tony responded with uncharacteristic sternness. He gripped Elizabeth's arm and she blinked up at him, startled. "You need each other more than ever, can't you see that?" His eyes burned into hers and she felt a thrill of excitement, and fear. "This . . . thing . . . is incredibly powerful, and incredibly evil. Our only hope of defeating it lies in banding together. Only that way, can we counter his strength, foil him in his wicked designs. Don't let yourself become the weak link, Elizabeth. Don't place yourself in the wolfman's path."

The door to the bedroom swung open and the intruder padded in on silent feet. Rearing back his head, his nostrils flared and he inhaled the feminine scents of the three girls who lived there—the perfumes, the shampoos and lotions, the delicate fabrics of their clothing.

One of the three girls held no interest for him, but the other two . . .

They have something of mine. They have something that can hurt me. That's why they went to Dr. Neville's.

Nanny Millie was out of the way, but the Wakefield twins still posed a threat, he knew it. He prowled over to a dressing table, his bloodshot eyes darting around the room. Yanking open a drawer, he pawed through the clothing, searching. Finding nothing, he hurled the stockings and slips and nightgowns angrily on the floor.

The next drawer yielded books and letters, one with the name Todd Wilkins on the return address.

He snarled, ripping the letter in two with his teeth. Then, glimpsing the manila folder at the bottom of the drawer, his eyes brightened. He removed it, reading the label: Robert Pembroke, Jr. *This is good, but it isn't all.*

He searched drawer after drawer, finding nothing. Panting and desperate, he ripped the sheets from the beds, slashed the pillows with his fingernails until feathers flew through the air like a snowstorm.

Under the mattress of one of the top bunks, he made his second discovery. Another one of Dr. Neville's files! With a triumphant yowl, he seized it. Annabelle S. *So they had found her, found out about her . . .*

Clever, clever, clever, hiding it so carefully, he thought as he paced the room. What else was hidden there? There was something—something important, essential, fateful. Yes—the silver bullet! *I must find it.*

He clawed through the dresser drawers again. Tearing the closet door half off its hinges, he dug through piles of shoes, tossed armfuls of jackets and dresses onto the floor.

Frustration boiled up inside him like volcanic lava. He ripped the room to pieces looking for the bullet, but to no avail. *They still have it,* he thought, slinking out of the room, out of the dorm, into the sheltering shadows of the park. *They are my enemies, then, to the death.*

Chapter 6

"This is shaping up nicely," Lucy said to Jessica late Monday afternoon after skimming Jessica's preliminary draft of a short biographical piece that would accompany Lucy's airline merger feature. "Sharp, stylish, succinct. You know, you could be a fine writer someday."

Jessica lifted her shoulders in a careless shrug. Her twin sister would do cartwheels over such praise from the editor-in-chief of the *London Journal*, but being a writer wasn't exactly Jessica's life's ambition. "Thanks."

"I'll scribble some comments and you can take a final crack at it in the morning. I guess that's all for today. You've been a terrific help."

"It was fun," Jessica said sincerely. "I'm really psyched to be your intern. See you tomorrow."

Her new desk was in the main newsroom just a

few steps from Lucy's office. *Miles away from Elizabeth and Tony,* Jessica thought as she sat down and reached under the desk for her shoulder bag. *But it's still not far enough.*

The whole office had been buzzing all afternoon, ever since Tony and Elizabeth returned from Pelham with a melodramatic accounting of the werewolf-style murder of the former Pembroke family nanny. Elizabeth hadn't spoken to Jessica about it, but a couple of times when they'd been in the same general vicinity, Jessica had caught her sister directing superior, self-righteous glances her way.

She's so sure she has it all figured out, Jessica fumed, unzipping the inside pocket of her bag and feeling around for a lipstick. *She acts like she's the head of Scotland Yard or something.* Instead of a lipstick case, her hand touched something cool and hard and unfamiliar. *A coin?* Jessica thought. *No, there's a chain attached. Jewelry . . . but what . . . ?*

Pulling a tarnished silver pendant from her purse, she recognized it immediately. "It's the tacky voodoo charm Luke gave Liz," Jessica muttered, tossing it disdainfully on her desk. "I can't believe she put it in there." Her anger flared. "She thinks Robert is the werewolf and is going to come after me!"

If it weren't so nasty, it would almost be funny, she reflected bitterly. *Sensible, smarty-pants Elizabeth, of all people, turning out to be totally, idiotically superstitious.*

Jessica glared at the pendant—at the face of the wolf baring its fangs inside the five-pointed star. An unaccountable shiver chased up her spine. Maybe there was some magic at work there. . . .

"No, it's just a stupid toy," she told herself. But against her will, she found herself picking up the pendant and looking at it more closely. The silver was solid, heavy—reassuring somehow. It quickly grew warm in her hand. Her first instinct had been to stalk over to Elizabeth's desk and throw the necklace in her face, but now Jessica didn't want to let it go.

She must have hated to part with it, Jessica mused. *Such a special gift from lover-boy. I guess she really is worried about me.*

The faintest, most begrudging of smiles curved Jessica's lips. Even though she was furious at her sister, she couldn't help being a tiny bit touched by Elizabeth's concern. *We haven't talked in days, but she's thinking about me,* Jessica realized. *She's worrying about me. Even though, of course, she's totally barking up the wrong tree—Robert hasn't committed any crimes and he wouldn't hurt me in a million years.*

Thoughtfully, Jessica turned the pendant over in her hand. On the back, a single initial had been engraved: a fancy, script "A," now nearly worn off. Jessica traced the letter with her fingertip. Something about it triggered a fuzzy, indefinite memory . . . but of what? She shook her head with a sigh. *It doesn't mean anything. It's just a letter, just someone's initial, the person who originally owned the necklace.*

She looked again at the werewolf and pentagram. "I'm not in any danger," she murmured to herself, "so I don't need any hoodoo voodoo potions and charms to protect me. But . . ." But she couldn't deny it. She wanted to clasp the smooth silver chain around her throat, to feel the pendant resting warm and heavy against her skin. "It is kind of pretty, kind of interesting."

Reaching back underneath her hair, Jessica fastened the necklace. *I'll wear it, but not so anyone can see,* she decided, tucking the pendant into her shirt. *There's no way I'm going to give Liz the satisfaction . . . !*

At the end of the day, Tony slipped his arms in the sleeves of his tweed jacket. Gripping the handle of his briefcase, he headed for the street.

Halfway across the newsroom, he halted. The editor-in-chief's door was ajar, and he could see Lucy still reading through some copy, her pumps kicked off and her stockinged feet on top of her desk.

Loosening his tie, Tony stuck his head in her office, smiling. "Good night, boss."

She didn't look up from her papers. "Night, Frank."

Tony lingered. "Uh, by the way. What did you think of my Mildred Price murder piece?"

Lucy glanced at him over the rims of her glasses. "Top-notch. I was impressed."

Tony practically levitated with joy at the compliment. Before he realized what he was saying, the words he'd been dying to utter for weeks spilled from his lips. "So, what do you say we talk about crime over a pint of ale and a bite of supper?"

Instantly, Tony regretted his audacity. "I'm not ready to call it a day yet," Lucy replied, her tone cool. "And besides. I have a philosophy, which I shared this morning with Jessica, about keeping one's private life out of the workplace. Let's keep it straight: you and I have a professional relationship, Frank. At least, that's what I'd call it on a good day," she added dryly.

"Point taken," Tony said with forced carelessness. "We all need to eat, that's all I was getting at. See you tomorrow."

He walked away whistling—he wouldn't give Lucy the satisfaction of seeing that she'd burst his dearest hopes like a balloon. But as soon as he was out of sight of her office, Tony's shoulders slumped dejectedly. *I guess that's it, ol' chap*, he thought to himself with a sigh. *It's hopeless*.

It was a gray London twilight as the twins walked in silence to the tube station a few blocks from the *London Journal* offices. Without exchanging a single word, they'd managed to leave the office at the same time, thanks to Jessica sauntering slowly by Elizabeth's desk and then waiting by the door, tapping her foot, until Elizabeth joined her.

She may be too blind to see that Robert is the werewolf, but she's not a complete idiot, Elizabeth reflected as they waited on the underground platform for the train. *She knows it's safer to stick together like this than to strike out on our own, especially after dark. She hasn't forgotten what happened to her down here last week. . . .*

Far away, they heard a rumbling. It grew louder and closer. Bright lights and a high-pitched metallic screeching filled the tunnel and a train roared into view. Car after car after car swept past as the train came to a stop.

There were quite a few other commuters standing on the platform, all dressed in work clothes and appearing sane and normal and nonthreatening; still, Elizabeth heaved a secret sigh of relief as she and Jessica sat down in a crowded car and the train leapt forward to speed like a bullet through the tunnel. *Why does life in London lately feel like one close call after another?* she wondered wearily. *Some vacation this is turning out to be!*

After a minute, the train rocked to a stop. People stood up and got off; others boarded and took the vacated seats. As the train proceeded, Elizabeth opened her mouth to ask Jessica a question. She was curious, and a little jealous: how had Jessica managed to get herself appointed Lucy's personal intern? What was it like working for the editor-in-chief?

But I'm not talking to her, Elizabeth reminded herself. *I'll have to ask Luke or Tony for the dirt.*

Jessica, meanwhile, glanced at Elizabeth out of the corner of her eye. Then, staring straight ahead, she said, as if to herself, "For such a smart, successful woman, Lucy Friday can really be a dope. Tony is so cute—all the women in the office think so. And she could have him, just like that." Jessica snapped her fingers to illustrate the point. "Why doesn't she snag him while she has the chance?"

"She's crazy about him and he's crazy about her, but they won't admit it," Elizabeth reflected, looking around idly—at everything and everyone but Jessica. "Tony thinks someone as feisty and brilliant as Lucy could never consider an ordinary chap like him, and Lucy thinks she's above romance—she thinks falling in love is incompatible with being a top-notch journalist."

"Now that she's the big boss and he's one of her underlings, they'll never get it together," Jessica concluded.

"Not without some help, anyway," mumbled Elizabeth. "Like a major push from a third party."

She felt a nostalgic pang and wondered if Jessica was thinking the same thing she was. *This would have been a natural for us in the old days. If we teamed up, it would take about five seconds to hatch up a plot to throw Lucy and Tony into each other's arms*. But if Jessica was entertaining fond reminiscences of past sisterly conspiracies, she didn't show it. Chin in the air, she kept a cool and expressionless profile turned to Elizabeth. Silence encircled them again, and this time it seemed unbreakable.

The underground ride, and their walk from the station to HIS, was uneventful. Entering the dorm, Jessica and Elizabeth climbed the stairs to the third floor, still in silence. When they opened their bedroom door, however, they both cried out simultaneously. "Ohmigod, what happened?" Jessica screeched.

"We've been robbed—ransacked," Elizabeth gasped.

Together, they stared at the wreckage of their room. Dresser drawers had been emptied willy-nilly on the floor, sheets and pillows thrown off the beds, the closets tumbled. Jessica put a hand over her mouth, speechless. Elizabeth also stood like a statue, paralyzed with shock.

Just then, they heard a sharp intake of breath behind them. Elizabeth jumped, her heart in her throat.

It was only Portia, who'd just returned from a rehearsal at the theater; there were no play performances on Monday evenings. "There's been an intruder," Portia exclaimed, her gray eyes wide. "Oh, look at that mess! I'll run down to Mrs. Bates and we'll call the police. You two start going through your things to find out what's missing."

Portia dashed off down the hall. Elizabeth took a tentative step into the room, her skin crawling. *An intruder . . . what if he's still here?* Her eyes darted to the open closet, its contents spilling out into the room. No, there was no place to hide—everything was torn open, exposed.

Jessica crossed the room, stirring up a cloud of goose feathers from the shredded pillows, and began sifting through her scattered belongings. "My jewelry's still here, and my money," she announced, holding up a quilted pouch.

"Mine, too," said Elizabeth. Bending, she picked up a torn fragment of notepaper. "My letter from Todd, all torn up! Who . . . why?"

"Look, Portia's dresser was hardly touched," Jessica observed.

Elizabeth glanced over. "Her bed, either."

"If the person didn't want to take money and jewelry, what did they want?" Jessica wondered. "Why do . . . this?"

"He—or she—must have been looking for something," Elizabeth said. She turned back to her dresser. "But what? And did he find it?"

Elizabeth kicked at a pile of things on the floor, then checked her drawers again. *Wait a minute,* she thought. Something was missing—the file she'd taken from Dr. Neville's!

"My file!" Elizabeth said out loud even as she realized that something else even more important had disappeared.

"My file!" Jessica burst out at the exact same moment.

The two sisters stared at each other. "And the silver bullet Luke gave me," Elizabeth gasped. "It's gone!"

"Silver bullet, I say, just like the movies, what?"

Both girls whirled. Sergeant Bumpo of Scotland Yard stood in the doorway, scratching his bald head.

"Oh, no," Jessica muttered, exchanging a glance with her sister. "I can't believe they sent him!"

If she weren't so upset, she would have laughed. Their very first day at the *London Journal*, Lucy Friday, then the crime editor, had assigned the twins to Sergeant Bumpo's beat. Initially, they'd been psyched as they fantasized about helping Scotland Yard crack open its toughest cases. It didn't take long to figure out, however, that Sergeant Bumpo was a comically inept buffoon who couldn't catch a criminal if his life depended on it.

They only give him the stupid, trivial cases, Jessica thought as the portly, red-faced detective stumbled into the room, tripping over a pile of clothes the intruder had dumped from a drawer. When Mrs. Bates called, the police must have written it off as a dorm prank.

"Yes, a silver bullet," Elizabeth explained. "It . . . it was just a trinket, a charm for a charm bracelet."

"Any other jewelry stolen?" asked Bumpo, wandering aimlessly around the disheveled room, pausing occasionally to examine something with a wise nod, as if he'd found a significant clue. *You can't fool me, Bumpo,* Jessica thought scornfully. *You're just going through the motions—you don't have the faintest idea what to look for!*

"No, no valuables—no money," said Elizabeth. "Only a file folder. Something I brought home from work, something worthless."

Elizabeth glanced at Jessica. Jessica cleared her throat. "Yes, a file of mine is missing, too." Not wanting to say anything about searching Dr. Neville's apartment, she simply repeated Elizabeth's remarks. "Something from work—I can't imagine why anyone would have thought it was interesting."

"Perhaps it was just a few of the boys from the dormitory having a lark, eh?" Bumpo proposed, appearing relieved that the case might wrap up so quickly and harmlessly.

"A lark?" Elizabeth glared at him. "Hardly! Whoever did this was violent—vicious."

"Well, hmm, I don't see why—if nothing was— but perhaps—" Sergeant Bumpo blustered.

Portia and Mrs. Bates had appeared in the doorway. Now Portia stepped into the room. "If it wasn't just an ordinary, random robber, can you think of anyone who might have wanted something from you?" Portia asked Jessica and Elizabeth. "To hurt you, or to take something from you?"

"Yes, of course, that was going to be my next

question. Right-o," interjected Bumpo, puffing out his chest and looking important. "Can you provide us with a list of possible suspects?"

Jessica felt Elizabeth's eyes boring into her. A nervous flush stole up her neck, staining her whole face pink. *Robert was here this morning, I know it,* Jessica thought, remembering her powerful intuition. *What if he had come back later and . . . ?*

"I have no idea who it might have been," Jessica told Sergeant Bumpo, her voice coming out in a nervous squeak.

Elizabeth continued to stare at Jessica hard. Jessica didn't meet her sister's gaze. Finally, Elizabeth shook her head. "Me, either," she said quietly.

"Well, I'll make a full report," Bumpo promised, giving the girls a gallant salute and marching toward the door. The closet door.

"What have we . . . ? Hmm, I say—" Bumpo backed up. More red-faced than ever, he took another shot at an exit, this time fortuitously landing in the hallway where a distracted Mrs. Bates stood wringing her hands. "Ring us up if you find anything else missing," the detective instructed the girls. "Cheerio!"

Elizabeth, Jessica, and Portia waved good-bye and Mrs. Bates accompanied Sergeant Bumpo down the hall. A moment later, there was a crashing sound, as if someone had fallen down the stairs. "My heavens," Portia declared, laughing. "I can't say that pathetic performance gives me much faith in Sergeant Bumpo's powers of detection, unless, of course, he's some kind of idiot savant."

"No, he's just an idiot, period," complained Elizabeth. "Talk about incompetence. He didn't come up with a single clue—he didn't even dust for fingerprints. We'll never know who did this!"

Jessica kept quiet. She was starting to feel glad that Bumpo had been sent to investigate, rather than someone else who might actually have found something. *I mean, of course it would be great if they catch the person, as it wasn't Robert,* she thought. *But just in case . . .*

Portia and Elizabeth began to clean up the room. Depressed and still more than a bit shaken, Jessica collapsed in an easy chair by the window. "Just leave my things," she told the other two. "I'll pick them up later."

Portia crossed the room to put a hand on Jessica's shoulder, giving her a warm, supportive squeeze. "Don't fret, Jess. Mrs. Bates will keep us all safe and sound. She's already sent David off to have copies of her front-door key made so we can each carry one—starting tonight, the dorm will be locked day and night. Besides," she joked, pointing out the window. "It looks like Bumpo's already got your man!"

Jessica peered into the gloomy dusk. Under a streetlight below, she saw a homeless man in a brown coat and cap weaving and shouting.

Elizabeth stepped over to the window to look. "I saw that man in the park the other day. He seemed harmless, but I guess he's drunk and causing a nuisance."

"I've seen him before, too," Jessica said, stifling a melancholy sigh. *This morning, when I ran outside looking for Robert.*

All three watched as the hapless detective struggled to get a pair of handcuffs on the uncooperative vagrant. "Poor Bumpo," they said in unison.

"Come on, Jessica," Portia urged a short while later, grabbing Jessica's hand and dragging her to her feet. "Let's go to supper—some hot soup will buck you up. Join us, Liz?"

"I'm going out in a bit, actually," Elizabeth replied. "See you later."

The door had only just closed behind Portia and Jessica when someone rapped sharply on it. "Come in," Elizabeth called.

Rene burst into the room. "Elizabeth!" he cried, dashing forward to take both her hands in his. "I just returned from the embassy and heard about the vandalism from Mrs. Bates. Are you all right?"

Rene squeezed her hands tightly and Elizabeth returned the pressure, smiling to reassure him. "I'm fine. It was pretty much of a mess, though."

"Thank goodness it was just the room that got torn apart." Rene's expression grew even more anxious and dark. "What if you or Jessica had been here when the perpetrator came in? What if—"

"Well, we weren't," Elizabeth cut in. "We're fine, really. Don't worry about us."

"I am worried," said Rene, "and you should be, too. I'm sure this wasn't a random act, Elizabeth. Someone is after you. You and Jessica must leave London immediately."

The urgency of Rene's tone struck an emotional chord in Elizabeth. She was more frightened than ever at the thought that the killer had penetrated the sanctuary of HIS, but she wasn't going to admit it. "Didn't we already have this conversation, Rene? We can't leave London," she reasoned. "It doesn't make sense, and besides it's not necessary. The police are investigating and they'll probably catch the person who did it and it will probably turn out to have nothing to do with the murders."

"You don't know that," insisted Rene. "And Portia told me about the detective who was here— a real clown, apparently. Please, Elizabeth. You and Jessica could spend the night at the embassy or a hotel and be on a plane home to the U.S. first thing in the morning. I'll make all the arrangements."

"No." Elizabeth shook her head firmly. "I appreciate your concern, Rene, but I'm staying in London and that's that. And now, I'm on my way out. Luke and I have a movie date."

Rene frowned. "Stay inside, Elizabeth," he begged. "Don't go out into the night."

Slipping on a jacket, Elizabeth laughed. "I'll be OK," she assured Rene. "Come on, walk downstairs with me."

Rene walked her to the front door of the dorm. As Elizabeth eased it open, she did have a brief instant of apprehension. *What if someone is out there, watching, waiting for another opportunity to strike?* she thought with a shiver.

But as she saw Luke striding up the walk, a welcoming smile on his face, her fears vanished like mist in the sun. The dark night held no danger, as long as Luke was by her side. "I'll be with Luke," Elizabeth told Rene as she stepped out the door and waved good-bye. "I'll be perfectly safe."

The top bunk creaked as Jessica rolled over. She burrowed more deeply under the covers, just the tip of her nose and her eyes peeking out.

The room is so dark, she thought, clenching her teeth to keep them from chattering. She felt like a baby, but she wished there were a night-light— something—*anything, but this spooky, haunted blackness.*

There's barely even a moon, Jessica noted, gazing out at the thin cold crescent visible through a break in the clouds. She remembered the full moon shining over Pembroke Manor the night Joy Singleton was murdered. *Maybe darkness isn't the worst thing,* Jessica decided with a shudder. *It's better than a full moon drawing the werewolf out of his lair!*

When she and Elizabeth had first arrived in London, they'd joked about the movie *An American Werewolf in London*, which they saw at a going-away party Lila Fowler gave for them before they went abroad. When Elizabeth and Luke started taking the werewolf business seriously, Jessica had ridiculed them. She was still highly skeptical that the murderer was actually a werewolf, but there was no doubt that the person responsible for the bloody rampage was less than human.

And there was also no doubt that Jessica Wakefield was scared out of her wits.

It's getting closer, she thought, wishing she could will the hands of the clock to speed forward toward sunrise. *The evil. It was here.*

She couldn't stop thinking about the smell of Robert's cologne lingering in her room. Once more, she forced herself to consider head-on the possibility that Robert had been the intruder. *No,* she concluded at last, her spirits lifting somewhat. *No. I know him. Yes, he's on the run—he's hiding somewhere, he's hiding something—but he didn't ransack this place. It just doesn't make sense. He wouldn't have made my bed for me in the morning and then come back later to tear it apart.*

Then who did? There were so many baffling questions. *Why was Robert here this morning?* Jessica asked herself, hugging her pillow. *Why didn't he leave a note—why doesn't he call me at work?*

And why did the intruder, whoever it was, steal the Annabelle S. file and Liz's stupid silver bullet?

Annabelle S., Annabelle S., she mused, her hand straying to her throat and the silver pendant. Suddenly, it hit her. The "A" on the pendant. What if it stood for Annabelle?

"Elizabeth!" Jessica hissed. "Elizabeth, wake up!"

"Hmm?" Elizabeth mumbled sleepily.

Jessica hung over the side of the bed. "I found the werewolf necklace you put in my purse," she whispered down to her sister. "It's Luke's, right? Where did he get it?"

"I thought we weren't talking," Elizabeth said, sounding tired and crabby.

"We're not. Just tell me where he got it."

Elizabeth rubbed her eyes. "His mother gave it to him."

His mother! Jessica's heart raced. Luke's mother was dead and so was Annabelle S. Annabelle S. could be Luke's mother—the S. could stand for Shepherd! "What was her name?" Jessica asked excitedly.

"Ann. Why?"

Ann, not Annabelle. *So much for that brilliant idea,* Jessica thought, disappointed. "No reason. Go back to sleep."

Jessica punched her pillow, frustrated and mystified. *Who on earth was Annabelle S.?* she wondered for about the thousandth time. She still didn't know, but Jessica felt certain now that

Annabelle S., dead for nine years, mattered somehow. Somehow, she figured into the puzzle. *Because the person who trashed our room took the file*, thought Jessica. *Maybe that's why he broke in in the first place!* Although that didn't really make sense, because who but the ghost of Dr. Neville could have known she had the file?

Jessica's eyelids drooped sleepily. The mystery had more angles every day, and it tired her out just thinking about it. She'd just have to redouble her investigative efforts in the morning.

Elizabeth lay in the dark, listening to her sister's steady breathing. Jessica had obviously dozed off, but now, Elizabeth was wide awake . . . and spooked.

Her skin crawled, thinking about a stranger entering their room, opening their drawers and closet, tearing the sheets off the beds. *Touching my clothes*, Elizabeth thought. *Reading my letters* . . .

She hadn't said anything to Sergeant Bumpo about Robert Pembroke. On the surface, there was no reason to connect the ransacked room with the manhunt for the alleged murderer, and Jessica's eyes had seemed to plead with her not to mention Robert's name. *But who else would want that medical file?* Elizabeth wondered. *And the silver bullet? It must have been the werewolf . . . Robert Pembroke himself.*

Elizabeth squeezed her eyes shut, trying to get back into the mood she'd been in on her date with Luke. After grabbing a bite to eat, they'd seen a movie, a lighthearted romantic comedy. Instead of the comedy, though, Elizabeth found herself thinking about another film she and Luke had gone to recently—*The Howling*, a horror movie. A werewolf movie . . .

Elizabeth heard a faint creaking sound and she held her breath, her heart thumping. What if the person who trashed the room came back?

The sound wasn't repeated; it was just the old house settling, Elizabeth decided. But she couldn't quite shake the sensation that something was stirring in the night, a shadowy, palpable presence. A werewolf's victims can't rest until their killer is destroyed, Elizabeth recalled, thinking about the storyline of *An American Werewolf in London*. Maybe all those poor lost souls are walking the earth: Nurse Handley, Dr. Neville, Joy, Maria the cook, Mrs. Price . . .

Gradually, Elizabeth slipped back into a troubled sleep, only to be visited again by the nightmare she'd had as the full moon hung over Pembroke Manor, the night Joy Singleton was murdered in Jessica's bed. Elizabeth stood helpless as the werewolf chased her sister, as he grasped Jessica with hairy, muscular arms, as he bent with a howl to tear her throat with his teeth. . . .

Wait a minute. . . . In her dream, Elizabeth

106

heard the snarl close to her own ear; she felt the claws digging into her flesh, the hot breath against her throat, the point of a knife-sharp fang. This time, the girl the werewolf was pursuing was herself.

Chapter 7

Jessica was just finishing her breakfast on Tuesday morning when her sister hurried into the dining room. She glanced at the clock over the mantel with a feeling of satisfaction. *Aha—look who overslept!* Jessica gloated silently. *Someone's going to be late for work today, and it's not me. For once, Liz will have to scramble—serves her right.*

As she walked to the tube station, however, Jessica's hard heart softened somewhat. She thought about the scene in the dorm room the previous evening, when they'd arrived home to find the place ransacked. *Sergeant Bumpo asked if we had any suspicions about who might have done it, and Liz looked right at me and I know she was thinking about Robert. But for once, she kept her big mouth shut.*

I should probably be grateful for small favors,

Jessica decided grudgingly. Stopping at a newsstand near the entrance to the tube, she lingered for ten minutes glancing through various glossy European fashion magazines. Just as she was about to blow Elizabeth off, her sister trotted up, panting. Without exchanging a word, the twins descended the escalator together.

A quarter of an hour later, as they pushed through the revolving doors of the newspaper building, Jessica experienced a strange feeling of déjà vu. An atmosphere of tense excitement filled the office; people were dashing distractedly in all directions. "This reminds me of the first day we came here," Jessica said, then bit her lip as she realized she'd inadvertently spoken to her sister. *A big story must be breaking,* she added to herself. *A story as big as the Dr. Neville murder!*

Immediately, a feeling of foreboding washed over her. "Please, God, not another murder," she heard Elizabeth whisper.

They hurried forward and Jessica grabbed a passing colleague by the arm. "Zena, what's going on?"

"There's been another attack—the werewolf struck again," Zena said dramatically. "The owner of the *Journal*, Lord Pembroke, was the victim!"

"Lord Pembroke!" Jessica gasped. Her knees buckled and a misty gray curtain seemed to fall before her eyes; she staggered forward, on the verge of fainting. "Ohmigod, Robert's father."

Elizabeth grabbed Jessica's elbow to support

her. "Lord Pembroke, dead!" she exclaimed. "I can't believe it."

"No, no, he's not dead," said Zena. "Not yet, anyway. He's in hospital. He survived the attack."

At Zena's words, Jessica snapped back into focus. Still pale, she shook off Elizabeth's arm and gaped at Zena. "He survived? Did he . . . did he get a look at— Did he identify his attacker?"

Please, don't let it be Robert, Jessica chanted in her brain. *Please, don't let it, don't let it, don't let it . . .*

Zena shook her head. "Supposedly, he didn't get a good look at the fellow. Or should I say creature? We don't have much information—the police weren't able to interview Lord Pembroke at any length. He's in critical condition."

"But there's no doubt it was the same person who killed the others?" said Elizabeth. "He was wounded in the same way?"

Zena nodded. "The throat," she said simply.

While Elizabeth plied Zena with more questions, Jessica wandered over to her desk near the editor-in-chief's office, dazed. *Lord Pembroke, brutally attacked!* she thought. *The poor, poor man.* Robert's father had been kind to Jessica, and she had a soft spot for him. *Critical condition— that's pretty bad. What if he doesn't make it? What will Robert do?*

A sudden, devastating thought struck Jessica. Robert had disappeared—he could be far away,

111

completely out of touch with the world. *What if he hasn't heard about this? What if Lord Pembroke dies in the hospital, and Robert isn't there to hold his hand, to say good-bye?*

"Jessica. Hullo, Jessica!"

Jessica blinked. Lucy Friday was standing in front of her desk, briskly snapping her fingers. "Oh, I'm sorry," said Jessica, her face flooding with color. "Do you have work for me? I was just—we heard when we came in— Oh, I'm so worried, about Lord Pembroke Senior and Robert and everything!"

She sniffled and gulped, on the verge of bursting into tears. In typical no-nonsense fashion, Lucy thrust a handkerchief at her. "Blow your nose and get yourself together," Lucy recommended, not unkindly. "Then come to my office."

Dutifully, Jessica blew her nose. Running over to the ladies' room, she splashed water on her face and brushed her hair. As she took a few deep breaths, gradually some of the tension began to drain from her body.

Her eyes dry, Jessica presented herself at Lucy's desk. Lucy waved her into a chair. "Now, are you just distressed in general or is there something specific troubling you?" she asked.

"I have to find Robert," said Jessica, anxiously clasping her hands together. "He's hiding somewhere—he might not even know about all this. I have to tell him."

"Hmm." Lucy tapped a pen on the desk. "What would you think if I told you it's more probable that Robert does know," she said flatly, "because he himself is the attacker?"

Jessica's eyes flashed. She responded without thinking. "I'd think maybe you weren't the great journalist you're cracked up to be. I'd think you were just listening to the stories everybody else was telling without going out there and finding out the truth for yourself."

Lucy stared at Jessica, momentarily taken aback. Then she smiled broadly. "You've got guts, Wakefield," she declared. "I admire that in a person. And even though I believe, for very good reasons and not just on the basis of hearsay, that Robert Pembroke Junior is guilty as all get-out, I sympathize with your situation. Take the morning off. Get to the bottom of this. Find Robert, if you can."

"But how?" Jessica asked.

Lucy considered for a moment. "Why don't you talk to Lord Pembroke?" she suggested at last. "He may know more about his son's whereabouts than he's let on to the police—he may still be protecting Robert."

Elizabeth, Luke, and Tony sat in chairs clustered around Tony's desk, cups of steaming tea in their hands. "Lord Pembroke was attacked in his study at Pembroke Green, the family's London residence," Tony related. Elizabeth thought he

113

sounded congested, as if he were coming down with a cold. "Around midnight, as he enjoyed a quiet, solitary pipe by candlelight before retiring."

Elizabeth shivered. "How could Rob—could anyone do such a thing?" she asked. "His own . . ."

She couldn't bear to put it into words. Luke, however, had no such hesitations. "His own father," he exclaimed, his eyes glittering strangely. "To try to kill one's own father!"

"It's the most heinous crime he's attempted yet," Tony agreed. "Clearly the boy went after his father to get back at him for turning against him."

"And also to prevent Lord Pembroke Senior from turning him in to the authorities," contributed Elizabeth.

"The werewolf's cruelty and fury knows no bounds," said Luke. "He knows no limits. Nothing . . . no one . . . is sacred."

Elizabeth and Tony both stared at Luke. Tony nodded, although Elizabeth could tell he thought Luke a bit batty. Even Elizabeth at times had to admit that Luke took things to an extreme. Poets are just like that, she'd tell herself.

But this morning, Luke's ominous, prophetic words seemed more than appropriate to the circumstances. *Maybe Robert's not a werewolf like the ones we see in the movies,* Elizabeth thought, *but he's a monster. The animal side of his nature has taken over.*

Another shiver shook her body from head to

toe. She'd decided not to tell Tony and Luke about the break-in at the dorm because she didn't want to worry them, but this latest development cast a new and terrible light on the incident. *The werewolf was in our room, and then he went to Pembroke Green. What if Jess or I had been home? Right now would one of us be lying in a hospital bed . . . or in the morgue?*

"It won't be long now, though," mused Tony, tipping back in his chair. "He's on the run, desperate, taking bigger risks than ever. And he's getting sloppy. He didn't finish the job—he left one alive."

Out of the corner of her eye, Elizabeth glimpsed a blur of color. Glancing over, she saw Jessica, in a bright yellow skirt and jacket and with her bag slung over her shoulder, dashing out the door of the office.

Elizabeth bit her lip anxiously. Where was Jessica off to in such a hurry? Was she planning to take bigger risks than ever, in the name of a misguided love? Could she still believe in Robert's innocence after this?

At enormous, sprawling London Hospital, Jessica learned from the receptionist that Lord Pembroke had been moved from intensive care to a private room on the third floor of Wing C.

"You're not from one of the newspapers, are you?" the receptionist asked suspiciously. "We'll have no reporters up there. A security guard just hauled off that sneaky young man from the *London Daily Post.*"

"Oh, no, I'm just a friend of the family," said Jessica.

She had to give the nurse on duty the same assurances. "All right," the nurse agreed, after eyeing Jessica up and down. "You can go in. But his wife is with him at the moment."

"I'll wait, then," Jessica murmured. "I don't want to disturb them."

A few minutes later, from her seat in the corner of the visitors' lounge, Jessica saw Lady Pembroke emerge from Room 21. The older woman was dabbing her eyes with a handkerchief; her thin face, always perfectly made-up, looked crumpled and careworn. Jessica had gotten the impression that the Pembroke marriage was mostly one of appearances at this point, but there must have been a trace of love left somewhere. Lady Pembroke was so distracted and upset, she didn't even notice Jessica as she walked past the lounge on her way to the nurses' station.

Rising, Jessica slipped unobtrusively into Room 21. Curtains darkened the windows; except for the sound of labored breathing, the room was silent.

At the sight of Lord Pembroke, tears of pity sprang into Jessica's eyes. A thick bandage muffled his throat; there was a tube in his nose to help him breathe and an IV hooked into his arm. The once hearty, vigorous man looked pale, diminished, and old, his body thin and frail under the sheet.

Lord Pembroke's eyes were closed. *Is he asleep?* Jessica wondered. *Unconscious?* She pulled a chair close to the bedside. "Lord Pembroke," she said softly. "It's Jessica Wakefield. How are you feeling?"

Lord Pembroke's eyelids fluttered, then opened. He gazed up at Jessica, but he didn't seem to really see her. "I wanted to catch a werewolf," he muttered.

He wanted to catch a werewolf? He must be hallucinating. "What do you mean?"

She had to lean close to hear his disjointed words. "My hobby . . . our hobby. I stalled the police investigation, thinking I might—but when the evidence started to point to my boy . . . Too many hurt, too many dead . . ."

Jessica patted his arm. "Ssh," she murmured. "Don't strain yourself."

Lord Pembroke made a visible effort to focus on her. A faint smile touched his haggard face. "My son loves you," he whispered.

Jessica took the thin hand that lay on top of the covers and squeezed it gently, her eyes brimming.

"He was a troublemaker as a boy, but he could never hurt anyone," Lord Pembroke continued. "Especially not his beloved nanny, or his own father . . ."

"I know," Jessica said. "I know."

Lord Pembroke continued to look up at her, his

117

gaze fond but foggy. Then suddenly, the expression in his eyes sharpened—they flashed with fire and he sat up in bed, fully awake. "The pendant," he declared accusingly. "Where did you get that?"

As she bent forward, Luke's silver werewolf pendant had slipped from behind the collar of Jessica's blouse. Startled, she raised a hand to tuck it back in. "My—my sister gave it to me," she stuttered. "It's—"

"Forgive me." Lord Pembroke's eyelids fluttered; he sank back weakly on the bed. "I didn't mean to scare you, my dear. It's just that it reminds me of the one I gave poor Annabelle."

"Annabelle?" Alarm bells sounded in Jessica's head. The file from Dr. Neville's—Annabelle S.!

"My lovely Annabelle," Lord Pembroke murmured. "The only woman I ever really . . ."

His voice trailed off; he seemed to be slipping back into semiconsciousness. Jessica gripped his hand, jiggling his arm a bit. She wasn't about to let him drift off to sleep now, not when she was on the verge of an important discovery. "Annabelle," she prompted, her tone urgent. "Who is she?"

When Lord Pembroke spoke again, it was clear his mind had gone off in another direction. "You must tell Robert something for me," he said.

Jessica sighed, swallowing her disappointment at not learning more about Annabelle. "Anything."

"Tell him . . ." Lord Pembroke's breathing was raspy and labored; every word was a struggle. "He has . . . a . . . brother."

"A brother?" Jessica gasped. "But . . ." But Robert was an only child! Or rather, she realized, Robert was the only child Lord Pembroke Senior had with Lady Pembroke. . . .

Her head whirled. Was Lord Pembroke trying to say that he'd had another son with another woman? That Robert had an illegitimate half brother he didn't even know about?

"Tell him," Lord Pembroke repeated feebly.

"Yes, of course," Jessica promised. "If I ever see him again, that is."

"You'll see him," Lord Pembroke assured her, his eyes closing. His final words were uttered in the faintest of whispers, but Jessica heard them and held them close to her heart. "He'll come back to you. He loves you. . . ."

Hunched over her desk at the *Journal*, Elizabeth thumbed through the notebook she'd been using to record interviews and observations relating to the werewolf case. *We know so much, and yet so little,* she thought, chewing on the end of a pencil. As much as she hated to admit it, Jessica was right—some of the evidence pointed to Robert, but not all of it. The question of motive remained elusive. What drove him to start killing? Why did he choose some of his victims? How did it all add up?

There was something very strange about the whole family, not just Robert, Elizabeth mused.

She'd sensed it at Pembroke Manor; the ancient house on the wild, barren moors reeked of secret passions, secret histories.

Elizabeth flipped back to the first few pages, rereading the notes she'd scribbled at Pembroke Manor, when the entire household was in disarray following the murder of Joy Singleton. After the local police interviewed family members, guests, and servants, Elizabeth had conducted some interviews of her own. *What did I learn, though?* she thought now, frustrated. *Nothing. A big zero, zip, zilch.*

Turning another page, a brief notation caught her eye. "All my love, Annabelle." Elizabeth squinted at the words, remembering their source. *Lord Pembroke's secret library—I copied that inscription from the flyleaf of a book about werewolves.*

She'd had no idea what to make of it then, and still didn't know if it possessed any significance. *But there's always a chance,* Elizabeth realized. *Who was Annabelle? Could she play a part in the mystery somehow?*

As she stared down at the note, a sudden, powerful hunch swept over Elizabeth. Annabelle was someone important. Annabelle might even hold the key. *All my love, Annabelle . . .*

"I've got to find her," Elizabeth said out loud. "Whoever she is, wherever she is, I bet she knows things about the Pembrokes that no one else does.

She might even be able to lead me to Robert!"

Jumping to her feet, Elizabeth stuck the notebook in her purse and reached for her sweater. It was time to make another visit to Pembroke Manor and the secret library. The answer was there—Elizabeth felt sure of it.

Chapter 8

And it's the perfect time to drop in at Pembroke Manor, Elizabeth reflected as she slipped a new cassette into her mini-corder. Lord and Lady Pembroke are both in the city, which means only servants are at the country estate. I shouldn't have any problem talking my way into the house.

After gathering her things together, she started instinctively in the direction of Luke's desk. Then she stopped, a pensive frown on her face. A week or so ago, Luke would have been psyched about the idea of sleuthing around Pembroke Manor—it wouldn't have occurred to her not to ask him to come along. But now . . .

He's been after me to stop investigating on my own, Elizabeth recalled. If I tell him where I'm going, he'll just say it's not safe and try to talk me out of it. And he'd have a point, Elizabeth had to acknowledge. The werewolf had already killed twice at Pembroke Manor. . . .

"But I have to go," Elizabeth murmured to herself. "Luke or no Luke."

Since this whole frightening drama had begun, she and Luke had shared everything with each other. She felt somewhat guilty leaving him out of her confidence. *It's for the best*, Elizabeth told herself. *I'll tell him about it afterward, when I've come back in one piece with some great new evidence. Then he'll have to admit I can take care of myself.*

So, it was settled: for the time being, Luke would remain in the dark about her plans to journey to Pembroke Manor. But she should tell someone where she was going, Elizabeth decided. Just in case . . .

Tony was a natural choice, as she needed his permission to take off from work anyhow. Elizabeth stepped over to the cubicle where Tony, a pencil stuck behind his ear, sat typing rapidly on his computer. "Hi, Tony, I wonder if—"

"Liz, there you are," he said, without looking up from the screen. "I have an assignment you might enjoy, a rather racy case of blackmail. I thought we could ah—ah—achew!"

The sneeze sent the pencil flying. Tony reached for a box of tissues. "Darn this cold," he muttered, blowing his nose with a loud honk. "What was I saying?"

"Something about a blackmail story, but I—"

"Oh, yes. I can get you an interview with the—" Tony cut his sentence short, holding up one hand in anticipation of another big sneeze.

Elizabeth took advantage of his momentary silence. "Actually, if you give me the green light, I already have a project in mind that will take the rest of the day," she said quickly. "I want to take the train to Pembroke Woods in order to . . ."

She told him about her Annabelle hunch. The sneeze on hold for the moment, Tony nodded, his watery eyes sparkling with interest. "By all means, we must go to Pembroke Manor," he agreed heartily.

Elizabeth raised her eyebrows. "We?"

"You shouldn't go alone, and two sleuths are better than one."

"What about your cold?" Elizabeth asked. "What about the blackmail case?"

"The blackmail case can wait," said Tony, grabbing a handful of tissues and stuffing them into his pockets. "And since when was a runny nose an excuse not to get a story? It wouldn't stop Adam Silver of the *London Daily Post*. Let's go!"

Lord Pembroke had dozed off. Carefully, Jessica removed her hand from his. Rising to her feet, she tiptoed from the room, easing the door closed behind her.

Tidbits from her strange, half-coherent conversation with Lord Pembroke buzzed through her brain like a swarm of excited bees. *Lord Pembroke is in love with a woman named Annabelle!* Jessica mused. *And Robert has a half brother he doesn't know about, Lord Pembroke's illegitimate son with Annabelle, I bet.* And Annabelle had a pendant similar to the one Jessica wore, which belonged originally to Luke Shepherd's mother, whose name was Ann, not Annabelle. Then there was the file she'd stolen from Dr. Neville's, and which someone else had stolen from her. Could Lord Pembroke's Annabelle be Annabelle S., who years ago died of pneumonia while under Dr. Neville's care? *She could be dead,* thought Jessica. *After all, Lord Pembroke called her "my poor Annabelle."*

Portia had hypothesized that Dr. Neville might have omitted Annabelle's full name from his records in order to preserve her anonymity because she was having an affair. *An affair with Lord Pembroke, Neville's best friend!* Jessica concluded. *It fits. That's what best friends are good for, keeping secrets.*

It wasn't hard to weave the fragments into a compelling story, but Jessica knew she was far from able to prove the truth of any of it, and far, also, from understanding what light the existence of Annabelle—living or dead—and her son might cast on what was happening now.

Lord Pembroke's Annabelle might not be the same as Dr. Neville's, Jessica thought as she strolled back toward the visitors' lounge. She could be alive—the affair could be going on now. Robert's brother might be a little kid, or even a baby.

She needed to know more, that was obvious. But Lord Pembroke had looked pretty ghastly. What if he died and she didn't get another chance to talk to him? There was one other person who might know something about Annabelle. . . .

Jessica peeked into the lounge. Lady Pembroke sat with her coat on, a Styrofoam cup of coffee in one gloved hand. *Tread carefully*, Jessica counseled herself as she stepped into the room. *Don't go blurting stuff out about Lord Pembroke's mistress. Lady P. might not even know about Annabelle. You don't want to scare her off.*

Jessica hesitated, then cleared her throat. "Hello, Lady Pembroke. I see you're about to leave, but I wondered if we could talk for a minute—"

Lady Pembroke glanced up, startled. "What are you doing here, you hateful, nosy American girl?" she cried shrilly.

Jessica blushed. "Well, I heard about Lord Pembroke's . . . accident," she stammered. "I wanted to pay my—"

"You have absolutely no right. You have no place here. Sticking your nose in where you don't belong . . . You're shameless, absolutely shameless!"

Jessica bit her lip. She couldn't blame Lady Pembroke for being so infuriated. *If only Liz hadn't barged in on her that time at Pembroke Green*, she thought, *pretending to be me so she could snoop around for clues . . .*

"Lady Pembroke, I know how hard all this is on you, how much stress you're under. I only wanted to—"

"To what?" Lady Pembroke snapped, her pale blue eyes flashing. "To intrude on my privacy? To satisfy your vulgar American curiosity—to gawk at an ancient, distinguished family falling to ruin?"

"It's not like that," Jessica said quietly. "I'm here because I'm truly concerned about Lord Pembroke, and about Robert."

At the mention of her son's name, what was left of Lady Pembroke's shattered composure crumbled into dust. Dropping her coffee cup on the floor, she rose to her feet, swaying slightly. "You were never any good for my son—all you did from the start was stir up trouble," she croaked hoarsely. "I don't ever want to speak to or lay eyes on you again. Clifford!" She clapped her gloved hands together imperiously. "Clifford!"

The family chauffeur materialized out of nowhere and solicitously offered Lady Pembroke his arm. "Take me home," she commanded.

With a swift, sympathetic glance at Jessica, Clifford ushered Lady Pembroke away. Jessica stood looking after them, remembering her high, glorious hopes when she first met Robert . . . and fell for him like a ton of bricks. She'd never forget their first date, when Clifford whisked them in a black limousine all over London. *I wanted so much to make a good impression on Lord and Lady*

Pembroke, Jessica thought sadly. *I wanted them to like me, to love me like a daughter.*

Instead, Lady Pembroke hated her with a passion that didn't appear likely to fade. In her relations with the Pembrokes—and in her attempt to fathom the mystery of Lord Pembroke's affair with Annabelle—Jessica had hit a dead end.

Tickets in hand, Elizabeth and Tony plunged into the sea of people at Victoria Station. "Our train leaves from track eleven in five minutes," Tony shouted. "We'd better hurry!"

Dodging around a large woman with an even larger suitcase, Elizabeth did her best to stay right behind Tony. For half a minute or so, she scrambled along, her eyes fixed on the back of a sandy-haired head and a tweed jacket. Then she realized something. Tony was wearing brown pants, not gray pants, and he wasn't that tall. She was following the wrong guy.

Halting, Elizabeth craned her neck, searching the crowd for her boss. "I'd better just get to the train," she decided. "If I miss it, I'm sunk!"

She hurried forward, her eyes still roving in hopes of spotting Tony. *It's hopeless,* she thought. *Tony is so typically English—half the men here have sandy hair and tweed jackets!* Then her eye was caught by someone who didn't blend into the scene quite so easily—a tall, dark-haired young man in a European-style double-breasted sports coat. Elizabeth blinked. *Rene?*

She stood on tiptoes and waved, trying to catch his eye. The young man didn't look in her direction, however; instead, he turned away and disappeared into the crowd.

Elizabeth shook her head as she trotted on. It must not have been him. What would Rene be doing at Victoria Station in the middle of a workday anyhow? *I probably just imagined I saw him because he's on my mind,* she decided, *because I keep thinking about how I'm always blowing him off.* From the moment she arrived at HIS, Rene had been so happy to resume their acquaintance, so attentive. *I haven't been a very good friend to him in return,* Elizabeth thought with a sigh of regret. She just didn't have the time. It sounded incredibly selfish, but it was true.

Tony was waiting for her at track eleven. "There you are!" he exclaimed with relief. "I thought I'd lost you—I thought I was going to have to figure out the secret door in Pembroke's library by myself."

As the train blew its whistle, an announcement echoed over the loudspeaker. "All aboard for the northwest express to Cauldmoor County. Leaving now, track eleven."

Taking Elizabeth's arm, Tony helped her onto the train. He jumped up behind her just as the doors slid shut. "And we're off," he said, fumbling in his pocket for a tissue. "Ah—ah—achew!"

•   •   •

Jessica sat at her desk at the *Journal*, eating french fries out of a paper bag. It had cheered her up a little to buy lunch at an American-style fast-food restaurant, but only a little.

I'm no Nancy Drew, she acknowledged glumly, squirting ketchup from a foil packet onto her hamburger. Robert was still in hiding somewhere, because he was still the prime suspect, because she hadn't figured out who the real killer was.

She licked her fingers and then fumbled in her shoulder bag for her reporter's notebook. Finding the page where she'd made a list of the werewolf's victims, she added Lord Pembroke's name. Then she scanned the list of possible suspects—people who'd had the opportunity to kill Joy Singleton.

"The servants at Pembroke Manor," Jessica mused aloud. "No, I don't think it's any of them. Most of the attacks have taken place in London— the killer must be based here."

She crossed off the servants. "The chief of police . . . hmm," she murmured. It would be pretty cool if he were the werewolf—just like a "bad cop" movie. Jessica tried the theory on for size. "Lord Pembroke made Thatcher hold off on the police investigation for a while, back when he was trying to protect Robert, even though of course the evidence against Robert is totally trumped up. That was pretty convenient for Thatcher! And it's pretty convenient to have control over the investigation— he can keep steering everybody after Robert, when meanwhile the dead bodies keep piling up."

She bit into her hamburger, pleased with this scenario. "Naturally, he was pretty devastated when he found out his fiancée had been murdered—because he'd meant to kill someone else. Me." A puzzled frown wrinkled her forehead. "Why would he want to kill me, though? Why would he want to kill any of these people? Just for the fun of it?"

She scrawled a question mark next to Andrew Thatcher's name and moved on down the list of suspects. Lady Pembroke. Now, there was an intriguing possibility. "She looked pretty upset at the hospital this morning, but that could have just been an act," Jessica reflected. "Maybe she went after Lord Pembroke herself, to get revenge because he had an affair!"

It was a juicy, workable theory, but it broke down as soon as Jessica pushed it a little further. What about all the other victims—why would Lady Pembroke kill them? And what about Robert? Would Lady Pembroke really just sit by and watch while her only beloved son went to jail in her place?

"Besides, she's too fastidious," Jessica decided. "She wouldn't want to mess up her hair and clothes—she's the type who'd hire someone else to do the dirty work for her."

Jessica gave Lady Pembroke a question mark. "Luke Shepherd." She popped a french fry in her mouth and tried to imagine Elizabeth's moony boyfriend prowling around London after dark and slashing people's throats. She laughed out loud. "Not that he isn't weird," she said with her mouth full. "He'd make a pretty good werewolf because he knows so much about them. And he's a loner, and serial killers are always loners." Still, it didn't jive. "People who write poetry are too wimpy to be murderers," Jessica concluded.

She started to scratch off Luke's name, then stopped herself. *Gotta keep him on the list—he's the easiest one to investigate!* she reasoned.

Wrapping up the rest of her hamburger, Jessica wiped her fingers on a paper napkin and got to her feet. Nonchalantly, she wandered across the office toward Luke's section.

The arts and entertainment staff were all out to lunch, so Jessica marched boldly up to Luke's desk and starting snooping through his stuff.

She found a coffee mug with some old, cold tea in the bottom, a book of English poetry, two half-finished movie reviews, and a handful of paper scraps—notes for stories in progress. *What did you expect?* Jessica asked herself, stifling a giggle. *A confession, signed "The Werewolf"?*

She opened a desk drawer. As she was about to pick up a fat spiral notebook with a red cover, she heard footsteps behind her. "May I help you?" Luke demanded.

Jessica turned, an innocent smile on her face.

"Who, me? Oh, yes. I just wanted to borrow . . . a stapler. Do you have one?"

Luke frowned, and then shrugged. Jessica stepped away from his desk, watching as he opened another drawer and pulled out a stapler. "Will this do?" he asked briskly.

"Thanks," said Jessica, taking the stapler. "I'll bring it back in a sec."

Luke waved her off. "Keep it."

Stapler in hand, Jessica sauntered back to the main newsroom. He definitely acted guilty, she decided. He must be hiding something in that desk. *Yeah, some gooey love poetry—"Ode to Elizabeth."*

Seated at her desk again, Jessica gave Luke a question mark. *I'm making great progress*, she thought sarcastically as she chewed a cold french fry. One question mark after another . . .

Two hours after boarding the train in Victoria Station, Elizabeth and Tony disembarked in the tiny country village of Pembroke Woods. "It's another world, eh?" remarked Tony, eyeing the cobblestone streets and ancient ivy-covered cottages.

"Another century," said Elizabeth. She felt the same way she had the first time she came to Pembroke Woods, as if she'd been transported back in time. "Robert told us those weavers' cottages were built four hundred years ago."

"And the town hasn't changed a whit since, I wager," said Tony. He gestured to a weathered wooden sign. "I'll find out from the tavern-keeper whether they run to such modern conveniences as taxicabs."

Tony ducked into the White Swan Inn and Elizabeth wandered onto a rickety wooden bridge. A pair of the majestic swans that gave the inn its name floated in the crystal-clear brook below, their dirty-gray cygnets paddling single file after them. It was hard to believe, Elizabeth thought, that two people were recently murdered just a few miles from this tranquil spot.

Turning back, Elizabeth saw Tony emerge from the inn, a heavyset farmer with a round, sunburnt face lumbering after him. "The bad news is, the town's one taxi is in the shop for repairs," Tony reported. "The good news is, this kind gentleman has offered to run us up to Pembroke Manor in his . . . conveyance."

The farmer's "conveyance" turned out to be a dilapidated pickup truck filled with grimy farm tools and dusty hay. Tony had a sneezing fit the instant he climbed in. "We should have skipped the train and hired a car in the city!" Tony hollered as the pickup rattled along a bumpy country road, he and Elizabeth bouncing around in the back.

The wind whipped Elizabeth's hair. "This makes it more of an adventure!"

The sensation of entering another world increased as they drove deeper into the woods outside the village. Elizabeth pointed out the ruins of

Woodleigh Abbey through the trees. "Haunted," she yelled to Tony.

"I believe it," he yelled back, tucking his chin down into the collar of his jacket.

There was one brief delay as the farmer stopped to let a flock of sheep meander across the road. Soon after, the truck crested a hill and Pembroke Manor appeared below them.

Elizabeth caught her breath, just as she had at her first sight of the stately fieldstone house built around an enormous emerald-green courtyard. With the rugged moors in the distance, it looked like the setting for a gothic novel.

At the top of the driveway, the farmer braked. "This is as far as I go," he called out the window to his passengers. "The family's nowt but bad luck lately. There's something gone wrong with that house and everyone in it. I'd be careful if I were you."

Tony and Elizabeth hopped down. Pulling a U-turn, the farmer sped off in a cloud of dust.

Together, the two faced Pembroke Manor. *There's no going back,* Elizabeth thought, taking a deep breath and starting forward.

"That was easier than I thought it would be," she whispered to Tony as they walked along the lofty, cathedral-like hall of Pembroke Manor toward the library.

"You heard that farmer—with a family member suspected of being a serial killer, the Pembrokes are probably having a tough time holding on to their help," said Tony. "It's a magnificent house, but it's acquiring a gruesome reputation. Can't say I'd want to spend a night under this roof!"

"Me, either," agreed Elizabeth. "Never again."

"What a fine collection of old books," Tony said as they entered Lord Pembroke's library, a typically English and very masculine room decorated with burgundy leather furniture and heavy brocade curtains.

Elizabeth stepped around the massive mahogany desk. "Watch this!"

As Tony watched in astonishment, she reached for a book on one of the shelves—a leatherbound edition of Robert Louis Stevenson's *The Strange Case of Dr. Jekyll and Mr. Hyde*. As she slowly removed the volume, a panel in the adjacent wall swung open to reveal a hidden door.

Tony's eyes nearly popped out of his head. "My, look at that! Just like in the films!"

Elizabeth slipped into the shadowy secret room, Tony following close behind her. She flipped on a light switch and he whistled. "Good heavens. I see why you've been calling it the wolf den!"

The walls of the small room were draped with wild animal skins and mounted trophy heads, mostly of wolves. "And all the books are about werewolves," Elizabeth told Tony. "It's Lord Pembroke Senior's big hobby."

"An obsession, more like," said Tony. "Robert must have known of this place, wouldn't you say?

He must have read some of these books—absorbed the lore. This is where he learned what kind of killer he wanted to become."

Elizabeth nodded. "It's a good theory. Here's the book from Annabelle." Taking it from the shelf, she offered it for Tony's inspection. "*Discours de la Lyncanthropie*—it's in French, from the sixteenth century. See?"

Tony read the inscription. "Well, let's get to work and see what else we can find."

Starting at opposite sides of the study, they began methodically examining each and every volume on the shelves. "Here's another one given to him by Annabelle!" Elizabeth cried after five minutes.

"Anything special about it?" asked Tony.

Elizabeth flipped through the pages. "Not particularly," she admitted, putting it back.

Twenty minutes later, they were nearly ready to give up. "We haven't learned anything new about Annabelle," declared Elizabeth, frustrated. "She gave Lord P. half a dozen books about werewolves, so we can conclude she was as interested in them as he was. But what kind of relationship did they have? Who was she?"

Tony shook his head. "She's a mystery woman."

"Well, let's get through these last two shelves," suggested Elizabeth. "Then we can look around some more in the big library."

Starting in on a new shelf, she looked at four books. Nothing. But there was something odd about the fifth book. *It's so light*, Elizabeth thought, weighing it in her hand. *It's almost as if it's . . .*

"Look!" she squealed. "This one's hollow—it's not really a book at all! It's a box that looks like a book." She lifted the front cover, the box's lid. "Something's inside." Her eyes widened with the thrill of discovery. "Letters!"

Eagerly, she removed a sheaf of old, faded letters from the box. Tony looked over her shoulder. "Don't tell me they're from—" he began.

Elizabeth glanced at the signature on the top letter. "Annabelle!" she confirmed excitedly.

They sat down cross-legged on the floor, the correspondence spread out before them, and each took a letter. As she read, Elizabeth's eyes grew rounder and rounder. The letter she'd chosen started, "My beloved Robert, I miss you more than I can say. It is such agony to be apart at a time like this. When can we be together?"

"They're love letters," Elizabeth gasped.

Tony nodded. "I'll say! And they go way back. This is twenty years old."

Elizabeth picked up another sheet of pale-pink paper covered with faded, graceful script. "This one is more recent, written only ten years ago."

"It must have been quite a love affair," remarked Tony.

"And quite a friendship," said Elizabeth, skimming a letter. "It's not all romantic stuff. Here she writes for a whole page about books she's read, and then for a page more about politics."

"Look at this one—I think it's the most recent."

Tony handed a letter to Elizabeth. It was dated just nine years ago. "Dear R.," it began simply. "I haven't much strength, so this will be brief. I haven't much time. . . . The doctor, your dear friend, is cheerful as always, but I see the truth in his eyes, and feel it in my heart. Pain and loneliness press down on me until I pray that I'll fall asleep and slip peacefully away—if only it didn't mean leaving my precious child, and you, my only love. How it hurts, more than any illness, to know I'll never see your face again! Forget me, Robert— it will be best. But take care of our son. I've never asked anything of you, and never will again, so please do just this one thing. . . ."

Elizabeth looked up from the letter, her eyes damp with sentimental tears. "Wow. They had a child together, and then she must have died. It's like a movie or something." Suddenly, something came together in her mind with an almost audible click. "The family scandal! Eliana couldn't remember what it was about, exactly, only that it took place a long time ago."

"Perhaps Lady Pembroke found out about the affair," deduced Tony. "I bet Annabelle's husband did, anyway. She doesn't mention him in the last batch of letters—he probably left her."

Elizabeth glanced down at the sheet of stationery. The words Annabelle had written so long ago seemed to jump off the page, to breathe with affection and vitality. *You, my only love* . . .

"They were so in love," she said as she copied the return address from one of the envelopes into her notebook. "And it was real. It lasted years and years. Why didn't they marry each other?"

"Love doesn't count for much in matters like these, especially with the aristocracy," Tony said, somewhat heartlessly, Elizabeth thought. "In this instance, clearly it wasn't enough to overcome the obstacle of class."

"Class? What do you mean?"

"Well, it's apparent from her letters that although Annabelle was extremely well-read and intelligent, she and Pembroke were of a different social status. It sounds like her husband was a shopkeeper of some sort, and here"—he pointed to one of the letters—"she writes about having to cut short a family holiday to the seaside because of financial constraints. I know it strikes a romantic American like you as odd, perhaps even despicable, but our class distinctions have long formed the basis of English civilization. The prince only marries the flower girl in fairy tales, or Hollywood movies. Knowing Lord Pembroke, that's why he wouldn't leave Lady Pembroke for Annabelle."

"Wow," Elizabeth said again. "It's so tragic. Poor Annabelle. And her little son—what do you think happened to him?" She clapped a hand over her mouth. "You don't suppose it's—"

"Little Lord Pembroke?" Tony shook his head. "No. Lady Pembroke would never have allowed her husband to raise the result of an adulterous affair in her home as her son. No, Annabelle and Lord Robert's progeny, who would be anywhere from nine to nineteen, is probably in an orphanage or on the street."

On the street . . . Elizabeth remembered the homeless man Sergeant Bumpo had carted off the day before. Her heart ached for the abandoned child, perhaps homeless himself, and the star-crossed lovers who had been his parents.

"We discovered the secret of Annabelle," Elizabeth said softly, holding the letters for a moment before returning them to their hiding place. "But this is all she's going to tell us."

Annabelle had long been silent. They'd reached a dead end.

"Ten minutes—grand," Tony said into the phone back in the main library. "We'll meet you in the drive." Hanging up, he turned to watch as Elizabeth pushed the Robert Louis Stevenson volume back into place and the trick panel swung shut, sealing off the secret room. "The town taxi is back in service and on its way to collect us."

"I guess Annabelle didn't turn out to be the key to the mystery," Elizabeth reflected as she and Tony headed back toward the entrance to the manor.

"Actually, maybe she is." Tony's eyes sparkled with inspiration. "Imagine it this way. Robert at some point discovered the werewolf room. Any boy or young man would be fascinated by such a place—he went there secretly to read the scary werewolf books. And one day . . . he does what you did. He picks the fake book from the shelf and discovers the love letters!"

"And so . . . ?"

"Perhaps finding out about Lord Pembroke's affair led to Robert's killing spree somehow. Perhaps Robert became unbalanced, fearing he might lose his inheritance or have to share it with Annabelle's son, or just from knowing what his father had done."

Elizabeth pondered this theory. "It could have happened that way," she conceded. "But it still doesn't explain everything, like why he chose some of his victims."

"If he chose at all," Tony pointed out. "Maybe he just snapped."

The main entry hall was deserted. Elizabeth and Tony paused there for a moment to look up at a large, ancient tapestry hanging on one of the stone walls. "The Pembroke family crest," Elizabeth told Tony. She pointed to the wolf in one of the shield's quadrants. "And guess what woodland creature happens to be the Pembrokes' patron saint?"

"Ironic, isn't it?" said Tony.

While they'd searched the secret room and perused Annabelle's letters, the sun had set. "The cab's not here yet," Tony observed, peering into the night. "I certainly hope it hasn't broken down again! Let's hope for the best and walk out to the main road to meet it, shall we?"

Elizabeth nodded reluctantly. On the one hand, she was glad to get out of Pembroke Manor; she was sure the old house was full of ghosts. But the inky darkness of the English countryside was hardly more comforting. The full moon that had been out the weekend she, Jessica, and Luke visited Pembroke Manor had been eerie and foreboding . . . and for Joy Singleton, fatal. Elizabeth shivered. *But this moonless gloom is almost worse. . . .*

They walked down the driveway without speaking, their feet crunching on the gravel. A light breeze stirred the leaves.

"What's that?" Elizabeth cried, stopping abruptly in her tracks.

"What's what?" Tony asked.

Her heart thumping, Elizabeth stood still as a statue and listened. There was nothing but the whispering of the trees. "I—I thought I heard something," she said apologetically. "I'm just a little jumpy, I guess."

"That makes two of us," Tony muttered, striding on.

Elizabeth trotted along next to him, her eyes darting from side to side. *Is that a person,* she thought, glimpsing a movement in the dark woods, *or just a tree shadow?*

She decided that, if she didn't want to keel over from fright, her best bet was to look straight ahead and walk as fast as she could. Which she did. But her skin continued to prickle, and logical or illogical, she was gripped by a disconcerting sensation that was starting to become familiar. She'd been getting it off and on all week. *Someone is out there in the dark and he's following me. . . .*

He watched the girl and the man from the shadowy woods. Snuffling the damp leaves and earth, he prowled closer to the edge of the trees. The two were alone and vulnerable, far from any human habitation. No one would hear them cry out. And if he dragged their bodies into the woods, chances were good they wouldn't be found for days or even weeks.

He rose to his full height, his muscles bunched and his jaw aching with the desire to rip and tear, to taste blood. He prepared to spring . . . and then dropped back down onto all fours, drawing back into the gloom.

No, now is not the time. There were two of them, and as the moon wasn't full, he wasn't at his full strength. *They are watching for me, hunting me, closing in. . . .*

But he wasn't cornered yet. He was still free, and he, too, was closer than ever to his goal.

145

The Wakefield girl and her companion disappeared around a bend in the drive and he loped toward the manor. The stately house towered above him, dark except for a few lights in the servants' quarters.

Stealing inside, he trailed the scent of the two visitors along the hallway, which was lit now by candles guttering in wall sconces. On noiseless feet, he padded into the library, sniffing. *They were here....*

Triggering the secret panel, he entered the werewolf study. *And here...*

He stood before the bookcase where Elizabeth had stood, and reached where she had reached. The fake book fell open in his clawed hand, revealing the packet of letters within. Lifting them reverently, he breathed the fragile, faded perfume of the woman who wrote them long ago and, lifting his head, howled balefully into the night.

Chapter 9

Jessica trudged dejectedly up the steps to the front door of HIS. Crossing the foyer, she paused at the bottom of the stairs and then started up, leaning on the banister with all her weight. She felt listless and spent; it was all she could do to lift one foot after the other. *I just want to sleep*, she thought sadly, *and wake up and be back in sunny Sweet Valley with all of this a crazy, terrible dream.*

Portia was knotting a silk scarf around her neck as Jessica shuffled into their bedroom and flung herself on the bottom bunk. "Look what the cat dragged in," said Portia. "Busy day at the newspaper, eh?"

"Umm," Jessica mumbled, rolling onto her back and closing her eyes.

Portia swept a brush through her cascading dark hair. "I'm running a bit late for the theater,

147

but I have a minute for supper. Join me for a bite downstairs?"

Jessica shook her head. "I'm too depressed to eat."

Portia sat down on the bed next to her. "Poor girl. What is it now?"

"Didn't you hear the news today?" asked Jessica. "Lord Pembroke was attacked by the werewolf!"

"No," Portia gasped. "How awful!"

"He survived, but he's at death's door. I visited him in the hospital and he looked horrible, but he was conscious and he recognized me. And he said the wildest things. He talked about someone named Annabelle."

"Annabelle. Like the name on the file you pinched from the dead doctor's office!" Portia exclaimed.

"Maybe. I don't know if she's the same," said Jessica. "But whoever she is, she and Lord P. had an affair—maybe they're still having one. And they had a kid. Robert has an illegitimate half brother somewhere!"

"Unbelievable. You're sure of all this?"

"The conversation was kind of sketchy and disjointed, and Lord Pembroke was pretty heavily sedated." Jessica sighed. "I don't know, maybe none of it's even true. Maybe he was just delirious."

Portia shook her head. "No, it's more likely that the truth would come out at a moment like that. What a shock, and how intriguing!"

Jessica sat up, propping her back against some pillows. "I can't help feeling that somehow this secret is really important, that it has something to do with the killings," she said, a measure of energy returning. "Robert's innocent—he would never hurt his father. But that means someone else is guilty, most likely someone connected to the Pembrokes somehow. Finding out about this other family breaks the whole thing wide open—there's a whole new direction."

"You need to learn more about Annabelle and her son," Portia agreed.

"After I saw Lord P., I tried to talk to Lady P. You know, just sound her out a bit. But she blew me off completely—she thinks I'm just looking to make trouble." Jessica punched the mattress, frustrated. "But she knows something, I'm sure she does. She could help me, she could help her son, if only she'd stop hiding her head in the sand. She'll never agree to see me, though—she's the most stubborn woman on earth."

Portia tipped her head to one side. "There must be a way we could break through her defenses," she mused. "Vain, self-important Lady Henrietta Pembroke . . ." Portia's gray eyes glinted with mischief. "I have an idea."

"What?"

Portia shook her head, smiling. "I'll tell you later, after I make sure we can pull it off." Rising, she slipped on a butter-soft black leather jacket and headed for the door. "Now I'm late in earnest—I'll have to go onstage without makeup at this rate!"

"Break a leg," Jessica called after her.

Portia stepped into the hallway and then turned back. "One other thing. You really should have some supper—you need to keep up your strength. And there's going to be a surprise in the dining room this evening."

"A surprise?" Despite her gloom, Jessica perked up. "What is it?"

But Portia had left. Jessica was alone.

For fifteen minutes, Jessica lay on her bed thinking hard about the Pembrokes. Finally, she stood up with a sigh. *I can't solve anything without more information. And if I don't get something to eat soon, I'm going to pass out.*

A surprise for dinner—wonder what it is? she thought as she thumped downstairs. *Something yummy for dessert, maybe.*

She entered the foyer just as the front door swung open. Elizabeth appeared, her cheeks flushed and her hair damp from the evening mist. Jessica bit back the question that jumped to her lips, even though she was dying to ask it. *Where were you all afternoon?*

Her chin in the air, Jessica breezed past Elizabeth into the dining room. She could hear her sister marching right behind her. *But I got here first*, Jessica thought maliciously. *I'll get to sit with Em and David and Gabe and she'll have to sit in the corner by herself. Ha!*

But as the twins appeared in the doorway, the

"surprise" jumped up and ran toward them. "Jessica! Elizabeth! It's so nice to see you!"

"Eliana!" Jessica and Elizabeth both exclaimed.

Their former dorm roommate, Princess Eliana, hugged each sister in turn, smiling radiantly. "I just had to come back for a visit. I really miss the old place!"

Taking Jessica with one arm and Elizabeth with the other, Eliana led them over to the table where Emily, Gabriello, and David were sitting. "Isn't this jolly?" Eliana declared. "Just like the good old days. Oh, I wish you could all live at the palace with me—wouldn't we have fun!"

"Sit, sit," Emily urged.

The three sat down, Jessica and Elizabeth facing each other across the table. "Doesn't she look great?" Emily asked the twins.

"I don't know," said David, smiling shyly. "I kind of miss the glasses and mousy brown hair."

Eliana tossed her pale blond hair, laughing. "Don't tease me," she begged. "I haven't gotten over worrying that you liked me better as Lina Smith."

"Eliana, what brings you to this neighborhood?" asked Elizabeth.

"Emily phoned to ask me over, and I just snuck off," said Eliana. When she saw Elizabeth's look, she laughed again. "Oh, I didn't sneak, literally. My running away days are over. This is part of my new freedom—I come and go as I please."

"With security guards and chauffeurs in tow, of course," remarked Gabriello.

"A fact of my life," Eliana conceded.

"So . . . Emily phoned you," said Elizabeth. She was smiling at Eliana with sincere warmth, but Jessica didn't need her twin intuition to pick up on a distinct sense of annoyance. *Liz sees right through this gimmick, too. They're trying to get us to make up. They knew we'd have to sit together, maybe even talk to each other, if Eliana came over.*

Freckle-faced Emily was the picture of innocence. "We were overdue for a reunion, don't you think?"

Jessica folded her arms across her chest and pushed out her lower lip, refusing to be manipulated.

Elizabeth shrugged. "Sure."

"So, these guys have filled me in on their exciting lives. Tell me what you've been up to," Eliana said to Jessica and Elizabeth. "How is the scene at the *London Journal*? What exciting story did you investigate today?"

Jessica looked at Elizabeth, waiting for her answer. Elizabeth toyed with her napkin. "I was out of the office most of the day, doing some . . . independent research," she mumbled.

"That sounds interesting," Eliana remarked. "What kind of independent research?"

"Yes, Liz, do tell us all about it," Jessica snapped, unable to restrain herself. "Were you snooping around the Pembrokes again, pretending to be me? Did you dig up some new dirt, find some new ways to trap and incriminate Robert?"

Elizabeth flushed a hot, angry red. "What about you? Where did you disappear to? Do you know where Robert's hiding—did you meet him someplace? How much longer are you planning to protect him, Jessica? Till he goes to the gas chamber as a convicted murderer?"

Jessica turned pale. Emily, David, and Gabriello looked shocked.

Eliana clapped her hands. "Elizabeth! Girls, please. This just won't do!"

"No, it won't." Jessica shoved back her chair and stood up. "Nice try, Eliana, but you can't order us around like the servants at Buckingham Palace. Don't you see why it won't work? Didn't you hear her? Well, I for one won't listen to garbage like that, but I guess the rest of you agree with her." Jessica glared tearfully at her friends, or the people she thought were her friends. In her whole life, she'd never been so angry; she'd never felt so hurt, so isolated. "I hate you, Elizabeth," she sobbed. "I hate you all!"

"I wish you'd go upstairs and say something to her," Eliana begged Elizabeth as they sat in the HIS library after dinner. "Anything, just a word or two. Tell her you're sorry and then leave her alone to get a grip on herself."

"Tell her I'm sorry?" Elizabeth scoffed. "For what? She's so unreasonable and ungrateful. Everything I've been doing, I've been doing for her. I'm trying to help solve this case so she'll be safe—so we'll all be safe. It's not my fault if she won't see that."

Eliana sighed, her bright blue eyes troubled. "I just hate seeing you feuding so bitterly at a time like this. I had such confidence that I'd be able to bring you back together, and now my hopes are dashed."

Elizabeth's expression softened. "You're sweet to care so much, Lina. Don't take what Jessica said too much to heart. She hates me, but she doesn't really hate you, and you should visit her again. Just don't," she added, "try to visit us both at the same time."

Eliana squeezed Elizabeth's hand and then stood up. "I won't give up that easily," she said with a smile. "I'm used to having things go my way. I'm a princess, remember!"

The royal limousine was parked in front of the dorm, its engine running. David joined Elizabeth and Eliana in the foyer. "I'll walk you out," he offered Eliana.

Eliana took David's hand, and with her other hand, blew a good-bye kiss to Elizabeth. Standing in the doorway, Elizabeth waved after them.

Just like the good old days—hardly, Elizabeth thought, turning away with a melancholy sigh. It was nice to see Eliana, but it wasn't the same when she was whisked in and out in royal fashion. It wasn't the same as when they were roommates, and could stay up late every night gabbing.

Elizabeth wandered back to the deserted library. The entire dorm seemed unnaturally quiet. *David has gone off with Eliana, Emily's cheering up Jessica, Gabriello is studying in his room,* Elizabeth thought, swamped by a sudden wave of loneliness. *There's absolutely no one to talk to.*

Or maybe there was. Walking upstairs, she paused on the second-floor landing. Mrs. Bates had strict rules: no girls on the boys' floor, no boys on the girls' floor. Elizabeth glanced over her shoulder. *Just this once . . . what are the odds I'll get caught? And so what if I do? Who really cares?*

Tiptoeing down the hall, she knocked softly on Rene's door. "Rene, psst!" she hissed. "It's Liz. Open up!"

She waited, but there was no response. She tried the doorknob: locked.

With a discouraged sigh, Elizabeth stomped back toward the stairs. "So much for Rene supposedly wanting so badly to be my friend," she grumbled to herself. "I can't believe I actually wasted time feeling guilty because we weren't seeing much of each other! He keeps spouting off about how worried he is about me, but from day one, he's always been too busy at the embassy to think of anything or anyone else."

No, he's never around when the chips are down, Elizabeth concluded. *He just shows up after the fact acting gallant and making promises he can't keep. Good thing I'm not counting on him to look out for me!*

Jessica was asleep when Elizabeth tiptoed into the dark bedroom at eleven o'clock. She undressed quietly, her teeth chattering as she slipped her flannel nightgown over her head; one of the windows was open a crack and a cold draft of very unsummerlike air brushed her bare skin like icy fingers.

Diving into bed, Elizabeth pulled the covers up to her nose, curling her body into a ball. Gradually, she started to warm up. *I'll never get used to this English weather,* she thought as she lay listening to the sound of rain pattering on the windowpane. Closing her eyes, she conjured up a vision of a balmy, fragrant summer night in Sweet Valley. She and Todd were walking barefoot on the beach in the moonlight, holding hands. *In just a few more weeks,* she thought.

The vision was as fragile as a candle flame in the wind. When Elizabeth opened her eyes again, it disappeared as if it had never existed—as if there were no such place as Sweet Valley, California, no such boy as Todd Wilkins, no such girl as Elizabeth Wakefield had been before she came to England to intern for the *London Journal*.

The only thing that was real was the present:

where she was now, who she was now. She was in London, a city terrorized by a brutal, demonic serial killer. She was trying to solve the mystery, to track the werewolf to his lair, without losing her own life in the process.

Propping herself up on one elbow, Elizabeth reached for her purse, which was on top of the bedside table. Taking out her notebook, she turned to the last note she'd made that afternoon at Pembroke Manor.

It was the return address she'd copied from the envelope of one of Annabelle's love letters to Lord Pembroke: A.C.S., Four Forget-Me-Not Lane.

Forget-Me-Not Lane—how appropriate, Elizabeth mused. Did Lord Pembroke think of her still? Did he look after their son as she asked on her deathbed? Did he store her letters in that box to keep them close at hand so he could read them, or was he hiding them away, out of sight and out of mind, forever?

Elizabeth tucked the notebook back in her purse and rested her head on the cool pillow. Her wide, sleepless eyes fixed on the dark window, she watched the raindrops streak down the glass. A gust of air, soft as a ghostly breath, lifted the curtain. It was as if the whole city sighed in sorrow for the lives that had been lost, Elizabeth thought fancifully. And somewhere, a murderer continued to prowl the black, rain-slick streets. . . .

"Annabelle," Elizabeth whispered. "If only you

were alive. Could you help me understand what happened to the Pembroke family? Could you tell me where Robert is, and why he's done what he's done?"

Jessica tossed in her sleep, caught in the grip of a dream in which she was running down the streets of London in the night, but whether running toward something or away from something, she wasn't sure. And now, from somewhere outside the dream, a voice called out to her, trying to wake her. *Annabelle,* the voice whispered. *Annabelle.*

Jessica's lips moved; her eyelids fluttered, but remained closed. In her dream, she stopped and stood on the sidewalk, peering around her into the fog. "Where are you, Annabelle?" Jessica asked in her dream. "Annabelle, is that you?"

Ahead, the fog thinned and the figure of a woman in a flowing white gown materialized. Jessica couldn't distinguish her features or even the color of her hair; still, she could see that the woman beckoned to her, inviting her to follow.

But before Jessica could take even one step forward, the woman disappeared, melting into the mist. Or was she just a wisp of fog all along, never really there at all?

"Annabelle!" Jessica called hopelessly. "Annabelle, where is your son? Do you know, Annabelle? Do you know who the werewolf is? Annabelle! Annabelle!"

In her dream, Jessica ran on into the night, her hands held out, hoping to grasp hold of Annabelle and her secrets, as all around her the fog echoed with the sound of a wild animal howling, a sound that drew closer and closer. . . .

Chapter 10

At the *Journal* offices Wednesday morning, Elizabeth hurried straight to Tony's desk to see what he thought of the idea of going to Forget-Me-Not Lane, even though of course Annabelle didn't live there anymore, having died years ago.

She found Tony standing at ironic attention with a box of tissues in his hand while the editor-in-chief, one hip perched on the edge of his desk, delivered a peppery lecture on the importance of timeliness in journalism.

"Let me get this straight," said Lucy, tossing back her long chestnut hair. "The blackmail article that I planned to put on the front page of the second section simply . . . doesn't exist."

"It's not written," Tony admitted cheerfully. "In fact, it's not even begun."

"And why is that, Mr. Crime Editor?" Lucy

crossed her arms. "What's been going on in this department since I left it?"

"Oh, lots," said Tony. Holding a tissue to his nose, he sneezed vigorously. "Achew! In fact, we have a whole new attitude toward reporting crime."

"I bet," said Lucy sarcastically. "Let me see. You imagine a fresh new focus on the subject, perhaps an angle inspired by your sojourn on the society page."

Tony cocked a finger, grinning. "How about, 'Hemlines, Hairstyles, and Homicide: The Hidden Connection'?"

"Seriously, Frank." Lucy fixed him with a stern glare, but Elizabeth saw her lips twitch. "You're accountable for a big department now and I want to see product. Where were you all day yesterday?"

Tony shot a glance at Elizabeth. "Liz and I were doing some more background work on the Pembrokes for the werewolf story."

Lucy held out her hand. "Let's see what you got."

"We don't know what we've got," Tony explained. "We don't know what it all adds up to yet. But when we do, you'll be the first to see it. You've got to trust us on this, Friday."

Lucy bit her lip. "I'm trusting you—this time. But let's get one thing straight, Frank. If you think you can cover up for substandard work or no work at all by flirting with me, you've got another think coming. A charming smile isn't going to win any journalism prizes . . . and it's not going to guarantee you keep your byline." Standing up, Lucy looked Tony straight in the eye. "Consider this your first and last warning. Don't blow it, Frank."

Lucy strode off, her hair bouncing on her shoulders. Tony stared after her, his eyes glassy. "Wow," he breathed. "She packs a powerful punch, doesn't she?"

"Are you OK?" Elizabeth asked. Tony's face was pale and his skin had a glossy sheen. "You look like you're running a fever."

"The boss has that effect on me," he said with a lopsided grin. "Did you hear that? She thinks I have a charming smile!"

"That's great," said Elizabeth. "But I wanted to ask you about something. What do you think about going to Annabelle's old house, just to see if we can find out anything from the people who live there now, or the neighbors?"

"Let's do it. I'm ready when you are!"

"Since it's not really official business, maybe we should wait until after work," Elizabeth suggested. "Otherwise Lucy might fire us."

"After work—it's a date." Tony blew his nose loudly. "We'll get to the bottom of the Annabelle mystery and find out if it's just a red herring or the key to the story of the century."

"We haven't been here in ages," Elizabeth said to Luke as they entered the Slaughtered Lamb at lunchtime. "Things have been so hectic lately!"

Luke had shared his favorite local pub with Elizabeth the very first day they met. She'd thought the name was creepy at first—there was a Slaughtered Lamb Pub in the movie *An American Werewolf in London*—but the restaurant turned out to be warm and homey and intimate and it had quickly become "their" place. For a while, they'd managed to drop in for lunch or tea nearly every day.

"I missed you yesterday," Luke told Elizabeth as they slid into a booth near the crackling fire. "I kept dropping by your desk, hoping for a chat, but you must have been off chasing a big story. Does Tony have you working on an interesting assignment?"

"Actually . . ." Elizabeth sipped from the mug of hot tea that the waitress had put in front of her. "I was chasing a big story, though it's not really a work assignment. I went back to Pembroke Manor."

Luke's face darkened. "Elizabeth, what were you thinking?" he cried, his blue eyes shooting sparks. "I've warned you that it's not safe. What if something had happened to you? What if—"

"I'm here, aren't I?" Elizabeth reasoned. "No harm came to me. And besides, I wasn't alone— Tony went with me."

Luke relaxed somewhat. "Thank goodness for that." He drew a hand across his forehead, and Elizabeth saw that he was shaking. "What would I have done," he murmured, almost to himself, "if anything had happened to you?"

Reaching out, Elizabeth touched his arm. "Nothing happened to me," she repeated. "I swear, I'm not taking any unnecessary chances." *Not many, anyhow,* she added silently. "And it was worth it. We made an incredible discovery!"

"You did?"

"Yes. We went back to look at the books in the secret werewolf library, to see if any more of them were from Annabelle or if there were any other clues to who she might be."

"Annabelle?" Luke sat forward. "You found books from someone named Annabelle in the werewolf library?"

"I found one the first time I was in there," said Elizabeth, "but I'd completely forgotten about it until I read through my notes yesterday morning. Then it occurred to me that maybe Annabelle was a person it would pay to learn more about."

"And what did you learn?"

"That she had an affair with Lord Pembroke!" Elizabeth revealed. "It lasted for years and years. In fact, they had a child together, a son. Robert's illegitimate half brother."

Luke sucked in his breath. "An affair . . . a son! How on earth did you . . . ?"

"Old love letters from Annabelle to Lord Pembroke—a boxful of them," said Elizabeth. "They told the whole story. Well, Annabelle's side of it, anyway."

"The whole story . . ." Luke raked a hand

through his black hair. "What does it mean, though? Do you think there's a connection to the murders? Could Robert know about this? What else did you find?"

He shot the questions at her machine-gun style. Elizabeth blinked at his intensity. "Nothing—we didn't find anything else. And I don't know if there's a connection. It's all still fuzzy and vague."

Elizabeth started to reach for her tea. Luke intercepted her hand, clasping it tightly in his own. "You're taking too many risks, Elizabeth. You mustn't visit the werewolf's haunts—you mustn't go where he might find you. If you were the next victim . . ." His voice cracked with emotion. "I wouldn't be able to bear it. I wouldn't be able to live."

Elizabeth's heart throbbed with pity and affection. Luke had lost someone he loved before—he was so vulnerable. *This isn't the time to tell him about Tony's and my plan to go to Annabelle's this afternoon,* she decided. "I'll be careful, but I won't just sit home," she told Luke, squeezing his hand. "It's too late for that—we've come too far. Don't you feel it? Don't you feel how close we are?"

"Close . . . yes." He nodded, his eyes somber. "Soon, he'll be cornered—we'll confront him, face-to-face. And if we're prepared, if we have the right weapons . . ."

Elizabeth thought about the silver bullet, now lost. Lost . . . or stolen by the werewolf himself?

"We can leave the weapons to the police," she said. "All we have to do is find him." As she and Luke clasped hands across the table, she felt it again, in her bones, in her blood. "And we're close," Elizabeth whispered. "So close . . ."

"I'm done with my work, but I can tell you're not done with yours," Jessica said to Lucy at five thirty Wednesday afternoon. "Should I stick around to help you out?"

Lucy waved a hand without looking up from the editorial she was composing. "I've got it under control. We had a productive day. Go on, get out of here."

Smiling, Jessica turned on her heel and breezed off. *I like that woman*, she thought. *She's gorgeous and smart and tough—she has style. Hey, maybe journalism wouldn't be such a bad career after all!*

It had been a good day, and the best part about it was that she hadn't bumped into Elizabeth once. *And if I never see her again in my life, that'll be too soon.* As she walked outside to the curb and boarded a double-decker bus, Jessica remembered their fight the previous evening at dinner—their worst fight yet. *Worst and last*, she thought. *Because I really, really don't ever plan to speak to her again. Although I do want to see her face when it's finally revealed that somebody else is the serial killer, not Robert. She'll have to speak to me then . . . to apologize and beg my forgiveness on her knees.*

The bus ambled along the busy city streets, heading in the direction of Pembroke Green, Robert's family's city home. Jessica had a date to meet Portia there to try Portia's still-secret scheme for getting Lady Pembroke to talk to her. Jessica gazed thoughtfully out the window. As the brick townhouses got fancier, the fences in front of them grew higher. *They're like fortresses—except they're missing moats. How does ol' Porsh expect to storm the gates of Pembroke Green?*

As she hopped off the bus half a block from Pembroke Green, Jessica spotted Portia waiting for her on the corner and saw the light immediately. Because Portia wasn't alone. Standing at her side was a tall, distinguished man with penetrating hawk-like eyes and a sweep of silver-streaked hair. Walking toward them, Jessica felt her knees weaken. The handsome man was larger than life; he exuded charisma. *Stage presence . . . and sex appeal,* Jessica thought. *Lady Pembroke will be putty in his hands!* But then, who wouldn't be putty in the hands of the finest and most famous Shakespearean actor in the world, Sir Montford Albert?

"Dad, you remember Jessica," said Portia.

Jessica shook Sir Montford's hand, a bedazzled smile on her face. "We met backstage at Portia's play."

"That's right," Sir Montford boomed. "Yes, Portia speaks often about you—I appreciate what a good, supportive friend you've been to her."

"Oh, well, I . . ." Jessica stuttered.

Taking Jessica's arm, Portia steered her toward Pembroke Green. "You see, when you and I were talking yesterday about how difficult Lady Pembroke was being, I suddenly remembered that she's a huge fan of Dad's. And there it was, the solution to your dilemma! You want Lady Pembroke to open the door to you, I guarantee she'll open the door to you . . . when Dad rings the bell."

"It's a stroke of genius," Jessica declared.

"Isn't it? And Dad's such a good sport." Portia blew a kiss to her father. "He just happened to be in town, and I promised it would only take five minutes of his time. It's all turning out as easy as pie!" she chirped cheerfully.

"The door's not open yet," Jessica reminded her.

"Oh, it will be," Portia said with utter confidence. "It will be."

The three strolled up the walk to Pembroke Green and Sir Montford pressed the bell. The butler answered, easing the door open a crack. "May I help you?" he asked in a clipped, discouraging manner.

"Please tell Lady Pembroke that Sir Montford Albert begs a minute of her time," the actor commanded.

The butler's jaw dropped to his chest. Taking advantage of this momentary lapse, Sir Montford stepped into the front hall, Portia and Jessica scooting in at his heels.

"As a matter of fact, she's—but I'm sure—just one—thank you, sir." The butler bowed. "I'll deliver the message."

The butler hurried off. A minute later, Lady Pembroke herself appeared. At the sight of Sir Montford, her blue eyes grew so big, Jessica thought they were going to pop out of her head. She took a step toward them, wobbling slightly. *For heaven's sake,* Jessica thought, astonished. *She's going to faint. Cold-as-ice, hard-as-a-diamond Lady Pembroke is swooning!*

"Oh, my," Lady Pembroke gasped, the handkerchief she clutched in one hand dancing up to her throat and then her lips. "I'm not receiving visitors—my husband is ill . . . but Sir Montford, do come in. Do come in!"

"I won't take but a minute of your time," he began.

"No, no, you must stay for tea," Lady Pembroke begged. "Have a seat . . . please make yourself at home . . . oh, my!"

Portia met Jessica's eye and grinned triumphantly. "We're in!" she whispered.

The handkerchief still fluttering, Lady Pembroke led them to the large, airy drawing room where Jessica had interviewed her a few weeks ago about her missing mink coat. When she and Sir Montford were seated side by side on a plush, brocade-covered sofa, Lady Pembroke seemed to notice Jessica and Portia for the first time. She narrowed her eyes, two spots of angry color rising in her pale, powdered cheeks. "Why, it's you!" she said to Jessica, balling the handkerchief up in her fist. "Who do you think—"

"Ah, you know Jessica," Sir Montford intervened smoothly. "My dear daughter Portia's friend. How delightful."

Lady Pembroke bit back any further nasty remark she was about to make. "Delightful—yes, it certainly is," she simpered. "But Sir Montford!" Lady Pembroke batted her eyelashes. "To what do I owe the honor—the profound honor—of this visit?"

"I come as a humble petitioner on behalf of my new Edinburgh Theater Company," Sir Montford explained, his voice warm and melodious. "As you know, it requires quite an investment to launch a new theatrical enterprise. Hence, in my capacity as director, I am approaching those very special people—a small group of deeply dedicated, highly cultured friends of the arts—whom I imagine, whom I fondly hope, will be persuaded to serve as patrons of the company. I count you, Lady Pembroke, among that number."

Lady Pembroke touched the diamond necklace encircling her throat. "You do?"

"But of course," Sir Montford said gallantly, accepting a cup from a maid who had just rolled in a teacart laden with china and silver. "There is no more devoted lover of the theater in all of London than Lady Henrietta Pembroke." He winked at Portia. "It's common knowledge."

"I try to do my part," Lady Pembroke said modestly. "And nothing would make me happier than to help further your efforts in Edinburgh. Please put me down for . . ."

She murmured an enormous monetary amount. Sir Montford clasped her bejeweled hand, raising it to his lips. "You are so generous. I cannot thank you enough."

"Oh, well, my . . ."

While Lady Pembroke blushed and babbled, Sir Montford shot a glance at his daughter. Portia nodded.

Releasing Lady Pembroke's hand, Sir Montford rose to his feet. "Thank you for your pledge, and for your hospitality, Lady Pembroke," he said. "And please extend my best wishes to Lord Pembroke for a speedy recovery."

"So soon? Well, this was—oh—good-bye!"

With a crisp bow, Sir Montford disappeared into the hallway. Lady Pembroke watched him until he was out of sight. Turning back, she saw the two girls still sitting in matching velvet wing chairs and jumped.

The expression that had softened for Sir Montford once again became cold and unyielding. Pointedly remaining standing, Lady Pembroke waited in hostile silence for Jessica and Portia to make their exits as well.

Calmly, Jessica lifted her teacup to her lips. "These cakes are delicious," she said, her eyes meanwhile adding, *and I'm not going anywhere, so don't bother glaring at me like that.*

Lady Pembroke sat down stiffly. *This is it,* Jessica thought, her throat suddenly dry. *This is my chance, the only one I'm going to get. I can't blow it. I can't let Robert down.*

Jessica looked at Portia for support and then put down her teacup. *Don't beat around the bush—don't give her time to make up any lies.* Staring straight at Lady Pembroke, Jessica aimed right for the bull's-eye. "I know about Annabelle," she bluffed. "Your husband told me everything."

Lady Pembroke had been leaning forward to spoon sugar into her tea. At Jessica's surprising declaration, she dropped the spoon into the cup, splashing tea onto the marble-topped coffee table.

It worked! Jessica thought. *I caught her off guard. She can't hide it—it's written all over her. She knows about Annabelle, too!*

Taking a damask napkin from the cart, Lady Pembroke dabbed at the spilled tea. Jessica and Portia held their breath.

When Lady Pembroke looked back up at Jessica, the surprise in her eyes had been replaced by a bitter, scornful glint. "Annabelle." Lady Pembroke spat out the name. "Then I suppose you know about the wretched boy."

The boy . . . Robert's brother. "Yes," said Jessica.

173

"Bad enough that Bobby was so tasteless as to be unfaithful with a low-class commoner. He could have walked away from his mistake—should have walked away. Instead, he seemed to feel somehow responsible," Lady Pembroke complained bitterly. "He was constantly throwing our money away on that urchin, but he could never do enough in her opinion. She always wanted more. It went on for years and years."

Lady Pembroke paused just long enough to catch her breath. "And of course, everything he gave to his misbegotten brat was something taken away from our own dear Robert. Why, Bobby even took away little Robert's nanny when Annabelle was sick with pneumonia! It wasn't enough that he had Cameron Neville making house calls every single day. Annabelle needed help, Bobby claimed—his bastard son needed Nanny Millie more than our sweet, pure Robert did."

Sick with pneumonia . . . house calls from Cameron Neville, Jessica thought, her heart racing with excitement. There was one answer already. *Then Lord Pembroke's Annabelle is Dr. Neville's Annabelle S.! And Nanny Millie knew her and the boy. Nanny Millie, who was one of the werewolf's victims!*

Silently, Jessica prayed that Lady Pembroke would keep talking. Appearing to have forgotten that the two girls were even there, Lady Pembroke ranted on to herself, venting the rage of years.

"Of course, everything he did for her had to be

hush-hush so her blind fool of a cuckolded husband wouldn't know that nasty child wasn't his own spawn," Lady Pembroke remembered. "Annabelle and Bobby agreed that she would pretend the money came from the *Journal*, her pension."

Jessica couldn't contain a gasp of surprise. "The *Journal*?"

"She'd worked there—that's how they met. Oh, she was a clever little thing, but it was her undoing. She should have been content with her lot in life instead of trying to steal what wasn't rightfully hers. The nanny incident was the last straw. It was the least he could do for them, Bobby said, but I said anything was too much." A malicious smile curved Lady Pembroke's thin, bloodless lips. "I cut him off. The money is mine, you know," she told her wide-eyed audience. "Bobby didn't bring a farthing into this marriage. Yes, I cut him off," she repeated, gloating and triumphant, "and I got Nanny Millie back. And when Annabelle finally died, I made Bobby swear never to lift a finger for that boy again."

The story of adultery, jealousy, and cruelty raised goose bumps on Jessica's skin. She felt chilled to the bone . . . but also electrified. *It's there, somewhere*, she thought, her head spinning as she struggled to untangle the narrative threads. *The nanny, killed by the werewolf, who isn't Robert so . . . who? Wait. Yes*, Jessica thought. *Yes, it could be . . .*

175

"The other son," she heard Portia whisper.

Jessica nodded. Of course! The other son, despised and rejected, denied his true father's name, left motherless, penniless . . . *Does the other son know this story?* Jessica wondered. *Could Lord Pembroke's illegitimate son, Robert's mysterious half brother, be the killer?*

Jessica opened her mouth to ask the burning, urgent question: Who is he and where is he now?

But Lady Pembroke spoke first. "Besides, I knew that boy was no good," she concluded. "I knew just from his name. Lucas is an evil name."

Lucas. The blood drained from Jessica's face, leaving her as white as the curtain that fluttered at the window, as white as the sheets that had been on her bed at Pembroke Manor. The sheets that she and Elizabeth and Luke saw soaked with Joy Singleton's blood that Saturday at dawn. Luke . . .

Luke, whose mother had worked for the *Journal* and died when he was a child. Luke, who was obsessed with werewolves . . .

Who would have a better motive? Jessica's heart leapt to her throat, choking her. "Luke Shepherd is Annabelle's son," she cried hoarsely. "Luke is the killer!"

Chapter 11

Without further explanation, Jessica sprang to her feet and bolted out of the drawing room and down the hallway, Portia sprinting after her.

"Jessica, wait!" Portia panted. "Have you gone crazy? What are you talking about? You can't mean Luke Shepherd, Liz's boyfriend from work, is—"

"That's exactly what I do mean," declared Jessica, brushing past the Pembrokes' startled butler and shoving open the heavy front door. "It all adds up, Porsh! Annabelle S., remember? S. is for Shepherd! It threw me off when Elizabeth said Luke's mother's name was Ann, but obviously Ann is just short for Annabelle. Or maybe Annabelle was Lord Pembroke's own private name for her. Whatever, it's the same woman, so Luke is Lord Pembroke's illegitimate son!"

"Wow," said Portia as they clattered onto the sidewalk. "So, where are we going now? To the police?"

"We have to go back to HIS first." Jessica waved her arms for a taxi as she jogged along. "We have to make sure Liz is OK and keep her away from Luke. God, why didn't I figure this out sooner? Why did I write Luke off as harmless?"

Spotting a red telephone booth, Jessica skidded to a stop. "I'm going to call the dorm," she told Portia. "We can't waste a minute. For all we know, she's getting ready for a date with Luke right now!"

Her hand was shaking so much, she could hardly insert the coins into the phone, and then her fingers felt so fat and clumsy, dialing the HIS hall phone number was almost impossible. And then it rang and rang and rang . . .

Pick up, somebody! Jessica thought desperately.

"Hello?" a voice said at last.

"David, is that you?" Jessica cried. "It's me, Jessica. I need to speak to my sister—it's a matter of life and death!"

"Hold on, I'll fetch her," David offered.

He seemed to be gone for an hour. Jessica stared through the glass panes of the phone booth, her brain fizzing with horrible images. Luke creeping into her bedroom at Pembroke Manor in Robert's silk bathrobe . . . returning to take care of the cook . . . going after the poor old nanny . . . attacking his own father. *And Elizabeth trusts him. Elizabeth loves him!*

"Jessica, are you still there?"

"Yes, yes!" she shouted. "Where is Elizabeth?"

"I don't know," said David. "Not here, anyway. I checked your room, and the dining room, and the library. Maybe she's working late."

"Working late," Jessica muttered. Hanging up on David, she stuck in another coin and dialed the *Journal*.

"No," said the receptionist, "she's not here. She left a while ago, with Tony."

Tony! Jessica's knees buckled with relief. *Of course, she's with Tony*. They probably had gone off to look into a story together, or maybe they'd just stopped for a cup of tea. They could be anywhere in London—that thought was somewhat distressing. But at least they were together.

"One more phone call," Jessica signaled to Portia. She might as well ring up Tony's home number. If nothing else, she could leave a message. It was time to start spreading the word about the danger, and she'd need Tony's advice about what to do next.

To her surprise, Tony himself answered the phone. "Hullo?" He sniffled.

"Tony, it's Jessica. Is Elizabeth there?"

She had to hold the phone away from her ear as Tony sneezed loudly on the other end. "Elizabeth? No, why do you ask?"

Jessica's heart dropped into her shoes. In an instant, her feelings of relief and security vanished like smoke, dread and uncertainty taking their place. "Where is she? Do you know?"

She heard Tony blow his nose. "She's doing some after-hours sleuthing. She went over to Annabelle's."

"Annabelle's?" Jessica gasped. "How did she find out about—but Annabelle is dead!"

"I know, but we found her address among Lord Pembroke's, um, papers. She's dead and buried, but Liz thinks there might be a connection between the story of the love affair and the murders. She's hoping to find some clues at Annabelle's old address that will lead her to . . . Excuse me, Jess—I know it hurts your feelings, but I must say it: to Robert."

No, Jessica thought. *It won't lead her to Robert . . . but it very well might lead her straight to the werewolf's lair!* "She went alone?"

"We'd planned to go together, but I'm feeling a bit under the weather." Tony sneezed as if to illustrate the point. "I insisted she take someone with her, though, as protection. The killer could strike again at any moment, and if it turns out that there is something important to be found at Annabelle's, that could make it a dangerous place. She said she'd ask . . ."

No, Jessica thought, knowing who Tony would name even before he said the word. *No. Anyone but . . .*

" . . . Luke."

"The address," Jessica choked out, her heart

freezing into a ball of ice in her chest. "Do you remember the address?"

"Well, let's see. I don't quite—not the exact number, no," said Tony, befuddled. "It's on Forget-Me-Not Lane somewhere. But, Jessica, why—"

Dropping the phone, Jessica exploded out of the booth. Eyes wide and hair flying, she ran out into the street, waving her arms madly. "Taxi!" she shouted. "Taxi!"

"Are you familiar with this part of London?" Elizabeth asked Luke as their cab whisked them through a residential area east of downtown.

Luke stared out the window at the city, gray and dusky in the twilight. "Yes, somewhat," he replied. "I know someone who lives around here."

"Who knows what we'll find at Annabelle's old address." Elizabeth pulled out her notebook and thumbed through it, pausing to skim the notes she'd scribbled after the previous day's visit to Pembroke Manor. "If nothing else, I guess I'm just curious to see where she lived." She looked at Luke, her eyes glowing. "Don't you wonder what she was like?"

Luke nodded without speaking, his own eyes dark and unreadable.

"I bet she was beautiful," Elizabeth mused. "Annabelle is a beautiful name, don't you think? There was something very special about her, anyway. But I think it's so sad that she and Lord

Pembroke couldn't love each other openly, couldn't lead a normal life."

Elizabeth tapped the page where she'd copied down a few lines from Annabelle's last letter to Lord Pembroke. "I wonder if they were still seeing each other at this point, or if they'd ended the affair. Lina said there was a scandal in the family, but eventually it must have blown over—she wasn't even able to remember what it was about. Do you think the scandal affected Annabelle's life?"

"Inevitably," Luke murmured.

"Inevitably . . . yes, of course, you're right," said Elizabeth. "Tony said her husband probably found out about it and left her. She probably had to take care of herself and the child." She shook her head. "That's the really sad part, if you ask me. All last night I lay awake wondering what happened to that poor little boy after his mother died."

Elizabeth bit her lip, wanting to curse herself for her tactlessness. *Duh, no wonder Luke's acting so quiet and withdrawn*, she thought. *Talking like this must remind him of his own mother dying.* Reaching across the wide backseat, she took his hand and squeezed it gently.

The last streaks of red and orange had faded from the western sky when the taxi turned onto Forget-Me-Not Lane, a quiet cul-de-sac in a modest neighborhood on the outskirts of town. Stepping out of the cab, Elizabeth and Luke stood side by side on the walk, gazing at number four, a small house in need of a new coat of paint, but with a well-tended little yard. "It's dark," observed Elizabeth. "No one's home." She pointed to the house next door. "How about talking to the neighbors? We could find out who lives here now—the neighbors might even remember back to the days of Annabelle."

Still staring at the dark house, Luke rocked back on his heels, his hands pushed deep in his trouser pockets. "Let's just try the door," he suggested. "If it's unlocked, we could take a quick look around."

Elizabeth hesitated, but only for an instant. They were so close to solving the mystery. . . . What if Annabelle's husband still lived there, and maybe even her child? It was a possibility. Just think of the clues she and Luke might find!

Breaking into someone's house was against the law, but under the circumstances it was also irresistibly tempting. "A really quick look," Elizabeth said as they strode up the walk. "I don't want to get caught."

On the front step, they looked around to make sure none of the neighbors were watching. The streets and sidewalks were empty, except for a homeless man about half a block away, pushing a grocery cart piled high with junk.

Luke put his hand on the doorknob. "Are you ready?" he asked, his voice low and vibrant.

Elizabeth nodded, a rush of adrenaline flooding her veins.

She held her breath as Luke turned the knob and gave a slight push. The door swung inward.

Tentatively, they stepped into the dark entryway. Elizabeth felt around on the wall for a light switch. She located one, but when she flicked the switch upward, the hall remained dark. "The light's not working," she told Luke.

He disappeared into the first room opening off the hallway. "No lights in there, either," he reported, returning a moment later. "The power must be out."

"Shoot," said Elizabeth. "Why didn't I bring a flashlight?"

They stood for a moment in the shadows. "We could leave," Luke said softly.

She couldn't read his expression in the darkness. "No," Elizabeth replied. "We're here. Let's go for it."

Crossing the dark hallway, Luke fumbled with the drawer of a table that was pushed up against the wall. Two empty brass candlesticks stood on top. "Candles," he declared, holding one up. "And matches."

"Then we're all set!"

There was a dry, raspy sound as Luke struck a match. Light flared. Lighting the candles, Luke handed one to Elizabeth. Then, taking the other, he nodded toward a door under the stairs. "I bet that's the basement," he said. "Why don't I check down there for a fuse box? Maybe I can get the power back on."

"I'll wait here," said Elizabeth, not terribly eager to explore the house by herself.

Luke disappeared through the door to the basement. Elizabeth listened to his footsteps creaking down the stairs. Then there was silence.

The candle flame flickered, wavering in the cool draft that had crept up from the basement. Elizabeth pressed her back against the wall, glancing around nervously. *What's taking him so long?* she wondered, even though she knew Luke had only been gone a minute or so.

The house was perfectly still and dark and quiet. Even so, it felt alive to Elizabeth—it seemed to breathe and pulse with ghosts. "Annabelle lived here," she whispered to herself. "She sat in one of these rooms and wrote letters to Lord Pembroke. She nursed their baby here. She died here."

What secrets were hidden in this haunted house?

A shiver shook Elizabeth's body from head to toe. Stepping forward, she paced down the hall. It definitely felt better to move around; it was too creepy just standing there waiting. *Besides, I don't want to be hanging out right there in case somebody comes in. . . .*

At the bottom of the staircase to the second floor, she paused, peering up into the darkness. Then, her candle held bravely out in front of her, she put her foot on the first step.

•   •   •

"Jessica? Jessica, are you there?" When there was no response, Tony replaced the telephone receiver, his brow furrowed. "Now, that was odd," he murmured. "Or maybe my head's just fuzzy from this cold. No . . ." He was contagious, maybe, but not delirious. "Something's wrong—something's very wrong."

Picking up the phone again, he dialed Lucy's home number. "Frank, what do you want?" she asked suspiciously when he identified himself.

"Don't worry, I'm not calling to ask you to go out with me," he said dryly. *Not that I wouldn't if I thought for a second that you'd say yes.* "I got your message about keeping work and personal life separate. But listen to this. . . ."

Quickly, he recounted his brief conversation with Jessica, filling Lucy in on the Annabelle angle at the same time. "Something's amiss," he concluded, sneezing. "Last I heard, Jessica wasn't speaking to Elizabeth. Now she's worried to death about her."

"To death. God, Frank, you don't think it has anything to do with . . ."

"With the murders? With Robert?" Tony said grimly. "It very well might. Liz may be in trouble—both girls may be in trouble. What do you say I come get you and we go to Annabelle's after them?"

He half expected Lucy to blow him off, to suspect that he was just trying to finagle a date, but she didn't hesitate. "We must," she agreed. "This sounds serious, Frank—you sound serious. And you're right, they're our interns. We have a responsibility to protect them."

"And to get the story," Tony added. "This could be it, Lucy."

"I'll be waiting for you on the curb," she said, ringing off.

Elizabeth walked slowly up the stairs, one hand shielding the candle flame. At the top of the stairs, she paused, listening to the silence. The dancing flame caused eerie shadows to flicker on the walls, shapes that seemed both to beckon her and to warn her back.

A doorway yawned, dark and intriguing. Elizabeth stepped through it, the candle held high to light her way.

The room was large but sparsely decorated, with only three pieces of furniture: a four-poster bed, matching antique dresser, and night table. The master bedroom, Elizabeth surmised.

The room was strangely bare of ornament: no pictures on the wall, no shoes on the floor, no clutter. It was a man's room, she decided after peeking into the walk-in closet and seeing no sign of a woman's clothing or toiletries.

Elizabeth wandered over to the dresser. Only two things rested on top of the recently dusted surface: an old-fashioned man's shaving brush in a china cup and a photograph in a silver frame.

Elizabeth lifted the photograph to look at it by the warm flickering light of the candle. It was a portrait of an exquisitely beautiful raven-haired woman holding a toddler with ringlets as dark as her own. The woman's smile was reminiscent of Mona Lisa's; her lips curved, but her eyes remained somehow shuttered and mysterious.

Studying the picture, Elizabeth's heart skipped a beat. Something about the woman's face was familiar. *Or is it the baby's face?* Elizabeth wondered. *Where have I seen these people before?*

Tucking the picture frame under her arm, she padded back out into the hallway. There were two other doors. The first turned out to be the bathroom. The second was another bedroom.

She pushed the bedroom door open, the candlelight preceding her into the room. Immediately, she was struck by the very different appearance of this bedroom. *It looks lived in,* she thought, taking another step forward. There were shelves overflowing with books and a desk cluttered with odds and ends. The walls were papered with photos and newspaper clippings—the whole room was like one big bulletin board.

A kid's room, Elizabeth thought, holding out the candle so she could get a better look at the stories tacked up on the wall. *A teenager—maybe someone my age. Someone with a lot of hobbies and interests!*

Curious, she held the candle closer in order to read one of the yellowed newspaper articles. The name in the headline jumped out at her, hitting her like a splash of cold water in the face. Pembroke.

"What's this?" Elizabeth said out loud. The candle nearly went out as she spun around to examine the other clippings. There was another and another and another about the Pembrokes, ranging from social-page items nearly a decade old to the latest newspaper coverage of Robert Junior being sought as a suspect in the werewolf killings.

No, Elizabeth thought, her blood slowly turning to ice in her veins. *They can't all be.* But they were. Every single clipping related to the Pembrokes.

Her teeth chattering, Elizabeth turned on her heel to survey each of the four walls in turn. "Who lives here?" she whispered to herself. "Who lives in Annabelle's old house?" It must have been someone who had known Annabelle . . . and who knew about Annabelle's connection to the Pembroke family. It was too coincidental otherwise. Was it Annabelle's son, all grown up?

At the desk, Elizabeth put down the candlestick and the silver-framed photograph. Picking up a red spiral notebook, she opened to a page at random. *It's a diary*, she realized. *I shouldn't read it. I'd hate it if a stranger read my journal. But* . . .

She couldn't tear her eyes from the page. Holding the notebook so that the candlelight fell on it, she read the first sentence. "I woke up again in a strange place, in the woods outside my father's country home." The script was slanted and dark, as if the person had scrawled the words quickly, pressing down hard with the pen. Elizabeth felt a shock of recognition. *I've seen this handwriting before . . . but where?*

She read on. "I don't know how I got there—I have no memory of journeying from London. My clothes were filthy and ripped and there were drops of blood spattered on my shirt . . . my own blood or someone else's? Did I try to prevent a crime . . . or did I commit one?"

Elizabeth dropped the notebook, her mouth suddenly dry with fear. She stared up at the werewolf clippings on the wall. *Who lives here?*

Behind her, she heard a creak . . . the door easing open. She whirled around, just as a muffled voice asked, "Do you like my collection?"

A scream of terror exploded from Elizabeth's throat, shattering the shadowy stillness of the house.

The werewolf crouched in the doorway. His eyes were red in the dim light and his fangs glistened; the flickering candle cast a huge, hairy, monstrous shadow on the wall behind him. Elizabeth screamed again.

At last, she had found the werewolf . . . or, rather, he had found her.

Chapter 12

Elizabeth stared at the wolfman, her heart pounding wildly. Each second that she waited for him to roar and leap forward to attack her seemed to last an eternity. *I'm going to die,* she thought, vivid memories of the recent tragedies flashing through her panicked brain. *With my throat ripped out, ravaged, in a pool of crimson blood, like Dr. Neville and Joy and Mildred Price....*

She clutched the desk behind her, her eyes darting around the room in search of a way to escape. The werewolf, meanwhile, didn't move.

As Elizabeth looked at him again, suddenly wondering if she were dreaming, if the ominous figure were just a figment of her imagination, she noticed something for the first time. The creature was wearing gray flannel trousers and a navy sweater over an Oxford shirt. *Ohmigod, it's not the werewolf at all. It's Luke!* she realized, her knees buckling with relief.

"Luke!" Elizabeth gasped, laughing at how fooled and frightened she'd been by the lifelike mask. "Oh, Luke, you scared me to death. Take that thing off and help me figure out what we've found here."

"I can't take it off, Elizabeth," Luke said hoarsely. "I can't take it off. Don't you see?"

He took a step toward her, his posture menacing. As he lifted his hands, Elizabeth saw that his fingers were clenched into claws; the muscles in his broad shoulders were bunched and tense. Through the holes in the mask, his eyes glittered at her—glittered with rage and hunger and despair. "I can't," Luke repeated, his voice a husky growl. "It's not a mask."

Do you like my collection? Don't you see?

In a lightning flash of illumination, Elizabeth did see . . . at long last, and all too clearly. "This is your room," she whispered. She shot a glance at the photograph resting on the desk. *Of course— she looks familiar because Luke showed me a picture of his mother the very first day we met.*

The picture was of Luke and his mother . . . Annabelle. Luke was Annabelle and Lord Pembroke's son.

And Luke, Elizabeth's dear friend . . . her love . . . was a madman. Luke was the werewolf of London.

• • •

Raindrops splattered on the windshield of Tony's car as he and Lucy sped through town toward Forget-Me-Not Lane. "I'll never forgive myself if anything happens to Luke or the girls," he muttered, flicking on the windshield wipers. The light at the intersection ahead turned red and he slammed on the brakes, cursing under his breath at the delay. "Why did I encourage Liz to stick out her neck like this, playing detective? She's just a summer intern, an amateur. I should have left her on Bumpo's beat where she'd be safe."

I didn't think this man ever took anything seriously, Lucy thought, touched. *But he's really worried—he really cares.* "Elizabeth may be young, but she's a journalist," Lucy consoled him. "Remember how she and her sister snuck over to the scene of the Neville murder behind my back? She follows her instincts—she follows the story. I don't think there's anything you could have done to stop her."

Tony raked a hand through his rumpled hair. "Still . . ."

"Still," Lucy agreed with an anxious sigh.

The light changed to green, and Tony stepped on the gas, tires squealing. Lucy studied his profile, a sudden and surprising feeling of warmth flooding through her. "You know, Frank," she said, "I think this is the first time we've ever seen eye-to-eye on anything."

He glanced at her, an ironic smile lifting one

corner of his mouth. "We must be getting soft in our dotage, Friday. We're like two old mother hens fussing about their chicks."

"I had been thinking about asking for your cooperation," she admitted, "to team up to get the girls to reconcile their differences."

Tony nodded. "It's crazy, don't you think, two sisters being so mad at each other for no good reason?"

"When underneath, they love each other more than anything," said Lucy. "I've never seen such stubbornness!"

"Sometimes the emotional wires get crossed," Tony reflected. "Two people think they can't stand each other, when, in fact, it's just the opposite. They put on a big act, pouring all their energy into a silly feud, but the whole time they really want to . . ."

His voice trailed off and a flush rose in his cheek. Lucy felt her own face grow hot. "Frank, are we still talking about Jessica and Elizabeth?"

Tony cleared his throat. "I thought we were, but . . ." They got stuck at another red light, but this time, Tony didn't seem to mind as much. He turned in his seat, fixing hopeful eyes on Lucy's expectant face. "The Wakefield twins aren't the only ones who've been holding each other at arm's length, are they?"

"No," Lucy said softly.

She took a deep breath and then, reaching across the space that separated them, she placed a hand on Tony's arm. Shyly, Tony covered her hand with his own. "I think the girls are going to work things out," he predicted. "How about us?"

Lucy smiled. "Let's tackle this late-breaking news story head-on—tell it like it is."

"It's our duty as investigative reporters, after all," Tony concurred. "All right—Friday. I mean, boss. I'm madly in love with you and I have been for months."

Bending over, Lucy pressed her lips against Tony's flushed cheek. "Me, too," she whispered.

The light turned green and the car shot forward into the rainy night.

"Can't you go any faster?" Jessica shouted desperately.

The driver met her eye in the rearview mirror and raised an eyebrow, scowling. Portia put a restraining hand on Jessica's arm. "He's already breaking the speed limit," she pointed out. "It would be foolish to risk an accident. We'll be there in a minute or two."

"But what if it's too late?" All traces of Jessica's anger at her sister for accusing Robert had disappeared. Tears streamed down her face. "Liz doesn't know—she doesn't even suspect! She gave the pendant to me, when really all the time she was the one dating a werewolf. She trusts Luke completely, she's totally at his mercy. What if he hurts her? What if . . ."

Jessica buried her face in her hands, tormented

by visions of Luke attacking her sister . . . of Elizabeth's lifeless body, the blood draining away . . .

Portia wrapped her arms around Jessica in a comforting hug. "Maybe Luke is the werewolf, but that doesn't mean he'd harm Elizabeth. They're friends—he loves her."

Jessica shook her head. "It doesn't matter. He's killed so many people, in such a cruel and horrible way. Do you really think he's capable of feeling compassion, or love?"

Portia was silent. The cab hurtled onward, city lights rushing past its windows in a rainy blur.

Jessica gripped the armrest so tightly her knuckles turned white. "It's all my fault," she said, choking back a sob. "If we weren't having this stupid fight, we would have been talking about the case, solving it together. Liz would have been with me at Pembroke Green to hear about Annabelle and Luke."

"Ssh," said Portia. "It's not your fault."

"It is," Jessica insisted. "I shouldn't have been so stubborn. I should have accepted that she was only trying to protect me. If anything happens to her . . ." The tears started to flow again. "I won't be able to go on living."

Portia patted Jessica's hand. Since there was no use yelling at the cabbie, Jessica squeezed her eyes shut and prayed. *Please, let me get there in time*, she chanted silently, rubbing Annabelle's silver pendant like a talisman. *Please, let me get there in time*. . . .

•   •   •

Still wearing the werewolf mask, Luke took another step toward Elizabeth. Edging around the desk, she flattened herself against the wall. "Luke, no," she whispered, terror robbing her of her voice.

As if in response to her plea, Luke froze in his tracks. Then Elizabeth saw that he was looking not at her, but at the framed photograph she'd carried from the other bedroom.

"My mother," Luke said, his rough voice softening. He lifted the picture and gazed at it reverently. "Ann . . . Annabelle. That's what my father—my real father—called her. He ruined her life, you know, the high and mighty Lord Pembroke. Abandoned her, abandoned both of us. Me, his own flesh and blood. Then, when she got sick, he let her die." Luke's voice cracked with remembered pain. "My other father, too—her husband. That quack doctor, Neville, and Nurse Handley. They all just let her die. They thought she was bad, but they were the bad ones. She was good—too good for this world. . . ."

Elizabeth stared at Luke, her breath coming fast. Luke had gone over the edge; he appeared to be in a sort of trance. The boy she knew . . . the boy she loved . . . would never hurt her, but this was someone else. Luke's animal side, his dark side had taken over, and it was far darker than Elizabeth ever could have guessed.

197

If I could only get the other Luke back, she thought desperately. *But how?* "Yes," she whispered, praying she would be able to keep the werewolf gentle. "She was too good."

His anger flaring again, Luke slammed the picture frame on the desk. Elizabeth jumped. "Can you imagine how I felt, that weekend at Pembroke Manor?" he snarled. "Seeing everything that should have been my mother's . . . that should have been mine. And your stupid sister, practically licking young Lord Robert's boots, and looking down her nose at me. Who did she think she was? Did she think she was going to be Lady Pembroke someday, when my own mother had been denied that privilege?"

Elizabeth licked her lips, which were as dry as paper. She was looking at the person who had stalked to Jessica's bedroom with murder on his mind . . . only to kill the wrong sleeping blond girl. "I—I—" she stuttered.

Luke cut her off, his hand slashing the air like a blade. "I was only eight years old as I stood by my mother's deathbed," he remembered. "With her last breath, she told me the truth. She told me who I really was. And I knew that someday . . ."

Elizabeth's eyes darted around the room. *There's got to be a way out. Someone has to come. Oh, please, don't let me die here.* "Someday . . . what?" she prompted, trying to keep Luke talking, knowing that her only hope was to stall for time.

"Someday I'd get back at the people who hurt her—the people who denied me. There have been so many." Luke's voice deepened to a hoarse, heartbroken growl. He took another step—he was only a few feet away from her now. "So many," he repeated, raising his arms as if to grasp Elizabeth by the throat. "But someday, I'd get them all."

"Luke, stop," Elizabeth begged, her throat constricting as if she could already feel the grip of sharp claws, the slash of beastly fangs. "Take off the mask. It's me. I can help you."

It was no use. Luke didn't see or hear her; he heard and saw only the demons in his own soul.

Elizabeth closed her eyes, trembling and dizzy with terror. Luke—her death—was almost upon her. She could feel the warmth of his breath . . . something furry brushed her arm. . . .

She waited for the blow to fall—she waited for the werewolf's bloodthirsty howl of triumph.

Instead, from the other side of the room, a strong male voice rang out, shattering the fateful silence. "Stop right there, Luke. Don't move another inch or I'll end it all. I have the silver bullet!"

Elizabeth's eyelids popped open. To her astonishment, the homeless man she'd seen outside with the grocery cart was now standing in the bedroom doorway, a gun raised and pointed straight at Luke's heart. With his grimy cap removed, Elizabeth recognized him instantly. "Robert!" she cried.

At that instant, another young man burst into the room, his face pale and his dark eyes wide. *Rene!* Even more incredible, right on Rene's heels was Sergeant Bumpo of Scotland Yard.

Luke whirled to face his challengers. "Robert, watch out!" Elizabeth screamed.

With an enraged roar, Luke lunged for Robert, grabbing the arm that held the gun. The two toppled to the floor, rolling over and over. Sergeant Bumpo and Rene dove into the fray, trying to seize Luke's arms and pin him, but Luke's madness seemed to give him the strength of ten men—he didn't relinquish his hold on Robert.

He'll kill him, Elizabeth thought, gnawing her fingernails. *Luke is going to kill Robert . . . his own half brother.*

There were groans and curses as the four men continued to scuffle frantically. Elizabeth held her breath, agonized by her helplessness. "Luke, stop," she cried. "Stop before it's too late."

It's over, Elizabeth thought a moment later. Robert appeared to have Luke pinned to the ground. But then, with a superhuman effort, Luke hurled Robert off him and leapt back to his feet. Robert lost his grip on the gun; it clattered to the ground. Elizabeth caught a glimpse of the weapon, but then it disappeared. Someone else had grabbed it . . . but who?

She started forward and then staggered back when a shot rang out. The blast was deafening in the small room. It echoed, penetrating Elizabeth's heart with a sharp knifelike pain as if she herself had been mortally wounded. "Who's been shot?" she cried out.

At the sound of the gunshot, all four men had frozen. Now three of them—Robert, Rene, and Sergeant Bumpo—remained standing. With a startled gasp, Luke toppled backward, a hole in the breast of his sweater where the bullet had torn through.

Rushing forward, Elizabeth knelt at Luke's side. The werewolf mask slipped off and she found herself gazing down at his face. It was the familiar, beloved face of the boy she'd met that first day at the *Journal*. The other Luke, the gentle, kind, poetic Luke, was back.

But not for long. Even though she was half blinded by tears, Elizabeth could see that Luke's fair skin was whiter than ever. His lifeblood was ebbing away, the light in the blue eyes growing dimmer and dimmer.

Clasping his hand in both of hers, Elizabeth willed Luke to hold on to life. But it was no use. "We did it, Elizabeth," Luke whispered, gazing up at her with a beatific smile. His eyelids fluttered and drooped. "We killed the werewolf."

Like a candle being snuffed out, the light in Luke's eyes flickered and died.

In front of the house at number four Forget-Me-Not Lane, Jessica and Portia converged with

Tony and Lucy. Guided by Tony's flashlight, all four dashed inside and up the stairs, following the sounds of shouting.

Halfway up the stairs, they heard the sharp crack of a pistol shot. "No!" Jessica cried. "Oh, God, he's killed her!"

They pounded down the hallway and then stopped at the door to a candelit bedroom, arrested by the somber tableau within.

Looking past Tony's shoulder, Jessica saw her sister bent over Luke Shepherd's motionless body. Rene Glize crouched next to Elizabeth, one hand resting on her shoulder.

Above them stood Sergeant Bumpo, a smoking gun in one hand and a walkie-talkie in the other. And next to the detective . . . Robert, dressed in the rags of a homeless person, gazing down remorsefully at his dead half brother.

The adrenaline that had fueled Jessica's body drained from her veins and she went limp. *It's over,* she realized numbly. *It's all over.*

Chapter 13

As the twins stepped out of the taxi in front of HIS, the first pink blush of dawn was just warming the eastern sky. Jessica stretched her arms over her head, yawning. "Talk about being late for curfew!" she joked tiredly. "Mrs. Bates will have our heads."

After talking all night with the police and Scotland Yard, with Tony and Lucy and Rene, and with her parents long distance, Elizabeth was too exhausted to speak or even smile. Her eyes on the ground, she turned away from the street to trudge slowly toward the dorm.

Before Elizabeth could insert her key in the door, Jessica touched her arm. "Let's not go in just yet," Jessica said softly. "Let's watch the sunrise."

Side by side, they sat down on the stone steps in front of HIS. In silence, they watched as the first faint streaks of pink brightened to orange and overhead the dark sky turned robin's-egg blue. "No fog, for once," observed Jessica. "It's going to be a sunny day."

Elizabeth drew in a deep, bracing breath of fresh morning air, her gaze fixed on the yellow rays of sunlight streaming through the trees in the park. *A new morning, a sunny day. For me and Jessica, maybe, but not for Luke. . . .*

A solitary tear trickled down Elizabeth's cheek. A second later, she felt Jessica pressing something into her hand. "A couple of Tony's tissues," Jessica explained wryly. "He had about ten boxes with him, so I snagged some."

Elizabeth dabbed her eyes and nose. "Thanks," she said, her voice scratchy. "And . . . thanks for forgiving me for all the bad and untrue things I said about Robert."

"You were only judging by the evidence," Jessica said generously. "And it's not like you were the only one. Everyone in London, including the police, saw it the same way."

"Still." Taking another tissue, Elizabeth blew her nose. "I kept accusing you of being blind and infatuated, when the whole time . . ."

"We were both doing the best we could with what we knew," said Jessica.

Elizabeth sighed. "I suppose you're right. It's funny, though, isn't it? We were both working on the Annabelle puzzle, but we didn't know it."

"That's right," said Jessica. "I found the file at Dr. Neville's—"

"And I found the books and love letters in the secret werewolf library."

"We both suspected she was important," said Jessica. "We were right, too."

"If only we could have solved the puzzle sooner." Elizabeth hugged her knees, fighting back another wave of bitter, regretful, pointless tears. "We might have prevented a lot of pain and grief. We might have saved lives. We might have saved . . ."

She didn't speak it, but the name hung in the cool morning air between them. *Luke. We might have saved Luke.*

"We should have been working together," Jessica agreed. "We always work best as a team."

Inching over on the step, Jessica wrapped an arm around her sister's shoulders. They sat that way for a few minutes, waiting for the sun to burst over the tops of the trees. At last it did, flooding the street and the yard with light and warmth.

Slowly, the twins rose to their feet. Jessica's words were still echoing in Elizabeth's head. *We always work best as a team.* "Let's never fight again," Elizabeth whispered to her sister.

Jessica folded Elizabeth in a warm, tight hug. "OK. Or at least," she added, a smile in her voice, "let's always fight on the same side."

●　　●　　●

There wasn't time to nap—Robert was picking her up in less than an hour to go visit his father in the hospital—but after a long, hot shower, Jessica felt wide awake and energized. Pirouetting in front of the mirror, she admired the crispness of her straw-colored linen suit and sage-green blouse. Just putting on clean clothes made a world of difference.

And breakfast, she thought, her mouth watering in anticipation of eggs, sausage, and home-baked scones. *I'm starving!*

When the Pembroke family limousine pulled up in front of HIS, Jessica flew down the walk to meet it, her body and heart feeling as light and free as a bird. The whole city was sparkling and beautiful . . . and safe. *We don't have to be afraid anymore,* she exulted. *The werewolf's reign of terror is over.*

Robert and the chauffeur stepped out of the limousine at the same time. With Clifford beaming his approval, Robert ran to meet her, and Jessica flung herself into his arms.

The limousine sped through town, Robert and Jessica snuggling close in the backseat. Robert ran a fingertip gently down the side of Jessica's face. "I can't believe I'm really touching you," he said, his voice gruff with emotion. "For a while, I thought I might never again be able to."

Jessica smiled, tugging playfully on the lapels of his navy blazer. "And I might not have let you, either, if you were still dressed in the smelly old rags you were wearing last night!"

Robert grinned. "I hadn't washed my hair for a week, either. Seriously, though." His expression grew solemn. "If I learned anything while I was undercover, it's how powerful personal appearances are. When you're dressed in expensive clothes, people are ready to respect you without knowing anything about you—before you even ask, they're bending over backward to be nice. But when you're grubby and ragged, people look right through you, as if you're less than human. You become invisible."

"That was why it was the best disguise," said Jessica. "You didn't have to leave London—you were right there, right under our eyes the whole time, but we didn't even see you."

"You were right under my eyes," Robert corrected her. "That was the whole point."

"Go back to the beginning," Jessica urged. "I got bits and pieces of it from everybody else last night, but I've been dying to hear the whole story from you."

"The beginning . . . all right," said Robert, stroking Jessica's hair. "You remember the last time we spoke, before I had to disappear?"

"We met for breakfast and you wouldn't tell me a thing," Jessica recalled. "I was so upset. And scared," she admitted. "I mean, not scared of you—scared for you."

"I was a bit scared myself," said Robert. "Who wouldn't be, after learning from my father that the police suspected me of being the most heinous serial killer to strike London since Jack the Ripper?"

"Your father didn't believe it, though," said Jessica. "And I didn't believe it."

"But the evidence was damaging," said Robert. "How did threads from my paisley robe get on the door frame to the room where Joy was murdered? No one was going to believe me if I said I hadn't worn the robe all weekend, much less gone to your room that night. And there was the cigarette case with my initials found by Dr. Neville's body."

"Luke was framing you!"

"Whether intentionally or unintentionally, we'll never know," Robert agreed. "Of course, I didn't suspect Luke at the time—I didn't know anything about him and Annabelle. But I knew someone was framing me, and I knew any jury would find me guilty if I didn't come up with real evidence that pointed to the real killer."

"You went to Nanny Millie's, didn't you?" said Jessica.

Robert nodded. "That first night. I needed a place to stay, and I also needed to talk to someone who had faith in me—who could lift my spirits and give me the courage to face the obstacles ahead of me. She was so kind, as always." Tears sparkled in Robert's deep-blue eyes and he clenched his teeth. "That woman never had anything but kindness for anyone. And to think I led that monster to her!"

"I don't think Luke going after her had anything to do with your visit," Jessica consoled him. "Poor Nanny Millie was already on Luke's list of people who'd betrayed him and his mother."

Robert sighed heavily. "Well, the next morning, the newspapers were all blaring the news—I was a werewolf and wanted for murder. Of course, Nanny didn't believe a word of it. She'd have stood staunchly by me if I'd sprouted fangs and hair right there in front of her. I didn't want to involve her, though, so I took off. If I'd known I'd never see her alive again . . . !"

Jessica squeezed his arm. "You couldn't have known, and you couldn't have prevented her death."

"I just didn't realize she was in any danger," said Robert. "I was too busy worrying about you."

"Me?" said Jessica, pleased.

Robert kissed the tip of her nose. "You. Someone—Luke, as it turns out—had tried to kill you at Pembroke Manor. If he tried again, I intended to be there to stop him. Going undercover as a homeless person, I was free to wander the streets any time of the day or night, to watch over you and Elizabeth and also do some sleuthing. My first day prowling around the park, I saw Luke give Elizabeth the silver bullet and decided I had to get hold of it. I was sure that, sooner or later, I'd come face-to-face with the killer, and I needed to be armed. So I went into your dorm room a few days later and took it from Elizabeth's drawer."

"I knew you were there that morning!" Jessica cried. "Oh, I wanted so much to see you!"

"For your own protection, I couldn't let that happen." Robert pressed a kiss on top of her hair. "But it broke my heart to see you crying."

"The silver bullet," Jessica mused, resting her cheek against Robert's broad chest. "Luke—werewolf Luke—must have been the one who tore our room apart later that same day. He must have known the bullet might be used against him."

"It was Luke," Robert confirmed. "When Sergeant Bumpo came back out of the dorm that evening, I pretended to be drunk—stumbling over my own feet and shouting obscenities at him. The poor man had no choice but to cuff me and take me in."

"But why did you do that?" asked Jessica. "You had to know the police were going to find out who you really were, and—"

"That was the point," Robert explained. "I revealed my true identity to Sergeant Bumpo on the way to the station. Was he flabbergasted! He thought that somehow he'd managed to catch the serial killer all by himself."

Jessica was beginning to feel lost in the complexity of Robert's tale. "Wait a minute. You said it was Luke who ransacked our room. How did you know?"

"I saw him enter HIS and then leave again not long before you and Liz came home and discovered the vandalism," he replied. "I told Bumpo, and he agreed Luke warranted watching. He also agreed not to turn me in—he booked me on vagrancy charges and I spent the night in a cell. That was the same night my father was attacked at Pembroke Green."

"So that proved you weren't the werewolf!" Jessica exclaimed.

"Right—it cleared me in Bumpo's mind and he decided I might be onto something. We both started watching Luke." Robert's face darkened. "But not quite closely enough. If it had taken us just a minute longer to get to the house on Forget-Me-Not Lane . . ."

"You got there in time. Thank God, you got there in time." Jessica threw her arms around Robert, her eyes brimming with grateful tears. "You're heroes, both of you. You saved my sister's life."

Robert returned Jessica's embrace. "But my brother lost his life," he said sadly. "My poor half brother. Will we ever understand what was really going on in his troubled, twisted mind?"

Elizabeth sat alone in her dorm room, an afghan wrapped around her legs and a red spiral notebook lying closed on her lap. She knew, at some point, Scotland Yard would want the notebook as evidence, but in the meantime, she needed it herself. She needed to read it, if she could force herself to. She needed to make one final effort to understand who Luke Shepherd really was.

It was the notebook Elizabeth had read from as she stood in Luke's bedroom in the house on Forget-Me-Not Lane. The same notebook that he'd been scribbling in when she surprised him at the *Journal* the day they met. *I caught him writing poetry,* she remembered. *He was so embarrassed.*

Elizabeth drew a deep, shaky breath, bracing herself. With trembling fingers, she opened the notebook.

It did contain poetry, but for the most part the notebook had been used as a journal. The first entries had been made when Luke was nine or ten. He had started writing things down after his mother died, Elizabeth observed. The poor little boy—he was so lonely, so confused!

In simple, childish diction, Luke wrote about missing his mother. Her death, and the secret she'd told him, had thrown his young life into disorder. He was curious about his "real" father, but also distressed. "How can Lord Pembroke be my daddy if I've never met him?" nine-year-old Luke had written. "What about the daddy I live with, who takes care of me? Since I'm not really his, he must not love me—he must only be pretending to love me. I wish that other family would come and take me away. Why don't they? Don't they want me?"

Elizabeth shook her head, her heart aching in sympathy. "He would have been better off not knowing the truth—Annabelle should never have told him," she said aloud. "How different things might have been!"

She turned a blank page and read on. Apparently, Luke had abandoned the diary for a number of years, taking it up again at the age of thirteen.

The tone had changed. Intense, focused bitterness took the place of the earlier childish uncertainty. The pages burned with anger at the biological father who had never acknowledged him, with resentment of the whole Pembroke family, especially the legitimate son and heir, Robert. "That spoiled boy has everything in the world," Luke wrote, underlining "spoiled" with dark strokes. "Today the whole city of London can read in the newspaper that he was expelled from another school. He has so many privileges, so many advantages, so much wealth, that he can afford to just throw it all away. There will always be more. How ashamed his father, our father, must be. If I had the chance, how proud I could make him!"

It was natural for him to be angry, Elizabeth reflected. Maybe even understandable that he would be sort of obsessed by the Pembrokes. But at some point, Luke had crossed over a line. His emotions had grown so warped, they took on a life of their own.

It's almost as if there were two Lukes, Elizabeth thought. One Luke continued to live the life of a normal teenaged boy, doing well in school and getting along superficially with his nominal father, Mr. Shepherd, who seemed never to have suspected that he wasn't Luke's real parent. While the other Luke . . .

At sixteen, Luke experienced his first blackout. As time passed, they became more and more frequent; not a week went by that he didn't wake up one morning in a strange place, with no idea of how he got there, whole blocks of time a blank in his memory. "What's happening to me?" Luke wrote, his script uneven. "Am I losing my mind?"

"Yes," Elizabeth whispered. "Yes, my poor Luke." He had begun the descent . . . into madness.

With tears in her eyes, she read the final portion of the journal, the entries written during the period that the werewolf was terrorizing London. Luke's split personality was starkly evident. "I finally met him, my own brother," Luke wrote about Robert Pembroke. "I set foot in Pembroke Manor—I shook my father's hand. I think he recognized me, my name, anyway, but he didn't acknowledge me. He won't, ever— He discarded me when he discarded my mother. But he will feel differently in the future. He will regret his mistake, when the entire world learns that his namesake is a killer . . . a werewolf!"

He really believed it was Robert, Elizabeth realized, recalling Luke's dying words. *He had no idea he himself was the murderer.*

Luke had realized that something was wrong with him, though; the diary recorded his growing sense of confusion. "I'm forgetting things," he wrote. "When Robert left his silver cigarette case at the office the other day, didn't I slip it into my pocket? I wanted something that belonged to him . . . it was so elegant, so rich. I held it in my hand, I know I did . . . but then, the case turned up next to Neville's corpse. So it must have fallen out of Robert's pocket, not mine. How could I have such a delusion?"

Elizabeth flipped back a page to an entry written at Pembroke Manor. "I snuck into Robert's room, just to see what it was like, just to imagine it was my room, as it should have been. That closet, full of the most elegant clothing! I couldn't resist slipping on the hunter-green paisley robe, just for a moment."

Elizabeth bit her lip until she tasted blood. *No, you took the robe, Luke. You wore it to Jessica's room that night. You wore it while you killed Joy. . . .*

A week later, Luke wrote of his fears for Elizabeth's safety. "I have vowed to protect her," he recorded. "I love her as I've loved no one since . . . But I begin to doubt my ability to keep her from harm. I begin to doubt myself. I am on the trail of the werewolf—I can feel how close we are to each other. I am just one step behind him. . . . But the blackouts trouble me, frighten me. What do they mean? What is my unconscious trying to tell me?"

The last entry was dated Tuesday, just two days earlier. *The day before his death,* Elizabeth thought, her throat tightening with tears.

"I am too exhausted, too feebleminded to work on the newspaper article my editor has told me she wants by the end of the day," Luke confided to the red spiral notebook. "I slept last night, but not a restful sleep—clearly not, since somehow, while in a dream or trancelike state, I found my way to the other side of town. The rain on my face woke me, as I lay in the leaves in a park just a block from Pembroke Green. There was blood on the sleeves and collar of my shirt . . . I let the rain pour down on me until it was washed away.

"This morning," the diary continued, "hearing the news, I see how close I am to my goal—to catching the werewolf. My father, Lord Pembroke, was attacked last night and I must have been there! I must have come upon the scene. Perhaps I touched my father's body, not knowing he still lived, or perhaps I grappled with the werewolf himself and that is how the blood came to stain me. I can not know for certain because I cannot remember. But it must have happened that way . . . mustn't it?"

I should have guessed, Elizabeth thought, her eyes brimming. *I should have seen that something was wrong. How can I say I loved him when I didn't even know him?*

216

Distractedly, Elizabeth turned the page. She'd thought she'd reached the end of Luke's diary, but now she found herself staring down at a short poem . . . a love sonnet titled, simply, "Elizabeth."

Elizabeth read the poem, her lips moving silently. *I did know Luke,* she realized, touching the lines on the page with her finger. *I knew this Luke. I loved this Luke. And he loved me. This side of Luke fought so hard against the other side . . . but it was a fight he couldn't win.*

The tears spilled forth, wetting her cheeks. She closed the notebook, whispering, "Good-bye, Luke."

The nurse on duty at the hospital gave Jessica and Robert permission to visit Lord Pembroke. "He's still quite weak, quite delicate, though," she cautioned. "He mustn't be agitated or excited."

Taking Jessica's hand, Robert walked purposefully toward his father's hospital room. Jessica could sense his powerful emotions: eagerness, anxiety, hope, fear, love. *He hasn't seen his father since the attack,* Jessica thought, *and the doctors say Lord Pembroke may not live. This may be the last time. . . .*

Hurrying to his father's bedside, Robert fell on his knees. He grasped the older man's hand and pressed his tear-streaked face against it.

Lord Pembroke had been dozing, but at the sight of Robert, his pale face brightened. "My son," he murmured, his voice trembling with emotion. "My son."

Jessica pulled up two chairs and she and Robert sat down. "So, I gather you've heard the news," Robert said to his father.

Lord Pembroke nodded. "I was told of your vindication, and of Luke's death. I don't know which is greater, my joy at the former or my sorrow at the latter."

"Why didn't you tell me?" Robert burst out. "Why didn't you tell me I had a brother?"

"Your mother couldn't bear for Luke to be part of our lives, and after what I'd done to her, I couldn't wrong her further. It was best for everyone, I thought, that there should be no contact. I had never even seen the boy," Lord Pembroke reminisced, "until the day he came to Pembroke Manor with the girls. When he spoke his name, I knew immediately. It was quite a shock. But it never occurred to me that he knew, that Annabelle had told him his true parentage." His watery eyes dimmed and he picked fretfully at the sheet. "I never meant for him to suffer. I tried to take care of them—I tried to protect them both."

"We know," Robert assured him. "We know you did what you thought best, under the circumstances."

"So many lost souls," Lord Pembroke mourned. "Annabelle, and now our son . . . and all the others. And your mother—I made her so unhappy. She never forgave me. I am responsible for all of it." His voice dropped to a tormented whisper. "Annabelle shared my passion for folklore, and we

218

transmitted it to our boy. I am the father of this tragedy, literally and figuratively."

"You mustn't blame yourself," Robert urged, leaning forward. "We have to put the past behind us. You must get better. I—" His voice cracked. "I need you."

Lord Pembroke grasped Robert's hand and Robert squeezed tightly. Jessica could almost see the life-giving strength flow from son to father. "I'll try, son," Lord Pembroke whispered.

"I always miss out on all the action," Emily bemoaned later that afternoon in the dorm dining room. "I can't believe I was working late on a boring BBC documentary about British immigration policy last night while you and Portia were cracking open the biggest murder case in the history of London!"

Jessica shrugged, feigning modesty. "I guess great detective work is half dumb luck—being in the right place at the right time. The other half, of course," she added with a smug smile, "is sheer raw brainpower."

"You wouldn't have wanted to be there," Portia told Emily. "It was horrible, seeing Luke right after he was shot. And poor Elizabeth, having to witness it. I'll never forget it as long as I live."

"That Luke seemed like a nice bloke." David shook his head. "Never would've picked him for a psycho."

"You can't tell—that's how they get away with it for so long," said Emily. "They look and act like anybody else—it's just underneath that they're ... off."

"The good news is, Robert turned up again and he's a hero," said Portia, smiling at Jessica. "Every cloud has a silver lining."

"I'm split in two," Jessica confessed. "I'm deliriously happy because of Robert, but at the same time I'm miserable for Liz. She wouldn't come down to dinner—she's just lying on her bed staring at the wall. Nothing I do or say seems to make her feel any better."

"She just needs time," said Portia. "Time to heal."

"Look," said Emily, nodding toward the entrance to the dining room. "Maybe she's starting to heal a little already."

After forcing herself to get out of bed, Elizabeth had walked downstairs and bumped into Rene outside the HIS dining room. "Elizabeth," he exclaimed, touching her arm. "I've been thinking about you all day at the embassy. You look well."

Elizabeth smiled tiredly. "No, I don't. I haven't slept in thirty-six hours. But thanks, anyway."

"How about some tea," suggested Rene, ushering her into the dining room.

Elizabeth glanced across the room to see Jessica, Emily, Portia, Gabriello, and David smiling encouragingly at her. Her resolve faltered. I can't deal with them—I'm just not ready. "I—I'll sit with you for a minute," she told Rene. "Here, this corner table."

Rene poured two cups of hot tea and filled a plate with scones and sandwiches. For a few minutes, they sat eating in silence. He seemed content just to keep her company; he didn't make conversation. Gratitude filled Elizabeth's grieving heart.

"I wanted to thank you, Rene," she said quietly. "For—for being there last night. "I know you were—I know you would have . . ." She choked on the words.

He put a finger to his lips. "Ssh. It's OK. We don't have to talk about it. I only did what any good friend would do."

She shook her head, smiling. "No, you went out of your way for me—way out of your way! When you couldn't talk me into leaving London, you decided to be my personal bodyguard . . . only, you had to do it from a distance because you knew I'd never put up with it otherwise."

Rene grinned. "It was a challenge. You get around, Elizabeth Wakefield!"

"You trailed me and Tony to Pelham that day," she recalled. "You weren't really visiting a friend of your mother's. And I saw you again at Victoria Station. And last night, you came to Forget-Me-Not Lane. It's funny, I kept getting the feeling that someone was following me. I didn't know I had a guardian angel—I thought it was . . . someone bad."

"I couldn't let anything happen to you," Rene

said simply. "But now, I don't have to play private eye anymore, and neither do you. We can return to our normal lives."

Elizabeth's lips trembled. "No, I don't think so," she whispered. "It's not that easy."

"I know it won't be easy." Rene squeezed her hand. "But it will happen. Your friends are here, and we'll help."

All day long, Elizabeth had been fighting back tears, struggling to keep from drowning in an ocean of loneliness and despair. Now, suddenly, she felt as if, against all odds, she'd managed to swim back to shore. The dangerous tide tugged at her ankles, but she was breathing the air—she was safe on the sand. *My friends . . . I'm not alone.*

The tears spilled forth, but they were tears of hope as well as sorrow. "Thanks," Elizabeth repeated. "Thanks for being my friend."

Chapter 14

"I never thought I'd see the day," said Zena, one of Jessica and Elizabeth's *Journal* co-workers, as they stood in a receiving line in the leafy courtyard of a fashionable London hotel on Saturday. "I never thought Tony would get Lucy on a date, much less to the altar!"

"Well, I knew they'd get together sooner or later," claimed Jessica. "I mean, it was inevitable. Like a force of nature or something."

"A force of nature, all right—a tornado," Robert interjected with a grin. "Didn't you say they fell in love on one day, and decided to get married the next?"

"Yes," said Jessica with a happy sigh. "Isn't it the most romantic thing you ever heard?"

In Jessica's opinion, Tony and Lucy couldn't have picked a better time to get swept off their feet by passion. It had been such a depressing week; they all needed a really good party to lift their spirits. And what could be more fun than a wedding?

Even Liz is having a good time, Jessica observed, watching out of the corner of her eye as Rene whispered something in Elizabeth's ear that made her smile. *It might take a while, but we're all going to get over this—all of us.*

It was their turn to greet the bride and groom. Lucy looked stunning and composed in a creamy, tea-length silk dress with her luxurious chestnut hair swept up on her head. Tony, in a suit and tie, looked dazed.

As Jessica flung her arms around Lucy, Robert pumped Tony's hand. "Congratulations, old chap. This is just grand!"

"Isn't it?" Tony marveled. "But I have this lurking suspicion that it's a fever-induced hallucination and any minute now I'll wake up and discover Lucy Friday won't give me the time of day."

His bride slipped a slender arm around his waist and planted a kiss on his cheek, causing him to flush profusely. "That's Lucy Friday Frank," she corrected him.

Tony shook his head, smiling at Jessica and Elizabeth. "I'm right, aren't I? This is a dream?"

"If it's a dream," said Lucy, her own eyes shining, "let's just hope it lasts a lifetime."

After filling their plates at the luncheon buffet

set up just inside the French doors in the airy, elegant dining room, the twins, Robert, and Rene scouted around for table seven. "There it is," said Elizabeth, pointing toward a table across the room near the band. "And you'll never guess who's sitting at the next table."

"The detective from Scotland Yard," exclaimed Rene.

"Sergeant Bumpo!" cried Jessica.

All four burst out laughing. "It's really kind of too bad that he's getting credit for solving such a big crime," mused Jessica. "He's just not going to be the same old bumbling Bumpo."

At that moment, in the process of rising to greet two ladies who were sharing his table, Sergeant Bumpo knocked over his chair. The chair crashed into a potted palm, which in turn toppled onto the startled band members.

"On the other hand, some people never change," said Jessica with a giggle. She hooked her arm through her sister's. "C'mon, Liz. Let's go say hi to the hero of Scotland Yard!"

After a number of friends and relatives had given toasts, Tony Frank himself rose to his feet. "We can't tell you how much it means to us that you were all able to be here on this special occasion, especially on such short notice!" A murmur of laughter ran around the room. "Now, I'd like you to raise a glass with me," Tony requested. Lifting his champagne, he turned to gaze adoringly down at Lucy. "And drink a toast to the most beautiful, talented, and intelligent woman in England, who on this day has made me the happiest man on earth. My wife, Lucy."

Elizabeth clinked her water glass against Jessica's. "Can you believe it was less than a week ago that we both wanted to fix Tony and Lucy up," said Jessica, "but because we weren't speaking to each other, we couldn't work together at it?"

Elizabeth laughed. "I guess they didn't wait around for us."

"Although I think we deserve at least some of the credit for getting this romance off the ground," Jessica declared. "Lucy said so herself. It was when they were frantic about us, and rushing to our aid, that it finally hit them that they were nuts about each other."

"Love always finds a way," said Robert, slipping an arm around Jessica's shoulders.

Jessica beamed up at him, her face glowing. "It does, doesn't it?"

Under the table, Rene reached for Elizabeth's hand to give it a supportive squeeze. Elizabeth made an effort to smile. "I'm OK," she whispered, although she wasn't at all sure she was . . . or would be, ever again.

When Tony sat down again, Lucy herself stood to address her guests. "I know it's not traditional for the bride to give a toast," she announced, "but then, I'm not a traditional bride. And this is not a traditional toast. I just wanted to take advantage of being the center of attention to share some good tidings. Robert Pembroke Junior tells us that his father has turned a corner for the better and will be released from hospital soon."

There were smiles and exclamations of relief at every table. Elizabeth felt her heart swell with emotion. Miraculously, one life that Luke had come so close to destroying had been saved.

"Of course, it will be a while before Lord Pembroke is fully recovered," Lucy continued. "Apparently, he is eager to turn some of the family business over to his highly capable son. One change is already official." Lucy flashed a smile at Robert. "As editor-in-chief of the *London Journal*, I'd like to bid a warm welcome to the new owner of the newspaper: Robert Pembroke Junior!"

A hearty cheer went up. Jessica threw her arms around Robert, bursting with pride. Elizabeth clapped along with the others. "You have to admit it now, Liz," Jessica whispered to her when the fuss finally died down. "Your first impression of Robert was way off base."

Elizabeth nodded. She wouldn't deny that Robert had struck her as self-centered and undeserving. But in recent weeks, faced with unjust accusations and mortal danger, he'd shown courage, initiative, and determination. "I've never claimed to be an infallible judge of character," she whis-

227

pered back, thinking about Luke Shepherd. "I was wrong about Robert, and I'm glad."

As Lucy and Tony cut the wedding cake, the band struck up a lively tune. Elizabeth smiled at the bride and groom, her eyes sparkling with sentimental tears. *I feel as if I've known them forever,* she reflected, accepting the linen handkerchief Rene offered her. *Tony, Lucy, Rene, the rest of the gang from the dorm . . . I guess because we've been through so much together.*

Her glance shifted from the newlyweds to Jessica and Robert, who stood with their arms wrapped around each other, gazing raptly into each other's eyes. Elizabeth hadn't seen her twin sister so radiantly happy in a long, long time. *She really does care for him,* Elizabeth realized. *Poor thing, her heart is going to break a week from now when our internships end and we have to fly back to the States.*

As for my heart . . . Elizabeth felt a pang for the special friend she'd lost. She thought about their lunches at the Slaughtered Lamb, their walks around the city, their lively discussions about literature and history, movies and art. If she closed her eyes, she could see the sparkle in Luke's lake-blue eyes, the shock of dark hair falling over his pale forehead; she could hear his sweet, adorable English voice; she could feel his hand in hers, the warmth of his lips as they kissed. *My heart has already been broken into a million pieces.*

Silently, deep in her being, Elizabeth said goodbye to the troubled soul of the boy she'd fallen in love with in London. *I'll keep the good memories separate from the bad,* she decided, *but good and bad both, it's time to put them away. It's time to put my heart back together.*

Almost imperceptibly, having made this determination, Elizabeth felt her spirits lift. Jessica had one week left with Robert, and Elizabeth had one week, too—one final week in which to enjoy the city and her job and the company of her friends with a clear, healing heart.

One week, Elizabeth thought, taking Rene's hand and leading him out onto the dance floor, *and then I'll be back in Sweet Valley. Back to my real life—the life I love. Back with my family, and Todd. Home.*

SWEET VALLEY HIGH™

Don't miss any of the latest fabulous Sweet Valley High Collections!

Double Love Collection

DOUBLE LOVE
SECRETS
PLAYING WITH FIRE

Summer Danger Collection

A STRANGER IN THE HOUSE
A KILLER ON BOARD

Château D'Amour Collection

ONCE UPON A TIME
TO CATCH A THIEF
HAPPILY EVER AFTER

Flair Collection

COVER GIRL
MODEL FLIRT
FASHION VICTIM